Rafael Sabatini, creator of som[...] was born in Italy in 1875 a[nd ...] Switzerland. He eventually settled in England in 1[...], by [which] time he was fluent in a total of five languages. He chose to write in English, claiming that 'all the best stories are written in English'.

His writing career was launched in the 1890s with a collection of short stories, and it was not until 1902 that his first novel was published. His fame, however, came with *Scaramouche*, the much-loved story of the French Revolution, which became an international bestseller. *Captain Blood* followed soon after which resulted in a renewed enthusiasm for his earlier work.

For many years a prolific writer, he was forced to abandon writing in the 1940s through illness and he eventually died in 1950.

Sabatini is best remembered for his heroic characters and high-spirited novels, many of which have been adapted into classic films, including *Scaramouche, Captain Blood* and *The Sea Hawk* starring Errol Flynn.

TITLES BY THE SAME AUTHOR
ALL PUBLISHED BY HOUSE OF STRATUS

FICTION:
ANTHONY WILDING
THE BANNER OF THE BULL
BARDELYS THE MAGNIFICENT
BELLARION
THE BLACK SWAN
CAPTAIN BLOOD
THE CAROLINIAN
CHIVALRY
THE CHRONICLES OF CAPTAIN BLOOD
COLUMBUS
FORTUNE'S FOOL
THE FORTUNES OF CAPTAIN BLOOD
THE GAMESTER
THE GATES OF DOOM
THE HOUNDS OF GOD
THE JUSTICE OF THE DUKE
THE LION'S SKIN
THE LOST KING
LOVE-AT-ARMS
THE MARQUIS OF CARABAS
THE MINION
THE NUPTIALS OF CORBAL
THE ROMANTIC PRINCE
SCARAMOUCHE
SCARAMOUCHE THE KING-MAKER
THE SEA HAWK
THE SHAME OF MOTLEY
THE SNARE
ST MARTIN'S SUMMER
THE STALKING-HORSE
THE STROLLING SAINT
THE TAVERN KNIGHT
THE TRAMPLING OF THE LILIES
TURBULENT TALES
VENETIAN MASQUE

NON-FICTION:
HEROIC LIVES
THE HISTORICAL NIGHTS' ENTERTAINMENT
KING IN PRUSSIA
THE LIFE OF CESARE BORGIA
TORQUEMADA AND THE SPANISH INQUISITION

The Sword of Islam

Rafael Sabatini

Copyright © Rafael Sabatini

All rights reserved. No part of this publication may be reproduced, stored in a retrieval system, or transmitted, in any form, or by any means (electronic, mechanical, photocopying, recording, or otherwise), without the prior permission of the publisher. Any person who does any unauthorised act in relation to this publication may be liable to criminal prosecution and civil claims for damages.

The right of Rafael Sabatini to be identified as the author of this work has been asserted.

This edition published in 2001 by House of Stratus, an imprint of Stratus Holdings plc, 24c Old Burlington Street, London, W1X 1RL, UK. Also at: Suite 210, 1270 Avenue of the Americas, New York, NY 10020, USA.

www.houseofstratus.com

Typeset, printed and bound by House of Stratus.

A catalogue record for this book is available from the British Library and the Library of Congress.

ISBN 1-84232-832-8

This book is sold subject to the condition that it shall not be lent, resold, hired out, or otherwise circulated without the publisher's express prior consent in any form of binding, or cover, other than the original as herein published and without a similar condition being imposed on any subsequent purchaser, or bona fide possessor.

This is a fictional work and all characters are drawn from the author's imagination. Any resemblances or similarities to persons either living or dead are entirely coincidental.

Contents

1	The Author of *the* Liguriad	1
2	The Doge	10
3	Surrender	15
4	The Castelletto	25
5	The Battle of Amalfi	31
6	The Prisoner	46
7	At Lerici	59
8	The City of Death	68
9	The Garden of Life	79
10	Waters of Lethe	93
11	Procida	103
12	The Amend	113
13	Mother and Son	124
14	Scipione de' Fieschi	130
15	The Adorno Honour	139
16	The Choice	157
17	Cherchell	171

18	Dragut's Prisoner	190
19	Monna Aurelia's Indiscretion	196
20	The Homecoming	206
21	Explanation	210
22	The Way Out	217
23	Capture	227
24	A Prize for Suleyman	236
25	The Trap	245
26	The Plan	260
27	The Reunion	270
28	At a Venture	277
29	The Return	286
30	Reparation	294
31	Mars Ultor	302
32	The Battle of Cape Mola	311
33	The Rehabilitation of an Emperor	327
34	The Discovery	335
35	The Last Hope	341
36	The Investiture	349

Chapter 1

The Author of the Liguriad

With banners limp in the breathless August noontide, the long line of blockading galleys rode drowsily at anchor, just out of gunshot from the shore, at a point where the water, smooth as an enamelled sheet, changed from emerald to sapphire.

From this station Andrea Doria commanded the gulf, from the rugged promontory of Portofino in the east to the distant Cape Melle in the west, and barred the sea approaches to Genoa the Superb, which rose, terrace upon terrace, in glittering marble splendour within the embrace of her encircling hills.

In the rear of his long line were stationed, as became an ancillary squadron, the seven red Pontifical galleys. Richly carved and gilded at stem and stern, they displayed at their mastheads the Papal vexilla: on one the keys of St Peter, on the other the besants of the Medici, the House from which His Holiness was sprung. From each red flank the thirty massive oars, thirty-six feet in length, were inclined astern and slightly upwards, presenting, thus at rest, the appearance of a gigantic, half-closed fan.

In the tabernacle – as the poop cabin was termed – of the rearmost galley, a sybaritic chamber, hung and carpeted with the glowing silks of Eastern looms, sat the Papal Captain, that Prospero Adorno who was at once a man of dreams and a man of action, a soldier and a poet. Other poets have acknowledged him a great soldier, and other soldiers have acknowledged him a great poet. Both state the truth and only jealousy makes them state it in this wise.

As a poet he lives on and sings to you from *The Liguriad*, that immortal epic of the sea, whose subject is proclaimed by its opening lines:

> *Io canto i prodi del liguro lido,*
> *Le armi loro e la lor' virtù.*

As a soldier let it be said at once that he achieved a celebrity never approached by the military deeds of any other poet. Just thirty years of age at the time of this blockade of Genoa, he was already famous as a naval condottiero. Four years ago in an action off Goialatta his skill and intrepidity had saved the great Andrea Doria from disaster at the hands of Dragut-Reis, the Anatolian who for his deeds had come to be known as The Drawn Sword of Islam.

Acclaimed as having plucked a Christian victory from an imminent defeat his fame had swept like a mistral across the Mediterranean, and it resulted naturally, that when, later, Doria passed into the service of the King of France, it was Prospero Adorno who succeeded him as Captain-General of the Pontifical navy.

Now that His Holiness had entered into alliance with France and Venice against the Emperor, whose troops had scandalized the world by the sack of Rome in May of that year 1527, Andrea Doria, as the Admiral of the King of France and the foremost seaman of his day, was in supreme command of the allied navies; and thus Prospero Adorno found himself once more serving under Doria's orders. Apparently it placed him in the invidious position of bearing arms against a republic of which his own father was the Doge. Actually, however, since the campaign had for object to break the Imperial yoke under which Genoa groaned, the blockade to which he brought his galleys sought to restore his native land to independence and change his father's status from that of a puppet-doge at the orders of an Imperial governor to that of an authoritative prince.

From where he now sat, just within the arched entrance of the tabernacle, his calm eyes, so dreamy and slow-moving that they appeared never to see anything, commanded the entire length of the vessel to its rambade, the raised bastion or forecastle in the prow, a hundred and twenty feet ahead of him. Along the narrow gang-deck between the rowers' benches two slave-wardens slowly paced, and under the arm of each was tucked his whip with the long lash of bullock-hide. On either side of this deck, and below the level of it, the idle slaves drowsed in their chains. There were five men to each oar, three hundred in all; unfortunates of many a race and creed: dusky, sullen Moors and Arabs, tough, enduring Turks, melancholy negroes from the Sus, and even some alien Christians, all rendered kin by misery. From where he sat the Captain could see only their shorn heads and naked weathered shoulders. Groups of soldiers paced or lounged in the dead-works of the galley, the galleries projecting over the water from the vessel's sides throughout her length; others squatted on the broad platform amidships, between the kitchen on one side and the heavy ordnance on the other, taking advantage of the shade cast by the sloop that was at rest there upon its blocks.

A sudden blare of trumpets snapped the thread of the Captain's dreaming. An officer, ascending the companion, rose into view, and stood before the entrance of the cabin.

"The Admiral's barge is coming alongside, Sir Captain."

Prospero came instantly to his feet with an effortless resilience. It was in this athletic ease of movement, in the long limbs and the broad shoulders, from which he tapered down over lean flanks, that you perceived the man of action. The width of his brow made his shaven countenance look narrow. In the wide wistful eyes of the visionary and the long mobile mouth you would have sought in vain the soldier. It was a face that had inherited none of the beauty so arresting in the portrait of his high-spirited, foolish, Florentine mother, that Aurelia Strozzi whom Titian painted. Only the bronze-coloured hair, and the vivid blue, though not the elongated shape, of her handsome eyes were repeated in her son. From the sombre richness of his dress, without ornament beyond the girdle of hammered gold slung diagonally over his hips to carry the heavy dagger, you might suppose that in matters of taste he had gone to school to that mirror of courtliness, Baldassare Castiglione.

He was waiting on the vestibule of the poop when the twelve-oared barge drew alongside, trailing a white standard, flecked with golden fleurs-de-lys. From her sternsheets three men rose and came up the short ladder to the deck. Two of them were big men, but of these the foremost, standing well over two yards high, was almost a half-head taller than the next. The third, more lightly built, was not above middle height.

They were Andrea Doria and his nephews Gianettino and Filippino. Comeliness was no characteristic of the males of the House of Doria, but in the aspect of the stalwart sexagenarian, with his fierce reddish eyebrows, his great promontory of a nose, and his long, fan-shaped, fulvid beard, there was something venerable, heightened by the stern controlled dignity in which he hedged himself about. There was strength in the long jaw, intelligence in the lofty brow, from which the thin hair was receding, and craft in the narrow, deep-set eyes. He carried his sixty years with the active, erect virility of a man of forty.

Gianettino, who immediately followed him aboard, was massive and ungainly. His face was a woman's, and without being ugly was repellent on that account. It was round and shaven, with a long, straight nose and a short chin. There was meanness in the beady eyes and petulance in the small mouth. In his endeavour to emulate the cold aloofness of his uncle he achieved no more than an aggressive arrogance. Men spoke and thought of him as Andrea Doria's nephew. Actually he was the son of a distant cousin in poor circumstances, and he might have pursued his father's trade as a silk-weaver had not his uncle, that childless nepotist, adopted and reared him, to pamper him with an indulgence that was destined ultimately to bring the upstart to an untimely end. In apparel he displayed the fundamental ostentation of his nature. His parti-coloured hose and parti-coloured sleeves, modishly puffed and slashed, made him a bewilderment to the eye, in black and white and yellow.

In age both nephews were approaching thirty. Both were black-haired, dark-complexioned men. Beyond this they presented no resemblance. Filippino, as restrained in his dress as Gianettino was flamboyant, displayed something of the same contrast in his person. Lithe and nimble, he moved with a quick, soft tread, stooping a little, where his cousin rolled and swaggered aggressively erect. Of the weakness in Gianettino's countenance there was no sign in Filippino's. A nose at once aquiline and fleshly overhung his short upper lip; his eyes, of the colour of mud, were prominent and low-lidded; the short black beard was of too feeble a growth to dissemble the narrowness of his jaw. He carried a bandaged right arm in a sling of black taffetas, and his manner was distempered and sullen.

Almost before they were well within the cabin, and without waiting, as deference dictated, for his uncle to speak, it was he who took the lead, his manner viperish.

"Our faith in your father, Sir Prospero, cost us rather dear last night. Close upon four hundred men lost, some seventy of them killed outright. You'll not yet have heard that our cousin Ettore has since died of the wounds he took. I have brought back this keepsake from Portofino." He pointed to his arm. "That I have brought back my life is no thanks to you."

Without pause his cousin followed up the onslaught that was taking Prospero completely by surprise. "The fact is that our faith has been abused. A trap has been sprung on us. A cursed treachery for which we have to thank Doge Adorno."

Prospero's clear eyes looked frigidly from one to other of the ranting twain. There was a stateliness in his self-control. "Sirs, I understand your words as little as your manner. You'll not imply that my father is responsible for the defeat of your rashly attempted landing?"

"Rashly attempted!" flared Filippino. "Lord God!"

"I judge from what I was told last night. To have been so instantly and heavily repulsed scarcely argues a properly cautious approach.

It was not to be supposed that the Spaniards would slumber at so vulnerable a point."

"Aye, if they had been Spaniards," bellowed Gianettino. "But Spaniards were not concerned."

"How, not concerned? Last night your tale was that Imperial troops had met your surprise party in overwhelming numbers."

At last Andrea Doria intervened. His quiet voice, his gravely placid manner contrasted with the violence of his nephews. Displays of heat were rare in him. "We know better today, Prospero. We have some prisoners. They are not Spaniards, but Genoese. Of the militia. And we know now that they were led by the Doge himself."

Prospero stared in blank surprise at each in turn. "My father led a Genoese force against you!" He almost laughed. "That is not credible. My father knows our aims."

"Does it follow that he is in sympathy with them?" asked Gianettino. "We have supposed – "

Warmly Prospero interrupted him. "To doubt it is to insult him."

The Lord Andrea intervened again, conciliatory. "You'll be patient with their heat. The death of Ettore has deeply affected us. After all, we must remember – perhaps we should have remembered before – that Doge Adorno holds the ducal crown from the Emperor. He may fear that what came with the Emperor may go with the Emperor."

"Why should he? Without Genoese support he could not have been elected. With it he cannot be deposed. Sirs, your information must be as false as your assumptions."

"Our information leaves no doubt," Filippino answered him. "As for the assumptions, your father will know that Cesare Fregoso is in command of the French troops investing him by land. He will not have forgotten that a Fregoso was dispossessed by him of the dogeship. That may make him doubt his own position should the French prevail."

Prospero shook his head. But before he could speak, Gianettino was adding stormily: "It's these accursed factions that poison faith; this ages-old struggle of Adorni, Fregosi, Spinoli, Fieschi and the rest. Each brawling for dominion in the State. For generations it has been the Republic's nightmare. It has rotted the sinews of this Genoa that once was mightier than Venice. Bled white by your cursed strife she has fallen under the heel of foreign despots. We are here," he bellowed, "to make an end of native factions as well as foreign usurpation. We are in arms to restore to Genoa her independence. We are here to…"

Prospero's patience gave out. "Sir, sir! Save the rest for the marketplace. No need here for orations in the manner of Titus Livy. Why we are besetting Genoa I know. Otherwise I should not be with you."

"That," said the elder Doria, quietly authoritative, "should be assurance enough for your father even if he forgets that I am Genoese to the marrow of my spine, and that the good of my country must always be my only object."

"My letters," said Prospero, "assured him that we serve the coalition only so that we may the better serve Genoa. I wrote of the undertaking to you from the King of France, that Genoa shall be restored at last to independence. It must be," he concluded, "that my letters never reached him."

"That is a possibility I have considered," said the Lord Andrea.

His volcanic nephews would have argued upon it. But quietly he repressed them.

"After all, it may be the explanation. The Milanese is full of de Leyva's Spaniards, and your courier may have been captured. So as to test it you shall write to him again. Thus bloodshed may be saved and the gates of Genoa opened to us. The Doge should have enough native militia to overpower the Spaniards in the place."

"How shall I get a letter to him now, from here?" asked Prospero.

The Lord Andrea sat down. He set one hand on his massive knee, and with the other thoughtfully stroked his length of beard. "You might send it openly, under a flag of truce."

Prospero moved slowly about the cabin, pondering. "It might be intercepted again by the Spaniards," he said at last, "and this time it might be dangerous for my father."

A shadow darkened the entrance of the tabernacle. Prospero's lieutenant stood on the threshold.

"Your pardon, Sir Captain. A fisherman of the gulf is alongside. He says he has letters for you; but will deliver them only into your own hands."

There was a pause of surprise. Then Gianettino swung round hotly upon Prospero. "Do you correspond then with the city? And you ask…"

"Patience!" his uncle suppressed him. "What profit is there in assumptions?"

Prospero glanced at Gianettino without affection. "Bring in this messenger," he shortly ordered.

And no more was said until a bare-legged youngster had pattered up the companion to the officer's beckoning, and was thrust into the tabernacle. The lad's dark eyes shifted keenly from one to another of the four men before him. "Messer Prospero Adorno?" he inquired.

Prospero stood forward. "I am he."

The fisherman drew a sealed package from the breast of his shirt and proffered it.

Prospero glanced at the superscription, and his fingers were scarcely steady when he broke the seal. Having read the contents with a darkening countenance, he looked up to find the eyes of the three Dorias watching him. He handed the letter in silence to the Lord Andrea. Then to his officer, indicating the fisherman, "Let him wait below," he said.

From the Lord Andrea came presently a sigh that was of relief. "At least this shows that your surmise was right, Prospero." He turned to his nephews. "And yours," he told them, "without justification."

"Let them read for themselves," said Prospero.

The Admiral handed the sheet to Gianettino.

"It's a warning to you both against rash assumptions," he gently chided his nephews. "I am glad to know that His Serenity's action comes from a lack of understanding of our aims. Once you will have informed him, Prospero, by the means now supplied you, we may confidently hope that Genoa's resistance will be at end."

There was a silence whilst the nephews together read the letter.

From prisoners taken last night at Portofino (wrote Antoniotto Adorno), *I learn with consternation that you are in command of the Papal squadron of the fleet blockading us. But for assurances which make doubt impossible, I could not credit that you are in arms against your native land, much less that you should be in arms against your own father. Although no explanation seems possible, yet unless something has happened to change your whole nature, some explanation there must be. A fisherman of the gulf will take this to you, and will no doubt be allowed to reach you. He will bring me your answer if you have one, which I pray God you may have.*

Filippino looked darkly at his uncle. "I share your hope, sir, but not your confidence. To me the Doge's tone is hostile."

"And to me," Gianettino agreed with him. He swung arrogantly to Prospero. "Make it plain to His Serenity that he can do himself no greater harm than by resisting us. In the end the might of France must prevail, and the Doge will be held responsible for any blood unnecessarily shed."

Prospero looked squarely and calmly into that countenance, so weak of feature and yet so bold of expression. "If you have such messages for my father, you may send them in your own hand. But I should not advise it. For I never yet knew an Adorno who would yield to bullying. You might remember that also, Gianettino, when you speak to me. If anyone has told you that there are no limits to my patience, he has lied to you."

It might have been the prelude to a very pretty quarrel if the Admiral had not been quick to smother further provocation from his bristling nephews. "Faith, you've been too patient already, Prospero, as I shall make these malaperts understand."

He rose. "No need to incommode you any longer, now that all is clear. We but delay the dispatch of your letter."

And he drove out the arrogant pair before they could work further mischief.

Chapter 2

The Doge

The patriotism of His Serenity the Doge Antoniotto Adorno stood high enough to surmount the tribulation of those days.

Behind her proud exterior, under her marble splendours, effulgent in the burning August sunshine, Genoa was succumbing to starvation. Of the troops sent by Marshal de Lautrec to invest her by land, she might be contemptuous. Abundantly were her flanks and rear protected by the towering natural ramparts, the bare craggy masses forming the amphitheatre in which she was set. If she was vulnerable along the narrow littoral at the base of these mountain bastions, yet here any attack, from east or west, would be as easy to repel as it would be hazardous to launch.

But the forces which knew themselves utterly inadequate to attempt an assault were more than adequate to cut off her supplies; and for ten days before the arrival of Doria in the gulf the sea approaches had effectively been guarded by seven Provençal war-galleys from Marseilles, which were now incorporated in the Admiral's fleet. So Genoa had begun to know starvation, and starvation never fostered heroism. A hungry population is prone to rebel against whatever government sits over it, visiting the blame for the famine upon its rulers. And lest the population of Genoa should be slow to rebel now, the Fregosi faction, in its rivalry of the Adorni for dominion in the Republic, perceived its opportunity and employed it ruthlessly. Those who form the populace are ever the ready gulls of the promises of crafty opportunists; and the populace of Genoa gave heed now to hollow promises of a golden age, to be ushered in by the King of France, which would not merely set a term to the present pangs of hunger, but create for all time an abiding and effortless abundance. So from artisans, from sailmakers, from fishermen who no longer dared put to sea, from stevedores' labourers, from carders, from sailors, from caulkers and all those who toiled in the shipbuilding yards, and from all those who made up the less defined sections of the people came the angrily swelling demand for surrender.

Up and down the streets of Genoa, so steep and narrow that a horse was rarely seen in them and the mule was the common beast of burden, moved with increasing menace in those hot days a people in revolt against a Doge who – because the devil he knew seemed preferable to the devil with whom he had yet to become acquainted – accounted it his duty to the Emperor to persist in holding out against the King of France and his Papal and Venetian allies.

With the menace from without he had shown last night at Portofino that he was competent to deal, whilst awaiting the relief that sooner or later should reach him from Don Antonio de Leyva, the Imperial Governor of Milan. But the menace from within was of graver sort. It left him to choose between impossible courses. Either he must employ his Spanish regiment to quell the insurgence, or else he must surrender the city to the French, who would probably deal with it as the German mercenaries had dealt with Rome. From this cruel dilemma Prospero's answer to his letter almost brought relief.

With that letter in his hand, the Doge now sat in a room of the Castelletto, the red fortress, deemed impregnable, that from the eastern heights dominated the city. The chamber was a small one in the eastern turret, hung with faded blue-grey tapestries, an eyrie commanding from its narrow windows a view of the city, the harbour, and the gulf beyond, where the blockading fleet rode on guard.

The Doge reclined in a high, broad chair of blue velvet, his right elbow on the heavy table. His left arm was in a sling, so as to ease the shoulder, in which he had taken a pike-thrust last night at Portofino. Perhaps because the heavy loss of blood left him chilled even in that sweltering heat, he was wrapped in a cloak. A flat cap was pulled down over his high, bald forehead, deepening the shadows in his pallid, hollow cheeks.

Beyond the table stood the Dogaressa. A woman moderately tall, and still, even now, in middle life, of a slender, graceful shape, retaining in her finely chiselled features much of the beauty that in her youth had been sung by poets and painted by the great Vecelli, she possessed the masterfulness that comes to all egoists who have been greatly courted.

With her were the middle-aged patrician captain, Agostino Spinola, and Scipione de' Fieschi, the handsome, elegant younger brother of the Count of Lavagna, who was a Prince of the Empire and of a lineage second to no man's in the State of Genoa.

Having read his son's letter once, the Lord Antoniotto sat long in a silence which not even his imperious lady ventured to disturb. Then he read it yet again before attempting to speak.

You cannot suppose (ran the vital part of it) *that I should be where I am if the cause we serve were not the cause of Genoa rather than that of the Alliance. We come, not to support the French, but supported by the French; not so much to promote French interests as to deliver Genoa from foreign thraldom and establish her independence. Therefore I have not hesitated to continue in command of a squadron that is bearing part in so laudable a task, confident that once you were made aware of the real aim you would join eager hands with us in this redemption of our native land.*

The Doge raised at last his troubled eyes, and looked from one to the other of his companions.

The Dogaressa's patience gave out. "Well?" she demanded. "What has he to say?"

He pushed the sheet across the table to her. "Read it for yourself. Read it to them."

She snatched it up and read it aloud, and when she had read she pronounced upon it. "God be praised! That should settle your doubts, Antoniotto."

"But is it to be believed?" he questioned gloomily.

"What else," Scipione asked him, "could explain Prospero's part?"

Less quietly the Dogaressa added the question: "Are you doubting your own son?"

"Not his faith. No. Never that. But the trust in others on which it stands."

Scipione, whose ambitious, intriguing soul was fierce with hatred of all the Doria brood, was quick to agree. But the Dogaressa paid no heed.

"Prospero is never rash. He is like me; more Florentine than Genoese. If he writes positively, it is because he is positive."

"That the French have no thought of profit? That is to be credulous."

"What do you gain by mistrust?" she demanded. "Can't even Prospero persuade you that if you hold your gates against Doria now, you hold them against the best interests of your country?"

"Dare I be persuaded? Heaven help me! I am in a fog. The only thing that I see clearly is that I hold the ducal crown from the Emperor. Have I, then, no duty to him?"

He seemed to put the question to them all. It was answered by Madonna Aurelia.

"Is not your highest duty to Genoa? Whilst you stand balancing between the cause of the Emperor and the cause of your own people, the only interest you are really serving is that of the Fregosi. Have no illusions upon that. Give heed to me. You should know by now that I am clear-sighted."

The Doge's heavy glance sought Spinola's, plainly asking a question. The stalwart captain raised shoulders and eyebrows expressively.

"To me it seems, Highness, that what Prospero tells us changes everything. As between the Emperor and the King of France, your duty, as you say, is clearly to the Emperor. But as between either of them and Genoa, your duty, as Prospero assumes, is still more clearly to Genoa. That is how I see the thing. But if your Serenity sees otherwise and is determined to resist, why then you must resolve to crush the mutineers."

Gloomily the Doge considered. Gloomily, at last, he sighed. "Yes. It is well argued, Agostino. Yes. And it is thus Prospero will have argued."

Scipione interposed: "His presence and his assurances would make the case for surrender very strong." But he added, with a tightening of the lips: "Provided that you could trust Andrea Doria."

"If I mistrust him, of what shall I mistrust him?"

"Of too much ambition. Of aspiring to become Prince of Genoa."

"With that danger we can deal when it arises. If it arises." He shook his head, and sighed. "I must not sacrifice the people and set Genoese blood flowing in the streets because of no more than that mistrust. So much, at least, seems clear."

"In that case," said Spinola, "nothing hinders your Serenity's decision."

"Saving, of course," Scipione added, and it is easy to conceive the sneer in his tone, "that for Prospero's faith there is no warrant but the word of Andrea Doria."

Chapter 3

Surrender

The account which Scipione de' Fieschi has left us of that scene in the grey chamber of the Castelletto ends abruptly on that answer of his. Either he was governed by a sense of drama, of which other traces are to be discovered in his writings, or else in what may have followed, the discussion did no more than trail to and fro over ground already covered.

He shows us plainly at least the decision towards which the Doge was leaning, and we know that late that evening messengers went to Doria aboard his flagship and to Cesare Fregoso at Veltri offering to surrender the city. The only condition made was that there should be no punitive action against any Genoese and that the Imperial troops should be allowed to march out with their arms.

This condition being agreed, Don Sancho Lopez departed with his regiment early on the morrow. The Spaniard had argued fiercely against surrender, urging that sooner or later Don Antonio de Leyva must come to their relief. But the Doge, fully persuaded at last that what he did was for Genoa's good, stood firm.

No sooner had the Spaniards marched out than Fregoso brought in three hundred of his French by the Lantern Gate to the acclamations of the populace who regarded them as liberators. Fregoso's main body remained in the camp at Veltri, since it was impossible to quarter so many upon a starving city.

Some two or three hours later, towards noon, the galleys were alongside the moles, and Doria was landing five hundred of his Provençal troops, whilst Prospero brought ashore three hundred of his Pontificals.

They were intended for purposes of parade, so as to lend a martial significance to the occasion. But before the last of them had landed, it was seen that they were needed in a very different sense.

It might be Cesare Fregoso's view that his French troops came to Genoa as deliverers of a people from oppression; but the actual troops seem to have been of a different opinion. To them Genoa was a conquered city, and they were not to be denied the rights over a conquered city in which your sixteenth century mercenary perceived the real inducement to adopt his trade. Only the fear of harsh repression, which they were not in sufficient force to have met, could have restrained their lusts. But in the very people who might have repressed them, the populace which for days now had been in a state of insurgence against the government, they discovered allies and supporters. No sooner had the French broken their ranks and committed one or two acts of violence than the famished rabble took the hint of how it might help itself. At first it was only in quest of food that these ruffians forced their way into the houses of wealthy merchants and the palaces of nobles. But once committed to this violence they did not confine it to the satisfaction of their hunger. After other forms of robbery came the sheer lust of destruction ever latent in the ape-like minds of those who know not how to build.

By the time the forces were landed from the galleys, Genoa was delivered over to all the horrors of a sack, with the added infamy that in this foulness some hundreds of her own children wrought side by side with the rapacious foreign soldiery.

In fury Prospero thrust his way through a group of officers about Doria on the mole. But his anger was silenced by the aspect of Doria's countenance, grey and drawn with a horror no less than Prospero's own.

The Admiral divined his object from the wrath in his eyes. "No words now, Prospero. No words. There is work to do. This foulness must be stemmed." And then his heavy glance alighted on another who strove to approach him, a short, thick-set man in a back-and-breast of black steel worn over a crimson doublet. Under his plumed steel cap the face, black-bearded and bony and disfigured by a scar that crossed his nose, was livid and his eyes were wild. It was Cesare Fregoso.

Doria's glance hardened. He spoke in a growl. "What order do you keep that such things can happen?"

That challenge went to swell the soldier's passion. "What order do I keep? Is the blame mine?"

"Whose else? Who else commands this French rabble?"

"Jesus God! Can a single man contain three hundred?"

"Three thousand if he's fitted for command." Doria's sternness was terrible in its calm.

Bubbles formed on Fregoso's writhing lips. In his anxiety to exonerate himself he was less than truthful. "Set the blame where it belongs: on that fool of a Doge, who out of servility to the Emperor, caring nothing for his country's good, drove the people mad with hunger."

And suddenly he found support from Filippino, who stood scowling at his uncle's side. "Faith, Ser Cesare sets his finger on the wound. The blame is Antoniotto Adorno's."

"As God's my life, it is," Fregoso raged. "These wretched starvelings were not to be restrained once the Spaniards were out of the place. Adorno's futile resistance had made them desperate. And so they go about helping themselves instead of helping Genoa to protect her property, as they would have done if – "

There Doria interrupted the ranter. "Is it a time to talk? Order must be restored. Words can come later."

Prospero leaned over, and touched Fregoso's arm. "And a word from me will be amongst them, Ser Cesare. Also a word to you, Filippino."

Doria denied them leisure in which to answer.

"Stir yourselves in the name of God. Leave bickering." He swung to Prospero. "You know what is to do. About it! Take the east side. I'll see to the west. And use a heavy hand."

So as to make it all the heavier, Prospero ordered one of his captains, a Neapolitan named Cattaneo, to land another two hundred men. He took the view that since the looters were roving the city in bands it was necessary to break up his troops similarly into bands, so as to deal with them. Accordingly he divided his forces into little companies of a score men, to each of which he appointed a leader.

Of one of these companies he assumed the command, himself; and almost at once, in the open space by the Fontanelle, not a hundred yards from the quays, he found employment for it in the violated dwelling of a merchant. A mixed band of French soldiers and waterside ruffians were actively looting the house, and Prospero caught them in the act of torturing the merchant, so as to make him disclose where he kept his gold.

Prospero hanged the leader, and left his body dangling above the doorway of the house he had outraged. The others, under the merciless blows of pike-butts, were driven forth as harbingers of the wrath that was loose against all pillagers.

From this stern beginning, Prospero swept on to pursue his work with swift and summary ruthlessness. Once when, perhaps, the poet in him inspired poetic justice, he caught the ringleader of a gang guzzling in a nobleman's wrecked cellar, he had the fellow thrust head foremost into a hogshead of wine, and submerged at least a dozen times almost to the point of drowning, so that for once he might drink his fill. In the main, however, he lost no time in such refinements. He did what was to do at speed, and at speed departed, never staying for the curses of those whose bones he broke or the thanks of those he delivered.

Working eastwards and upwards to the heights of Carignano, he came towards noon into a little space before a tiny church, where acacia trees made a square about a plot of grass. It was a pleasant, peaceful spot, all bathed in sunlight, fragrant with the blossoms that clustered like berries of gold on the feathery branches. He paused there to assemble his men, so that they might keep together, for some five of them, who had been hurt in the course of their repressive activities, were lagging in the rear.

A distant sound of male voices, raucous with mirth, flowed out of an alley on the left of the church and above the level of the square, reached by six steps rising under an arch. Suddenly, as Prospero listened, there was a swift succession of crashes, as of timbers being rent by heavy blows. Laughter rose louder, receded, and then, like a clarion call came the piercing scream of a woman.

Up the steps with every sound man of his company at his heels leapt Prospero. The way was gloomy, lying between high walls, the one on his right being thick with ivy from foot to summit. Twenty paces on a patch of sunshine broke the gloom, where a doorway gaped, the door hanging battered on its hinges. To this he was guided by repeated screams, and the sounds of ugly laughter that were hideously mingled with them.

Under the lintel Prospero paused at gaze. He had a fleeting glimpse of a wide garden space, of greensward, trim hedges, flowering shrubs, a vast fountain splashing into a pool, the white gleam of statuary against the green, and as a background to it all the wide façade of a palace in black and white marbles rising above a delicate, Romanesque colonnade. Of all this his impression was no more than vague. His attention went first to a youth in a plain livery that betokened the servant, who lay prone upon the grass in a curious twisted way, with arms outflung; near him sat an older man, his elbows on his knees, his head in his hands, and blood streaming between the fingers of them. The continuing outcries drew his glance on to behold a woman, whose upper garments hung torn about her waist, fleeing in terror. After her through the shrubs, with whoops of laughter, crashed a pair of ruffians, whilst away on Prospero's left, against the garden's high wall, stood another woman, tall, slim and straight, confronting wide-eyed the menacing mockery of yet another of these brigands.

Seeking afterwards to evoke in memory her image, all that he could remember was that she was dressed in white with a glint of jewels from the caul that confined her dark hair, so fleeting had been his glance, so intent his mind upon his purpose there.

He stepped clear of the threshold to give admission to his men.

"Make an end of that," was his sharp, brief order.

Instantly a half-dozen of his troopers plunged after those who were hunting the woman in the garden's depth, whilst others made for the rascal who was baiting the lady in white.

The man had spun round at the stir behind him, and by instinct rather than by reason dropped a hand to his hilt. But before he could draw they were upon him. His steel cap was knocked off, his sword-belt was removed and the straps of his back-and-breast were severed by a knife. Thus deprived of arms and armour, pike-butts thrust him towards the doorway, pikestaffs fell about his shoulders until he cried out in pain and terror whilst stumbling blindly forward. His two companions came similarly driven, until a pikestaff taking one of them across the head, laid him senseless on the turf. They took him by the heels and hauled him out and along the alley, down which his fellows were now being swept. They dragged him down the steps into the little square, reckless of how they bumped his head, and at last abandoned him senseless on the plot of grass under the acacia trees. Prospero following close upon their heels, had had no more thought here than elsewhere to wait for the thanks of those he had delivered. The urgency of his business never suffered him to linger.

And the men from his galleys, well-disciplined and imbued with something of his own spirit, displayed all the promptitude and impartiality he could desire of them, dealing alike with all marauders, whether French or Genoese, clearing assaulted houses and sweeping the looters before them with many a bleeding head.

Late in the afternoon, when, weary and sickened by his task, Prospero could account it performed and order restored, he set out with his little band of followers to make his way at last to the ducal palace and present himself to his father.

They came by way of Sarzano, and thence climbed the steep ways that led to San Lorenzo and the ducal palace. Although of rapine there were no further signs, yet the city was naturally in a ferment, and Prospero's progress lay through streets that were thronged and noisy with people, most of whom were moving now in the same uphill direction.

As he advanced he was joined by successive bodies of his soldiers returning from similar labours, and one of these was led by Cattaneo. Before San Lorenzo was reached his following amounted to fully a hundred and fifty men. They made up a fairly solid phalanx, favourably viewed by citizens of the better sort, but scowled upon by the populace for the roughness of the repression they had used.

Doria's methods had been more gentle. Whilst Prospero had dispatched five hundred men in twenty-five detachments of a score apiece to bludgeon the pillagers into decency, the Admiral had used two hundred men to form a line across half the city; then he had sent in four companies, each of a hundred men, with rolling drums and blaring trumpets, and it had needed little more than this loud advertisement of coming repression to put the delinquents to flight. The ruffians of the populace went to earth in their hovels, and the ruffians of Fregoso's French troops made off as unobtrusively as they could to the quarters assigned to them in the great barrack opposite the Cappucini. Thus Doria had avoided arousing any of that fierce resentment of which Prospero perceived himself the object as he marched his swelling troop towards San Lorenzo.

There, in the square before the ducal palace, he found a throng so dense that it seemed impossible to cleave a passage through it. A double file of pikemen of Doria's Provençal troops was ranged before the palace in a barrier to restrain the multitude, whilst from a balcony immediately above the wide portal a booming voice was compelling a hushed attention.

Looking up over the rippling sea of heads, Prospero recognized in the speaker, a big man, grey-headed and elderly, Ottaviano Fregoso, who had been Doge when last the French were in possession of

Genoa. His heart was tightened by bewildered apprehension. For if the ducal chlamys in which Ottaviano Fregoso was now arrayed bore evidence of anything, it was that with the return of the French he had been restored to the ducal office. On his left stood his cousin Cesare Fregoso, on his right towered the majestic figure of Andrea Doria.

Holding his breath, so that he should miss no word that might explain this ill-omened portent, Prospero heard the fulsome terms in which Ottaviano was announcing that the Lord Andrea Doria, the first of their fellow-citizens, the very father of his country, was come to deliver Genoa from foreign oppression. No more should the Ligurian Republic be taxed in levies to maintain the Imperial armies in Italy. Those Spanish shackles were broken. Under the benevolent protection of the King of France, Genoa would henceforth be free, and for this great boon their thanks were due to the Lord Andrea Doria, that lion of the sea.

There he paused, like an actor inviting applause, and at once it came in roars of "Long live Doria!"

It was the Lord Andrea, himself, whose raised hand at last restored the silence in which Ottaviano Fregoso might continue.

He came to more immediate and concrete benefits resulting from the events. Grain ships were already unloading in the port, and there was bread for all. His cousin Cesare's men were driving in cattle to be slaughtered, and there was an end to the famine they had been suffering. Again a rolling thunder applauded him; and this time the cry was: "Long live the Doge Fregoso!"

After that came assurances from Messer Ottaviano that the people's sufferings should not go unpunished. Those responsible for all the misery endured should be called to account; those who, so as to maintain Genoa under the heel of a foreign tyrant, had not scrupled to subject the people to starvation should be brought speedily to justice. With a crude eloquence Ottaviano painted the maleficence of those who for their own unpatriotic ends had visited the city with those hardships, and he worked himself up into such a frenzy of indignation that very soon it was communicated to his vast audience. He was answered with fierce shouts of "Death to the Adorni!" "Death to the betrayers of the Republic!"

From the petrification of horror into which that speech, its insidious implications and its answering clamour, had brought him, Prospero was roused by a vigorous plucking at his sleeve, and a voice in his ear.

"Well found, at last, Prospero. I have been seeking you these two hours and more."

Scipione de' Fieschi, flushed and out of breath, stood at his elbow.

"Since you'll have heard that mountebank, you'll know what is doing; though hardly all, or you would not be here."

"I was on my way to the palace when this press brought me to a standstill."

"If you seek your father, you'll not find him in the palace. He is in the Castelletto. A prisoner."

"God of Heaven!"

"Do you wonder? The Fregosi mean to cast his head to the mob so as to ingratiate themselves. To destroy the old Doge is to make things safe for the new. Those who are loyal to the Adorni must be left without a rallying-point. Most logical." Abruptly, his eye ranged over the serried ordered ranks aflash with steel that were now wedged into the throng. "Are these your men and can you trust them? If so, you had best act promptly if you would save your father."

In a face white with distress Prospero's lips parted to ask a question: "My mother?"

"With your father. Sharing his prison."

"Forward, then. My men shall open me a way to the palace. I will see the Admiral at once."

"The Admiral? Doria?" In his scorn, Scipione almost laughed. "As well make your appeal to Fregoso himself. It is Doria who has proclaimed him Doge. Words won't avail here, my Prospero. This calls for action. Swift and prompt. The French troops in the Castelletto are not more than fifty, and the gates are open. This is your opportunity, so that you are sure of these men of yours."

Prospero beckoned Cattaneo forward and gave an order. It was passed swiftly and quietly along the ranks, and soon that martial phalanx was writhing itself a way out of the press that hemmed it in. To go forward was impossible. It remained only to retreat and to take another road to the heights whence the Castelletto dominated the city.

Chapter 4

The Castelletto

On the balcony the new Doge was resuming his harangue; and because the stir of Prospero's troop was not accomplished without some roughness and some noise, the mob would have passed from protests to menaces and perhaps to violence but for the formidable glitter of that compact and full-armed body.

They won out at last and gained the less encumbered spaces before the Cathedral, where, however, they still had to breast the stream of townsfolk advancing in the opposite direction. Beyond that space, as they ascended a steep street leading to the Campetto, they moved more freely and in orderly formation, their pikes at the slope. Active interference with them none dared to venture. But more than once, recognized for the foreign troops of Prospero Adorno, responsible for the harsh measures of that day, jeers and insults greeted and followed them from some of those who had been repressed. Answering taunt with laughing taunt as they marched, they pressed on, Prospero in the rear with Scipione, his countenance white and wicked.

In the Campetto they were met by another of Prospero's captains, who with some sixty men he had assembled was on his way downhill in quest of the main body. Thus when at last Prospero reached the red walls of the Castelletto, flushed now by the setting sun, he brought at his heels a force more than two hundred strong.

The arched gateway yawned open, and they went through at the double. The men who sprang forth to challenge them as their accelerated steps clattered past the gatehouse were swept aside like twigs on the edges of a torrent.

In the courtyard, one half of which lay already in shadow, more men confronted them, and the officer in charge, a Provençal of Doria's following, recognizing the Pontifical Captain, stepped forward briskly.

"In what can I serve you, Sir Captain?" The deference of the question was purely mechanical. The Provençal knew enough of what had happened that day in Genoa to be made uneasy by this invasion in strength.

Prospero was short. "You will place the Castelletto in my charge."

Dismay overspread the man's swarthy countenance. It was a moment before he found his voice. "With deference, Sir Captain, that I cannot do. Messer Cesare Fregoso has placed me in command here, and here I must remain until Messer Cesare relieves me."

"Or until I sweep you out. You've heard me, sir. Willingly or unwillingly you'll obey."

The officer attempted bluster. A big man, his proportions seemed to swell. "Sir Captain, I cannot take your orders. I – "

Prospero waved his attention to the men now in ordered ranks behind him. "There is the argument that will compel you."

A gloomy laugh followed upon a grimace of malevolence. "Ah, Ventre Dieu! If you take that tone, what can I do?"

"What I bid you. It will save trouble."

"For me, perhaps. But for you, sir, it may make it."

"That is my affair, I think."

"I hope you'll like it." The fellow swung on his heel, bawling orders in a voice like a trumpet call. Men came at the double in response to it, formed their ranks across the courtyard, and within ten minutes were marching out of the fortress to the tune of "*En Revenant d'Espagne*". The officer going last swept Prospero a bow that was full of mockery and the menace of things to come.

Prospero went in, to find his father, and was led by Scipione up a narrow stone staircase to a portal guarded by two sentries, who were summarily dismissed to rejoin their company. Then Prospero unlocked the door, and across an antechamber bare as a prison, came to that little closet tapestried in blue and grey.

On a day-bed set under one of those narrow windows that commanded a view of the city, the harbour and the gulf beyond, Antoniotto Adorno reclined in a drowsiness of exhaustion. Despite the heat he was wrapped in a long black houppelande that was heavy with dark fur. His lady, slim and youthful in a stiff high-corsaged gown of purple shot with gold, occupied an arm-chair at the head of his couch.

A table in mid-chamber was encumbered with the remnants of the very simplest of meals: the half of a loaf of rye bread, a hemisphere of Lombard cheese, a dish of fruit, figs, peaches and grapes from some patrician garden, a tall silver beaker of wine and some glasses.

The creak of the door on its hinges roused Monna Aurelia. She looked over her shoulder and her face went pale under the black, peaked headdress at the sight of Prospero almost hesitant upon the threshold. Then she was on her feet, with heaving bosom and a cry that caused her lord to raise his heavy eyelids and look round in his turn. Beyond a wider opening of the kindly generous old eyes, Antoniotto's countenance showed no change. His voice spoke so quietly that it was impossible to suspect any emotion.

"Ah! It is you, Prospero. You arrive at a sad moment, as you see."

But if his father had no further reproach for him, Prospero in that hour was not disposed to be tender with himself. "You may marvel, sir, that I should come at all." He advanced, Scipione following and closing the door.

"No, no. I hoped you would. You will have something to tell me."

"Only that you have a fool for a son, which will be no news to you, unless you have supposed him also a knave." He was bitter. "I was too easily duped by that rascal Doria."

Antoniotto's nether lip was protruded deprecatingly. "No more easily than I," said he, and added: "Like father, like child."

Shamed as no invective could have shamed him, Prospero's pained eyes sought his mother. In a whorl of maternal emotion, she was holding out her hands to him. He stepped quickly to her, caught them in his own and bowed to kiss each of them in turn.

"For once your father is just," she greeted him. "Your fault is no worse than his own, as he says. His obstinacy is to blame for all." Her voice hardened shrewishly. "He should have done the will of the people. He should have surrendered when they desired it. Then they would have supported him. Instead, he left them to starve into exasperation, and then to mutiny against him at the bidding of the Fregosi. That is where the blame lies."

Thereafter they wrangled fruitlessly; she intent upon being his advocate, Prospero insistently self-condemnatory. Antoniotto listened listlessly, almost drowsily. At last Scipione reminded them that it was more important now to discover an issue from their peril than to dispute as to how it had arisen.

"The issue at least I can provide," Prospero asserted. "To that extent I can repair my fault. I have a sufficient force at hand."

"Is that an issue?" cried his mother. "Flight? Forsaking everything? A fine issue that for the Doge of Genoa, leaving the Fregosi and these Doria rogues triumphant."

"In the pass to which things have come, Madonna," ventured Scipione, "I'd be glad even to be sure of that for you. Do you suppose, Prospero, that you have men enough? That you will be suffered to reach your galleys? Or, if you reach them, that Doria will allow you to depart?"

Antoniotto roused himself. "Ask, rather: Will the Fregosi? It is they who are now the real masters. Can you doubt they will require that no Adorno be left alive to come back and dispute their usurpation?"

"Whilst I hold this fortress – "

"Dismiss the thought," his father interrupted him. "You cannot hold it for a day. Troops must be fed. We are without victuals."

This was a stab in the back to all Prospero's hopes. Blank consternation overspread his face. "What, then, remains?"

"Since we haven't wings, or even a flying-machine, like that idiot who broke his neck off the Tower of Sant' Angelo, it remains only to recommend our souls to God."

And there they might have left it had not Scipione brought his wits to their assistance. "Your way out," he said, "lies not in force through the city, but alone by way of the open country."

Under their questioning eyes he explained himself. The eastern face of the Castelletto rose upon the wall of the city itself. From the roofed battlements that crowned the summit of the fortress to the rocks at the base of the city wall it was a cliff of seventy feet of masonry.

"You will leave Genoa," said Scipione, "as St Paul left Damascus. In default of a basket, a cradle is easily made, and easily lowered by ropes."

Antoniotto's eyes remained unresponsively dull. He reminded them of his condition. His wound put it beyond his power to go that way. It had drained his strength. Besides, what did he matter now? Having lost all that he valued, he was ready to face with indifference whatever might follow. He would be glad, he assured them with a sincerity they could not doubt, to come to rest. Let Prospero and his mother make the attempt, unencumbered by a sick and helpless man.

Neither Prospero nor his mother, however, would give heed to this. Either he went with them or they remained with him. Confronted with these alternatives, Antoniotto ended by yielding, and it remained only to prepare for flight.

By dusk all was ready, and later, under cover of darkness, the improvised cradle, bearing each of the three fugitives in turn, was lowered from the battlements by men acting under the directions of Scipione.

Thus furtively ended the Adorno rule in Genoa, and whilst Madonna Aurelia raged against Doria and Fregosi alike, Prospero reviled only himself for having been used as the instrument of the perfidy that had encompassed the ruin of the father whose faltering steps he supported in that ignominious flight.

Chapter 5

The Battle of Amalfi

It was in the first days of August of 1527 that Doria took possession of Genoa for the King of France, and Prospero Adorno, in flight from the city, abandoned his command of the Papal navy.

Less than a year later – towards the end of May of 1528 – we find him in Naples, as an Imperial Captain, serving under Don Hugo de Moncada, the Emperor's Viceroy.

His father had perished miserably, be it from an aggravation of his infirm condition as a result of hardships endured in the escape, be it from a loss of the will to live, be it from a combination of the two. He was a dying man when at last they had reached Milan and the shelter which Antonio de Leyva, the Imperial Governor, so readily afforded them. There, in the great castle of Porta Giovio, Antoniotto Adorno had yielded up his life within three days of arrival.

The first explosion of his widow's grief was of a violence that took Prospero by surprise. Reluctantly he had regarded his mother as one who loved herself too well to be deeply stirred by whatever might happen to another, no matter how near of kin. In the hour of his own grief he found some consolation in that under the hard surface of his mother's nature a depth of feeling made of their bereavement a bond between them.

All of a day and a night she was in a state of prostration. But thirty hours after Antoniotto's death she came, in black velvet, to stand with Prospero beside his father's bier.

Often he had heard the voice of this daughter of the Strozzi hard to the pitch of cruelty, but never so hard as now.

"Your father lies here murdered. You know his murderers, and where to find them. It is the Dorias, greedy, perfidious, faithless and unscrupulous, who have brought him, broken-hearted, to this miserable end. Never forget that, Prospero."

"I am not likely to forget it."

She touched his arm, her voice deepening in solemnity. "Kneel, my child. Kneel. Place your hand on the bier. There, where his heart should be. It is cold now; but it was warm once with love of you. Make oath upon that heart never to rest until you've brought the House of Doria as low as Andrea Doria has brought Antoniotto Adorno. Swear that, my son. Let it be as a last prayer, to give your father peace."

He knelt and put forth his hand. Remembering the perfidy which had made him the instrument of his father's ruin, his voice pronounced the oath with an intensity as fierce as that which administered it.

The first step towards its fulfilment was taken when Prospero embraced the chance which de Leyva afforded him of entering the Emperor's service.

In the year that was sped since that was done, as if the curse which Charles V had invited by the sack of Rome were paralysing his strength, the campaign had gone steadily against the Imperial arms. Marshal de Lautrec, who had made himself master of Upper Italy, had for two months now been encamped before Naples with thirty thousand men. The siege had brought the city to the point of famine; and in the wake of this the foul spectre of the plague was already stalking. Co-operating with Lautrec, Doria's galleys had come to bar the sea approaches. But the Lord Andrea, himself, was not in command. He had been content to let Filippino take his place, himself remaining in Genoa. To the mystery of this the key was supplied by Scipione de' Fieschi. He had contrived to maintain a correspondence with Prospero, and in his later letters there was news of bitter unrest in Genoa. He wrote that the fate of politicians who do not fulfil their promises was overtaking Andrea Doria, and that his dominant position in the Republic had never stood so near destruction.

The French protection, accepted on Doria's assurances that under it the Ligurian Republic would at last be free, was proving a tyranny as harsh and exacting as any that the State had known, and the hero's aureole was fading fast from the Lord Andrea's head. Matters had been brought to a climax by the French endeavour to build up the port of Savona at the expense of Genoa. In this, if it were continued, the Genoese foresaw their own inevitable ruin; and Doria was being held responsible for it, since the change of masters which produced this threat had certainly been his work. Even the Fregosi, whom he had set up, were in the swelling movement against him.

Thus threatened with the extinction of the credit upon which he depended, Doria sought refuge in proclaiming that France had broken faith with him, and that he would quit the service of King Francis if these wrongs were not righted.

Scipione wrote of these things in obvious malicious satisfaction, and from the events he drew inferences which, whilst dictated by the same malice, were yet irresistible.

They explained, he thought, why instead of going, himself, to Naples, Andrea Doria had sent his nephew Filippino. He was afraid to leave Genoa at such a moment. He must remain, so that the honesty of his intentions should appear, and so as to defend what was left him of his reputation. Scipione accounted it certain that self-defence must drive him the length of quitting French service. And there were rumours, too, of personal grievances. It was said that money was not forthcoming from King Francis. The knightly monarch's ladies absorbed the gold that should have come to pay and feed the troops. Doria, already heavily out of pocket and vainly clamouring for arrears, was notoriously as implacable as any other mercenary where money was concerned.

Scipione ventured the opinion that in this occasion, if properly employed, lay the means to mend the Emperor's fortunes in Italy. To extricate himself from his present difficulties Doria would sell his services and his galleys on almost any terms.

Prospero perfectly understood the malicious hope that Scipione fostered. If Doria, being tempted, should succumb, and abandoning the service of France to which he was pledged, pass over to the enemy, he might win the immediate approval of the Genoese, but at the price of the world's contempt; and once Genoa perceived this, Scipione conceived it unlikely that Doria would count for much in the councils of the Republic.

With the letter that contained all this, Prospero sought the Marquis del Vasto, who was lodged in the Castel Nuovo regally, as became a consequence derived not only from his relationship with the great Pescara, but from the intimacy in which he was held by Charles V. Deep in the confidence of the Emperor, Alfonso d'Avalos was regarded in Naples as more closely representing His Majesty than even the Viceroy himself.

The young Marquis – he was, like the Emperor, in his twenty-eighth year – darkly handsome of person and of easy courtly manners, received his visitor with affability. Prospero went without preamble to the matter that brought him.

"You know my views, my lord, of the action to which the Viceroy is being driven by counsels of despair."

"More than that." Del Vasto smiled. "I share them."

"Why, then, here is something that may persuade him to stay his hand awhile." He proffered his letter.

It was a day of gloom and storm, and del Vasto moved to the window, against which the rain was beating, seeking light by which to read. He was a long time reading, fingering his little pointed beard the while, and a longer time considering, whilst the only sounds were the lashing of the rain and dull boom of the waves upon the rocks at the castle's base.

At last, when he turned again to face his companion there was a faint flush glowing through his olive skin and a glitter in his dark eyes, betraying a queer excitement.

"Is the writer trustworthy?" he asked, sharply. "Can you depend upon his opinions?"

"If his opinions were all, I should not have troubled you. What he believes is of no consequence. We can draw inferences for ourselves. What matter are the facts which he reports, the events in Genoa. To these we can add our knowledge of Doria ambition. He must extricate himself from his difficulty, or become the last man in the State, where he had hoped to be the first."

"Yes. I see that." The frowning Marquis toyed absently with his thumb-ring. "But it is possible that he speaks the truth when he declares that he was betrayed by France. More, it is probable; for King Francis is of a shifty nature, reckless of promises, grudging of fulfilment."

"That is no matter." Prospero displayed impatience. This defence of Doria irritated him. "It does not affect the situation."

"Believe me, it does; for if I were persuaded that Doria is untrustworthy, I should not care to deal with him."

He looked at Prospero as if inviting an answer. But Prospero subdued himself. It was inevitable that he should share Scipione's hope of seeing Doria unmasked; and having sought del Vasto so as to further that aim, it was not for him to raise obstacles against it.

In the face of Prospero's silence, the Marquis resumed. "I know, of course, that you have very cause to think the worst of Doria. The appearances justify you. But they are still only appearances."

"My father did not die merely in appearance," said Prospero, unable to repress at least that protest.

Slowly del Vasto came forward until one of his fine hands was resting on Prospero's shoulder. He spoke softly. "I know. I know. That must colour all your view." He paused a moment, then became brisk. "I'll borrow the courier who brought you this letter. He shall bear me a word to Andrea Doria that will put Messer de' Fieschi's judgment to the test."

"Have you in mind to make him a proposal? Would you go as far as that, my lord?"

"At need I'll go further. I know the Emperor's mind in this as I know my own. He accounts Doria the greatest captain of the age, as, indeed, do we all. It is his firm conviction that whom Doria serves will be master of the Mediterranean Sea. If Fieschi is right, here is the chance to win him for the Emperor's service, and His Majesty would never forgive me if I missed it. I'll write to Madrid at once. And meanwhile I shall open negotiations with Messer Andrea." His hand closed again on Prospero's shoulder with more than ordinary warmth. "I shall owe you an increase of credit with my master. The inspiration to bring me this letter was as shrewd as it was friendly. I am very grateful to you."

Prospero returned the smile of those dark liquid eyes. "That is an even better recompense than the arresting of this ill-conceived project to break the blockade."

But when they came later in the day to the meeting of the Viceroy's Council they found that ill-conceived project none so easy to arrest.

Hugo de Moncada sat with his captains in the Chamber of the Angels in the Beverello Tower, a chamber so called from the angelic mural paintings of Bicazzo.

They were famous captains all: the hard-bitten Neapolitan, Cesare Fieramosca; the sombre Ascanio Colonna; Girolami da Trani, the Grand-Master of the artillery, and the hunchback Giustiniani, accounted one of the foremost naval commanders of the day. There was also Philibert of Chalons, Prince of Orange, who like Alfonso of Avalos had not yet reached the age of thirty, but whose celebrity and authority stood high. Prospero came to the council-table with Scipione's letter, and made known its contents, which, he opined, should bear upon the matter they were gathered to consider.

When he paused, having read the vital phrase: "If time be not lost in seizing the moment, Charles V may buy Doria and his galleys on almost any terms," del Vasto interposed. "I may tell you, sirs, that no time is being lost. I have already dispatched a proposal to Andrea Doria in my master's name."

There was a general movement of startled surprise, which the Prince of Orange allayed almost at once.

"There was no rashness in that. His Majesty's confirmation may confidently be assumed."

"That being the situation," said del Vasto, "the gods having tossed this gift into our lap, we are relieved, I think, of the necessity of pursuing this matter of attempting to break the blockade. We can wait."

The hunchback Giustiniani threw himself back in his chair with an audible sigh of relief.

"God be thanked for that. For the business was desperate."

But they reckoned without the obstinacy of Moncada. The swarthy, stockily built Aragonese at the table's head was contemptuous.

"Are you supposing that with Naples starving and pest-ridden, we can wait whilst couriers come and go, and terms are settled?" He leaned forward and with a powerful brown finger punctuated what he had to say by taps upon the table. "Andrea Doria may be for sale, or he may not. The one thing certain is that he can't be bought today or this week. The transaction will need time, and we command none. Send off your couriers, by all means, Lord Marquis; but meanwhile I must bring food into Naples, and I can't do that until I've chased Filippino Doria from the Gulf."

"Which I've already declared to be a task beyond the resources at our command," grumbled Giustiniani. "And I know something of these matters."

Moncada, however, was not to be intimidated. A soldier of fortune, nobly born and of a wide experience gathered under Cesare Borgia and the great Gonsalvo de Cordoba, he had fought at sea against the Moors and at one time had been Admiral of the Imperial fleet. He was of a boldness almost without parallel in his day, and he indulged it now. From dockyard and arsenal he had scraped together a force of six ordinary traffic galleys, four feluccas, a couple of brigantines and some fishing boats. With this ramshackle fleet he proposed to assail the eight powerful, well-found war galleys with which Filippino held the Gulf. He possessed no adequate ordnance, but what he lacked in this he would make up in man-power by embarking a thousand Spanish arquebusiers. That there were risks, grave risks, he was ready to admit. But they had reached the desperate stage in which any risk must be accepted, and, impatient of opposition, he looked to his captains to remember it.

When he had forcibly expressed himself, del Vasto was the only one who still ventured to oppose him. Such was his confidence that he would willingly let Naples suffer plague and famine yet awhile; but so as to save time, he would not hesitate to go to Genoa in person at once and negotiate with Doria in the Emperor's name.

It was all in vain. There was no swaying Moncada. A Venetian fleet under Lando was known to be on its way to reinforce Filippino. Once it arrived, all chance of a breakthrough would be gone. He dared not delay.

On that the council broke up, and the captains went about their preparations for the adventure.

It proved an ill-conducted affair from the outset. The only chance of an inferior force's success against a superior one lies in surprise, and the chance of this which might so easily have been his, Moncada threw away.

In the dark hours before the dawn of a calm day of late May the fleet, with the Viceroy himself in command, left the roadstead under the heights of Posilipo, and reached its station on the eastern side of Capri just as the sunrise cast a rosy glow upon the island bluffs. The intention had been to set out at midnight so that under cover of darkness they might lie in wait for Filippino as he cruised in the Gulf of Salerno. But such had been the delays that the light of day came to reveal the fleet to hostile eyes before the headlands of Capri could supply a dissembling background.

To make matters worse, the chance of a night surprise being lost, Moncada, that carefree soldier of fortune who for thirty years had gaily carried his life in his hands, prepared for battle as for a wedding. He landed his forces and feasted them on the island; and after this, delayed further whilst they listened to a sermon preached them by a friar. Then when at last he took the sea to meet Filippino's galleys which advanced in the far-flung line abreast that best disposed them to any evolution, Moncada went in such a bravery of banners and with such flourishes of trumpets that he might have been upon a Venetian water festival in time of Carnival.

Prospero, who had been given command of the *Sicama*, one of the best of the Neapolitan galleys, observed all this with gloomy forebodings. They were headed south, the six galleys forming line abreast like their opponents, with the lesser vessels straggling after them. As if expressing Moncada's impatience to be at grips, their speed was an ever-increasing one, mercilessly wrung by the whips of the wardens from the slaves at the oars.

As they came abreast of Amalfi they observed that three of the Genoese galleys at the seaward end of Filippino's line veered away from it and made for the open.

Too rashly the Spaniards interpreted that action. "They are in flight!" was the cry that ran from vessel to vessel, and more fiercely fell the lashes of the wardens on the straining backs of the panting oarsmen.

Prospero, however, saw the thing quite differently, and said so to del Vasto, who stood with him on the poop of the *Sicama*. Deliberately the Marquis, who was without experience of naval action, had chosen to serve as lieutenant to this young captain, whose fame he knew.

"That is no flight." Prospero pointed to a flag that had broken from the poop of the galley that now occupied the middle position of Filippino's line "Those three obey a signal, and the signalling galley is the capitana. That the plan was preconcerted is clear from the capitana's present position in the line. The departing galleys held their stations only temporarily. Filippino is forming a reserve, with which to strike as the events may dictate."

All that Moncada perceived was that his six galleys were now confronted by no more than five. Encouraged, he drove forward the more furiously in his haste to come to close quarters, so as to neutralize the enemy's superior artillery. So intent was he upon this that he disdained to open fire, the advice offered by Trani, who was with him on his flagship.

"That is merely to invite the like answer from them. I want to do this business with cold steel."

Filippino, however, trusting to his superior ordnance, was just as anxious to avoid boarding tactics. Flame and smoke belched from the great basilisk on the prow of his capitana, and launched upon Moncada a stone shot, two hundred pounds in weight. The monstrous projectile, truly aimed, enfiladed the capitana of Naples from stem to stern; it shore away rostrum and rambade, and dealing death and destruction in its passage, it crashed through the tabernacle astern and went to spend itself in the waters of the gulf.

Moncada and Trani were smothered where they stood in the blood of those on the vestibule whom the shot had shattered. The oars faltered, fell into confusion, ceased as a result of death and panic among the slaves. Two surviving half-demented wardens flung themselves at the gang to restore order, summoning soldiers to assist them to drag out the cumbering dead and wounded, and plying their lashes to subdue the living.

Across the shambles of the gang-deck, Girolamo da Trani leapt, himself to replace the gunners who had been swept away from the guns on the starboard side of the rambade. From the deck he snatched up a glowing match, fallen from a hand now dead, and touched off one of the falconets. But the galley had yawed from her course, and the shot went wide and harmless. An officer with furious vigour, making himself heard above the general din, was assembling and posting arquebusiers under cover of the wreckage of the rambade, and Trani was desperately seeking cannoneers for their other guns, when a second burst of fire swept their deck from the enemy capitana, which had now ceased to ply her oars.

Perceiving in this Filippino's design to avoid battle at close quarters, Moncada roared orders to his wardens to get the oars going, so as to come to grapples with the Genoese.

On either side of the two flagships the other galleys had now opened fire on one another, and for a little while the engagement resolved itself into a number of artillery duels with no particular advantage yet to either side. During this the Genoese capitana drew so far ahead of her line that, at last, she was midway between the two fleets. So much fire had Filippino pumped by now into Moncada's galley, as to be sure that her power of resistance was so broken that she might with confidence be boarded and carried. To this end he was bearing down upon her when Prospero, from his station on the extreme right of the line, swung the *Sicama* inwards across the bows of his neighbour, the *Villamarina*, signalling to her to veer with him. If he exposed his flank to the enemy fire, he had taken the precaution of ordering his men to lie prone, so that the shot should sweep over them. His aim was to engage Filippino with a superior force, not only so as to arrest the advance upon Moncada's crippled galley, but so that by striking at the head of the enemy fleet, he might perhaps force a quick decision.

Cesare Fieramosca who commanded the Villamarina, quick to perceive his aim, instantly obeyed the summons, and swung with him to intercept the Genoese. But Filippino perceived it, too, and as instantly signalled to the two galleys on his left to meet and hold off the menace.

It became a race between the Spanish galleys to intercept Filippino and the Genoese to intercept the Spaniards. Vainly did Prospero call to his wardens to lash the last ounce of power out of his rowers and vainly did the slaves respond. Unable to elude the two Genoese, Prospero was forced to engage them, and soon the four galleys locked together were at death grips, whilst Filippino bore on to administer the coup-de-grâce to the half-shattered Spanish capitana.

Giustiniani on the *Gobba*, seeing in that battle of four galleys at close quarters the very heart of the engagement, sped to the assistance of Prospero, leaving the two remaining Spaniards to engage the two remaining Genoese. As for the feluccas and the fishing-boats, without adequate leadership or armament, they were kept at a respectful distance by the enemy's fire.

Prospero meanwhile, in back-and-breast and steel cap, and wielding a two-handed sword, had led a charge aboard the *Pellegrina* that swept her from end to end and reduced her into possession. This enabled him to pass on to swell Fieramosca's forces that were beating down the resistance of the other galley, the *Donzella*. And a terrible resistance it proved, in which the Spaniards faced not only the arquebusiers of Lautrec, but the actual slave-gangs, a horde of half naked Barbary fighters, armed with target and sword. Relieved of their chains, and given by Filippino under solemn oath a promise that they should be restored to liberty if victory favoured them, they fought with the desperate fury which such a hope inspired. Nevertheless, assailed on both quarters, despite their superior numbers, the two Genoese galleys were at last overpowered. But even as the last blow was struck that gave the victory to the Spaniards, Prospero, foul with grime and sweat and the blood of the carnage through which he had come, realized from the poop of the *Donzella* that this victory came too late.

The three galleys that had stood off were now coming back at speed into the fray, proving themselves the reserve he had pronounced them. His lingering hope was that their purpose would be to attempt to wrest from him the vessels he had captured. But Lomellino, who commanded that reserve, knew better, or had been better schooled. His blow was to be struck at the head, at Moncada's capitana, which at grips with Filippino and despite her battered state was still valiantly holding her own.

Straight for Moncada raced Lomellino's three vessels. The spur of one of them shore away the rudder of the Spaniard, whilst a second one rammed her amidships, and the noise of the breaking oars made one with the screams of the slaves whose ribs were being crushed by the impact. It brought the mainmast smashing murderously down to put an end by its fall to the agony of some of these wretches, and amongst others whom it crushed to death was Girolamo da Trani who was still directing the galley's fire.

Then the third of Lomellino's galleys drove her rostrum over the space whence the rostrum of the capitana had been shorn away by the first shot of the battle.

Moncada, seeing his danger of being boarded on three sides at once, leapt, sword in hand, from the poop to the deck below, roaring a rallying-cry to his men. The shot of an arquebuse shattered his right arm, another ploughed deeply through his left thigh. He went down in a welter of blood, strove for a moment to rise again as the sound of the enemy rushing his decks rolled to him like thunder; then he passed into an unconsciousness from which he was never to return.

Ascanio Colonna saw him go down, and sprang to his aid, to be felled, himself, momentarily dazed. A fire-pot flung by one of the men on the cross-trees of Lomellino's galley had almost crushed his helmet.

A rapidly diminishing line of arquebusiers still held the space between the stern and the middle platform where the stump of the mainmast sprouted from the deck. They were ringed about by fire and steel, deafened by yells and screams, by shots, the clang of metal and the crash of timbers. And then even this space was being invaded on the starboard quarter through a breach in the galley's deadworks.

At the head of this fresh party of boarders, yet without knowing how he came there, Colonna, who had staggered, bleeding, to his feet, recognized Filippino Doria, himself.

He took his sword by the blade and reeled forward.

"You arrive opportunely," he greeted the Genoese. His voice was drowned in that infernal uproar, but the sword, proffered hilt foremost conveyed a clear message, and Filippino, recognizing him, raised hand and voice to stem the carnage on the galley that at last surrendered.

That surrender, however, Filippino was regarding as of small account. Two of his galleys, smashed by gunfire, and one of these in flames, barely kept themselves afloat. Two more were in the grip of Prospero's contingent, and even as Moncada's colours were hauled down, Prospero, leaving a prize crew to hold the captured vessels, was free at last to succour his admiral and redeem the day. Once more aboard the *Sicama*, he led the *Villamarina* and the *Gobba* to the rescue, whilst Lomellino backed his three galleys away from the conquered capitana, and swung to engage these newcomers. The superior ordnance of the Genoese smothered the *Villamarina* in a murderous fire, and an arquebuse ball ended the intrepid life of Cesare Fieramosca. His galley fell behind in confusion, staggered by a blow that in slaying her captain left her without direction.

But the *Sicama* and the *Gobba*, running in through the fire, were at grips with Lomellino's three. Their force reduced by the men left in possession of the captured Genoese, Prospero, his hopes now running high, enjoined a purely defensive action until one or the other of the two remaining imperial galleys, the *Perpignana* and the *Oria*, could come to their support. Largely as a result of his vision and promptitude the fortunes of the day were turning strongly in favour of Naples. Let the *Perpignana* and the *Oria* now be prompt, and as a naval commander Filippino Doria's course would be run and the seas would be open for the relief of Naples.

There was no time to lose. Already the Genoese were on the forward platform of the *Sicama*, driving back the Spaniards and making themselves masters of the rambade. And then, as things became desperate aboard his own galley, Prospero saw to his anger and dismay that the *Perpignana* and the *Oria*, upon which he counted, were standing off ignoring his signalled summons. As the Genoese stormed his rambade he beheld the two Neapolitan galleys actually in flight, followed by what remained of the lesser craft. Because they had seen Moncada's flag hauled down, they had chosen to consider that the day was lost, and they were speeding to safety.

The captain of the *Perpignana* was to explain himself ashore to the Prince of Orange, who had remained there in command during Moncada's absence. He propounded to the Prince that he had accounted it his duty to save his galley for the Emperor, for which conception of duty Orange hanged him out of hand. As for the captain of the *Oria*, intelligent enough to foresee what might happen to him in Naples, he carried his defection to its logical conclusion, and went eventually to range himself and his galley under the Doria banner.

Prospero's hopes, which had been running so high, were utterly shattered by that cowardly desertion. In despair he realized that nothing that he might now do could redeem their fortunes. A fourth galley, Filippino's own, was coming up to join the assailants of the only two imperial vessels that still resisted.

Del Vasto touched his arm. "It is finished, my friend. Those traitors have stolen a victory that would have been yours alone. It will not profit the Emperor that you die here."

To this proposal to surrender Prospero could oppose no reason.

"Better to live, so that we may die some other day to better purpose."

As Lautrec's arquebusiers broke through the rambade to the gang-deck, where his last line of defence was ranged, Prospero hauled down his flag so that he might put an end to a slaughter that was now useless.

Chapter 6

The Prisoner

Messer Prospero Adorno, naked to the waist, his red-brown hair cropped short, savoured the ignominy of the rowers' bench.

Chained by the leg, his body broiled by the ardent midsummer sun of Southern Italy and scarified by the lash of the warden's whip, he toiled at the oar, slept in his place with no more than a strip of verminous cowhide between his body and the unyielding wood, and was nourished on the galley-slave's fare of some thirty ounces of biscuit daily with a bucket of water from which to slake his thirst.

For a man fastidious by nature and by habit there could scarcely be a lower depth of animal existence. Only an abnormal fortitude in that situation could prevent the degradation of the body from inducing a similar degradation of the soul, until of humanity only the outward form remains.

Of such fortitude an example was offered to Prospero by his immediate oar-companion on the padrona galley of the fleet, the fifty-six oared *Mora*, under that Niccolò Lomellino who at the Battle of Amalfi had commanded the reserve. The black eyes of that stalwart, brown-bodied fellow-slave had opened wide, first with amazement and then with laughter in their depths, when Prospero was brought to the place made vacant for him. In that swarthy, aquiline face with its black stubble of beard, its vivid, full red lips that parted at last in a broad grin to display two lines of strong white teeth, Prospero had recognized the great Corsair commander Dragut-Reis, the first of the captains of Kheyred-Din, Barbarossa. That he should happen to be chained to the same oar as this Dragut, his own captive, taken in the famous action of Goialatta, had seemed to Prospero, as it had seemed to Dragut, much more than coincidence.

"Ya anta!" the Muslim had cried when he recovered from his stupor. "Bismillah! Unfathomable are the ways of the One." Then he had laughed his deep rich laugh, and in a queer mixture of Spanish and Italian he had exclaimed: "The usage of war, Don Prospero!"

The armourer was making fast Messer Prospero's gyves, whilst Lomellino, himself, a tall limber man of forty, with a narrow, stern patrician face, looked on, his eyes dark and troubled. Yet, not to be outdone by an infidel in light-heartedness under misfortune, Prospero laughed to the tune of the clanging metal.

"And a change of fortune for both of us, Señor Dragut."

The trouble in Lomellino's eyes deepened as he listened.

"So the axe goes to the wood from which it had its helve," said Dragut. "But be welcome. Marhaba fik! If I must defile my shoulder against that of an unbeliever, be it at least the shoulder of an unbeliever such as thou. Yet I say again, unfathomable are the ways of Allah the Pitiful."

"I think, Señor Dragut, we have to do with the fathomable ways of man." For it became plain to him that he was being chained at Dragut's side in a superlative expression of that vindictiveness which inspired Filippino Doria to doom a prisoner of Prospero's station to the oar.

At Amalfi, on the day after that bloody encounter in which two thousand men had lost their lives and a half score of officers of rank had fallen captive to the Genoese commander, the weedy Filippino's mud-coloured eyes had gleamed when in the line of prisoners ranged on his deck he had beheld Prospero Adorno. From the arched entrance of the tabernacle he had looked down in appraisal, whilst an officer at his elbow made the captives known to him by name. Then, his gaze upon Prospero, he had slowly descended the steps to the vestibule, and had come to take his stooping stand before him.

"Well come," was his greeting, with a sneering twist to his thick lips. "There was talk of a reckoning when last we were together, and you made some boast. We shall see now how you fulfil it." On that he had turned, and summoning Lomellino from among his captains, he had issued aloud the order which doomed Prospero Adorno to the oar.

It brought an explosion of indignation from Prospero's fellow prisoners. With one voice they cried shame upon Filippino, whilst Alfonso of Avalos went further.

"Sir, you think to dishonour by that sentence. And so you do. You dishonour yourself."

Filippino had winced. A man of less consequence than del Vasto might for that speech have gone to join Prospero on the rowers' bench. But this intimate of an Emperor must be used more gently. Charles V had a long arm. So, swallowing his gall, Filippino condescended to explain.

"My Lord Marquis, if you conceive me moved by personal rancour, you do me wrong. It has no part in the order I have given. This man is no ordinary prisoner of war. Last year, when in command of the fleet of our ally the Pope, he deserted his post; and for this he is required to answer to Pontifical justice. With duty to the King of France goes a duty to His Majesty's ally, the Holy Father; and in the fulfilment of this I must treat this deserter as a felon until I can hand him over to the Pontifical authorities so that he may purge his felony on the gallows." He humped his round shoulders and spread his hands. He smiled odiously. "You will see, my Lord Marquis, that I have no choice."

But the young Marquis, very cold and haughty, answered with insult piled on insult. "What I see is that you are skilled in subterfuge, or else that your conception of duty is such as any man of honour must despise. It does not become a gentleman to play the catchpoll, Messer Doria."

Filippino shook with anger.

"Whilst you are my prisoner, my lord, you will oblige me by keeping to matters that are your own concern," was all that he could find to say. He turned his back upon the Marquis, and curtly ordered Lomellino to convey his prisoner aboard the *Mora*.

Lomellino did not obey until he had remonstrated that it was to him that Prospero Adorno had surrendered, and that therefore, by all the usages of war, he possessed the right to dispose of him, whilst holding him to ransom. But he had been stormily overborne.

"Did you not hear me say that he is no ordinary prisoner of war? That he is a felon, and that it is my duty to hand him over to justice? Am I to betray my duty for the sake of some ducats that he might bring you?"

To Lomellino the hypocrisy was clear; yet he dared not denounce it, since fundamentally Prospero's guilt of desertion made good Filippino's shabby pretence.

Meanwhile del Vasto, raging on his friend's behalf, had done what he could. Treated, like the rest of the officers captured, as became his rank, and kept aboard Filippino's galley merely on parole, he contrived to send a strong letter of protest to Marshal de Lautrec. Chivalrously to oblige him, Lautrec, as the supreme commander of the forces before Naples, demanded of Filippino the surrender to him of the prisoners taken at Amalfi. But Filippino with his private spite to pursue, and with that eye to profit which distinguished every member of his family, returned the answer that the prisoners belonged to the Lord Andrea Doria, for whom he acted. Lautrec insisted, with a stern reminder that Andrea Doria was but the servant of the King of France, whose chief representative in Italy was Lautrec himself. In that quality he demanded once again, peremptorily, that the captives be delivered to him. Filippino's obstinacy was shaken, but by no means quelled. He replied that it was in his instructions that by the terms of Andrea Doria's service, all prisoners taken were the Admiral's property, their ransom to be regarded as his prizes of war; but in view of the Marshal's insistence, Filippino would write at once to his uncle for definite orders.

There the matter hung, and Filippino, in angry uneasiness, kept his prisoners. He cared little about the main body of them or the ransoms they would bring his uncle, and he would have surrendered them rather than give Lautrec a cause for grievance, if from their surrender he could have excepted Prospero. It was not only that he was urged by rancour. He feared the vengeance of the House of Adorno, and he beheld in the enterprising and turbulent spirit of its present head a menace to Doria supremacy in the Ligurian Republic. Rancour, however, was probably the only mean emotion that spurred him one day to visit Messer Adorno in his chains.

With Lomellino and a warden to attend him Filippino sauntered down the gang-deck of the *Mora* until he came to the oar at which Prospero sat, with Dragut beside him. Looking past Prospero, he addressed the Corsair, and his metallic voice was keenly edged with malice.

"I hope you like the company I've provided for you, Messer Dragut. Your sometime captor is now your fellow-captive at the same oar. That is delicately to avenge you. Is it not?"

Dragut looked up at him, frank and fearless, his lip curling.

"Which of us do you mock in your knightly valour?" he asked.

Filippino's eyes narrowed.

"Separately at the oar, either of you would be a diverting sight. Conjointly you are something more; you make a spectacle that should amuse the Lord Andrea Doria when he comes to view it."

"Or any other shameless dastard," said Prospero.

"Ha!" Filippino's grin drew his long lip back from his teeth. He fingered his ragged beard. "You mention shame, you poor runagate?"

"I mentioned shamelessness, which you should better understand. The sight of Dragut-Reis and me at the one oar may remind you of how I saved my Lord Andrea's reputation at Goialatta. For that you may call me a fool, and I'll agree with you. But I was young, you see. I hadn't learnt my world. I still believed in chivalry and in gratitude, in honour and nobility of heart, and other such qualities with which you have no acquaintance."

Filippino swung to the warden who stood behind him. "Give me your whip," he said.

But Lomellino, who had looked on with just such trouble in his eyes as when Prospero had been chained to the bench, now intervened. It may be that his sense of decency revolted. Or it may be that, aware of how things stood in Genoa, he feared a Doria eclipse which would carry the Fregosi with them and bring the Adorni back to power with sorry consequences to those who had abused them in the hour of their defeat. Be that as it may, he put forth a restraining hand.

"What would you do?"

"What would I do? Let me have that whip, and you shall see."

Lomellino waved back the warden. His narrow face was set. "It was to me that Prospero Adorno surrendered. Enough that you should filch the ransom. He is still my prisoner. I have yielded to you in this matter of putting him to an oar. That is shame enough for both of us."

"Niccolò!" Filippino was angrily aghast. "Did you hear what the dog said to me?"

"And what you said to him. I heard."

For a moment Filippino continued to glare; then he laughed to cover his embarrassment. "And as for his being your prisoner, that is a matter you can argue with my Lord Andrea. But listen, my friend." He took him by the sleeve, and drew him away, Prospero apparently forgotten. Just below the poop they stood awhile in very earnest talk, then Filippino stepped down into his barge and was pulled back to his own galley.

"May dogs defile his grave," was the pious prayer of Dragut, careless of who heard him. "Aye, and the great Andrea's, who doomed me to this hell." Then he looked at Prospero, and flashed his teeth in a grin. "The nephew has avenged me on you more subtly than he knows. Had Allah shown me what was in store I'd have died fighting on my deck before ever I'd have surrendered. And so, I take it, would you."

Prospero shook his head. A smile was trembling on his lips, his glance that of a man who looks inwards rather than outwards.

"Ah, no," he said. "To me life is a necessity. There are three things that I must do before I die."

"You will do them if it is written that you shall. But being dead it will not matter that you did none of them."

"Not to me. No. But it will matter to others."

"What you shall do is not what you intend, but what Allah wills. What is written is written."

"I think that Allah must have written these three things for me. So I'll be thankful to be even abjectly alive, here at the oar."

For the best part of a month he continued so to toil in those Neapolitan waters, and it was a month of unparalleled hardship which took heavy toll even from a frame so hardy and vigorous as his own. And there were indignities the least of which was the warden's lash which fell across his shoulders from time to time. For whilst Lomellino might have refused to have him flogged from personal spite, yet he could do nothing in the matter of the whip impersonally employed by the wardens on the gang when the galley in its patrolling required more than ordinary speed.

Thus for a month, and then at last came the long expected Venetian galleys under Lando. Originally awaited so that they might reinforce the Genoese, now that they arrived they were destined, instead, to replace them. For on the same day came a swift sailing felucca from Genoa with letters commanding Filippino's immediate return. Filippino welcomed the order; for there was no love between those jealous rivals, Genoa and Venice, and he had viewed with no satisfaction the association which France imposed upon him. Additional orders in Andrea Doria's letters were of such a nature that he found it necessary to request the presence of the Marquis del Vasto in the tabernacle of the capitana. He sent the request almost reluctantly. For the relations between himself and the most exalted of his prisoners, so inauspiciously begun, had never warmed to any cordiality. But there was no help for it. The Lord Andrea's commands were as definite as they were startling.

Del Vasto came promptly in response, his manner smooth and urbane.

"I am ordered here," Filippino announced, tapping the papers spread on his table, "to return immediately to Genoa with my galleys."

"Ah!" Del Vasto's dark, patrician countenance was instantly alert. "And this blockade?"

"The Venetians will suffice for that." Filippino's tone was careless. "The siege cannot in any case continue long. If they are starving and pest-ridden in Naples, Lautrec is in no better case. The plague has spread to his camp. Indeed, it seems to be spreading over Italy. I hear of outbreaks in Genoa.

"I warned Lautrec when he was opening entrenchments not to interfere with the water-courses. But he would not heed me. Self-opinionated and omniscient, like all Frenchmen."

At this sudden depreciation of the French del Vasto raised his brows; but he offered no comment. He let Filippino run on.

"Perhaps he knows better now. The waters have oozed over the land to rot there and poison the air. And in this climate. I told him that he could not take liberties with a Neapolitan summer. But you can teach a Frenchman nothing. Thank God my uncle seems to have realized it."

"Ah!" said del Vasto again. "May I sit?" He moved into the depths of the cabin and sank to a chair. He was without weapons, of course, but brilliantly dressed in sulphur-coloured silk, his sleeves fashionably puffed, a girdle set with cabochon emeralds at his waist. He had been permitted to procure from Naples his wardrobe, money, and what else he needed, as well as to receive such letters as had arrived there for him. He spoke very quietly. "So Messer Andrea has discovered that he serves the wrong master."

Almost Filippino took alarm. "That is not to say that he has decided upon a change."

"It will follow, I hope." Del Vasto was of a cool suavity that continued to disconcert the less subtle Genoese.

"That will depend."

"Ah? Upon what?"

Filippino crossed to the table. "I have a letter for you. Better begin by reading it."

The Marquis received it, broke the seal, and read. When next he looked up he was quietly serious. "Messer Andrea asks for nothing that I am not prepared to concede in the Emperor's name."

"In the Emperor's name? Let us be quite plain, my lord. Have you His Majesty's authority for the proposals which I understand that you have sent my uncle?"

Del Vasto drew a letter from his breast, unfolded and proffered it. "This is in His Majesty's own hand. It came to me a week ago. You see that it gives me the fullest powers. Is that enough?"

"Provided that you are willing to pledge His Majesty to the extent required." Filippino returned the letter. "My uncle is exigent. First the stipend and the other moneys. You have seen his demands."

"They are heavy. But the Emperor is munificent. He does not stint his captains like the knightly King of France, whose substance goes in harlotry and the like. Give yourself no thought on that score."

"Then there is the condition touching prizes of war, the booty and the prisoners. The King of France claimed a share of the first and the whole of the second."

"The Emperor is not a pedlar. Messer Andrea shall have the whole of one and the other."

Filippino, keeping a solemn face, inclined his head.

"There remains the question of Genoa; and that is grave."

Del Vasto smiled. "So grave that I should have thought you would have begun with it."

Filippino was annoyed. He did not like the suspicion of contempt in del Vasto's tone, or the expression, faintly amusedly scornful on that handsome olive face. Besides, del Vasto seemed to know too much. How much he knew he now went on to disclose.

"It is no secret to me that French greed has made it impossible for Messer Andrea to fulfil the promise to the Genoese under which he induced them to accept the protection of the King of France. His Very Christian Majesty has proved not the King Log your uncle promised them, but a very voracious King Stork; and your uncle's position in Genoa becomes difficult; even, I think, precarious. My knowledge seems to take you by surprise. Yet it need not, Messer Filippino. Without it I should scarcely have ventured to invite negotiations so delicate. It was my perception of Messer Andrea's need to put himself right with the people of Genoa that encouraged me. For, of course, he cannot accomplish that so long as he is in the service of the King of France."

"Do not assume too much." Filippino spoke with a sharpness of annoyance. "I can tell you this: my uncle will make no pact with anyone who does not accord full independence to Genoa."

"None could reasonably ask him to do anything so dangerous to himself."

"He is not thinking of the danger. He is thinking of Genoa."

"Of course. Of course."

Filippino looked at him sharply. Did this Imperial favourite permit himself sarcasm?

"The Republic," he asserted aggressively, "must be emancipated from all foreign dominion."

"I understand. But unless the Emperor emancipates her, none other will, for none other has the power."

"The question is: Will the Emperor emancipate her? That is the question upon which this agreement depends. For I am to tell you frankly that unless His Majesty pledges himself to this, there can be no agreement between us."

"To the Emperor Genoa is no more than a bridgehead. Provided that he is given the freedom of the port, the Genoese may govern themselves as they please. He will see that no one else does."

"And there must be no levies on the Republic for the Imperial troops in Italy."

"I have said, I think, that the freedom of the port is all that His Majesty will require in return for his protection."

Filippino could scarcely conceal his satisfaction. "Since you can say so much for His Majesty I am prepared on my side to say for the

Lord Andrea Doria that you may account the matter settled, all but the signing."

"That is excellent." The Marquis rose. "We have accomplished, I think, a happy piece of work, Ser Filippino. It follows, of course, that there will no longer be any question of ransom for the prisoners you took at Amalfi."

Filippino's satisfaction visibly diminished. His greedy eyes were startled. "That is a matter best left to the Lord Andrea. By our accord itself, all prisoners of war are to be his property."

There was a shade of contempt in del Vasto's smile. "Ser Filippino, that answer might serve for Monsieur de Lautrec. It will not serve for the Emperor, or, meanwhile, for me. By the accord, your uncle becomes the servant of the Emperor. He can hardly pretend to hold fellow-servants to ransom."

"Hardly, as you say," Filippino grudgingly admitted. He studied del Vasto's face and found it uncompromising. "I think I can promise that the signing of the agreement will relieve these gentlemen of their parole and leave them free."

"It will have to," del Vasto insisted. "Still, on this matter of your prisoners, there is one that cannot wait until the signing. I require the deliverance of Messer Prospero Adorno from his present situation, and that he be treated as his rank requires."

The colour darkened in Filippino's sallow face. It was a moment before he replied. "You do not know what you are asking, my lord. Prospero Adorno is not an ordinary prisoner of war. He is a felon, who..."

Peremptorily del Vasto interrupted. "I've heard that already. It will not profit you to repeat it." He advanced to the table's edge, and stood eye to eye with the Genoese. "I cannot suffer you to pursue for another moment a personal vindictiveness against a captain in the Imperial service, and one with whose high worth I propose to acquaint His Majesty."

As much the words as the manner of them were fuel to Filippino's inward wrath. Del Vasto's tone was that of the master, and whilst Filippino might take such hectoring from the Emperor, he would take it from no one of lesser rank. At least so he told himself, and on that thought he snarled a timely reminder.

"We are not yet in the Emperor's service, we Dorias."

"And you never will be if you oppose me in this," was the swift, alarming counter. The Marquis smote the table. "What is the fact? Do you hire the Emperor, or does the Emperor hire you? So far I've heard a deal of your conditions. You must have this, you must have that, you must have the other. Well, well! Now you've heard of something that we must have."

If that did not extinguish Filippino's wrath, at least it had the effect of submerging it in the fear of wrecking a compact that was nothing short of a necessity to Andrea Doria if he was to save his credit and authority in Genoa.

"But consider, sir," he pleaded, "that this man is not as the others. They are gentlemen of untarnished honour. He is – "

The Marquis cut him short. "He is my friend."

Filippino bowed a little, spreading his hands. "Even so, my lord. There is here a question of duty for me. A year ago, when in the Pope's service, Adorno abandoned his command, and – "

"That is the Pope's affair. Not yours."

"Ours, too, permit me. The Pope is in alliance with the King of France, whom we serve."

"I have already expressed myself upon that quibble. Do not force me to repeat unpleasant words. And, anyway, that alliance is at an end, all but the signing as you've said."

"But it existed at the time of the offence, and it remains that – "

Yet again del Vasto interrupted him. "No more!" He was peremptory, contemptuous. "You merely shame yourself in vain by this mean subterfuge. Do you suppose that I do not know from what it was that Messer Adorno deserted, as you call it in your duplicity?"

"My lord, this is not to be endured!"

"You would have it by your insistence."

"But duplicity!"

"I can find another name for it if you are not satisfied with that."

Filippino faced him in angry silence for a long moment, breathing hard, his nostrils dilated. Then he recovered himself.

"Your lordship does me a great wrong. With me this is purely a matter of duty. My motives are no more than I have said."

"Then they are worthless." On that del Vasto lowered his tone. Who holds the whip is not always in need of using it. "Come, sir. To wrangle over this is a foolish waste. The facts are too stubborn. It is not to be forgotten that Prospero Adorno's father was driven to flight from Genoa so as to escape assassination for his loyalty to the Emperor. For it amounts to that. This being so, do you conceive that His Majesty would condone any such action as you may have contemplated; or that I, acting for the Emperor, could tolerate it? A word in season, Messer Filippino. Do not compel me to draw the Emperor's attention to Prospero Adorno's case. It would not make a good impression. It might provoke the Imperial wrath, against those responsible for what you describe as a desertion. What then would become of our agreement?"

That word in season scared Filippino at last into a reluctant, mortified surrender. His low-lidded eyes sullenly considered the haughty countenance of the Imperial representative. Then he turned, and paced away, still battling with his chagrin.

"For myself," he said at last, "I'd yield the point. But..."

"Yield it," del Vasto advised him.

Filippino shrugged away the sweet cup of rancorous gratification, and quaffed instead the draught that the Marquis thrust upon him.

Chapter 7

At Lerici

The nine galleys in line ahead, the capitana leading, were steering northwards through the Canal of Piombino, the narrow sea between the Island of Elba and the mainland. A gentle wind from the southeast, which when it comes to blow with strength is known to Italian sailors as Libeccio and is held in dread, was bellying the big lateen sails, and speeding the fleet smoothly on its way, the oars at rest, like pinions folded astern. To westward the sun was stooping towards the mass of the Monte Grosso, its mellowing light gilding the Massoncello and the green Tuscan hills to starboard.

The *Signora*, on which del Vasto and three other captives of Amalfi were now housed, was the penultimate galley in the line. The last was Lomellino's *Mora*, from an oar of which Prospero Adorno had that morning been delivered. He had been given for his quarters a small chamber below deck astern, entered by a scuttle from the tabernacle. Del Vasto's wardrobe had enabled him to restore himself to an appearance suiting his station. Of the choice del Vasto had sent him he had availed himself, as became a disciple of Castiglione, of a doublet of black damask thinly edged with sable and girdled by a black belt with a gold buckle. Black too were the hose he took and the long boots of soft Cordovan leather, of which the Moors had left the secret with the Spaniards. A black bonnet covered his cropped head, the only lingering evidence of the condition from which he had been rescued.

With his rescuer, who came that afternoon to visit him aboard the *Mora*, he paced the narrow gang-deck, and heard at last the arguments by which Filippino had been brought to reason.

"That was to prove a friend," said Prospero.

"It was merely to display a conscience."

They had reached the raised platform of the forecastle, and del Vasto ascended the steps. "The air is purer here." He had been making play before his nostrils with a pomander ball, so as to exclude the strong odour of the slaves as they paced between their idle ranks. He left it now to dangle from his wrist, and took a full breath of the clean sea air. "I owe it to you and the news of Doria's predicament which you gave us in Naples that I am able to gratify the Emperor's most ardent wish. His Majesty perfectly understands that there can be no dominion of Italy for him without dominion of the Mediterranean, and in this sea Doria has shown himself the master, both by his address and by the powerful fleet maintained at his own charges."

Leaning on the rail, his eyes on the white wave that curled away from the thrusting prow as earth curls from the plough, Prospero laughed softly. "It is very well. It could not be better. The world will now see Doria for what he is. When yielding to the lure of ducats he shall have sold his French master and transferred himself to the service of Spain, his name should stink in its true odours. That is very well."

"And that is all that matters to you?"

"I have a sense of justice. It is gratified."

"I wonder. After all, his insistence upon the independence of Genoa was even greater than his insistence upon ducats. He made it clear that without this there could be no agreement no matter what were offered him."

"Of course. For in that case nothing offered him would be of any value. He made the same condition when he took service under King Francis. Thus he gilds his venality."

"May he not have been sincere? And may not his change of sides result from France's betrayal of him?"

"So he will contend. But the world will not be deceived. It will supply a new motto for his house. *Pecuniae obediunt.*"

Del Vasto looked at him with speculative eyes. "That is merely what you hope?"

Prospero straightened himself. "I should be inhuman if it were not. My father died broken-hearted, an exile, driven forth by the enemies this high-souled admiral loosed upon him."

"It may not have been in Doria's power to restrain them. The Fregosi were frankly in the French interest – "

"And Doria was in the Fregosi interest. Because it suited his ends. The Fregosi are of the material of which puppets are made. We Adorni are not, so Doria would have none of us. He would have exterminated us."

"Assumptions," said del Vasto.

"Is it an assumption that this Filippino chained me to an oar like a felon, and would have delivered me up to the justice of the Pope?"

"But Filippino is not his uncle. He pursues his own spite."

"I wonder that you trouble to defend Doria, Alfonso."

Del Vasto shrugged. "I do not want to have it on my mind that I have lured for the Emperor a greedy adventurer who will betray him when there is greater profit elsewhere."

"Be at ease. The Emperor is rich enough to see that that never happens."

"I would have him sure of it on other grounds."

"You ask too much. Like me, you should be content with what there is. Though I doubt if I've much reason for content. Now that you've contrived that the Pope is not to be used as the hired assassin of the Dorias and destroyed even Filippino's chance of having me beaten to death at the oar, there will probably be a knife between my ribs one of these dark nights. In one way if not in another they'll have my skin. Depend upon it."

"They would be made to pay dearly for it," swore the Marquis.

"And flowers of vengeance will blossom on my grave. A sweet consoling thought."

"I think not, Prospero." Del Vasto laid an affectionate hand upon his shoulder. "I do not trust a judgment that, like yours, is prejudiced by avowed enmity. But just as the Emperor's shadow has frustrated your being sent in chains to Rome, so it shall continue to protect you. You are a captain in his service. I'll remind the Dorias of that in terms that will convert them into your life-guards."

As a pledge of friendship this was valuable, and Prospero prized it. As a prognostication he did not rate it quite so highly, nor did it turn him from the determination to take his own precautions.

A way to take them seemed to him offered by Lomellino. He remembered Lomellino's snarl when Filippino had called for a whip that day on board the *Mora*: "Enough that you should wish to filch his ransom." And he remembered something else. Ironically, Prospero derived a curious advantage from the vindictive treatment he had received. Unlike the other prisoners of Amalfi, who had been honourably treated, he was bound by no parole. When his deliverance from the oar had followed, the matter had been overlooked. The only thing to prevent him from casting himself overboard at once and attempting to swim ashore was the certainty of being detected and recaptured. But it might with luck be done without detection on some dark night, whilst the galleys were in port at anchor. Or he might make a plea to Lomellino backed by a note of hand for the ransom that should be established.

These were the alternatives he weighed. As things fell out, the decision he ultimately took was a combination of the two, and this not until they had reached their destination, which, as it happened, was not Genoa at all, but the Gulf of Spezia. Here the Castle of Lerici, dominating a landscape of languid beauty in that evening light, reared its square reddish mass that looked like a part of the promontory in which its enormous plinth was rooted. Into this fortress, which was his property, Andrea Doria had retired whilst waiting for his future to take definite shape.

Under that promontory the galleys came to anchor as the dusk of the summer day was deepening, and the order went forth from the capitana that the commanders should render themselves ashore, and that the officers taken at Amalfi should accompany them, to wait upon the Lord Andrea Doria.

Lomellino received his orders like the rest, and Prospero was amongst those to whom it was communicated. It was an unexpected turn of events, and it called for a quick decision. Prospero made it. He was with Lomellino at the entrance of the tabernacle when the captain ordered one of his wardens to man a six-oared barge.

Lomellino in preparation for going ashore had flung across his shoulders a scarlet cloak of ample folds, for the wind had suddenly turned chilly at sunset and the captain was very sensitive to cold.

The three great lanterns on the poop had just been lighted and glowed golden above and behind the tabernacle.

This, however, remained in shadow, as did the vestibule deck immediately below it. In that shadow the two men were but darker shadows.

Prospero spoke softly, almost on a sigh. "I have a presentiment against going to Lerici."

"Why should you have? You'll be given a proper bed tonight."

"And I should, therefore, sleep soundly. That's it. An Adorno might sleep too soundly on a bed of Doria's making."

Lomellino sucked in his breath and turned to peer at him. But the gloom concealed the expression of his face.

"That's a monstrous fancy."

"Monstrous perhaps. But is it fancy? Would the rancour that set me at the oar grow less because of the powerful insistence that delivered me?"

"It would be curbed. That is, if it really menaced you. But the Dorias are not assassins."

"Not yet, perhaps. But they may be by tomorrow. I'd sooner trust to you, Ser Niccolò. I am your prisoner, not Filippino's. Why do you fear to claim your rights?"

"Fear!" growled Lomellino.

"If you don't, then name my ransom. Or shall I name it? Would two thousand ducats satisfy you?"

"Two thousand ducats! Body of God! You don't hold yourself cheaply."

"None ever shall. You accept then?"

"Softly, softly, my friend. Who is to pay this ransom?"

"The Bank of St George. You shall have my note of hand at once, before I depart."

Lomellino laughed and sighed in one. "Faith, I'd be glad of such a parting. But… I must give you reason when you said I fear to claim my rights. One does not jest with Andrea Doria."

"You mean that you don't. I must go to the castle, then?"

"Alas! I see no help for it."

"A pity. But so be it. A moment." He stepped back into the cabin, as if for something that he had forgotten. From the deep gloom of the cavernous interior the captain heard him cry out in astonishment: "Why! What have we here?"

Lomellino followed him into the shadows. "What is it?"

"I can't find…" He did not say what it was he sought by groping, moving hither and thither.

"Stay, while I make a light."

"No matter." He was now behind Lomellino, and suddenly the captain of the *Mora* found his neck in the crook of Prospero's arm, and one of Prospero's knees at the base of his spine. "What's to be done is done better in the dark."

Wrenched backwards, and powerless in that master-hold which at the same time choked him, so that he could not so much as cry out, he felt Prospero's free hand come under his cloak, questing for the dagger at his hip. Half-strangled, he sought vainly with his own hand to anticipate that theft.

"It distresses me," Prospero was murmuring, "to appear so unfriendly. You should have taken the ducats. For whatever happens, I'll not sleep at Lerici."

He drew his victim farther back, and dragged him towards the scuttle that led to the chamber below, a scuttle which Prospero had opened as soon as he had stepped into the cabin. For some seconds that seemed endless where every second might bring discovery, he put forth all his strength to hold the desperately writhing man. Then, at last, suddenly Lomellino's body went limp, and sagged against him. Slackening at once his strangling grip, Prospero eased the unconscious body to the ground.

A moment he knelt over him, assuring himself that he still lived. Then, working swiftly, he removed the captain's belt and sword, rolled him over to lie prone, pulled away and cast aside his cloak, and with his own girdle made fast his victim's wrists behind him. He dragged the limp body to the gaping scuttle. To gag the captain would have taken too long, and he dared not delay. He must take his chance of the duration of the unconsciousness. Gently he lowered him along the ladder, then let him slide down the few remaining feet to settle in a heap at the base of it. He closed the scuttle, reached for Lomellino's cloak and sword-belt, flung the cloak over his own shoulders, and buckled on the sword-belt as he went.

From beginning to end less than three minutes had been consumed.

The warden, waiting on the platform below, beheld a tall figure in a cloak and a flat cap emerge from the tabernacle and come at leisure down the steps. The cloak glowed scarlet as the light of the poop lamps caught it. One wing was worn over the left shoulder at a height that covered the lower half of the face.

The warden stepped to the entrance ladder. "All is ready, captain."

"Forward, then," said a muffled voice, and a hand waved the subordinate peremptorily on.

The warden stepped down into the sternsheets of the waiting barge, and took the tiller. Prospero followed to a place beside him.

The warden waited. "Messer Prospero?" he enquired.

"Give way," was the sharp command from the cloak.

The warden may have thought it odd. But it was not for him to comment.

The barge was pushed out from the galley's side, the oars creaked on the thole pins, and they began to move through the water, heading for the shore. Midway thither, less than a quarter of a mile from the station taken by Filippino's galleys, of which no more than the poop-lamps were now visible against the night, the cloaked figure in the sternsheets stretched forth a hand to grasp the arm of the warden at the tiller.

"Put about," was the command.

"Put about?" echoed the warden.

"That's what I said. At once."

He let the cloak fall from him. His face may have been no more than a grey blur in the gloom; yet something in the shape of it – the lack of beard, perhaps – made the warden lean forward to peer more closely. Then with an oath he was on his feet, which was as Prospero wanted him, for a standing man is easily knocked overboard. And overboard the warden splashed before he could add another word, whilst the amazed slaves stopped rowing.

Prospero standing where a moment ago the warden had stood was grasping the tiller and putting it hard over.

"Now, my lads, pull away," he bade them. "Pull away for freedom. And bend your backs as you've never bent them yet; for presently there will be pursuit, and to be overtaken is to sleep in Hell. So give way there with a will."

It needed no more to explain the situation. There was a splutter of chuckles and some morphological oaths of amazement from six Spanish throats, for they were Spaniards all, and then they bent to their oars almost with frenzy, whilst Prospero put the boat about.

From the water, the swimming warden alternated curses with supplications. In return, all he got from the slaves, exhilarated by the scent of freedom already in their nostrils, was derision.

"Ply your whip now, you son of a dog."

"Swim for it, you carrion."

"Drown and be damned, you bastard."

Thus until they were out of earshot of the swimmer, and pulling for the open sea.

Prospero looked over his shoulder. Aboard the *Mora* lanterns were moving like will-o'-the-wisps at play upon the deck.

Chapter 8

The City of Death

All through the summer night those men rowed under the spur of hope as they had never rowed under the warden's lash.

When about a mile out to sea, as he estimated, Prospero had headed the barge westward, so that their course should lie parallel with the coast. His aim was to reach Genoa. He did not overlook the dangers that might await him there. But he was without alternative, since only there could he obtain the supplies that were indispensable. To the sword-belt of which he had deprived Lomellino was attached, in addition to sword and dagger, a leather scrip in which Prospero found a gold comfit-box, a notebook and six ducats. These he must borrow for immediate needs. It was his intention to attempt to rejoin the Prince of Orange, going by way of Florence, so that he might pay a visit to his mother.

They made such good progress that daybreak found them off that fold in the hilly coast within which Lavanto is almost hidden. Behind them to the eastern horizon aglow with the fires of dawn the sea was empty. Of pursuit there was as yet no sign.

They put in at Lavanto, and Prospero went ashore and adventured into the awakening village. He roused a still slumbering taverner, and after him a shopkeeper, and when he came back to the boat he was accompanied by a boy laden with loaves of rye bread, flasks of wine and a half-dozen shirts and caps for the men, who were naked save for their cotton drawers. He brought also a couple of files, with which they might deliver their legs from the gyves.

As the barge emerged again from the bay, having cleared the headland, one of the men pointed astern in alarm. A sail had appeared on the horizon. Under a quickening breeze that had sprung up at daybreak a galley was ploughing westward in their wake.

That vessels would have been flung out in pursuit in every direction was not to be doubted, and this might well be one of them.

Prospero, thankful for the breeze, ordered their own triangular sail to be hoisted, and as the light barge plunged forward before the wind, the weary men ate and drank, and then set themselves to file away their fetters.

By the time this was done, they were abreast of the village of Bonassola, perched white against the grey-green of olive trees on a slope above a little cove.

Behind them the galley, not more now than three miles astern, was gaining rapidly. In less than another hour at this rate they would be overtaken, and if the vessel proved a pursuer, as there was every reason to suppose, that would be the end of their adventure. The slaves would be flogged to the bone, and as for himself, it might well be found that he had supplied such reasons for his condemnation that not even del Vasto's great influence might avail him.

"We must take to the land," he decided, to the great relief of the men.

On the golden sands under Bonassola he shared his meagre resources with them, a half ducat to each, which earned him their grateful blessings. When they had kissed his hands and gone their ways, he went up alone into the village, and contrived to hire a mule that bore him over twenty miles of rugged coastland, to Chiavari. There he exchanged the mule for a post-horse, and on this came in the summer dusk to the walls of Genoa.

Because the Angelus was tolling from a dozen belfries as he approached the Porta del Arco, he spurred on so as to cross the threshold before the gate should close. Nearer at hand there was another sound of ringing, a clang so harsh and insistent as to seem fraught with menace. A man, at the head of a team of mules harnessed to a cart whose sides were boarded high, swung a bell as he advanced. The cart was followed by two men who carried queer implements that resembled grappling irons. They leered up at Prospero as they passed him under the deep arch of the gateway.

"Didn't you hear the bell?" grumbled one of them, and trudged on without staying for an answer.

A sentry with a halbert, lounging on the steps of the guardhouse eyed him incuriously. None challenged him, for whilst war might be sweeping over the rest of Italy, here in Genoa there was yet no menace of it; nor did Trivulzio, whose government, whatever the factionaries might pretend, was mild and benevolent, apprehend any.

Prospero rode on, following the Via Giulia, past San Domenico, through the Campetto, and then by narrower streets climbing upwards towards San Siro, where dwelt Scipione de' Fieschi upon whom he was now depending. As he went, the uneasy feeling grew upon him that he moved in an unnatural atmosphere through a city mysteriously stricken, paralysed and almost lifeless. It was not only that never had he seen the streets so empty, but the few whom he met or overtook appeared to move in furtive haste, like wild creatures scuttling to cover against an enemy's approach. There were no saunterers as might have been expected on so warm a summer evening, no loiterers, and, above all, no groups. The echoing of his horse's hoofbeats stressed the sepulchral silence of the city. As darkness deepened, the gloom was relieved by few lighted windows or open, friendly doorways. The very inns seemed dead, save one near San Domenico, whence light and hilarity fell almost startlingly upon the black, empty street. Here at least men were alive and gay, yet to Prospero this gaiety contained an excessive abandoned note. Upon the sensuous acuity which is the poet's equipment, the sound smote horribly. It held an obscene ring. In fancy he likened it to the laughter of ghouls in a charnel house, and thereby went nearer to the truth than he yet suspected.

Emerging into the open space of the Campetto, where all was again silence, his horse shied suddenly and swerved to avoid a man lying prone upon the ground. Prospero drew rein, dismounted, and bent over the body, to discover that it was stiff and cold. He drew back, and stood up again.

Across the square a man was moving quickly, the only other human thing in sight. "Hi!" Prospero called to him. "There's a dead man here."

The wayfarer never checked his stride. "He'll have to lie till morning now," he called back, and added cryptically: "They've already gone."

To Prospero the answer was not merely cynical. It was senseless. He stood hesitating whilst the man hurried away. Did no watch patrol the streets at night under this French government? Then it occurred to him that if he roused the place he would probably be asked to account for himself, which might offer inconvenience. So he climbed his horse again and pursued his way.

He came at last to San Siro and the Fieschi palace. It was completely in darkness, and the heavy doors that normally stood open to the courtyard were now ominously closed. With a stone he hammered on one of the panels, sending a hollow echo through the mansion. After a silent while he knocked again, and was answered at last by shuffling steps within. The drawing of a bolt rang like a shot on the uncanny stillness, and a small, narrow door practised within the greater one swung inwards. A lantern was hoisted to the level of Prospero's face; a querulous, elderly voice assailed his ears.

"What do you want?"

Behind the lantern an old man's eyes, rheumy and malevolent, were considering him. "Who are you? Why do you knock?"

"Faith, we're gracious," said Prospero. "I seek Messer Scipione. Is he within?"

"Within? Messer Scipione? Why should he be? Gesù! Who are you to ask such a question?"

"I'd thank you to begin by answering it."

"Why, good sir, Messer Scipione has been gone these weeks. Like all the rest."

"Gone? Where has he gone?"

"Where? What do I know? To Lavagna perhaps, or perhaps to his country house at Acqui. Perhaps farther. How could you think to find him here?"

"In God's name, what ails the place? What is amiss with you all?"

"Amiss?" The old voice chuckled scornfully. "Have you landed from the New World, or whence?" He stepped out through the narrow doorway, and held the lantern higher so that its rays reached a doorway across the narrow street. He pointed. "See that?"

But Prospero saw nothing. "See what?" he asked.

From the old man at his elbow there was again that ghoulish chuckle. "The cross, noble sir. The cross."

Prospero looked again, more intently. Very faintly he could discern on the door opposite the sign of a cross that was rudely smeared in red. "The cross?" he echoed. "What then?"

"What then? Why – Gesùmaria! – an infected house. The plague has been that way. They're all dead."

"The plague?" Prospero was stricken into ice. "You have the plague here?"

"It has fallen on us from the hands of a God weary of men's iniquities; fallen on us as the fire fell on Sodom and Gomorrah. They say it was brought here from Naples, where it was first sent to destroy the godless bandits who laid the hand of sacrilege on Rome and the Holy Father. Many have fled, like Messer Scipione, as if God's punishment can be escaped. Messer Trivulzio and his French have shut themselves up in the Castelletto, as if its walls could defy God's wrath. Faith, noble sir, you come to Genoa in an evil hour. Here we have only the dead who care not, and the poor like myself who have nowhere else to go." Again he muttered his malevolent little laugh, and turned to re-enter the house. "Go with God, noble sir. Go with God."

But Prospero did not yet depart. Even when the door had closed, he remained there listening to the retreating shuffle of the steps beyond it. At last he shook off his palsy, climbed again to the saddle, and with the nausea of a fastidious man in an unclean environment took his way through the darkness of steep, narrow, tortuous streets down towards the waterfront.

His horse was to be surrendered at the hostelry of the Mercanti, facing the quay of the same name, between which and the inn at Chiavari where Prospero had hired it a posting service was established.

Since the friend upon whom he depended was no longer in Genoa to house him, since others to whom he might have turned would no doubt be similarly absent, and since the city gates would now be shut, so that he could not if he would escape from this necropolis, he must hope to lie the night at this inn of the Mercanti. Tomorrow he would consider what to do.

He went slowly and cautiously on a horse that slithered under him on the steep declivity and at moments would stand still, shivering in the dark. He met no one. Twice only was that graveyard silence broken, and then by sounds of lamentation from houses that he passed.

He came at last from the blackness of the steep, narrow ways into the open lighter space at the waterside. A sickle of moon was rising over the sea, and in the faint light the old mole made a long black silhouette athwart the dark gleam of water. Lofty rigging of galleons and shorter rigging of galleys at anchor in the spacious harbour reared a faint tracery against the sky. Here where normally even to a late hour the activity was that of a hive, there were at least some feeble signs of life. He met odd stragglers who called a greeting to him as they went. And at a distance of half a bowshot from where he had emerged a rhomb of yellow light clove the darkness to illumine the quay of the Mercanti and the boats that were moored against it. He caught oddly discordant sounds of hilarious voices, snatches of song and the twanging of some string instrument. This would be the inn of the Mercanti. At least they were alive here, though Prospero wondered was this liveliness less than horrible. Again, and more vividly now, because he was more informed, he gathered the impression of ghouls at play, of creatures obscenely merry in a graveyard. And the impression when presently, his horse surrendered, he beheld the company, was confirmed.

Hitherto he had known that inn as a house frequented by the better class of those concerned with the business of the port: merchants, officers from the ships or of the harbour, owners of vessels, and even some of the lesser patricians whose interests were maritime, whilst women were never seen, at least in the public apartments of the hostelry. But tonight, under the vaulted ceiling of the long common-room, the company at the trestle tables was made up of the scourings of the port. The best of them were underwardens from the galleys or the bagnio, the worst just common seamen and quayside porters with a sprinkling of the waterside queans and harpies who in every port lie in wait for seafaring men, but none of whom in ordinary times would have dared to cross the threshold of the Mercanti.

And they were gay in there, under the smoking oil-lamps that hung from the beams overhead, gay with a noisy, hysterical, abandoned gaiety into which fear and defiance seemed compounded. It was laughter with a shudder behind it; the loud, hollow laughter with which men dissemble the panic in their hearts whilst they deride their gods. Just so, must Prospero have thought, might they laugh in Hell, for so he expresses it in a line of *The Liguriad*:

Cosi ridean i pravi in Malebolge.

His advent among them gave a moment's pause to their mirth.

A pale, lean youth bestrode a table twanging a lute to accompany the bawdy lyrics sung in alternate couplets by two women improvisers. The song broke off, and with it the chatter and the laughter, whilst the obscene crowd stared at this courtly stranger who in that foul environment was like a being from another world. For he still wore del Vasto's finery of black damask and Lomellino's brave scarlet cloak.

For perhaps a dozen heartbeats the astounded silence reigned. Then like an explosion came the renewal of hilarity, louder and fiercer than before. With rattle of discarded drinking-cans and a crash of overturned stools they came in a rush to press about him, to hail him, to leer at him, to bid him welcome to their revels.

"Back!" he stormed. "Give me air. Into what ante-room of Hell have I blundered?"

Some laughed the louder. Others growled. Others, more daring, still laid hold of his cloak to draw him with them. And then, cleaving roughly through the crowd at speed, came Marcantonio, the landlord, a big, hot man who showed little regard for his patrons.

In a moment, with cuffs and roars, he had cleared himself a space in which to stand and bow to this newcomer, panting from exertion and emotion. "My Lord Prospero! My Lord Prospero!"

"What witches' sabbath do you hold in the Mercanti?"

The booming voice fell to a whine. "These are the only patrons the times have left us. You return in an evil hour, my lord. But come with me, I beg you. There are rooms above. All my house is your nobility's. An honour. Come, my lord. Come."

Marcantonio led him down the long room, clearing a way ahead by objurgations and by arms that waved as if to scare vermin from their path. The revellers gave way, with jests and gibes that provoked screeches of revolting laughter. The nobleman, they jeered, was too fine for such humble company. Perhaps he'd be less proud when the pestilence made free with his nobility. Wait till the swellings showed. He'd remember then that he was as mortal as the meanest. A great leveller the plague. Long live the plague!

At last he was out of their foul company, and, lighted by a serving-wench who tripped ahead, he was going up a winding stair, with Marcantonio now following. He was ushered into a room of fair proportions and decent furnishings, but close-smelling and stiflingly hot, the windows shuttered.

From the candle she bore, the girl was lighting others in a copper branch on the table. Marcantonio, mopping his red face, confronted his guest with tragic eyes.

"God have mercy on us. The hand of affliction is heavy upon us all."

"And Genoa grows lewd in the shadow of death. Most reasonable."

"Men's reasons are turned, my lord."

"Into swines' I see."

"Compassionate them, my lord. They are mad with terror. They try to smother it in drunkenness and debauchery. God help us all. Times have been hard since Messer Doria brought in the French to govern us. There's many a fool who listened to him and lent a hand in the change who's cursed himself since and wished himself back in the days when your nobility's father was Doge – God rest his soul!" Marcantonio crossed himself. "And now, for our sins, this exterminating pestilence is upon us. But your nobility's commands? Your needs?"

For that night his needs were supper and a bed. Tomorrow he would take order for the future.

He was provided. The windows were flung wide despite the prejudice against it, from the belief that to let in the air was to let in the plague with which it was laden. Supper was served him with abject excuses for its quality from a host who in happier times had ever been proud of the fare he set before his guests, and in the adjacent room a bed was made ready.

Eufemia, the girl who had lighted him, was left to minister to his wants. She was young, plump and black-haired, with a moist red mouth that smiled readily, and dark moist eyes of deliberate wantonness. In her ministerings she was assiduous. She poured water for him, so that he might wash, and added to it a quantity of vinegar, assuring him that it was a safeguard against infection. He must preserve himself from that, and she would help him. To this end she fetched some glowing charcoal in a copper dish, and cast on this some aromatic herbs, to fumigate the chamber. Herself, she informed him, she had no fear of the infection, being protected from it by a scapulary she wore, which had been blessed on the coffin of St John the Baptist in the Church of the martyred St Lawrence. Not for all the gold of the New World would she part with it. But his nobility might ask for anything else that was hers, she assured him, and the inviting smile on the red mouth, the languishing glance of the velvet eyes left him in no doubt of the potency she attributed to her prophylactic. She was clearly persuaded that not even wantonness could impair its efficacy.

She waited upon him at table with the same solicitous assiduity. Boiled kid was the backbone of the meal. She protested that it was nauseous food to set before his nobility, thus repeating the apologies of Marcantonio; but it had been boiled with plenty of vinegar, and that made it safe from the contagion. At the end of the meal she urged him to drink more wine, and uninvited set him the example by pouring for herself. She knew that it was harsh and acid. But that made it all the better medicine against the plague.

She made bold to pledge their better acquaintance. She liked him, she confessed.

"You are kind," he mumbled drowsily.

The food was acting as a drug upon his weary body. All last night awake at the tiller, all today in the saddle, and some emotional labours as well, from the smothering of Lomellino to the discovery of the plague in Genoa, left him exhausted. His chin drooped to his breast, and the girl's crooning tone as she babbled on of kindness and how kind she would be to him became gradually fainter until he heard it no more.

He awoke with a start to find an arm about his neck, and a cheek against his cheek.

To come to his feet and hurl her violently from him was a single action, and more instinctive than reasoned. For not until he had seen her white face and fiercely puckered mouth was he fully awake. Then, realizing the situation, he laughed.

"It's the plague, I suppose."

"The plague?" There was almost a note of hope in the question. "Did you think I have it?"

Fate was astir to prompt the jesting answer. "A plague of some sort is certainly at work in you, my girl. You need to wear an amulet of another kind."

Very gradually there came a kindling of hatred in those dark liquid eyes that had been so fond. Then, abruptly, she was gone.

With a shrug of disdain he staggered off to find his couch, and there sink into an exhausted sleep, undisturbed by the roar of revelry below, which did not cease until the break of day.

Chapter 9

The Garden of Life

You are next to see the very noble Messer Prospero Adorno running for his life.

We gather from what he related later of the matter that he was acutely conscious of the indignity, and that anger was the dominant emotion as of necessity he fled. He ran, he says, not because he was afraid to die, but because he desired to live. A nice distinction.

The thing happened late next day; and whilst he was well aware at the time of how it had been provoked, yet it was not until later, much later, that he came to realize how big with Fate had been the moment when he flung a jesting dismissal at the black-eyed Eufemia, and how by a half-dozen contemptuous words he had determined the shape of all his later life.

He had spent that morrow of his coming to Genoa in a fruitless pilgrimage from one to another of those patrician houses, beginning with that of the Spinola, to which friendship gave him the right to look for assistance. All were closed, or else tenanted only by custodians, the families having fled the place.

Of the desolation left in the city by a scourge that was now, at last, diminishing daily in virulence, the signs were everywhere: the negligible traffic of the streets, the hurrying furtiveness of those he met, the shuttered houses, and on many a door the red cross that announced infection, and once he met again that gruesome mule-drawn cart preceded by its bell-ringer.

As a last resource he was constrained to disclose himself to the Bank of St George. In that unrivalled financial establishment, almost the only one of its kind in Europe, he found one of the governors to whom he was known, a Messer Taddeo del Campo, who remained at his post despite the pestilence. On his note of hand he obtained here a loan of fifty ducats, sufficient for his immediate needs and for the fulfilment of his present intention, which was to return at once to Naples.

Now whilst he was engaged with Messer del Campo upon this matter it happened that three tall fellows of a bearing at once soldierly and rascally rode up to the Mercanti and incontinently asked for him. In this there was neither chance nor coincidence. They had picked up his trail at Bonassola, followed it to Chiavari, and there at the leading hostelry they had been naturally informed of the posting service established between that house and the Mercanti. At the Mercanti, therefore, they sought him.

Marcantonio admitted without thought that the Lord Prospero had arrived last night, and only realized afterwards with what he had to deal. The men dismounted in high good humour, announcing that the bird was caught, and requiring the host to conduct them to him at once. Marcantonio sought to retreat in good order.

"How should I know where he is now?"

At this the leader swore so lewdly that if Marcantonio had still doubted their intentions, he could doubt no longer. "Do you mean he's gone again?"

"Just that," said Marcantonio, and then Eufemia, who had slunk to his elbow, all agrin as if she did something clever, added: "But he's coming back. He's lodged here."

"Lodged here? Come. That's better." The rascal grinned his relief, whilst Marcantonio silently promised Eufemia the soundest beating she had ever known.

"Won't you come in and wait?" said Eufemia. "The wine of the house is good."

The wine and the girl so engaged them that they paid no heed to Marcantonio. Eufemia, however, kept an eye on the taverner, and seeing him presently slink out, suspected that his purpose might be to parade the waterfront so as to intercept Messer Prospero and give him timely warning.

This was exactly what Marcantonio was about. Nor was his patience tried; for very soon he caught a glimpse of his guest stepping out from under the arcades of the Bank of St George. He reached him at speed, thrust him back under the shadow of those arches, and in a dozen words told him of the arrivals.

"You'll know what it means, my lord."

Too well did Prospero know. He would have stayed to thank the taverner, but Marcantonio cut him short. "Don't delay here. God be with you, my lord." He stepped out from the arcade again, and then checked on an oath.

"That misbegotten slut has set them on. Away with you! Away!"

He started to move forward so as to put himself in the way, and he was almost rolled over by the rush of the three bravos. But by this time, Prospero, who had acted upon swift instinct, was vanishing round the corner at the far end of the long building.

The glimpse they had of that fleeing figure was enough. They were after him like hounds upon a trail. But they were stiff from the saddle, whilst Prospero was comparatively fresh, and he was naturally fleet of foot. He ran in a cold rage at this ignominy of having to save his life by his heels, but in the conviction that if he were overtaken a swift death on the spot would be the best for which he could hope. And he would ensure it, he vowed, if overtaken he were. Meanwhile he ran only until he could find a position of advantage that held out some hope of dealing with these pursuers. Then he would accept the odds of three to one.

The chase went away past the Cathedral and across the square before the ducal palace, where a year ago his father had reigned. Beyond that he took to narrow alley-ways on the rising ground towards Carignano. Deliberately he chose this daedalus of little winding streets as affording the best means of perhaps yet baffling the pursuit. Deserted though these alleys were, they were not so deserted but that here and there someone was astir to stand gaping at his flight and to inform his pursuers of the way he had taken.

The pace and the acclivity were beginning to wind him, and he was thinking of doubling back so that he might go downhill once more, when a twist of the alley which he followed brought him suddenly into a diminutive square: a plot of grass within a frame of acacia trees, overlooked by small houses, all of which were closeshuttered and dominated by a little church the door of which was closed.

It was a place familiar to him with the vague familiarity of something seen in a dream. Four ways led out of it. The way on his right was the narrowest. Six steps led through an archway up to it, and on that narrow summit he would make a stand. But having reached it he was lured on by the deep shadows of the narrow way beyond, running between high blank walls, like a gully between cliffs. He supposed them to enclose the gardens of palaces set here on the heights of Carignano. And soon the assumption was confirmed. The wall on his right was for a considerable space thickly clad in ivy. Then it was broken by an embrasure within the shadow of which there was a door. The sight of it awoke in him a memory of a year ago. Through that doorway he had driven a party of looters on the day Genoa was opened to the French. There was a debt of which this was the moment to claim payment.

He flung himself at the door to find it barred. He looked up. The low lintel made a narrow edge. About it for a yard or so the ivy exposed a trunk as thick as a man's arm. He was inspired to see in it a ladder lowered by Fate for his salvation, provided that the claspers of the ivy would hold to the summit, some fifteen feet above.

As he paused, breathing hard, the loud, discordant voices of his pursuers reached him from the little square. He gathered that they were at fault and knew not which of the four ways to take. But the devil might easily guide them aright.

So he went up the ivy.

Its grip proved as stout as he could have hoped. Generations old, the trunk upon which he depended had long since surmounted the wall and taken a firm hold along its crown. True, when the journey was almost accomplished the growth began to yield under his weight. But by then he was within reach of the summit, and a quick, desperate upward clutch made him safe. He drew himself up, and sat astride for a moment. A backward glance showed him the gloomy lane still empty, but the footfalls of his pursuers warned him that they had chosen aright, and sent him down the other side in haste. There was only one method of descent. He lowered himself to his full length, then loosed his hold and fell slithering to earth.

He gathered himself up, dusted mould and crushed umbels from his hands and garments, straightened sword-belt and doublet, and took stock of his surroundings.

His memories were vague, as if in some remote past time he had walked in this very noble garden which had for background a palace, proclaimed patrician not only by its proportions but by the alternating layers of black-and-white marble with which it was faced and the Romanesque colonnade of slender pillars, delicately carved. The garden itself, as he observed it now in the twilight of that summer evening, was a place of enchantment, of lawns and walks set between hedges of yew and of boxwood. Here clustering roses, and lilies yonder by a pool. Tall cypresses, like vast black spears, were set about another, larger pool that was rimmed in stone and mirrored the white marble of a triton coldly carved, whose fishtail legs bestrode a rock, whilst, with head thrown back, his lips flung aloft a crystal column that broke and fell in spray upon the mermaids on the plinth. And beyond that, of marble, too, gleamed white a round pavilion, a temple in little, with a domed roof that was carried on a peristyle. Pigeons circled above it in the evening sky. It was hedged about its base by shrubs and trees, the deep green of lemon, the grey-green of quince and the lucent green of pomegranate splashed with vivid scarlet flowers.

But for all its beauty the place was overhung by an air of neglect. The grass of the lawns was rank and scorched, the hedges were dishevelled, fallen leaves and withered petals lay rotting on the unswept paths.

He was disturbed by a faint sound behind him. He span round, and beheld, as he afterwards declared, the noblest sight this garden had yet revealed.

She came sedately towards him over the unkempt lawn, evincing no surprise, or haste, or fear, or emotion of any kind that he could discern.

She was moderately tall, and she wore a gown of silver brocade, which borrowed from the broad black arabesques that were wrought upon it an almost funereal splendour. In her long, slim hands, gauntleted in white with silver fringes, she bore a little ivory coffer with gilt pillars, between every two of which a scene was painted. Her head was small, the dark-brown hair so neatly set that in itself it seemed to form a cap within the pearl-studded net that confined it. Pearl-studded, too, was the net that rose from the straight line of corsage to cover her white shoulders, and of pearls was the slender stole she wore and even the tassels in which it ended. Her face was long and pale, and at present almost mask-like in its calm. The wide-set eyes were dark, and so gravely thoughtful as to seem sad. The lips were moderately full and only moderately red.

He could not conceive that this was the lady he had served a year ago. For this lady was unforgettable, and she had no place in his memory. Her beauty none would have denied, though none might have deemed it unearthly, as Prospero deemed it. Its power lay in some inner grace, reflected in those grave eyes, in her serenity and steady poise.

She was attended by an elderly woman in black, who remained like a sentry on the lawn's edge, with folded hands.

Her voice came level and deep-toned. "You choose an odd way to enter. Or do you drop from Heaven?"

Breathing hard he answered her. "Into Heaven, I think."

"Into the way of it, perhaps." But although there was a faint smile on her lips, the sadness of her eyes appeared to deepen. "It is rash to leap without looking. Never so rash as now. What do you want here?"

He was frank. "Sanctuary. I am in flight from death."

"Into the very arms of it. Poor man! This is an infected house."

"Infected?" She mistook the sudden horror in his eyes, but only until he spoke again. "Not you? Ah, never you! The plague cannot have touched you."

"You think it discriminates? Perhaps it does. I have had it. I am healed again. But it may be that I am not yet safe to approach. And all is poisoned here. Corruption stirs under the fair surface of this place."

"Let it stir," said he. "It shall not make me sorry that I came."

"Yet it should, if you come seeking life."

"I have found it," he dared to answer.

She played the game he set. "To die perhaps tomorrow."

"No matter. At least I shall have lived a day. A day in thirty years."

"We toy with words, I think," said she, her calm unruffled. "Perhaps you think I jest, to punish your intrusion; and you answer me in kind."

"I had no thought to be merry, madam."

"It's as well. This is not a merry place. Shall we leave pretty insincerities?"

"They have never been among my accomplishments," he assured her. But she was not heeding his words. Her eyes were intent upon his face; her expression was no longer of a frozen calm.

"I seem to know you," she said at last.

This startled him. Could it, then be? Had he been so blinded by the frenzy of that day, a year ago, that he had not really seen her?

"Who are you?" she asked him.

Straight, tall and vigorously slender he stood before her in del Vasto's finery of black brocade with sable edge. Lomellino's gaudy cloak had been left behind at the Mercanti.

"My name is Prospero Adorno, madam, to serve you."

The announcement disturbed her miraculous composure. Her eyes dilated. Her voice, however, remained as level as before.

"I have heard of you."

"Nothing to my hurt, I hope."

"Are you not he who deserted from the Papal fleet?"

"That is the slanderous way of saying that I fled from assassins."

"What assassins?"

"The same as now. Doria assassins."

"Doria assassins! What tale is that?"

"A true one. My existence incommodes that noble house."

He saw a frown deepening on her brow, and wondered. Then it was dispelled. "Now I know," she exclaimed, and there was sudden warmth in her voice. "Now I remember. You are he who on a day a year ago rescued me from some French soldiers in this garden."

"I was hoping that it might be so. It would supply the reason why I was begotten."

Frowning again she scanned his face more closely. "You hoped? Don't you remember that you rescued two women from insult and worse on the day when the French entered Genoa?"

"Faith, yes, I remember. There was a man spread-eagled on the grass there, and yonder another, grey-haired, who sat nursing a broken head. And you – " He broke off. Impossible to confess that he had borne away no recollection of her face. He deserved to have his eyes plucked out.

Steps pattered in the lane, and there was a muttering by the door above which the ivy hung dishevelled. It struck them into a listening silence.

From beyond the wall there was a rending sound, an outcry, a thud, an oath and an excited chatter.

Prospero's lean face grew alight with humorous malice. "Now there," he murmured, "is evidence that the saints protect and guide me. The ivy that stood my friend when I climbed, has stood my friend again when another seeks to follow. I'll hang a golden heart on the altar of St Lawrence if that dog has broken his evil neck."

The lady's calm had completely disappeared. She looked with startled eyes at the summit of the wall whence the ivy had been rent.

"Gesùmaria!" she exclaimed. "Come with me. Into the house I dare not take you, for the infection. But in the pavilion, there, it may be safe. Since your evil star has brought you here, you must accept the risk. God help you."

"Lady, I would not malign that star of mine."

"Please come."

He moved beside her, and the elderly woman moved with them at my lady's beckoning, yet keeping her distance. A dozen paces brought them abreast of the door that was practised in the wall, and at that moment a shower of blows fell on its timbers, to shouts of "Holà there! Open! Open!"

The lady looked at him, and all her face was set in gravity. He smiled in answer, displaying again the humorously attractive lines of his wide mouth.

"Peremptory gentlemen," he murmured. And asked: "Is the door stout?"

"Not stout enough to give you time to reach the pavilion." She pointed to the tall yew hedge of an enclosed garden. "In there," she ordered him.

He turned to her, aghast. "How long will that hide me?" Impatiently he added: "Have you no men at hand?"

"Two, besides yourself. But one is too old and feeble to be counted, and the other lies sick of the plague."

"In short, you have none. And there are three of them." He felt for his weapons. His right hand fell to his sword, his left to the dagger on his hip. "You shall have some entertainment," he said.

Her hand came to his arm and clutched it. Her voice quivered from its even level. "Time enough for that if they discover you. And they will not if you'll conceal yourself." Once more she pointed to the hedge.

Blows fell again upon the door, but as they ceased, a revolting oath was screamed by one of those who knocked. For an instant their voices rose in incoherent chatter; then there was a scurry, ending in the thud of racing feet that receded swiftly.

Prospero and the lady stood arrested, listening until those fleeing footsteps had faded out of earshot, he in bewildered surprise, she with the quiet smile of understanding.

"What can have scared them?" he asked at last.

"The spectre of the plague. They saw the cross upon the door. I meant to show it to them had they broken in. It's a sight few men can bear." She dismissed the matter in a sigh, and looked at him sadly. "This will be something towards the debt I owe you. I am thankful for the chance."

"There was less chance in it than you suppose. None beyond the fact that I fled this way. Finding myself here, I thought I might claim payment."

"I see," she said. "I would that I could offer more. But it is not wise to linger here. It is not safe to breathe this air."

"Is safety all?"

"Wasn't that what you were seeking when you came?"

"But that was in a former life. I've been born again since then."

There was still light enough to show him the frown of her displeasure. "Sir, since I cannot accord you the hospitality of my house, there is no excuse for keeping you."

"No excuse, perhaps. But some reason. If I go from here it will be to lose the life that you've preserved. There is no safety for me in Genoa."

"What prevents you from leaving it?"

The Angelus was ringing as she spoke. "That answers you," he said. "The gates will be closing. I am shut in at least until tomorrow."

Not at once did she reply. She crossed herself, and like her woman, stood with bent head murmuring the Aves to which the bell was a summons. Prospero bared his head and kept them company in that prayer.

When it was done, her eyes sought his face in the dusk.

Quietly she explained herself. Into the house she dared not take him. The infection there would strike him like a sword. One of her servants lay dying of the pestilence. There remained the pavilion, which she had used since her recovery. Even the air of that might be tainted. Still, if in his desperate plight he chose to accept the risk, she would not deny him; the hospitality of it was at his disposal.

"Madam," he reassured her, "I take no risk there that is not present everywhere in Genoa."

"So be it. Come then." She led him across the ill-kempt lawns and by yew-bordered paths past the pond where the triton gleamed palely in the dusk, and so came at last to the steps of the temple to be met by a rush of wings of the pigeons that descended in a cloud about her.

"Oh, my poor birds, have I neglected you?" She raised the lid of the casket and scattered grain in handfuls. "They are more fortunate than you, who must go supperless to bed. Wine we can give you, and eggs, too. They are safe if you will break them for yourself. But other food from that house will be as poison."

She called her woman, who had followed them, and sent her ahead to make a light. When this had been kindled, she conducted him up to the peristyle and into a circular chamber that was lined in coloured marbles, paved in porphyry and furnished with that luxury suggestive of the East as often found in Genoese houses as in patrician houses of Venice, the rival maritime republic. There was a divan spread with a silken carpet from Persian looms; a table of bronze and porphyry bore a sheaf of lilies in a crystal bowl; an archlute lay beside it and some volumes bound in vellum. There were velvet chairs and a painted bridal chest, and on a pillar of malachite a graceful Theban Bacchus in bronze, vine and ivy crowned, standing some two feet high.

He surveyed the place in the soft radiance from the two hanging lamps that the woman Bona had lighted, and told himself that it was just such a temple as he might have imagined for the divinity who normally inhabited it.

Bona was dispatched to the house for those things which it was permissible to supply him, the wine and the eggs. "And say no word of this to Ambrogio," my lady warned the waiting-woman.

She invited Prospero to sit and take his ease.

"I need none, having found sanctuary; and in a shrine."

"Of a pagan god, you mean." Her eyes swept to the laughing Bacchus. "It is scarcely so much, although I've brought him to preside here. But a sanctuary may it prove to you, not only from the evil that you flee but from the evil to which you've fled."

She gave him no time to answer, but went on to talk of her own situation, as if to explain. And now he learnt that she was alone in that great palace, save for the woman Bona and the two men of whom she had spoken, one of whom was old and feeble and the other so sick of the pestilence that he was like to die of it. Herself she had caught the contagion in its early days, two months ago. She was an orphan of the noble house of Montaldi, and lived here in the palace of her uncle, the Marquis of Fenaro. Some time before she had been smitten with the pestilence, the Marquis had fallen sick in Padua, and her aunt had hurried off to him. Since then he had died, and his widow dared not return to Genoa whilst the pestilence raged. She went on to tell him that it was to Bona, who had been her nurse, and who would die sooner than forsake her in her need, that she owed her life. The faithful soul had been at her bedside to fight the disease, and she had conquered it, herself immune because, like old Ambrogio, she had suffered from it in youth. Beppo, the only other of her servants who had not fled, had miraculously escaped the contagion until these last few days.

So much he learnt from what she told him between the going and returning of her woman.

When Bona, out of breath, came hurrying in, my lady rose. "I'll leave you now. Bona will supply your needs to the poor extent my house permits. I shall see you in the morning before you go."

He was on his feet, tall and lithe, and for a moment they stood face to face in solemn consideration each of the other.

"In that sad hour," said he, "I shall seek in vain for words to thank you."

She shook her head. "You forget," said that level voice, "that I pay a debt. Good night, sir, and good repose."

She rustled out in her stiff silver brocade, and he coming to the peristyle followed with his eyes the faintly shimmering figure until it was lost in the darkness.

Behind him Bona spoke. She had brought a flask of wine, some eggs in a basket, a drinking glass, a crystal bowl and a vase of honey.

"So much at least is safe," he heard her say. "No hands but mine have touched these vessels. All have been wiped in vinegar. The honey is good medicine for the infection, so you need have no fear of it. The eggs you may break for yourself. Is there anything else you lack, sir?"

He had turned with a sigh when she began to speak. As he now met her gaze, he smiled into her broad, honest peasant face, and his was a smile that won him friends. He thanked her and dismissed her. But he seemed in no haste to sup. For when she was gone he came to the peristyle again, and leaning against one of the pillars he remained there. As his eyes became accustomed to the gloom, shapes formed themselves to his gaze: the cypresses so still in the tepid summer night, the steely gleam of water, the pale glow of the marble triton poised above it, and in the background the long mass of the Carreto Palace. As he looked, a window glowed with sudden light, like an eye that opened to return his gaze. He did not stir again until that light went out. Then slowly he entered the pavilion, and closed the door. He poured wine and drank, and found it rich and good. He loosed and removed his sword-belt and its weapons, and flung them on a chair. But there was yet no thought of seeking rest. A volcano was in his mind. His face was flushed, and his eyes glittered as if he were in prey to fever. He opened an ebony cabinet that stood against a wall, found pens and paper, and drew up a chair.

You know the sonnet in his collected verses, whose first lines run:

Fù nel fuggir la morte che in vita
Io mi trovai qual' uno nuovo nato.

which roughly may be Englished:

It was in flight from death that into life
I leapt, and found myself as one new-born.

It was written that night in the garden pavilion of the Carreto Palace in Genoa. It was an attempt to express what had happened to him in that garden, and the addition it brought to the purposes that governed his existence.

Chapter 10

Waters of Lethe

On that July night, in the garden pavilion, Prospero Adorno fell into a sleep that was destined to be heavy and long.

When the awakening came, full and clear, it brought the faint dream memory of an earlier awakening in the hour of dawn. His head, he had dreamed, was a globe of pain, and of such a leaden weight that he could scarcely raise it from the pillow. On his breast he had found livid blotches, which he had recognized for the fingerprints of the pestilence. After this had followed other, later dreams of which his memories were imperfect and confused.

But he was awake now, and only momentarily was he bewildered by the walls of coloured marbles aglow in sunshine, with the graceful, youthful Bacchus smiling upon him from the summit of his malachite pillar. Full recognition of his surroundings followed almost at once.

Then he discovered that the divan on which he had lain down half-clad had been transmuted whilst he slept into a proper bed, with sheets of fine linen and a silken coverlet, and that his body had unaccountably been stripped. Amazed by all this he struggled up, only then to become aware of a feebleness such as he had never known in all his vigorous young life. His startled, bewildered gaze met the eyes of a small man, bald and grey-bearded and benign as old Silenus, who stood at the bed's foot.

"God save me!" cried Prospero, and found his voice as weak as all the rest of him. Exerting it, "What's o'clock?" he croaked, and "Who are you?"

"Sh!" The old man came round to his side. "The Saints be praised! Your soul has returned at last. But lie still." Gently he thrust Prospero down again upon pillows swiftly and deftly adjusted. A cool, bony hand soothed Prospero's brow. "The fever's gone. All will now be well. Courage, my master."

Prospero stared up at him. "But what ails me, then? And," he asked again, "what's o'clock?"

The gentle, deeply-lined old face was smiling. "It is close on noon, and the day is the feast of the blessed St Lawrence: the tenth of August."

Prospero absorbed the information slowly. "You've left out the year," he complained.

"He! he! You can laugh already! That's good. That's good. You're clearly cured."

"But of what, if you please?"

"Why, of the plague, to be sure. What else? Aye, of the plague. For a fortnight you've lain there sweating the poison until at times we thought you'd sweat your life out with it. But you're a lusty lad, if your nobility will forgive the expression, and you've cheated Messer Death."

"The plague!" He felt a nausea stir in him. "And I've lain here a fortnight? A fortnight! What a Lethean draught was that." He half closed his eyes, and lay very still and thoughtful, realizing himself. Then he addressed the old man again. "Who are you?"

"They call me Ambrogio, may it please your nobility. I am the servant of Madonna."

"Ah, yes, Madonna. Madonna who?"

A shadow fell from the open door across the chamber. There was a quick gasp, the rustle of a gown, and the lady herself was at his side.

"He is conscious!"

Ambrogio rubbed bony hands together. "He! He! Did I not say he was healed and would soon awaken? Trust old Ambrogio, my lady. In seventy years one has time to learn a deal, God be praised."

Prospero's eyes glowed unnaturally large in their sunken sockets as he now contemplated her, standing there so straight and slim and gathering height from a blue mantle tied across her breast by long, tasselled cords.

"Madam, this is to abuse hospitality. To crave shelter for a night, and to stay two weeks…"

"Sh!" she admonished him in a whisper, appalled by the weakness of his voice. "You are to rest. We'll talk when you are stronger."

He grew stronger more swiftly than he would at that moment have deemed possible.

Well nourished, and at an increasing rate, by Ambrogio and Bona, his vigour was of hourly growth. And once each day Madonna would come to visit him, bringing fresh flowers to deck the place. Whilst she moved stately and unhurried, his glance never left her, lest he should miss a facet of the incomparable grace that he discovered in her. In delight he watched the play of light about her sleek brown head, upon her white slender throat and her incomparable hands. But when he would detain her in talk she denied him with a gentle solemnity which he found adorable even when the denial tormented him. They would talk, she promised him, when he was afoot again.

Hence an impatience to be afoot, which made him on the fourth morning demand a mirror that he might study his condition in his countenance. The sight appalled him. His sense of touch had warned him of the shaggy growth of reddish beard that disfigured him, but it had not prepared him for its hideous aspect on his sunken cheeks and hollowed eyes. He was made impatient and masterful, and he imposed upon Ambrogio obedience to commands which the old man accounted unreasonable.

As a result when towards noon my lady came to pay her daily visit, she discovered a gentleman strongly resembling the one who had climbed her wall. Shaved by Ambrogio, his cropped head reasonably dressed, and his long spare person arrayed once more in its black brocade, Prospero, pallid but smiling, bowed to her from the threshold.

He earned reproaches for this premature forsaking of his couch. These he bore with a becoming penitence, at once obeying her commands to sit, and permitting her to set cushions for him with her own hands.

"You suffer it like a martyr," she rallied him.

"Like a martyr who has reached Paradise."

"The way to that is through the gates of death, and those were closed against you."

"Not so. It was over a wall. For the rest, I refused to be ferried over Styx since I had discovered Elysium on this side."

"Is that your gratitude to us who held you back?"

"If I can express it in better words you shall teach me them."

She stood looking down at him. "Words? What store you set by words. I suspect that to you they are as bright beads, which you string into pretty patterns for your own delight."

"Oh, and for the delight of others, I hope, Madonna…" He looked up. "I owe you so much, and yet I do not even know your name."

"My name? My friends call me Gianna."

"Then let me, too, call you Gianna. For I should be more than a friend; almost your child; indeed, twice your child, for you have twice given me life."

"So be it, my son, provided you'll be filial."

"In piety I shall be more than that."

"I am content, since that includes obedience."

She stayed for little more that day, but on the next she delighted him by coming to dine with him in the pavilion, where Bona and Ambrogio waited on them. From that hour this interlude in that fair garden into which chance had brought him assumed more and more the aspect of a lovely dream.

As the days sped and his strength increased she gave him more and more of her company. Seven such days there were from that of his first rising, days in which the world was forgotten and past and future blotted from the present. He was in an oasis in time, akin to the oasis of this garden set in the heart of a plague-stricken city. Into this oasis filtered scraps of news, of which Ambrogio was the bearer. They were chiefly concerned with the conditions in Genoa, sometimes rumours relating to the war in which the tide seemed to be turning against the French, and once there was a tale that Messer Andrea Doria, having broken with the King of France, sat close in his Castle of Lerici, assembling men for the galleys he was equipping. Italy watched him, wondering what this might portend.

That brought a laugh from Prospero. "I could guess. He'll take the pay of the Emperor and restore Genoa to the Imperial protection from which he wrested it when he took the pay of France."

Madonna broke a lance with him on that. "Don't you suspect that it is just your hatred shapes your views?"

"I am aware of it. Can you blame me after what I've told you of myself?"

"Why, no. Perhaps it was enough to warp your judgment."

"It is not my judgment that is warped."

"Yet you refuse to see the other reason for my Lord Andrea's change. King Francis did not keep his bargain where Genoa is concerned."

"So Doria says, to justify himself. And you believe it?"

"There are no wrongs to blind me. Upon what evidence do you disbelieve?"

It was a moment before he answered. "There is a proverb: Vox populi, vox Dei. Do the people of Genoa believe it?"

"They will when by driving out the French he shall have made good his error."

"Therefore be sure that he will drive them out. Thus he will restore his damaged credit, and be once more the great man in the State."

She sighed. "You are very bitter."

"In that I hold him faithless? Have I no reason? What other have I found him? Did he not break faith with me, so that my father, whom I shall ever feel that I betrayed, was forced to flee, and died of it?"

"But that was the work of the Fregosi."

"Without Andrea Doria the Fregosi are nothing and could have accomplished nothing. And to make Ottaviano Doge! A fine Doge, as God's my witness. The plague here in Genoa, and this Fregoso, this worthy creature of the Doria, fled in panic, away from the post of duty so that he may save his skin."

She set a restraining hand upon his sleeve. "I understand. But..." She hesitated, then in a gust that was almost passionate, she went on. "Oh, but that you should make of vengeance the purpose of your life! It's a black thing to carry in your heart, a sort of pestilence to the soul."

The sentiment must have left him unmoved, for to him it was hollow. But the tone of passionate concern from one who seemed to him placidity incarnate stirred him. He could do no more than sigh, and answer wistfully.

"It's a duty. A duty to my house, whose members are in exile."

"Because they were against the French party. If that is overthrown they will return. Would not reconciliation then be possible?"

"Reconciliation!" He felt the blood rising to his cheeks. But he curbed himself. He shook his head. "There must be expiation first."

She faced him squarely, and he saw how solemn was that long, sweet face, how sad were the eyes under the broad brow.

"Monna Gianna, my troubles must not burden you. Myself, I bear them lightly."

But even as he protested it he knew that it was not true. For that talk had served to shatter the dream in which he lived, had awakened consciousness of the forgotten past and disregarded future. He was a whole man again, and he had no right to tarry lotus-eating here. His duty as an Imperial officer was in Naples with the Prince of Orange. Doria's defection from France and the withdrawal of his fleet supplied occasions for which a naval commander would be needed. Yet another duty was to his mother, now in Florence, to whom he owed at least a visit of reassurance.

He announced this to Madonna Gianna on the morrow, and there was no exaggeration in the description he gave to his emotions. "It is as if I tore body and soul asunder."

They were alone together in the pavilion, and it was eventide. She wore, as when he had first beheld her, that funereal splendour of silver slashed with black.

She made him no immediate answer. But after a little spell of silence she took up the arch-lute which lay near, and as the strings throbbed under her long hands, she began slowly to chant:

"Fù nel fuggir la morte che in vita
Io mi trovai qual' uno nuovo nato."

In thrall at once to amazement, joy and awe, he sat and listened to the song he had made when his blood was already tainted with the pestilence, the song which had been inspired by his first sight of her.

The last line expired softly on her lips: "*Con i ginnochi chini a tua beltade.*" – On bended knees before thy beauty.

The lute ceased.

"Just words," she said. "The brightly coloured beads you string to make a necklace for the creature of a dream."

He shook his head. His face was very pale. "Not brightly coloured. No. Nor beads. Pearls, madonna. For pearls are the symbols of our tears, and there are tears in that; tears bright and pure and true as any that were ever shed. How came you by those lines?"

"They were on a paper yonder, on the morning when we found you ill. They bore a title: 'To My Lady in Silver'. I thought at first it was a note you had left for me."

"So I suppose it was. And then?"

She looked away. "And then I read them, and I hoped it was."

"You hoped? You hoped!" He was looking at her, his face transfigured, aglow as with some inner light. And then, as if she realized how much she had avowed, a panic took her. Her cheeks were drained of colour, and the dark, grave eyes were hidden from him.

"Gianna," he said softly, "if that is true – as I pray God and Our Lady that it may be – then we should neither lack words now nor need them. You claimed me for your own in that blessed hour of our meeting as I claimed you for mine."

Without looking up she answered him. "My first dread was that the sonnet lied; that you had not fled from death to life, but from death to death. When you were well again my dread was almost greater: that the sonnet was but a toy for the soul, such as poets will be making."

"Dear love," he murmured, "I have no art to compass all the glorious truth. But I shall try. If it is in me to make songs at all, I should sing now, easily, as sings the lark, from its heart's ecstasy."

"But if you go?" she cried.

"Can I linger? There is a duty that I must fulfil. Until then I do not belong to myself. When it is done I shall come back. Will you wait, Gianna?"

Slowly she raised her eyes to meet his ardent, hungry glance.

"Wait?" she asked. And never had he seen that solemn loveliness more solemn. "Wait whilst you pursue a vengeance? Wait until you can come to me with blood upon your hands? Is that your prayer?"

He was chilled. "Dare I come whilst this is in my future?"

There was a long pause before she answered him. Her elbow was on her knee, her chin cupped in her hand. She did not move as she spoke.

"You say you love me, Prospero."

"I say much more than that."

"I ask no more. None could. And you have said that I have some claim on you. Once you bade me regard you as my child, since twice I had given you life."

"That is so, and, therefore, this life belongs to you. Do with it as you please."

She looked up now. "You are sincere? These are not just words? Then, Prospero, I require that you put this vengeance from you."

"My father's ghost would haunt me."

"The dead are at peace. They are not disturbed by our follies."

"There are still the living. In the eyes of every Adorno I should be a thing of scorn, an outcast, if I renounced this task. Would you mate with such a man?"

"I should be proud to. For he would be a man of courage. But vengeance being the vile thing it is in the sight of God, could I mate with one who pursued it?"

He moved away from her side, hanging his head. "Gianna, you break my heart. To refuse your first request, when I would yield up my life to serve you!"

"I ask much less than that."

"Much more. You ask my honour."

"Only your misconception of it. What honour is there in revenge? Have you not been taught by Mother Church that it is a mortal sin?"

"It may be so. But I swore an oath on my father's bier."

"From such an oath the first priest will absolve you."

"But can I absolve myself? Gianna! Dear Gianna!"

Her lips trembled, so moved was she by the anguished entreaty in his voice. "Dear love, do not ask more than conscience suffers me to give. Take thought upon it, lest it should be that we have met only to part again."

"That could never be. Do you suppose that it was merest chance we met? It was predestined."

"If you believe that, you will do nothing to thwart Destiny's fulfilment. It lies with you, my dear."

"It is a choice you offer me," he cried in pain.

"Alas! What else? But at least you know how I shall pray that you may choose."

She rose. He sprang to her as if to take her in his arms. Gently she denied him. "Not yet, my dear. First cast this dark evil from your soul. Then claim me when you please."

Breathing hard, he looked at her in sorrow. And under the sorrow there was anger kindling. "You reduce me to despair. Better to have let me perish of the pestilence."

"Better for us both if you say that," she answered sadly. "I will go now. To pray for you, Prospero, yes and for myself. If you can make your choice before you leave, send me word. If not…why then, my dear, God give us strength. I know that I shall need it."

Abruptly she moved towards the threshold and the dusk. He sprang to check her. "Gianna, at least I shall see you before I go."

She considered him, and her eyes showed large and bright with tears in her white face. "That would be to give needless pain where there is pain enough – unless you should choose as I would have you choose."

"To find you so hard," he complained softly, "who have seemed to me an incarnation of gentleness and pity."

"Is what I ask ungentle, then? Reflect, Prospero. It may help you to see with my own eyes. Pray God you may."

She moved out, and down the steps.

He made no further movement to detain her. He watched the silvery figure inciting into the dusk as he had watched it on his first night in that garden. But the difference. Then there had been wonder and exaltation in his soul. Now there was pain and anger so closely blent that he knew not where one ceased and the other began. His lovely dream was shattered. She asked too high a price for herself: a price he had not the means to pay; and obstinately she refused to recognize it.

In passion he demanded of the gods to know why he had met her. The answer came with a tinge of cynicism. So that he might be spared for the three tasks before him: to pull down the House of Doria, and so win honour; to write *The Liguriad*, and so achieve immortality; to drive the Infidel from the Mediterranean Sea, and so come by treasure in Heaven. Thus Monna Gianna would have served Fate's purpose in his life.

He laughed at the irony, laughed aloud until the laughter cracked on a sob.

Chapter 11

Procida

He did not see her again before he went. But at the moment of departure on the morrow, when Ambrogio led him to the garden gate, on which the red cross still warned the world to keep its distance, he gave the old servant a note for his mistress. It contained his Twentieth Sonnet, the Farewell to Joy, which opens:

"*Amando men', l'onor saria men' caro.*"

Lovelace may or may not have known it. Through the *Farewell to Lucasta*, however, runs no such deep note of hopelessness as in Prospero's sonnet, and none of the bitterness of his last line, equivalent to: "Take thou these last few pearls mine art has strung."

Together with that written scrap he pressed five gold ducats into Ambrogio's hand, before mounting the horse the old man had procured him.

He rode away, leaving his heart behind him, and carrying with him in exchange a deeper rancour against the House of Doria, for he added his present heart-break to the reckoning it must one day be called upon to pay.

Where Monna Gianna was concerned, however, there came to him as he rode a change of mind, an understanding that the barrier she had raised she would not have raised had she not been what she was, the adorable woman of his adoration; and since it went to establish the virtue, the rectitude and the sweetness of which her nature was compounded he must account it proper that she should have raised it.

He journeyed without adventures, and came through the drizzle of an August evening into Florence and to the poor house on Lung' Arno where his mother dwelt on the charity of the Strozzi and in a state scarcely befitting a daughter of that proud patrician house.

She gave him a tenderly effusive welcome. She had been awaiting him for weeks, she said. Alfonso of Avalos had had the thought to write to her from Lerici to tell her of her son's escape. But as time passed she had grown anxious for his safety. After that, as the excitement of this reunion waned, her querulousness came to the surface. She dwelt bitterly upon the discomforts to which she found herself condemned. When he spoke of the indignity of the oar to which Filippino had subjected him, she made light of it by contrast with the indignity endured in such unworthy surroundings as these by a woman of her descent and station. After all, what had befallen him was all in the way of a soldier's trade; the fortune of war. What she suffered, she plaintively complained, came to her by no fault of her own, but from the misfortune of having married a husband infirm of purpose and begotten a son upon the unhappy pattern of his father.

Her reproach of himself he passed over in silence. But against the slur upon his father's memory he raised a protest.

"I say of him dead nothing that I did not say to him living," he was answered, which was true enough, for she was of those, as she also reminded him, who must be saying exactly what she thought.

He expressed the opinion that those who say exactly what they think, seldom think correctly and never pleasantly, which merely brought upon him a fresh display of unpalatable candour. In the course of it she inveighed fiercely against the Dorias as a prelude to inveighing against Prospero for his dilatoriness in squaring the account with them. He pleaded in vain the lack of opportunity. A man of energy and strength of purpose, he was answered, did not wait for opportunities; he created them. But so long as his own life was soft, she added with the cruelty of the selfish, she supposed it would not trouble him to see his mother living meanly in exile.

Yet when it came to parting with him – having given him so little encouragement to protract his stay – this woman who still possessed something of the beauty of her girlhood, folded him passionately to her breast, and wept bitterly at losing him again so soon.

Two days only had he spent with her, and he left more bruised in spirit than he had come. Having inherited none of her egotism he could actually discover some justification for her laments. And he was tormented by the unfulfillable desire to ease her lot.

He went on to Leghorn, and there found a ship to carry him to Naples, running the blockade of the bay one dark night. It was no difficult feat, for the siege was breaking down by now. Lautrec might persist in it with futile obstinacy, but his troops, decimated by the plague, which had spread from the city to his insalubrious quarters, were no longer of a strength to tighten the cord of strangulation. And the Venetian galleys under Lando that kept the bay grew careless from the commander's sense of their futility.

At the Castel Nuovo, the tall, fair-headed Prince of Orange gave him a welcome as glad as it was surprised. Prospero could not, the Viceroy declared, have arrived more opportunely. Supply ships were being laden at Piombino, and an Imperial captain, Don Ramon Vargas, had been secretly assembling a small fleet of galleys, picking them up as he could, one at a time, and manning them, for lack of slaves, with hireling rowers known as buonevoglie. Five of these vessels were in readiness and well-equipped to convoy the supply ships. But they lacked a commander of experience. Don Ramon was without knowledge of the sea, and the Prince had been casting about him without yet finding one whom he could trust with that hazardous command. He offered it to Prospero.

"If you can break through the blockade," the Prince assured him, "you may save the Emperor's cause in Naples; for once we are strengthened by these fresh supplies it should be easy to hold out until the French demoralization is complete."

There was no more to be said. Glad of activities to turn his mind from thoughts that brought him heartache, he departed again at once. Two days later he was with Vargas at Piombino, and found all in readiness. To the five galleys mentioned by the Prince of Orange, Vargas had added at the last moment a sixth. They were well-found, and well-manned with buonevoglie. The supply ships, too, were six in number: two brigantines and a felucca packed with grain, and three clumsy swag-bellied galleons laden almost beyond the point of safety.

With this fleet Prospero left Piombino immediately, and well served by the wind he brought it safely to shelter on the northern side of the Island of Procida, off the northern horn of the Bay of Naples, just before daybreak one day exactly a week from that on which he had quitted the Viceroy, so as to go and take command of it. The wind had failed them at the end of the voyage, and all through that last night the galleys had towed the round ships. Prospero had insisted upon this because it was a part of his design to complete his approach under cover of night, so that the Venetians should have no warning of it.

His carefully considered plan was inspired by the situation of this little Island of Procida, set midway between the mainland on the east and the greater Island of Ischia on the west, the straits on either side being some two miles wide.

Having taken up his station there, behind the island, he gave his rowers five hours to sleep before he would call on them again. Himself, ashore meanwhile, and from the heights above and behind the castle-crowned Point Rocciosa he surveyed the vast bay that was spread before him, beyond Baiae of which Horace sang, to the hazy headland of Posilipo, that screened Naples from his view, and to the Vesuvian peaks in the further distance, above which a dense white cloud of ever-shifting shape was suspended in the blue. Below him on his right, as if crawling up the flank of the castle hill, he beheld the flat-roofed houses of the little awakening town of Procida, set in vineyards and in gardens.

From his eminence he studied the narrow straits between the island and the mainland. The sea, reflecting from the sky the flush of approaching sunrise, was all a sparkling opalescence. To the west, a couple of miles away, beyond the flat crescent-shaped little Island of Vivara, rose precipitously the coast of Ischia. The green island, dominated by the volcanic mass of Epoemo – the Epopus of the Greeks – was the homeland of his friend del Vasto and the birthplace of the great Pescara. But Prospero's interest now was in the narrow waters separating it from Procida, as if expressly fashioned for the game of hide-and-seek he meant to play with the Venetians.

There as a sentinel he remained until he beheld, somewhere in the neighbourhood of nine o'clock, the blockading fleet coming into view round the headland of Posilipo. Ten galleys he counted moving out in line ahead on their patrol. He judged their rate of progress to be scarcely more than two miles an hour.

Briskly then he went down by vine-clad sparsely tenanted northern slopes to the cove in which his fleet had so far remained unobserved.

Back aboard, he summoned Vargas, placed him in command of a division of three galleys with explicit instructions of how he should employ them.

An hour or so later, which is to say at something after ten o'clock that morning, one of Lando's captains, looking aft, beheld to his amazement, emerging from the Straits of Procida, three miles astern of him, a brigantine close-hauled to the southerly breeze, and three galleys that appeared to be convoying her.

"If these be Spaniards making for Naples," said he, "let me admire their impudence."

Lando must have been of the same mind, for at that moment from his capitana came a trumpet signal to go about.

"Sia voga!" ran the command from galley to galley, and the slaves on the larboard side rose in their places and turned to face the prow, thus pulling backwards whilst the starboard gang continued to pull forward. The ponderous vessels swung round as if on pivots and came on towards Procida, the formation changing as they advanced from line ahead to a crescent that should envelop the enemy.

The brigantine, which was approaching Cape Miseno on an easterly tack, as if belatedly aware of the trap into which she was blundering, went about and headed not merely west, but slightly north. Better favoured now by the wind, her speed, still all too sluggish, was slightly increased. The convoying galleys, with every sign of haste and confusion, swung to follow and to form a rearguard.

Across the southern face of Procida they raced, and soon it became plain that they were making for the Straits of Ischia, with intent to escape that way.

Lando, launching himself in pursuit, was checked by a suspicion that this might be a ruse. He perceived that with a start of nearly three miles even if those Spaniards proved no fleeter than his own galleys, they could lead him round the island, and, coming well ahead of him, once more into the bay by the Straits of Procida, find the way clear for a dash into Naples harbour and the shelter of the forts. Convinced that this must be the plan, Messer Lando was amused. It was astute. But not astute enough. To frustrate that pretty piece of strategy he left four of his galleys under an able, experienced captain named Feliciani, on patrol whilst with the other six he continued the pursuit.

The brigantine rounding Point Succiaro entered the narrows between the two islands, and with the wind now astern, sped like a bird along the green coast of Ischia, outstripping the three escorting galleys and leaving them to labour after her.

By the time the Venetians reached the entrance of the straits the Imperialists were out of sight, from which it was clear that they had veered to the north of Procida. They were adopting, then, precisely the tactics Lando had suspected, leading him round the island, so that they might have a clear run for Naples. Chuckling with satisfaction in his shrewdness, which had so disposed that he must come upon their rear whilst they were held ahead by Feliciani, making their capture easy and assured, Lando pressed on.

Meanwhile Feliciani's division, moving slowly forward, entered the eastern channel. Because, so as to conceal himself, Feliciani hugged the coast of the island, he did not see the three galleys that came into the straits round Point Chiupetto until they were almost upon him. Their appearance, so much sooner than was possible for the three he had seen enter the Straits of Ischia, told him at once that these could not possibly be the vessels of which Lando had gone in pursuit. He was confronted, he realized, with a strategy far deeper than his admiral suspected. Caught unawares, he was still considering how to meet an advance so resolute that it seemed to take no account of the fact that the odds were by one quarter in the Venetian favour. The Imperialists, coming on abreast, offered such narrow targets that Feliciani, in haste and confusion, felt the need to bring to bear upon them his heaviest guns, emplaced on the platform amidships. His trumpets blared the order, and the four galleys swung their prows to the land.

With an enemy less prompt and resolute than Prospero, his aim might have succeeded. As it was, with execution almost as swift as perception of the sudden advantage, the guns on the bows of the three Imperialists were touched off as one, at the broad marks Feliciani offered them. And it was by Prospero's orders, too, that those six guns were trained low. As a result, with not more than three hundred yards separating the fleets, the execution done was terrible. Feliciani's own galley took a shot between wind and water, whilst another cannon-ball ricocheting from the waves, crashed into the crowd of arquebusiers assembled on the rambade. In the flank of another galley a gap had been opened with such execution to the rowers that she was momentarily helpless. Upon the remaining two, which had escaped damage, the three enemy galleys were now swiftly converging.

The Venetians met the onslaught by a discharge of their heavy stone-mortars which took some effect. Then the assailants were upon them, and with crash of fractured oars and splintered pavisades drove their rostra across the Venetian decks. Prospero's arquebusiers led the boarding, whilst his buonevoglie, quitting the oars, seized their weapons and followed.

The fight was still on, and watched by the islanders crowding the heights from Rocciola to Chiupetto, when round the latter point came sailing the six supply ships, followed presently by the three galleys under Vargas. The ships passed on, holding to their course, as previously determined, and heading straight for the harbour of Naples. Two of the galleys came speeding into the fight, and by their very presence determined it. The third pushed on to engage the less damaged of the two Venetians that had been the first to suffer, but which by now had contrived to clear again for action. As for Feliciani's vessel, an attempt to jettison her guns, so as to lighten her and bring her wound clear of the water, had been made too late. She was sinking.

Lando was still behind the island, a good two miles away. But he no longer laughed. The sound of gunfire had changed his amused satisfaction into a dreadful conviction that he had somehow been tricked, for it reached him whilst the fugitives he hunted were still in view to the north of Procida. In a fury he recklessly flogged the last ounce of effort from his slaves. With backs streaming blood and chests convulsively heaving, they pulled him round Chiupetto, and there to his dismay Lando found himself faced by six Imperial galleys in line abreast, whilst of Feliciani's four only three were visible, and these partly dismantled and obviously captured. Away in the direction of Posilipo three galleons and three lesser craft under sail were running unopposed for Naples.

"Sia scorre!" The command to back the vessels was the cry.

But in response to it there was no arising and turning of the slaves, so as to row with their faces to the prow. The majority of the wretches, brutally driven to exhaustion by the frenzy of the last hour, merely ceased to row and collapsed gasping over the oars. Only the hardiest amongst them could even reach for their water-buckets to slake their burning thirst.

The wardens looked to their captains for orders, the captains to Lando's galley. Lando with hell in his heart and a thundercloud on his brow, erect on the poop, weighed the evil situation. His gangs were in no case to carry the vessels forward at once. No flogging could stimulate again those fainting slaves until they had rested, and with the wind now blowing in his face he could make no use of sails. Six galleys opposed his six. To pass they would certainly not allow him, and unless he could pass at once, without being delayed by an engagement, those supply ships would reach harbour. This he recognized, raging, was in any case inevitable now. Only vengeance remained: to destroy this Imperial captain who had so cunningly outwitted him and crippled him already of almost half his strength. But before he could think even of that, he must rest his gangs which had been too hard and recklessly driven at the desperate rate of nearly thirty strokes a minute. And meanwhile if the enemy, observing him a mile away, should decide upon attack, Lando would hardly find himself at his best to meet it. He realized it.

"Serve wine," he ordered in a voice that shook, his face livid above his black beard.

Wardens and sub-wardens moved at speed along the gang-decks with wine-skins and drinking-cans for the slaves.

On Prospero's side, however, there was no incentive to further engagement. The supply ships were already under the shadow of Posilipo, and he did not hesitate to leave the enemy in possession of the field of battle, since having fully accomplished his purpose the victory lay certainly with him.

So he gave the order to go about, and headed for Naples, taking with him the three captured galleys, in charge of a sufficiency of his soldiers and wardens to see that the rowers plied the oars. If Lando chose to pursue him it was unlikely that he would get within range before the harbour was reached. Should he, nevertheless, do so, and press Prospero too hard, it would be time enough to consider renewing the action.

But Lando did not pursue, and so, still early in the afternoon, Prospero followed the supply ships into harbour, to receive there such an ovation as had not often fallen to a seaman's lot. And this not only from the people that lined the waterfront and crowded the mole, drawn thither by the report of the arriving relief, but from the crews of the supply ships now at anchor. As his capitana went past them at the head of the line of homing galleys, their crews lined the bulwarks and roared their acclamations. He landed on the mole under the Tower of St Vincent, which controls the sluices of the moat, and here the Prince of Orange, who was waiting to give him welcome, opened his arms to embrace him like a brother, whilst the hungry populace cheered with frenzied enthusiasm the hero who had brought them food.

Generous were the expressions of the young Viceroy's delight.

"As pretty a piece of work as ever was seen," he declared it. "To go out with six galleys and come back with nine after defeating a fleet of twice your strength is in itself a matter for pride. But it is the art you displayed in the use you made of the island that proclaims the master. It is a tale that will rejoice the Emperor, and he shall have it, for my own sake as well as yours. For to me will be the credit of having chosen you for the enterprise."

Chapter 12

The Amend

What the Prince of Orange said that day, the world was saying before September was out. By then the brave tale of that brief naval battle in the Straits of Procida, magnified in the telling, had flamed over Italy; it had crossed the Alps; it had reached the Emperor in Madrid, and was to be memorable to him as the one bright piece of news amidst all the gloomy reports that came to him out of Italy.

Prospero's mother heard it in Florence, and went swollen with pride in her son. It was told in Genoa, and it rejoiced a people ever jealous of Venice that the hero of it should be a Genoese. It brought the name of Adorno into a sudden esteem that went to increase the continuing disfavour of the Dorias, against whom it was remembered that they were responsible for the exile of the Adorni. Within a few days Genoa was clamouring for their recall.

It was heard with joy by del Vasto at the Imperial court, with mortification by Filippino Doria at Lerici. In Filippino's view it raised a fresh difficulty to the reckoning which he hoped to present. And the debt had meanwhile grown. For when Andrea Doria had heard that Prospero had been set to the oar he had for once been moved to wrath with his nephew.

"Must I account you a fool?" he had asked him. "Have you yet to learn that there's no profit in pursuing rancour? That it merely breeds rancour in return? This was a brutal act."

"You did no less, yourself, by Dragut-Reis," the nephew sullenly retorted. "I chained them side by side."

"And you see no difference? God teach me to suffer fools! Dragut is an enemy in race and creed."

"Leaving out the race and the creed, is Prospero Adorno less?"

"Not now perhaps. Not now that you've confirmed in enmity a man whom you might profitably have studied to make a friend. If this recoils on you, don't look to me for help. You'll take your wages."

Yet in spite of that, Filippino went grumbling now to his uncle of the clamour in Genoa over the Battle of Procida. The old man offered him no sympathy.

"What then? What then? Haven't you yet done with spite? When will you learn that it diminishes a man? Leave it to women, Filippino, and attend to men's work. Heaven knows we've enough of it on our hands."

There was the fleet he was assembling, equipping and manning at his own charges, enough to engage not only their minds, but their resources, especially as the King of France was not likely now to reimburse his Admiral of all the treasure he had spent in that royal service. Among the various measures the Lord Andrea had taken to raise money was that of allowing every Infidel prisoner of worth to be ransomed, and Dragut-Reis had been in the number of these. The Genoese had accepted the three thousand ducats offered by Kheyr-ed-Din for the return of this famous captain.

It made some stir when it was known, and when Prospero heard of it in Naples he was sardonic on the subject of Doria avarice that thus defrauded him. For Dragut had been his prisoner, and when he would have held him to ransom as was his right, Doria had opposed it on the ground that Christianity could not suffer so redoubtable an Infidel to be loose again upon the seas.

Meanwhile Imperial profit from the Battle of Procida became increasingly manifest. It had given the death-blow to the siege of Naples. Lando was constrained to raise the blockade and withdraw what remained him of a fleet, no longer equal to resisting a Neapolitan attack once Prospero should have repaired and re-equipped the galleys he had captured. And this, Prospero, now in command of harbour and arsenal, was losing no time in doing.

Thus the tables were completely turned. The Imperialists, masters of the sea approaches, were able to bring in supplies and reinforcements, whilst preventing the like from reaching the besiegers. The French, demoralized by the plague and finally dejected by the loss of Marshal de Lautrec who had succumbed to it, realized the futility of continuing to hold entrenchments in which only disease and death awaited them. They folded their tents, and commenced a retreat which was converted into a rout by the troops the Prince of Orange launched in pursuit.

That was the end of the French supremacy in Italy, and for his signal contribution Prospero Adorno was by the Emperor appointed to the office of Captain-General of the Neapolitan fleet. And there were letters for him from Madrid in which the Marquis del Vasto, felicitating him upon the glory he had earned, assured him of the high commendation of his action by the Emperor.

From Genoa, meanwhile, came news of another sort.

Andrea Doria had concluded the agreement with Charles V whereby he was appointed Imperial Admiral of the Mediterranean. It had become widely known of late that the Emperor was proposing to take him into his service. But only one or two, who like del Vasto were very close in His Majesty's confidence, were aware that it was his intention to give him the supreme command of the Mediterranean fleets. At the last moment when this intention became of necessity divulged, there was frank and hostile criticism of it from the Spanish nobles about His Majesty's person. They were hot with resentment that such an office should be entrusted to a foreigner, considering that their own ranks contained so many seamen whom they accounted of at least equal merit.

A prince less resolute or obstinate than Charles V might have bowed before so formidable a body of opposition. But the young Emperor, in what they accounted his infatuation, was not to be dissuaded.

Following almost immediately upon his appointment, Andrea Doria had moved out of Lerici, had landed a force in Genoa, and had taken possession of a city too weakened by the visitation of the plague to offer any resistance. This done, he had proceeded to reform the government, and to persuade the people that under Imperial protection he brought them at last liberty and autonomy. He protested that he had quitted the service of France because in this very matter King Francis had broken faith with him, and that his one aim and endeavour had been to deliver his country from foreign vassalage.

The reaction of public feeling in his favour was immediate. Hailed as the saviour of Genoa, he was insistently offered the ducal crown, which had been borne by so many of his forebears. Firmly he refused, and thereby increased his credit. He could continue, he asserted, to serve the Republic better on the seas. At the same time the new constitution which he established considerably curtailed the Doge's power and left him under the tutelage of five censors. These were to be periodically elected, with the exception of Doria, himself, who accepted the appointment of censor for life. Thus, without assuming any trappings of office, he made himself the real and paramount master of the State.

It was not quite as Scipione had counted or as Prospero had hoped when they set afoot the movement that had brought the Lord Andrea to change sides.

Next came news of his marriage with the wealthy Madonna Peretta Usodimare, a niece of Pope Innocent VIII and widow of the Marquis of Fenaro, and they heard in Naples of the great festivities with which were celebrated the nuptials of that evergreen sexagenarian. For the pleasantries with which the world was greeting the event Prospero had not so much as a smile. Doria's appointment as Admiral of the Mediterranean meant for Prospero that as Captain-General of Naples he would be under Doria's orders once again. It only remained for him to offer his resignation to the Prince of Orange. His Highness, passing from dismay to anger, declined to accept it even when Prospero had candidly stated his reasons. They were met with arguments that he would be abundantly protected from Doria rancour not only by the Emperor's favour, but by that of his Genoese compatriots. Did Prospero know, stormed the Viceroy, that the Genoese were clamouring for the return amongst them of the man who had whipped the Venetians? Did Prospero suppose that in such circumstances the Dorias would venture to do other than conciliate him? Prospero did suppose it, and, therefore, he must hold to his resolve. And hold to it he would have done had not persuasion ultimately reached him in the very last form in which he could have expected it.

Gianettino Doria, with three galleys, had come to cast anchor off Ischia, and thence on an October day of fog and drizzle he crossed to Naples. Having discharged his courtesy duties to the Viceroy, he desired a word with Messer Prospero Adorno, and Prospero was fetched.

Gianettino advanced as if to greet an old friend. He bulked large in a red doublet that was laced in gold across the square opening on his broad chest. His voice boomed importantly, and the poise of his head was arrogant as ever, but his words were of the utmost cordiality. He shared, he announced, the pride of all Genoa in their valiant fellow countryman. He came to offer his felicitations, and to inform him, in his uncle's name, that the Admiral was proud to confirm Prospero in the command of the Neapolitan squadron. Volubly he boomed on. The Lord Andrea Doria desired him to say with what satisfaction he viewed this renewal of an old association.

Frosty-eyed, Prospero considered Gianettino, caressing the while his shaven chin.

"For your felicitations, my thanks," he said in a voice which the Prince of Orange accounted too cold. "For the rest, in the office bestowed upon me here I was confirmed already."

Gianettino winced, but kept himself in hand. No doubt he had been rigorously schooled. "Respectfully, Ser Prospero, let me observe that in all matters concerning the Imperial fleet, the Admiral my uncle is the chief authority under the Emperor."

"Under the Emperor. My confirmation comes from His Majesty."

The Viceroy, seeing which way the wind was setting, made haste to interpose. "But since of necessity, Prospero, you will serve under the Lord Andrea Doria's orders, you cannot be indifferent to the cordiality with which he welcomes you."

"Your Highness already knows that it is not my intention to continue in this service."

There was angry dismay in Gianettino's big round face. But the Prince forestalled any interpolation of his. "I still hope that you will change your mind, and I look to Messer Gianettino to assist me in persuading you." He turned to Gianettino with a laugh that took some of the sting out of his words. "Faith, sir, there are obstacles to an accord for which I think that your family must take some blame. You'll need patience to overcome them."

Prospero looked for an outburst from the Genoese. Instead, he seemed almost false to his arrogant nature. "Alas! Am I not aware of it? I bring not only patience, but penitence, Ser Prospero."

"You hear!" said Orange, encouragingly.

Prospero heard, but waited to hear more, and Gianettino scarcely paused. "You must perceive, Ser Prospero, that things have changed since…"

He hesitated, and Prospero was quick to supply the sequel. "Since your cousin chained me to an oar, you would say; or since he proposed to deliver me up to the Papal Justiciar in the hope to see me hanged; or since the Lord Andrea broke faith with me and drove my father from the ducal office, so as to replace him by a creature of his own."

Gianettino's colour darkened, there was a scowl on his black brows. The Viceroy was distressed, and looked it. He fetched a sigh, and shook his golden head. "My dear Prospero, as things are now what good can come of these recriminations?"

"Your Highness thinks that I should turn the other cheek?"

"That is not apt. Ser Gianettino's hand is not raised to strike. It is offered in reconciliation."

"And it is not empty," Gianettino made haste to assert. "I come as an ambassador of peace. Freely we acknowledge the errors of the past. But if looked at squarely, it will be seen that in all that has occurred to embitter you against the Lord Andrea, the service of the State has been his only guide. He betrayed you, you say. But is it not, rather, that he was, himself, betrayed? In single-minded patriotism it is difficult not to do hurt to some. In your patriotism, Ser Prospero, you should recognize it."

"No doubt I lack the Doria high-mindedness."

"Or faith in our present good intentions."

"Or that."

"Yet I bring some proof of them. There is the matter of Dragut, who was your prisoner."

"Appropriated by the Lord Andrea out of a patriotism which has not prevented him from selling Dragut to Kheyr-ed-Din for three thousand ducats. We've heard, you see, of that transaction."

But now Gianettino laughed. "I wish it were as easy to show the groundlessness of your mistrust in all the rest. That three thousand ducats have been deposited for you with the Bank of St George. I bring you a note of it." He plucked a paper from his scrip and proffered it.

For a moment Prospero was taken aback. Then he reflected that if he accepted this payment of a legitimate debt as proof of Doria honesty, he could not permit himself to be deceived as to the forces that made this honesty politic. He was still silently conning the note when Gianettino resumed, and he was as one reciting a lesson learnt.

"My uncle the Lord Andrea bids me say that he offers this as an earnest of intentions towards you which have never been other than good, whatever the appearances. It is important for Genoa's sake that you should realize it. A man who can render his country such great service upon the seas as that of Procida must not be lost to the State. And so, Ser Prospero, your house in Genoa now awaits you. The Adorni need no longer regard themselves as exiles. The Lord Andrea answers for it that their return will be welcomed."

"Sir, you pile gift upon gift." The irony of his tone made unnecessary the line he added with a bitter smile: "Timeo Danaos et dona ferentes."

Again the blood darkened Gianettino's cheeks. "By god, sir, you make my mission a hard one."

The Viceroy came to set a hand upon Prospero's shoulder. "Come, my friend. Make an end of these difficulties. There is the Empire to be considered and there is your native Genoa. Sheathe the sword. You and the Dorias are now aboard one galley."

"I am aware of it. Ser Gianettino has made me aware of it. But it gives me no guarantees of what will happen when the Dorias again change sides."

"That is an unworthy taunt," cried Gianettino, losing his hold upon a slippery patience. "It is to be calculatedly offensive. If you were concerned to be other, you would see in this very change of sides the proof that in what you call his betrayal of you, my uncle was himself the man betrayed. When we urged that your father should open the gates of Genoa to the French, we trusted the pledge of the King of France that Genoa should be made free and independent. What followed was the result of the French King's faithlessness."

"I know the argument," said Prospero coldly.

"But it has no weight with you? You do not trust it? Then – Body of God! – perhaps you will trust this. You spoke of guarantees. Guarantees of our good faith. It happens that I have guarantees to offer you. From all that we have heard, we expected your mistrust. So as to allay it once for all, so as finally to extinguish this unhappy feud, the Lord Andrea offers you an alliance with our house. He offers you the hand in marriage of his niece Maria Giovanna, who will bring a dowry of thirty thousand ducats and the rich lands of Paracotti."

There he paused, hand on hip, head thrown back, a triumphant defiance on his woman's face. Then in a voice that was like the roar of a cannon, he added the question: "Is that guarantee enough?"

Prospero's eyes had opened very wide. Slowly they narrowed again, whilst the Viceroy at his side, clapping his shoulder once more, was summing up the Doria bid for his friendship.

"Three thousand ducats, the ransom of Dragut, the restoration of the Adorni to their Genoese possessions, and a wife dowered like a princess. You'll sheathe the sword at last, Prospero."

"In God's name!" Gianettino appealed to him.

Slowly in silence Prospero turned away. He paced to the window, and paused there looking out upon the misty rain and the grey sea. Urgent, indeed, to the House of Doria must have become the need to make peace with him that they should go to such lengths as these. And he weighed the offer. In one scale he set all that had been enumerated; in the other his love and his righteous hate; his Lady of the Garden, his Madonna dell' Orta as he called her in his latest sonnet upon which the ink was scarcely dry, and the manner of his father's death.

His father was gone, and his Lady of the Garden perhaps beyond his reach. But could he sacrifice to worldly advancement his duty to the memory of the one and his hopes, however slender, of the other? Could he do this without abiding self-contempt? It was said that every man had his price. But what man of honour would admit that the saying was true of himself? And must he not have to admit it hereafter if he took now the proffered Doria hand?

He turned at last to those two who watched and waited. His eyes were grave to the point of wistfulness. He spoke slowly, almost sadly.

"Once I read on a sword-blade that was forged in Toledo the motto: 'Draw me not without reason. Sheathe me not without honour.' That is an injunction of which to be mindful. This sword of which we speak, Gianettino, was certainly not drawn without reason. Abundant reason. It certainly cannot be sheathed again without honour."

There was a long silence. The Viceroy's eyes were troubled, Gianettino's angry. Then the latter burst into stormy speech.

"Body of God! Do you say that there is no honour in what we offer? It is an amend, no less. And what an amend! An amend not to be surpassed in generosity. Certainly not to be received in churlishness. If you will not…"

The Viceroy interposed, a steadying hand upon Gianettino's arm.

"It might be well to wait; to give Ser Prospero time to digest this thing. It comes upon him very abruptly. He will scarcely yet realize all that your offer really means. A decision taken thus without reflection would be fair to neither of you. Let him carefully weigh the matter before you insist upon an answer, and forget meanwhile what has been said." He looked beyond Gianettino at Prospero. "At least you will consent to take time for thought," he begged.

"Since you urge it." Prospero shrugged. "But I am sure that it can alter nothing."

Despite the little hope of agreement that was left by the finality of his tone, the Prince of Orange, that night, when they were alone, laboured hard to persuade him, moved no less by friendship than by anxiety to retain in the Imperial ranks a captain of such proven worth. And he even employed among his arguments the great career which lay before Prospero in these ranks, the heights to which he might rise in the service of an Emperor already so prepossessed in his favour. Here was something of incalculable worth that Prospero would be forfeiting in addition to all that the Dorias offered him, if he should obstinately remain entrenched in his grievance.

So little, however, did Prospero show himself moved by the Viceroy's efforts at persuasion that it was matter for astonishment as startled as it was glad when on the following morning he announced that a night's reflection had produced in him a yielding mood.

"I do not know when I heard better news," the uplifted Viceroy exclaimed. "Glad on every score, I am most glad for you: glad that you have come to perceive how prejudice has blinded you."

"I did not say that I perceived that."

"But you must. Or else you would never have taken this wise decision. Just as at last you must be persuaded of the good faith of the Dorias. It required only reflection. The guarantee they supply could hardly be stouter."

Prospero looked at him with a crooked smile. "You think so? It has not occurred to you that the proposed marriage is to be a guarantee not of their good faith, but of mine. I was slow to perceive it, myself."

The Prince of Orange's face was blank. "Oh, come! That is an extreme view. At most, the guarantee is mutual."

But Prospero slowly shook his head. "Nothing short of that would assure them that they can trust me really to have sheathed the sword."

The Prince was momentarily thoughtful. Then he shrugged. "What then? What matters is that sheathed it is."

Chapter 13

Mother and Son

"Judas Adorno. That is what the men of your blood will henceforth call you."

Thus his mother in Florence, a fortnight later, when he had told her of the accord.

So as to visit her he had snatched a few days from the heavy duties that would demand until the following spring his presence in Naples. As Commander of the Neapolitan squadron, he assumed the burden of its reorganization, entailing the building, equipping, arming and manning of galleys, all of which would require his constant supervision. Not until it was done – or so he chose to decide – could he leave the post of duty, and go to receive in Genoa the welcome awaiting him, and the bride, this poor Iphigenia who was to be immolated in the cause of Doria ambition.

In the meantime his mother was to be delivered from her Florentine penury, and to this end he had made haste to seek her. Her satisfaction in the visit was changed to horror when he had rendered his accounts, and the eyes that glared at him out of that angelic countenance were the eyes of a Maenad.

"You have made your peace with those assassins?" She was hoarse with unbelief. "You have taken a hand that is stained with your father's blood? You can enter into alliance with that infamous family? And you are so shameless that you come here to boast of it?"

It was precisely what he had expected from her. Yet he could no more keep the pain from his countenance than from his soul.

"So much has been explained," he weakly announced.

"Explained? Can explanation change the face of truth?"

He looked at her where she sat by her window above the Arno, so gracefully slight and miraculously youthful, and he fetched a sigh. "What, after all is truth? No more than a mind's conception of a fact, and it may differ in one mind from another."

This merely put her further out of temper. "There was never a knave but could make of philosophy a cloak for his dishonour. You have sold yourself. That is the plain truth of this; one truth at least about which no two minds can differ. Three thousand ducats for Dragut. Thirty thousand as a dowry for your Doria bride. The figures suit the deal. Thirty hundreds and then thirty thousands. Thirty pieces was the Iscariot's price." And then came that cruel phrase: "Judas Adorno! That is what the men of your blood will call you henceforth."

He passed a hand wearily over his brow, thrusting back the chestnut hair which was now once more abundant as of old. "There was so much to consider."

"So much profit to yourself, you mean."

"And for others. The ban against the Adorni is lifted. They may return when they please to their Genoese possessions. If they choose to profit by my deed whilst cursing it, why, let them. It is very human."

"Do you sneer?"

He let the question pass. "There was also some thought for you in the transaction."

"Thought for me? What lie is that? When was there ever thought for me? When did any ever think of me – who like a fool have wasted my life in thought for others?"

"There are the privations you suffer here. This will make an end of them."

"Privations? What do I care about privations?"

"You complained of them very bitterly," he reminded her. "You even blamed me for them."

"And is shame to be preferred? Hypocrite! Could you suppose that I should set plenty in dishonour against an honourable famine? I was born a Strozzi, God be thanked; not a child of Genoa. Oh, God! The bitterness of this! After all that I have suffered! I shall die of it."

She was in tears. Covering her face with her almost translucent hands, she sat and rocked herself in grief.

Prospero approached her. Lines of pain deepened across his brow as he stood beside her tall chair.

"Mother!"

She became theatrical. "Never call me by that name again. Go. Leave me to die of grief and shame. Go to Genoa, to which you belong – that country of sea without fish, mountains without trees, men without honour and women without shame. Go back to the ease and plenty that are the price of your dishonour. Enjoy them until, infirm of purpose like your father, you will end like him."

The allusion to his father stirred him to wrath as always. "Confine your insults, madam, to me, who can answer them. Let my father rest in God's peace."

"Do you think he can rest now?" she shrilled at him. "Go, I tell you. Leave me." Her ready tears flowed faster. Sobs tore her. The rocking of her frail body grew more violent.

Prospero moved about the sparsely furnished room, clenching and unclenching his hands, a man distracted. For a moment he came to stand again beside her, and again looked from the window upon the dreary winter view, the Arno flowing steel-grey under grey skies, and the row of yellow houses on the Old Bridge. Then he went pacing away again, her sobbing in his ears. He was fighting a battle with his prudence, and prudence was reluctant to yield.

"Mother, you must trust my judgment," he desperately insisted, knowing the plea an idle one.

"Your judgment! God save us! And I must trust it? After this?"

He ignored the fresh taunt. He appealed to her love of ease, to her sensuousness. "You will leave this parsimonious Strozzi hospitality, and return to enjoy your own in Genoa."

"A curse on your Genoa, and all it holds," she raged through her weeping. "A curse on it. I never want to see the place again. But you would have me go. Yes. So that I should become the accomplice of your shame. So that I should be pointed at as the mother of the Adorno who walks in the way of Judas." There was an explosion of dreadful laughter from her, that was all grief and anger. "Here I stay. For here, at least, I can hide myself. Go, I tell you. You have all but killed me, as you all but killed your father. You can do no more."

"How unjust you are!" he lamented. "And how quick to blame!"

"Shall I praise you? Is that what you deserve of me?"

"I deserve, madam, that you should trust me to do what is right."

"You have done it, have you not – by your lights?"

And there at last his prudence went down in ruins. He beheld her torment and could not endure it to continue. She must have the truth, and he must hope for her discretion, well though he knew how little it was to be relied upon.

"Yes. I have done it." There was a bitter impatience in his voice. "But you do not guess what it is that I have done. Judas, you call me. And the name fits me. But not as you are supposing. There's a difference. I did not bestow the kiss. I merely submitted to it."

There was a frowning perplexity on her tear-stained face. He answered it with a grim smile.

"Now, madam, you have all the truth. You have wrung it from me with your never-ending plaints. See to it that you guard it more sacredly than I have guarded it from you. See to it that you never make me repent this confidence."

"What truth?" she faltered. "Of what are you ranting? What do you mean?"

"Don't you understand even yet? Shamelessly, because it suits their policy, these Dorias came to me with rich gifts in their bloody hands. As shamelessly, if you will, because it suits mine – ut clavus clavo retundatur – I take their offerings, accept their kiss of peace.

But I do this only because if I had rejected their advances I must have left them on their guard against me, and so frustrated my hopes of their ultimate ruin. Am I plain now?"

That full disclosure brought her gasping to her feet. She crossed to him quickly, and reached up her long slim hands, to set them on his shoulders. Her wet eyes looked squarely into his own. "You are not deceiving me, Prospero? This is really the truth?"

"Does it not seem so, if you reflect? Was anything else possible?"

"Nothing else should be to a son of mine. But this marriage? That is to push the deception very far. To do what may never be undone."

He set an arm about her shoulders, and led her back to her chair.

"Sit down, madam, and listen," he bade her, and when she was seated again, he went down on one knee beside her.

He was quiet now and gentle as a child at his mother's lap, or as a penitent at the knees of his confessor. And the confession that he made concerned his Lady of the Garden. He took his mother into the secret places of his heart; there he showed her Monna Gianna, and disclosed the vow he had made that if he could not win to wife that exquisite lady he would live a celibate all his days, his manhood offered up in sacrifice to a love as pure and noble as man had ever known or woman ever been worthy to inspire.

"I could be false to my name and to the memory of my father's wrongs before I could be false to that. So give peace to your doubts. Betrothal there may be; there must be, of course. This seal they offer to set upon the bond does not deceive me. It is offered as a guarantee of their good faith. But it is in their calculations that it will be a guarantee of mine. They are subtle these Dorias. I merely borrow a little of their subtlety. The marriage will never follow. I shall discover reason upon reason to postpone it during the time that I must wait to see my purposes fulfilled. Now, madam, I have told you all."

"Why did you not tell me at first? Why did you torment me with that incomplete tale?"

"Because it is dangerous to speak such things. Almost I am afraid to think them, lest some sense of my thoughts should reach the

Dorias. Therefore, mother, put it from your mind. Never even think of it again."

"You can trust me," she assured him, a close smile on that tear-stained face. "The secret is safe with me. But not to think of it... I shall think of nothing else. It will warm me to think of the Dorias in all their craft marching blindly upon destruction. The fools! And that woman of theirs, whom they had the insolence to thrust upon you, given to the humiliation she deserves."

"Ah! That, no! This poor lady deserves no hurt, and she shall take none that I can spare her. That she is in it at all is the one ugly flaw that I deplore."

"Need you be squeamish over a decoy? For that is what they've made her. The rest is their affair."

"Mine, too," he insisted. "And she shall not be hurt if I can help it. Not in her heart, at least. A mere betrothal to a stranger need not matter. She's but a victim of their plans. It should be a relief to her that they are not to be carried out. If I had not so argued, this would have been impossible."

She leaned over him. "When did they ever think to spare our women? Did they spare me? You have seen the pain and hardships, the dangers to which your mother has been subjected. They would have had my life had I not fled with your father from the Castelletto on that dreadful night. Let no thought for this girl trouble you."

His only answer was a sigh as he knelt ever at her side, his brows contracted. Coaxingly she asked him for an account of his plans. But to this he shook his head. "I have formed none yet. Opportunity must guide me."

"I see," she said, and put her arms about him. "My child, you are more Florentine than Genoese."

He sighed again. "That may be true."

Fiercely she retorted, "I thank God for it."

Chapter 14

Scipione de' Fieschi

Summer had come again by the time that Prospero Adorno appeared in Genoa, and it is certain that he would not have appeared there even then had not further postponement been made impossible by the events. His work in the Neapolitan arsenal and shipyards was complete and could not be urged as a reason for further delay without betraying that it was no more than a pretext. In addition to this a summons had reached him which could not be ignored.

The Emperor, himself, was on his way to the Ligurian capital, and he commanded Prospero's presence with that of other captains, so that on the occasion of this visit order might be taken for sweeping the insolent Infidel from the Mediterranean. Kheyr-ed-Din's audacity could no longer be endured. Firmly established now in Algiers, the entire province recognized the Corsair's authority and was under his rule. Until lately the actual city of Algiers had been dominated by the Spanish guns of the fort on the island in the bay, and this had been as a thorn in the flesh of the Moslem commander, whose hands were tied by lack of ordnance.

But on a recent raid Kheyr-ed-Din had captured some French vessels and had possessed himself of their guns, whilst Dragut-Reis had celebrated his restoration to liberty by the seizure of a Venetian fleet, which he had stripped of munitions and gunpowder. Thus equipped, Kheyr-ed-Din went vigorously about justifying his assumed title of King of Algiers by making himself fully master of the place. After ten days of bombardment, his Moslems had carried the Peñon – as the fort was called – by assault, and thereafter some five hundred Spaniards of the garrison who had escaped the Turkish scimitars were set to work to demolish that stronghold. With the stones of it they built a mole that should afford shelter to the Turkish galleys.

In the meantime nine transport vessels laden with troops, provisions and war material coming to reinforce the Spaniards in the Peñon brought up before Algiers to look in vain for the castle. Its absence was beginning to persuade the Spanish captains that their landfall had been mistaken, when suddenly the Turks swarmed about them. That was a fine day for Islam. Close upon three thousand Spanish prisoners went to join their five hundred fellow countrymen in the bagnio of Algiers.

Spain shook with indignation at the news, and the Emperor, turning his mind to the matter and giving it precedence of all others that might engage his ambition, determined to let the Infidel feel the full weight of his might.

By his orders an expedition was preparing in Genoa under the direction of Andrea Doria, and to this expedition Prospero Adorno was now commanded to bring his Neapolitan galleys.

So, however reluctant, he must at long last repair to Genoa, there to avow by his formal betrothal to Madonna Maria Giovanna his reconciliation and alliance with the House of Doria.

The announcement of this had played meanwhile at least some small part in further enhancing Doria credit. Remembering the feud between Doria and Adorno men pointed to this reconciliation as an instance of the Lord Andrea's generosity and greatness, which placed the advantage of the State above all petty personal considerations. It was worthy of the man who was now virtually in the position of Prince Paramount of the Ligurian Republic. He might, for the asking, have been now also its titular prince. Esteeming this great seaman as he did, the Emperor would never have hesitated to bestow upon him a title which, anyway, would have cost the Emperor nothing. But

Doria perceived reasons of policy against it, and he knew perhaps that power that is masked goes more securely than power that is bare of face. He contented himself with permitting the Emperor to create him Duke of Melfi.

However the Adorni and their factionaries might view the power which Andrea Doria now firmly grasped, it is certain that this power was benignly exercised. If a despot, he was a benevolent one. Not only did his measures sternly and effectively repress the factions that had hitherto divided and distracted the Republic, but under his influence the Imperial undertaking to leave Genoa free to govern herself in her own fashion was meticulously fulfilled. Of the form of government adopted, Doria was the architect. He instituted on the Venetian model a Grand Council and a Lesser Council, with Doge, Senators and Procurators; but with this difference, that the Doge was elected every two years, whilst the chief power in the State was vested in the five censors, who held office for four years, guarded the constitution and controlled the Doge and Senators. Andrea Doria's refusal of the titular Lordship of Genoa having led to his being elected censor for life and supreme Admiral, it followed that the virtual lordship was his in a dissembled form.

Nor was this the end of the marks he received of his restoration to popular favour from his temporary eclipse. A grateful State bestowed upon him the ancient, princely Fassuolo Palace, on the western side of the harbour, and this palace he was rebuilding with a magnificence that should render it remarkable even in that city of splendid mansions. He brought Montorsoli, that great pupil of Michelangelo's, to Genoa, to be his architect; and in stone of Lavagna and marble of Carrara, the princely dwelling, with its galleries and colonnades, set in the heart of a vast garden bordering the sea, rose swiftly to be one of the marvels of Liguria. Montorsoli worked too, in shaping those gardens, so as to render the setting worthy of the jewel. He erected terraces, laid out avenues, planted choice shrubberies, and built fountains, over one of which presided a Neptune in the likeness of Andrea Doria himself.

For the interior decoration the Duke of Melfi employed Raphael's pupil Pierino della Vaga to paint him frescoes and portraits which should lend the Palace some of the opulence which Raphael's art had added to the Vatican. To enhance it, Doria had levied heavy toll upon the East. Silken hangings from Ispahan, carpets from Smyrna and Bokhara, Moorish divans, Greek vases supplied their sumptuous backgrounds to the rich furniture, much of it brought from France and Spain, that equipped the vast apartments.

Amid these splendours, the great Admiral received Messer Prospero Adorno on that day of May which witnessed his landing in Genoa, and by that reception supplied a fitting sequel to the acclamations with which the city had that morning surprised the young captain.

That the victory of Procida had placed him high in the esteem of his fellow countrymen he was, of course, aware. But not until he came ashore to face the multitude, to tread the flower-strewn paths to the Ducal Palace, whither he was bidden so that he might be welcomed home in lyrical terms by a new Doge supported by the red-robed senate of Doria's institution, did he realize that by his spectacular defeat of the detested Venetians he was become a national hero.

From this triumph he had escaped at last, to go and embrace his mother in the black and white marble palace where she kept the state to which her son's achievements had restored her. And with his mother he had found his old friend Scipione de' Fieschi awaiting him, and awaiting in impatience.

Scipione had not been idle in these months. With his gift of intrigue and urged ever by his ambition for his house, he had been diligently undermining the soil upon which Andrea Doria stood so firmly planted. With his preparations complete he accounted that the moment had arrived to spring the mine.

He had heard, as all Genoa had heard, of the reconciliation cemented by the betrothal of Prospero and the Lord Andrea's niece. But Scipione had not for a moment permitted himself to be deceived either by the reconciliation or the proposed marriage. He perceived, he thought, not only why the Dorias had sought to be reconciled with one who had suddenly risen in the public favour, but also why Prospero should have appeared to lend himself to that reconciliation. It was a strategy that Scipione's tortuous mind entirely approved, and the more warmly since it guaranteed him, as he supposed, a valuable ally in his own projects. A bitter disillusion awaited him at the hands of Prospero himself, who came now with flushed cheeks and sparkling eyes from the acclamations that had hailed his landing.

Madonna Aurelia took him to her slender, shapely arms. "You are happy, my child?" she asked him.

He returned her kiss, and stood back to give a hand to Scipione. He laughed shortly. "It would all be amusing if it were less tedious."

"Amusing?"

"The voices that acclaim me today are the same that were clamouring for our blood when last I heard them. Isn't that matter for laughter?"

Scipione could have had no better cue. "Let it warn you, my friend, to seize the mood before it changes. The men of Genoa belong to you today. This is your opportunity."

Prospero's face was blank to that vehemence. He was conducting his mother to her chair by a little table of ebony inlaid with ivory cupids. They occupied a small room she had made peculiarly her own in the great palace. It was hung with ivory damask and softly lighted by a window which bore in stained glass a figure of St Michael. He seated her, and himself took a stool beside her. Thence he looked up at Scipione, who remained standing.

"My opportunity for what?"

"For what?" Scipione repeated himself: "The men of Genoa belong to you today." And he added significantly: "It is for you to lead them. You are the man."

"Perhaps. But this is not the hour. Indeed, none could be worse chosen. The Emperor will arrive in two days' time. Am I to present him with a revolution?"

"Well conducted, it will be accomplished in two days. The means are under my hand."

"Means to what?"

"To sweep these Dorias finally to Hell."

"They'll not be swept so easily. The Lord Andrea never stood more firmly than at this moment." He shook his head. "Decidedly it is not the hour. The gamble would be a desperate one."

Scipione was annoyed. "It might be if I had prepared less soundly. I am not without the support of France."

"So I was supposing when you spoke of the means under your hand. But, for myself, I must prefer the Emperor. That is why I will not present him with a revolution when he arrives."

"The Emperor? Are you then concerned to serve him?"

"I am not concerned to serve France, which would be the consequence of receiving French support. My service is to Genoa and the Adorni, and this the Emperor is likelier to further."

"And Doria, then?" cried Scipione, exasperated by this phlegm. "Does he not rely upon Imperial support? Isn't Charles V beglamoured by the Admiral?"

"That is why we must begin by dispelling the Imperial illusion. Before we can bring Doria down, we must pull away his Imperial prop; cause the Emperor to see for himself that this man's fame is a superstition, a bubble blown by Fortune."

Scipione was changing colour. His eyes were angry. "How long will this take to accomplish?"

"I don't know, Scipione. But nothing can be done until accomplished it is. It is necessary to have patience. Perhaps this will not be tried too hard. We are about to take the seas against the Turk. War has a way of supplying opportunities both for making and for destroying reputations. I think of Goialatta and in what case I might there have left Andrea Doria."

"That is to trust too much to chance. Suppose that the coming war affords you none. Suppose, instead, that it is your own reputation that is destroyed, and with it the ascendancy you enjoy at this moment. What then?"

"Faith, I am not a prophet. I cannot speak to the future. But I can speak to the present, and the present I tell you again is not our moment."

"You tell me so." Scipione was now utterly out of patience. "You do not even trouble to ask what are the means of which I speak. Listen, Prospero. I have three hundred French troops at Lavagna to supply a cutting edge to the axe."

"But where is the axe?"

"Here. In your hands. The populace offers itself as a weapon to you, as it may never offer itself again. You have but to parade your wrongs, demand vengeance for the death of your father, and the people will rally to you, the hero of the hour. With my French to open the way, we storm the Fassuolo Palace, and the day of Doria dominion in Genoa is at an end."

"After which, if even so much were possible, we can sit down and wait for the Emperor to avenge the Lord Andrea. You look at only one side of the coin. No, no, Scipione. Before I attempt to strike down the Duke of Melfi I shall have removed the Imperial shield that covers him."

In despair, Scipione turned to Madonna Aurelia, and vehemently, with outflung arms, implored her to try to move her son from this obstinacy. But for once Madonna Aurelia was in complete agreement with Prospero.

"I think I understand his views," she said. "Believe me, Scipione, he knows what he is doing. He may move slowly, but only so that he may strike more surely. Trust him as I do."

"Trust him?" Scipione echoed, and his handsome face was further darkened now. In his deep chagrin, confronted with the frustration of all his measures to procure a revolution, deprived of the master-weapon upon which he had so confidently counted, a sudden suspicion came to explain his failure. He stood squarely before Prospero, his hands on his hips, his dark, handsome eyes fiercely intent upon his friend's calm countenance.

"Will you be open with me?" he asked.

"Have you ever found me otherwise?"

"You may never before have had occasion for deceit with me."

"I do not think I like the implication. But no matter. What do you want to ask me?"

"On this matter of your alliance by marriage... That you agreed to it I understand. At least, I thought I understood. I thought I knew you well enough. I judged that you found it necessary; that you agreed so as to lull them whilst you heated your irons. But now that the moment to strike has come, and you refuse to profit by it, I ask myself did I misjudge you. I ask myself..." He paused there, then added brutally: "Do you play a double game with us?"

"A double game?" said Prospero. He remained bland. "And with you, do you say? I play no game with you at all. I play my own game, in my own way. I welcome those who join me, amongst whom I have reckoned you. But this does not make me the servant of their aims." He laughed. "You have shown me something, Scipione. Let me disabuse your mind. I shall not spend myself to crush the Dorias so as to further your ambition, the French ambition, or the ambition of any faction."

And now Scipione was viperishly contemptuous. "I've shown you something, have I? But what have you shown me?"

"You shall tell me."

"First answer me this: Now that you are here, do you go forward with this Doria marriage?"

"The betrothal will be formally announced tonight."

"That is the answer I was already expecting. All is explained, I think." There was horror and loathing in his glance. "You disclose at last the comfortable bed you've made yourself. You take the easier way to advancement. You accept even the helping hand of your father's murderers. You urge pretexts for postponing a justice which you no longer intend to execute. And I have loved you. I have thought you were a man."

"At need I could prove that you were right."

"You've proved all that I need to know of you. You've found your profit in eating from the hand that slew your father. May it choke you, Prospero. And be sure it will. God will see to that."

He swung in fury on his heel, to depart.

Madonna Aurelia leapt from her chair. Her cry was vibrant. "Stay, Scipione! Wait!"

"Nay, madam, let him go," said Prospero, who had risen with her.

The door slammed behind the departing nobleman; the damask hangings quivered in the draught of it. Madonna Aurelia stared in wild distress at her son. "You see! This is but the beginning of the storm."

"I'll weather it." He set a soothing hand upon her shoulder.

"Surely it were better to tell him. To – "

"And so tell the world," he interrupted. "It is what would follow. And then?" He smiled wistfully, as he shook his head. "This is a thing with which we can trust nobody. Besides, in what is it Scipione's affair that he should rage at me? He suffers the fury of the thwarted plotter. He would have used me to the profit of the Fieschi. Haven't you understood?" And with a little laugh of bitterness he added: "My friend!"

She sank thoughtfully to her seat again. He remained standing over her. "The world must think what it will. I know what I do. That is enough. Whatever obloquy may come must be borne in silence until the end is reached."

She bowed her head in afflicted acquiescence. But when presently he reminded her that they were awaited at the Fassuolo Palace, that a banquet was to be spread there in honour of the betrothal to be announced, she shuddered in horror. She could not go. She would not go. In vain he urged her. Her answer was that he must make excuses for her. Let him plead that the emotions of the day had left her exhausted. Face the Dorias at such a time and on such a matter she could not.

So in the end he kissed her cheek, and departed on that errand with a self-loathing inferior only to his resolve to discharge in full a debt that could not be forgone.

Chapter 15

The Adorno Honour

In his vast, glittering halls, the Duke of Melfi had assembled all that was noblest in Genoa, the Lomellini, the Gaspari, the Grimani, the Fregosi and the rest. But there was no Adorno present. Although invited, the members of that noble house remained absent. They might allow the feud to slumber, but they would not go the lengths of denying its existence by accepting Doria hospitality.

Their absence cast no cloud upon the splendid gathering. It represented a state of things which if not yet extinct was to be extinguished by what was to be done that day. Since the greatest of the Adorni, the recognized head of the house, was to be present, publicly to receive the honour of the Doria alliance, it mattered little what other Adorno stayed away. So the new Duke of Melfi waited calmly with his patrician guests, assembled to witness the formal betrothal that was to consolidate Prospero Adorno's alliance with the House of Doria.

To that feast came Prospero more gaily dressed than his habit, but no more gaily than the occasion craved, in kilted tunic of cloth of silver above hose that was striped red and white, the colours of Genoa. He would have denied that he had been at any pains to make himself attractive, for he desired nothing less than that the prospective bride should find him so. His chestnut hair hung severe and sleek to the nape of his neck. His weathered, shaven, rather bony face, for all its pensive cast looked singularly youthful.

Andrea Doria, detaching himself from a courtly throng of guests, advanced to meet him, and opened wide his mighty arms to enfold the young captain. His words matched in breadth the gesture.

"Be welcome to my house as to my heart, Prospero. It is the prayer of an old man that the alliance between our houses may endure forever to the magnification of our fatherland."

Then came Gianettino, big and showy in a round cloak of maroon sarcenet the points of which were modishly knotted. He rolled forward with a swagger and a grin, and after him followed Filippino, slim and sly, his goggle eyes uneasy as he smiled upon this new-found brother whom once he had chained to an oar.

Under the watchful eye of his uncle he proffered his hand. "If there have been errors," he muttered, "let no rankling memory remain to taint an association that is offered in friendship."

Prospero took the proffered hand. He smiled.

"This day begins a new chapter," he answered, and they thought it was well said, perceiving no ambiguity or evasion.

There was no time for more, for Madonna Peretta, the new Duchess of Melfi, was approaching and not to be kept waiting. With her came a dark, bright-eyed boy, her son Marcantonio del Carretto, who now added the name of Doria to his own. Prospero was presented to her, and bowed low, bearing to his lips the hand she gave him. She was a small, neatly shaped woman of forty, who contrived to look demure despite the glitter of jewels that decked her.

After that the crowd pressed about Prospero, to greet him. There were Lomellini and even Fregosi among the men with whom those of his blood had always been at feud, who came to fawn upon him now and to present him to their smirking women. And there were those, like the Spinoli and the Grimani, with whom the Adorni had ever been allied, who may have been disposed to marvel. But clearly all were here to hold obsequies upon the past.

Prospero stood gravely attentive to their compliments. But behind the solemnity with which he masked himself there was grim amusement at so much adulation where he knew there was no love, simply because a deed of arms – and a friend at court to make the most of it – had won him Imperial favour and had earned him the worship of the populace, ephemeral if omnipotent whilst in being.

Abruptly that secret amusement was jarred and checked. Ahead of him, where he stood with Andrea Doria towering at his side, a gap had opened in the glittering, chattering crowd, and at Madonna Peretta's side a lady stood revealed to him, in a gown of silver that was shot with black arabesques. She was young and moderately tall. A pearl-studded caul confined her smoothly dressed brown hair. A twisted rope of pearls fell like a stole over her white bosom to end in a tassel of pearls at the level of her waist.

Across the intervening space her eyes were steadily regarding him with a glint that was almost as of tears, whilst at the corners of her lips quivered faintly something that was neither laughter nor weeping, and yet both.

Prospero had caught his breath, and he felt the blood ebbing from his cheeks. Swift upon the first surge of joyous wonder had followed blank dismay to meet here again, in this evil hour of his mock betrothal, his Lady of the Garden.

The Lord Andrea, smiling through narrowed eyes as he watched him, leaned from his towering height to murmur: "A very lovely lady. Is she not?"

Prospero's answer was mechanical. "The loveliest I have ever seen."

He heard the Lord Andrea's soft laugh, ushering his next words. "Yours, Prospero, is the most enviable of all human states. If you still think yourself injured at Doria's hands, this should make the most abundant of amends. Come, sir. Your bride is waiting there to greet you."

"My…" He checked open-mouthed, and was half-turning to the Admiral, when the Admiral took him by the arm, and pressed him forward with a jocularly impatient, "Come, sir."

He moved like a sleep-walker until brought to a halt within a yard of the lady, conscious of no other presence in that crowded room. Her smile was no longer dubious or elusive. It was the smile he knew so well, tender, yet of a calm restraint, almost belied by the glow of her dark eyes and the gentle heave of her white breast in its square corsage.

Doria was speaking. "Here, Gianna, is your Prospero as I promised you."

Prospero's senses were too dazed to note the oddness of that presentation. He commanded himself, bowed low over the proffered hands, and bore each in turn to his dry lips, but still mechanically, bewildered, almost scared by the incredible thing with which he was confronted, and the dark mystery of it. Some instinct warned him not to probe this mystery, but to possess himself until it should come to be unfolded to him.

Therefore, and because, half-stupefied, he stood silent before her, whilst on her side she waited for him to speak, the awkward moment was ended by Madonna Peretta. She touched her husband's arm.

"We embarrass the children, Andrea. We make a show of them. But at least we need not stand there eavesdropping. Leave them to unload their hearts."

Not only did she take the Duke away, she so well contrived to remove others, that in a moment there was an empty space about the pair. If they remained the object of attention of all curious eyes, at least they were sufficiently alone to speak softly without fear of being overheard.

"How long you have kept me waiting, Prospero," were the first amazing words that added to his confusion. It was a lament rather than a reproach. "What endless months in which to practise patience. And now that at last you are here…" She paused. She was scanning his face, so grim and solemn. "Have you nothing to say to me?"

"More than I could say in a lifetime." His voice trembled.

"It is…what you would wish?" There was hesitancy in the question.

"A queer trick of Fate's, to bring us thus together again," he answered dully. "Who could believe in so tremendous a coincidence?"

By that question he resolved her doubts into relieved amusement. "Why, nobody, of course. For there is no coincidence. The trick is not Fate's. It is mine. How came you not to guess it? Had you so little faith in me? Had you no sense of the depth of my sincerity? Could you conceive it just a coincidence that they should offer you my hand in marriage?"

Into his staggering, groping senses came the recollection of a gibe, flung by his mother or Scipione, that the all-absorbing Doria upon his marriage had imposed his name upon Madonna Peretta's son and even upon her niece. He remembered, too, that Gianna – the diminutive of Giovanna – was a niece of that Marquis of Fenaro who had been Madonna Peretta's first husband.

He stood foolishly tongue-tied, faced with the horror of confessing that he had never suspected the identity of the bride they offered him, yet realizing how impossible was that confession unless he added unthinkable explanations.

Fortunately she took her answer from his silence. "I see that you did not. Perhaps you accounted me too guileless. Oh, but I can be guileful, Prospero, as you'll find. You just accepted me as a gift – a bountiful gift, I hope – from the hands of Madam Fortune. That is to be over full of faith in Fortune. When I tell you all, I hope you will have as much faith in me. Then, perhaps, you'll become more like the Prospero I remember. So far, my dear, I scarcely recognize you for my songster of the garden."

He murmured airy evasions, whilst she led him to the embrasure of a mullioned window that looked across the miracle of a garden Montorsoli had created to the gleaming harbour, where Prospero's galleys rode amid the crowd of shipping. In that embrasure, as in an alcove, whilst still in view, there was a sense of being private. A chair of embossed and painted leather, craftsmanship of the Moors of Spain, had been set there. Gianna sank to it, and calmly composed her silver gown about her. Quietly she told her tale.

Heaven had offered her the chance to make her happiness and Prospero's, and she had seized it. That, she declared, was all the concern that Chance was allowed in what had happened.

At a time when the Lord Andrea was being deeply wounded by the hostility towards him of the Genoese, his distress was increased when, after the victory of Procida, his fellow countrymen added to other grievances against him the exile of the Adorni. Gianna's aunt Peretta was by then the Admiral's wife, and Gianna had come with her to take up her residence at the Fassuolo Palace. The Lord Andrea, who was her godfather, had, after a fashion, now adopted her; and the orphan had willingly assumed his name to mark her sense of the great kindness that she owed him. He honoured her with much of his confidence, and from himself she learnt that the unhappy feud with the Adorni resulted entirely from the breach of faith of which King Francis had been guilty. Unfortunately, he explained, it had been aggravated by rash words, and then by the arrogance and unforgivable blundering of Filippino. When he spoke wistfully of it as a breach which he would give much to close, she had perceived her opportunity. She thought she knew, she told him, how a bridge might be cast across the gulf. Let him send Prospero Adorno an offer of reconciliation backed by the proposal of an alliance by marriage in proof of its sincerity.

"My Lord Andrea did not hesitate to ask me whether I was merely a fool, or whether I permitted myself to be merry out of season at his expense. Where, he had asked, even if disposed to such a step, should he find him a daughter?"

"A god-daughter should suffice," I answered him. "And you dispose of a dutiful one in me."

She went on then to relate how she had met the Admiral's incredulity by a frank confession. She had told him how she had sheltered Prospero and had cared for him in his need; how they had come to love each other, and how they had parted in the end because this very feud stood as an obstacle between them. Having begun by urging the Admiral to take this means to heal the feud for his own sake, she ended by pleading with him for hers. And at last, between one and the other, she had prevailed. Perhaps because the Lord Andrea was so recently a bridegroom himself he was the more understanding.

The tale was long in telling, and by the time the end was reached Prospero had resumed command of his wits. Amongst other things that he perceived was the source of the urgency she had used to turn him from his task of vengeance. Not alone, if indeed at all, was the barrier that had risen between them a year ago due to considerations of abstract virtue, but, rather, to the ties existing between her house and the house of Doria and the unsuspected spiritual relationship in which she stood to the Lord Andrea.

"So," he said. "That was the way of it. It was your doing. The mystery is dispelled. Meddlesome Fate is dismissed the scene. The miracle becomes as all miracles once the explanation is supplied."

There was almost a note of bitterness in his voice, and she could not discern the source of it, could not guess that he was being bitter with himself, derisive of the vanity that had so grossly misled him. Presumptuously he had supposed the Adorno friendship so necessary to the Dorias that to procure it they had been ready to stifle their pride and abase themselves, to come to him with gifts. The veil was now torn from his error. More, far more, than by their own need had they been moved by Andrea Doria's fond readiness to cast into Gianna's lap the gift she told him that she needed for her own happiness. Prospero's complacent vanity was brought in shame to the dust by this revelation.

He found her eyes were searching his face, and they were troubled. "Still so cold and formal, Prospero? What is amiss? I have been looking for applause from you for the part I have played. You do not even say that you are glad."

He forced himself to smile into those reproachful eyes. "Are you glad, Gianna?"

"So glad," she answered him candidly. "And not only for myself. For you, too, whom I have now delivered from your dreadful burden of vengeance."

"You perceive that, do you?"

"Naturally. You could not have accepted this alliance unless your reconciliation is sincere."

"Yes. It should be sincere, should it not?"

"Of course. When the Lord Andrea consented, he said that it would provide the test."

"Yes, yes." The odd smile was again on Prospero's lips. "In that, at least, I was right, as I told the Prince of Orange. The alliance was proposed as a guarantee of Doria good faith. I saw in it the need for a guarantee of mine."

"It is mutual," she answered him. "It establishes the faith of each in the other, and so makes for the happiness of all."

He went forward from her a little, and stared through the window at the play of sunlight on the distant water, striving to master the pain and perplexity which his face was in danger of betraying. She rose, and came to his elbow.

"Prospero," she asked him again, on an urgent note, "is anything amiss?"

"Amiss?" Hating himself, he commanded a smile that was purely of reassurance. "Now? What could there be?"

She was searching his face again with those eyes that in their calm gentleness were so like a hind's, but a wrinkle stood between them. "You are so strange. So solemn. So...so cold."

"Not cold. No. Not cold, dear Gianna. A little bewildered...and solemn. Yes. The occasion is solemn. Besides..." He half turned, and seemed to indicate the ever-shifting, chattering throng. "We are very public here."

"Ah yes," she agreed, with a little smiling sigh. "It is not quite so that I had pictured our first meeting. But it is as the Lord Andrea would have it." Then with a hand on his arm, its touch a caress that thrilled him, she added: "Come to me tomorrow. I'll show you the glories Montorsoli has fashioned in these gardens. They make a poor thing of the garden in which we dwelt awhile, you and I."

"Will you blaspheme? That garden was my paradise."

She brightened. "There speaks at last my Adam. Did you remark my robe, Prospero? It is a copy of the one I wore when first you saw me. It was my whim to appear so today. And I was glad to see you, too, in silver. It was as if you wore my livery. A sweet homage, my Prospero."

Her glance, all tenderness, sought his own, but failed to find it, for in fresh shame at the necessary lie of silence, his eyes were averted. That and his lack of answer and the grim set of his long mouth chilled her again with a sense of something incomprehensible, of something that had changed him.

Then the Lord Andrea advanced upon them, tolerantly grumbling that they had been private long enough and that his guests desired their company at closer quarters.

To Prospero the interruption brought relief. He had need of time in which to adjust his mind to a situation so different from all that he had expected, a situation which might have lifted him to exalted heights of joy, but for the accompanying horror that weighed him down. He had come prepared to dissemble, but not to dissemble to Gianna. This seemed to him monstrous, not merely because he loved her, but because the clear, shining purity of her which had first compelled his worship must ever put dissimulation to flight in shame. Yet what but dissimulation had he used already? What but dissimulation must he continue to use, unless he were to tell her the vile truth?

For that she must dismiss him in pain and contempt, not because he was a foe, but because he was a treacherous foe. It came to him, as if in a flash of revelation, not only that this is how her noble mind would regard him, but that it was the only way in which he was to be regarded by every honourable eye. Hitherto he had complacently viewed his action with a vision obfuscated and distorted by rancour and vindictiveness. Now, suddenly, it was as if he had borrowed her own clear, honest sight. It was the startled apprehension of how she would view it that had shown him how it should be viewed. Those eyes of hers had become as a mirror of truth in which he saw himself reflected in a garb that appalled him. Yet in that garb he must continue, since he could discover no means of discarding it. In that travesty he went presently to take his place at the betrothal banquet.

Against the frescoed walls two tables ran the length of the great hall and were united at their upper extremities by a third that crossed the chamber. Thus united they formed the three sides of a parallelogram within which a regiment of servants in red and white liveries with the eagle badge of the Dorias wrought in gold upon their breasts moved under the command of the steward of the household to wait upon a hundred guests.

At the upper table sat Andrea Doria, Duke of Melfi, between his Duchess and Giovanna Maria, and on Giovanna Maria's left sat Prospero, with hell in his heart and a smile of make-believe happiness frozen on his lips. And make-believe inspired his words whether addressed to her or to the florid Archbishop of Palermo on his other hand. It was horrible. He was caught in the toils of his own deceit, and could perceive from it none but an agonizing deliverance.

There was worse to follow on the morrow when he came as Gianna had commanded him, and was taken by her to view the Montorsoli marvels in the terraced gardens. This, however, as he well knew, was merely so as to furnish the occasion to be alone, and to talk not of Montorsoli, but of themselves.

To Prospero at the moment no subject could be more repellent. A sleepless night of dreary pondering had brought him no nearer to a solution of his difficulties. It was a relief to him when near the great Neptune statue, in features modelled upon those of Doria himself, they were joined by the Lord Andrea. The Admiral was urbane and gracious and he used more words than were common with him. A man as sparing normally of praise as of censure, he commended at generous length the Neapolitan squadron. He had visited the galleys that morning, and he professed himself filled with wonder for Prospero's labours in perfecting them. In building, arming and equipment the squadron could not be bettered, and it would supply a formidable addition to the fleet for the expedition against Kheyr-ed-Din upon which the Emperor had set his heart. He brought news that a fast trireme from Monaco had just arrived with word that His Majesty would be in Genoa on Saturday. This was already Thursday, but fortunately all was in readiness for His Majesty's reception.

Thus he talked on, genial, amiable, almost garrulous, until the suspicion grew in Prospero that it was not merely for such chatter as this that he had joined them. At last, all other themes exhausted, he came to the real business. He stroked his long grey beard. He cleared his throat, and plunged.

"And now to talk of something nearer to your hearts. Our time is short. The Emperor's visit is almost the signal for departure. In a week or so we shall be putting to sea. There is the question of your marriage. You'll naturally be impatient." And he smiled down upon them, a benign match-making giant.

Prospero, ill at ease, stared out to sea. Gianna looked at him shyly, and then away. Neither spoke.

"Come, come," said the Duke. "You'll have thought of it. You'll have views."

"Oh, yes. Yes." Prospero spoke jerkily. "But there is the expedition."

"To be sure there is, and hence the need for haste." The Duke faced them, leaning his back against the marble balustrade that edged the terrace. "And that I take it will not be displeasing. Eh?"

"The haste, no," said Prospero instantly. With repugnance choking him he followed in dissimulation the only avenue of escape that he perceived. "For my happiness the date could not be too soon. But there is this expedition."

"So you said before. What then?"

"There are the risks it brings." This was a subterfuge long since prepared against the danger that they should press him to immediate marriage. That he should be employing it so as to postpone marriage with Gianna was circumstance's cruel revenge upon him for the deceit to which he was committed. He went on, devil-driven as it seemed to him. "If I should not return... To embark on marriage with that chance before me would be a grievous wrong to your niece, my lord."

She set a hand upon his sleeve. She spoke softly, with the artless candour that revealed the strength and fineness of her spirit. "That need not be counted. I would sooner live as your widow than as the wife of another man."

"Dear Gianna, no man lives who is worthy that you should say that to him." And in this at least he was sincere.

"If I should choose to think so; that there is one man?"

"I should prove to you that I am not he if I were to take you at your word."

"Not if that were my own wish."

"Even then. I must protect you against yourself." Because this had a noble, lofty sound, he hated himself the more for uttering it.

"Well, then? What then?" grumbled Doria, frowning from one to other of them.

The lady sighed and smiled in one. "It shall be as Prospero wishes. I would not persuade him from what he thinks right and fitting."

This was to turn the sword in the wound for him. The Duke, however, would not leave it there. "Things do not become fit and proper, my dear, just because he accounts them so. I have given the world to understand that the marriage will take place at once. I was supposing, Prospero, that you would pay my niece the compliment of impatience."

"Whereas I pay her a still higher compliment by my restraint," said he, made inwardly sick by his own hypocrisy. "Let the hope of this marriage spur me to those high deeds of which it shall be the reward. Believe me, my lord, thus I shall be the better soldier in the expedition ahead of us."

Again the Duke looked from one to the other without satisfaction. Again he passed a meditative hand over his long beard. "Faith, you're laggard lovers," he disapproved. "But be it so, since you're of a mind. Though devil take me if I can understand such coolness in young blood."

To Prospero's unutterable relief this was the end of the argument. But it was by no means the end of the troubles the situation brought him.

Returning home that afternoon he found a storm in progress in his mother's ivory-hung closet. There were present with her his uncles Giovacchino Adorno, who was Cardinal of Santa Barbara, and Rainaldo Adorno, the latter accompanied by his two tall sons, Annibale and Taddeo. Their raised voices had warned him of their presence as he approached, and it was easy to guess the subject that was being discussed with so much heat. For this, however, he was prepared. Already he had been given a taste of it by others. Yesterday at the Fassuolo Palace one of the Grimani had turned his back upon him without acknowledging his greeting. Agostino Spinola, on the other hand, had spoken with the blunt freedom of the hard-bitten old soldier that he was.

"So your noble father is forgotten, his wrongs forgiven. Ha! It may be the way of the world, when interest beckons. But I had not thought it would have been your way, Prospero."

Prospero had defended himself. "Nor is it. I have no need to follow the beckoning of interest."

"True, your father left you rich. The more reason not to kiss the hands of his enemies."

"Were they that? Or did it merely seem so? The King of France it was who broke faith."

"So they say. And to be sure it will suit you to believe it," Spinola had quietly sneered, and on that he had passed on.

Prospero had quivered under the insult. Yet he had swallowed it. Impossible to demand satisfaction on such a matter of one who had been his father's loyal friend.

Now the like awaited him, no doubt, again. He went boldly in to face it.

His mother looked round quickly when the door opened. Her countenance was flushed and angry. "Thank God you're come at last to answer for yourself," she greeted him. "I am driven crazy with seeking to answer for you."

"That was surely unnecessary." He closed the door, and stood with his back to it, considering his uncles and his cousins in simulated calm. Behind it his temper was worn raw. "I trust that I shall be ready always to answer for myself."

"There's the need for it now, as God's in Heaven," stormed his uncle Rainaldo. He was a big, hearty man, all jowl and beard, in nothing resembling Prospero's dead father. More like the departed Antoniotto was the Cardinal, spare and tall of frame, almost ascetic of countenance, with gentle dark eyes and a sensitive mouth. His lips murmured something now. His fine hand was extended to restrain his burly brother. But Rainaldo shook it off impatiently.

"This is no matter for priests or women." He glared at Prospero. "What's this of your marrying into the House of Doria?"

"Have you only just heard of it?"

"I have only just been brought to believe it."

"Then why ask me about it? I am betrothed to Maddona Giovanna Maria Monaldi. Is that what you mean?"

"What else should I mean?"

"You are not pleased about it?"

"Pleased? Do you laugh at me? I see my brother's son marrying into the house of my brother's butcher, and you ask me am I not pleased about it."

The Cardinal made a sound of sorrowful disapproval. "Why must you overstate, Rainaldo? Blood-guilt at least there was not…"

"Leave me to judge," Rainaldo roared at him.

"The lady," said Prospero quietly, "is of the House of Monaldi. Not of the House of Doria."

"It makes a difference, Rainaldo," the Cardinal purred.

But Rainaldo brought his fist down with a crash on the table by which he stood. "God's blood! Will you quibble? Has she not become Andrea's niece by marriage? Has she not assumed his name?"

Madonna Aurelia interposed. "You forget that I am present, I think. Don't bellow, sir. It hurts my head."

"Your head, madam? What of your heart? Is that as insensible as your son's?"

"God give me patience with you. I'll not be stormed at in my own house."

"No, no," the Cardinal supported her. "It is unseemly. Most unseemly, Rainaldo. You should consider Aurelia."

"I am considering our honour," said the fierce Rainaldo.

"You are considering mine, I think," said Prospero. "I wonder why you should find it necessary."

His uncle was robbed of breath. "For impudence," he said when he had recovered it, "you deserve a crown."

"Shameful," muttered Annibale.

"Say shameless," Taddeo corrected.

"Say anything you please," quoth Prospero. "It shall not move me. I recognize no right in any of you to dictate my actions."

"We don't dictate," said Rainaldo. "We judge."

"No, no," the Cardinal disagreed. "It is not ours to judge."

"It may not be yours..." Rainaldo was beginning, when the Cardinal interrupted him.

"Mine more than yours, by virtue of my office. But I am less presumptuous. I do not usurp the divine functions. You may censure, by your poor lights, Rainaldo. But you shall not blaspheme of judging, for you have not the right."

"Keep to your breviary, man. Keep to what you understand. I have no right, you say. Have I no rights in decency, in honour, in duty to our name? The shame that Prospero earns falls upon every Adorno."

"Yet you do not scruple to profit by it," Prospero taunted him.

Rainaldo and his two sons flung back the taunt at him in a roar. In fury now, himself, he laughed upon their fury. "Were you not in needy exile, all of you; not daring to approach Genoa or claim your own until six months ago when my reconciliation with the Dorias lifted the ban and allowed you to come back? You knew the terms of it, I suppose. Or you could have discovered them. Did any sense of this decency, this honour, this duty to our name of which you prattle, prevent you from returning whilst the wrong was unavenged? It did not, in such haste were you to run back to your ease and your fleshpots. Yet you presume to spurn the act that made it possible."

There was a tight-lipped smile on the prelate's lips. His eyes were veiled. He folded his hands. "Consider that, my virtuous, self-righteous brother," he softly murmured. "Ponder it."

But Rainaldo did not heed him. His bulging eyes stared at Prospero in horrified amazement. Then he shifted his glance to his scowling sons. "The man's demented," he declared.

"Not he," said Taddeo. "Do you suppose this is sincere? He has craft enough for arguments to make himself a mask." He advanced upon Prospero, and his voice rose with his swelling anger. "Did we know when the ban was lifted that this was the infamous price?"

"Did you not? Then you were not curious enough. But you know it now. What will you do? Will you cease to profit by it? Will you go forth again as homeless wanderers, or will you eat the bread my treachery earns you? Or will you discover your duty in some even more heroic course? Until you do, you'll be sparing of a contempt that recoils upon you. You'll remember that as great a thief as he who robs the orchard is he who watches at the gate."

The three glowered at him in dumb hatred. The Cardinal watched their discomfiture for a moment from under his brows. Then, "You have your answer, I think," he told them, and so stirred them into life again.

Rainaldo reached for his hat, which he had cast upon the table. He looked at his sons. His voice was hard and dry. "Come," he said. "Here is no more to be done." He strode to the door. Prospero stood aside to let him pass. From the threshold Rainaldo looked back, and scowled at the tall scarlet figure of his brother.

"You will remain, of course, Giovacchino," he sneered.

"For a moment," the Cardinal mildly answered, and added, with gentle irony: "Do not quit Genoa without coming to take leave of me."

Rainaldo and his sons went out in fury.

From the chair in which she sat stiffly upright, mother looked at son. Her tight lips parted. "You made the best of it," she admitted. "So much I grant. But what is the best worth? That boy Taddeo was right. Your arguments were those of a crafty advocate, reckless of truth. They did not persuade."

"At least they silenced," said Prospero wearily.

"Oh, and they persuaded," his uncle supported him. He came forward with a rustle of his silken robe and set a delicate hand on Madonna Aurelia's shoulder. "They persuaded because they are true. You are wrong, Aurelia, to describe them as you do. It is easy to be lofty in judgment where there is no price to pay. Rainaldo has shown you that. Now let him judge himself by the same harsh standards that he sets, and refuse to profit by what he calls a treachery." The Cardinal smiled. "Do you think that he will?"

"But the treachery remains," she said.

"By certain canons, you may say so," she was answered. "But what are those canons worth? What is the Christian view of them? If wrong is ever to call for wrong, and pardon never to make peace between men, then we need not wait for death to find ourselves in Hell." He looked at Prospero, and sighed. "I do not know the motives in your heart, nor do I ask them. Even as an Adorno I am not sure that I should condemn your action. For it seems to me that a man of honour should travel cautiously when rancour is the signpost." And thoughtfully he quoted Juvenal: "Nunquam ad liquidam fama perducitur. As a priest, however, I am clear. I should commit a treachery if I did not oppose vindictiveness. And the view of the priest goes deeper than the view of the man." He gathered his scarlet cloak about him. "Follow the voice of your conscience, Prospero, whatever men may say." He raised his hand in benediction. "God be with you."

Madonna Aurelia was silent only until the door had closed upon the departing prelate. "That is but the view of a priest," she said in scorn. "It will not help you with the world."

But Prospero did not answer her. The view of the priest had profoundly startled him, and left him deep in thought. Seeing him silent, his head bowed, as she supposed in sorrow, she spoke again. "You would have done better to have told Rainaldo the whole truth."

He roused himself.

"So that he may publish it?"

"He would keep faith with you."

"Would he?" He passed a hand over his pale brow in a gesture of distress. "Does their contempt matter? You heard what the Cardinal said? Was it less than true? This uncle and these cousins swollen with indignation at the lack in me of the virtue they think I should possess. What virtue is in them? What sacrifice have they ever made? By what means do they propose to avenge the Adorno honour?"

Chapter 16

The Choice

Prospero walked with his uncle Giovacchino in the Cardinal's garden, where azaleas, lately brought from the New World which a Genoese had discovered, blazed in the early morning sunlight.

The disturbance the Cardinal had stirred in his soul only the Cardinal could allay.

So he had sought in confession an easement of his tormenting perplexities, taking his uncle for his confessor.

Now as they sauntered between trim boxwood hedges centuries old, their talk being concerned with what had been confessed was still under seal. The confession itself, full and frank, had been sterile.

"My son, I cannot grant you absolution," the Cardinal had wistfully told him. "There must first be a purpose of amendment. Until you cast out from your heart all thought of vengeance you continue in a state of sin."

"There is no issue from it save by the pathway of dishonour." Thus argued Prospero in the secret hope that the argument might be refuted. It was not.

"That may be man's judgment. I am concerned with God's. I can do no more for you, child, until you can announce a change of heart."

So the penitent who was not truly penitent had risen unshriven from his knees. But though the Cardinal as priest could do no more for him, as man he still sought to help him, and to this end had brought him to the garden.

"There is no clear issue, Prospero, from the tangle in which you are caught. If piety alone inspired you it would be easy. In setting your duty to God above the opinions of the world you would find abundant strength to bear censure with indifference. But your only inspiration lies in your own passions; in a worldly love. Even if you were to forgo that vengeance which you conceive a filial duty, you would forgo it out of no Christian principle, but only for your own gratification. You would hate the sin not because the sin is hateful, but because it stands in the path of your desires."

"I have not said so much," Prospero protested. "I stand at the parting of the ways. What I must forgo is not vengeance, but justice upon my father's slayers, or else forgo my hopes of happiness. That is my choice."

"You merely say in other words what I have said. If you forgo vengeance so that you may gain the alternative, where is the merit?"

"Your Eminence is an Adorno as well as a priest. As an Adorno would you see merit in forgoing this just vengeance?"

"It is written: 'Vengeance is Mine'."

"That is the answer of the priest."

"It is God's law. The layman is not exempt from it, save at the peril of his soul."

"Would you have me believe that if you were not a priest you would have me forgive the Dorias?"

The Cardinal's smile was very gentle. "Being an Adorno, it is possible that I might not. But since clearly I should be wrong, what need that matter? Though a priest, I am still an Adorno, still your father's brother. Yet I swear to you there is no thirst in me for Doria blood. But I will not say, being weak and subject to passions as we all are, that, priest though I may be, I should not thirst for it if there were real blood-guilt."

Prospero halted in amazement. "But is there not?"

The Cardinal halted with him. He passed a narrow delicate hand over the summit of the boxwood hedge, where diamonds of dew still sparkled. He withdrew it moist, and inhaled the fragrance.

"In my opinion there is not. To speak of the Dorias as your father's assassins is to speak in hyperbole. The worst that can be truthfully said is that Antoniotto died as a result of certain actions of theirs, actions, however, which did not aim at his life, or, for that matter, even at his office. His life, to my knowledge, Andrea Doria would have saved. He brought his troops ashore early on the morning after your flight."

"So as to protect my father's life?" Prospero was almost derisive.

"Why else? So as to destroy it he had but to remain inactive."

This was a forcible answer, as Prospero was constrained to admit. "He had promised to provide an escort," Prospero remembered. "But why was I never told that he kept his word?"

The Cardinal smiled. "Your hatred drew to you only enemies of the Dorias, and their only aim would be to feed your rancour."

"But his alliance with the Fregosi? The deposition of my father?"

"That would be imposed upon him by the King of France. We may believe that Doria had no purpose but the deliverance of Genoa, and that he believed that King Francis would promote it. The King broke faith with him."

"That has been Doria's explanation. You believe it?"

"I hold it to be true. I have been at pains to ascertain." And again the deprecating smile broke on his ascetic face. "After all, I am an Adorno, and I conceived it my concern to discover the truth. I pray that it may help you."

"I'll need some proof."

His Eminence nodded understanding. "Seek it, and God send you find it. Then you can purge your vindictiveness out of pure motives, and not merely barter it for something you desire. Thus you make your peace with God, and you will be able to meet censure with the strength of a conscience at peace."

Meanwhile, however, peace for that conscience was not discoverable to Prospero, tangled as matters were by Gianna's presence in them and the deceit he was meanwhile practising upon her whatever might be the ultimate unpredictable issue.

He inclined to adopt the Cardinal's view that, after all, there was no blood-guilt. Belief in it rested upon assumptions which disappeared when all was sifted. In Filippino's hostility towards him and the outrage of chaining him to the oar, he could perceive a rancour sown by fear of the vindictiveness he professed. It grew clear, and would have grown clearer had not Prospero recoiled from the vision in suspicion that it took shape from his own desires.

It was a gloomy bedevilled Prospero who waited on the morrow in one of the foremost places, assigned to him by the Duke of Melfi, in the patrician and military ranks that were ranged to receive the Emperor at his landing.

To the roar of guns, the flourish of trumpets and the thundered acclamations of the multitude, Charles V stepped ashore from the great gilded galley that in a bravery of pennants and streamers led an escorting fleet into the harbour gaily bedizened for so tremendous an occasion.

Along the Ripa, behind the glittering lines of troops, seethed in a dense mass the clamorous crowds of Genoese, against a brilliant background of tapestries and spreads of cloth of gold and of silver, waving banners that transfigured the shops and houses of the waterfront. Within the clear space that the soldiers kept, the gonfaloniers of the wards, each with his standard aloft, stood ranged in a line at the head of which fluttered the white banner bearing the griffin and the cross.

The Emperor set foot ashore on the mole of Carignano, where a triumphal arch had been erected, bearing a label inscribed with Genoa's welcome to the most potent monarch of the earth. A short flight of carpeted steps made easy the imperial descent from the galley, and at the foot of them waited Doria with a score of nobles whom he had honoured with invitations to attend him. Behind these were ranged the new Doge in cloth of gold with his scarlet senators and his thirty trumpeters in red and white silk, whose embannered silver trumpets rang clear in greeting.

The tall, spare figure of the young monarch detached by its sombreness from the glittering throng of courtiers that attended him ashore. All in black, his only ornaments were the Golden Fleece on his breast with its pale blue ribbon and the pearls thickly sown on the high collar of his mantle. He was excellently made, and credited with the shapeliest leg in Europe. But there the beauty of him ended. His long face was unhealthily pallid. His brow, hidden now under a flat velvet cap, was fine and lofty, and his eyes, on the rare occasions when he allowed them to be fully perceived, were seen to be bright and eloquent. But his nose was of excessive length and set askew upon his countenance. His thinly-bearded lower jaw protruded heavily, and his lips, thick, shapeless, and ever parted, lent him an expression dull and vacuous.

He put forth a beautiful hand, unadorned by any ring, to raise the kneeling Doria to his feet, and then stood to hear the address of welcome in Latin uttered by the Archbishop of Genoa. His own brief reply was rendered by his nasal tone and stammering speech almost unintelligible. To deliver it, he stood slightly in advance of his two immediate followers, one of whom, in flaming scarlet, was his confessor, Cardinal Garcia de Loyasa, the other, clad almost as soberly as his Imperial master, Alfonso d'Avalos, Marquis of Vasto, whose questing eyes had found Prospero and smiled a greeting to him.

Some brief presentations followed by the Duke of Melfi; first his nephews Gianettino and Filippino. Prospero Adorno was next, as became a captain who as commander of the Neapolitan fleet stood high in the Imperial service. Doria was generous in his terms.

"Messer Prospero Adorno has already earned Your Majesty's esteem."

"With God's help," stammered Majesty, "my service shall leave no earnings unpaid." And with a nod and a smile he would have passed on, accounting the debt discharged by so much condescension, but for Alfonso of Avalos.

"By your gracious leave, sire, this is that Adorno who at Procida won the victory which Your Majesty was pleased to admire."

"So! So! I thank you, Marquis, for that word." He vouchsafed Prospero a full sight of his Imperial eyes. "I felicitate myself upon counting you among my officers. I shall desire your better acquaintance, sir."

He passed on, drawing Doria with him, to be greeted next by the Doge, and to receive from the gonfaloniers the homage of lowered standards, whilst from the throats of all Genoa came the roar of welcome reserved for one in whom they beheld their liberator. With that roar, like a salvo of artillery in his ears, the young Emperor mounted a white mule richly bedecked with purple housings, and rode up the steep streets that were overhung with banners, past palaces festooned in rich tapestries and carpets from eastern looms, and so came to the Cathedral, there to inaugurate his presence in Genoa by a thanksgiving. His next visit was one of ceremony to the Ducal Palace, and when that was done, he rode away on his white mule to Doria's palace and the princely hospitality he was to enjoy there during his sojourn.

That night, whilst Genoa celebrated with revelry and illuminations the great occasion, a banquet was spread by the Duke of Melfi, followed by an eastern masque and this again by dancing.

At table Prospero was placed with Monna Gianna on his right and a lady of the house of Giustiniano on his other hand. Both found him poor company, a matter which exercised Leonora di Giustiniano not at all, but left Giovanna Maria Monaldi deeply troubled.

"Gianettino told me that the Emperor had special words of commendation for you at his landing," she said.

"Gianettino would be pleased," said he.

"Were not you?"

"I? Oh, to be sure I was."

"You scarcely betray it. And why sneer at Gianettino?"

"From my consciousness of how they love me, your adopted cousins."

"But will you let them? Will you still not bury the past?"

"It requires so deep a grave," he said.

"Yet they, themselves, have dug it for you. Why will you not set the stone in place?"

"Perhaps I find it a little heavy for my strength."

"I will help you, Prospero," she promised him, and turned back to speak again of the favour the Emperor had shown him. "I was so proud to know it. Have you no pride in it, yourself, Prospero?"

"Pride? Why yes."

"Then why so glum, my dear?"

He roused himself to play his hateful part. He looked at her, and smiled. "Can I be gay when in less than a week I shall have sailed away from you?"

This summoned a tender gravity to her glance. "Is that the cause?"

"Is it not cause enough?"

"If you say it is." She spoke on a sigh, expressing a hope rather than a conviction.

Later she danced with him, and her misgivings were renewed by the joyless correctness of his steps. His spirit had settled into a gloom from which not even a further and very public display of Imperial favour could deliver him.

Alfonso of Avalos, who of all the imperial following held the chief attention of the Genoese, as much by the brilliance of his person as by his fame as courtier and soldier and the knowledge of his influence with Charles V, sought Prospero out to conduct him to his master's presence.

His Majesty held him long enough in talk to give matter for comment. He spoke again of Procida and desired from Prospero himself closer details than had yet been furnished him.

Of a boundless ambition, this monarch upon whose dominions the sun never set was imbued with a chivalry very different from the theatrical parade of chivalry of King Francis. Valorous himself, he prized above all other qualities valour and daring when allied with skill and judgment, for he was shrewdly aware of their value to himself. It was the perception of just these qualities in Andrea Doria which had awakened the Emperor's desire at all costs to enlist the Genoese seaman in his service. It was the perception of them in

Prospero's feat of arms at Procida, which in itself had so richly served the Imperial ambition, that disposed him now so favourably towards the young Genoese captain.

He questioned him closely on the number, character and equipment of the Neapolitan galleys, and when he learnt the strength to which since his appointment Prospero had brought the squadron, he generously expressed his wonder not only that so much should have been done in so little time, but that his Neapolitan subjects should have been able to provide so richly.

On this Prospero smiled. "They were not overtaxed, sire. Seven of the twelve galleys are my own property, built, equipped and armed at my own charges."

The brows of Majesty were raised. The eyes were a shade less friendly. But d'Avalos, who made the third in this little group, aloof from the assembled company, was quick to interpose. "My friend Prospero follows, like my Lord Duke of Melfi, the custom of the Italian condottiero."

It was a timely reminder to check if not to extinguish Imperial displeasure. "But with the Duke of Melfi we have an agreement, definitely engaging his services and that of his galleys," came the mumbling, stammering speech, rendered more indistinct than usual by His Majesty's haste to express himself. "With yours, sir, we have none. Yours is but an ordinary enlistment."

"Pardon, sire. The engagement exists. His Highness of Orange was careful to make it in Your Majesty's name. I am hired with my galleys to serve you for a term of five years. My hope is to be continued in Your Majesty's service for as long as I have a deck under my feet."

Majesty unbent. "It shall be my hope, too, sir, if your service continues as it has begun."

D'Avalos permitted himself again an interjection. "If Prospero's counsel had been heeded at Amalfi, the issue might have been very different, despite the odds. Even as it was, it might have been different if two captains had not played the coward."

Majesty desired more knowledge of this and was impressed when it had been supplied. "I felicitated myself this morning upon numbering you among my captains. I was not then aware of the extent of my good fortune. I knew that I possessed in Genoa the first sea captain of the age; I was not aware that I possessed also the second."

"They may change places, sire, before all is done," said the smiling Avalos.

Upon that pleasantry His Majesty frowned, his Doria infatuation mildly offended. "That were a foolish because excessive hope. Let us be content with what we possess, recognizing it, so that we may know with what we have to build." Almost abruptly he added: "You have leave to go, Messer Adorno." Then, more gently, as Prospero was bowing himself away, he added: "I am in your debt, sir, and I was in your father's too; for the Duke of Melfi has reminded me that he suffered for his loyalty to me. These things shall not be forgotten. I must study to repay."

Upon that uplifting dismissal Prospero withdrew from an interview the length and intimacy of which procured him now the increased regard of the assembly. But it did not uplift him. It would have left him indifferent but for the Emperor's assertion that it was from Andrea Doria that His Majesty had learnt of Antoniotto Adorno's case. Here was confirmation of a sort of Cardinal Adorno's opinion that Doria had been the victim of circumstances resulting from King Francis' breach of faith, and that the matter of Doria's calculated hostility to the Adorni for his own ambitious ends rested, after all, upon assumptions that may well have been too hasty. Yet again, because it opened the gates to his heart's desire, Prospero was held mistrustfully back from that comforting belief.

His credit, enhanced that night, continued steadily to grow during those days of the Imperial visit. There were solemn intervals in the festivities and revelries provided. In one of these there was an intimate conference to which the Emperor admitted only a half-dozen besides Andrea Doria. Whilst Gianettino was of the number, Filippino was excluded from it. It was concerned with the forthcoming expedition, and in the discussions Prospero was prominent and impressive. He found Doria generously supporting him, free of all petty jealousies such as an old commander might bring to criticize the opinions of a young one who was in danger of shining too brilliantly.

If Prospero aroused other jealousies by his increasing credit it remained unuttered. Not so, however, the contempt that was being stirred in the men of his own house. His cousin Taddeo gave tongue to it one day when he met Prospero in the street. He put himself aggressively in his way.

"You swell daily in consequence, cousin, like the frog in the fable. And the water that swells you is that in which your honour lies drowned."

Prospero covered his anger by a mask of pleasant laughter. "Yet you drink of it, Taddeo. And grow sleek with drinking." And he passed on.

Another day it was another cousin, of a more remote degree, who doffed a hat to him in mock reverence. "We uncover before you nowadays, so high do you stand in the Imperial regard and the Doria favour, however low in that of honourable men. Beware the fate of Icarus, my cousin. You fly too near the sun."

"That is why I cannot discern you. Be thankful," was all the answer Prospero flung at him.

But the sting of such taunts abode to poison him. Fortunately the time was as short as it was crowded. Matters concerned with the forthcoming expedition busied him perhaps more than they need have done. They served as pretexts to avoid as many as possible of the festive events demanded by the Emperor's presence, where Prospero was in danger on the one hand of slights and insults from those of the Adorno faction, and under the necessity, on the other, to play his loathsome part with Gianna. Unwittingly he found himself increased in the Imperial regard by these very absences. The Emperor, informed of their ostensible occasion, deepened Prospero's sense of ignobility by commending his diligence.

"I would I were so served by all," His Majesty told del Vasto.

To which del Vasto, loyal to his friend, made answer: "You are so served, sire, by all who are of Prospero Adorno's worth."

"Unfortunately they are few. Command him from me to make holiday tonight. I desire to see him at the Admiral's revels."

It was the eve of departure, and these revels, by which Doria planned to outshine all that had gone before, were held just after dusk in the illuminated gardens of the Fassuolo. Prospero, Gianna, and the Duchess of Melfi composed a small group which was included in the party of the more illustrious patricians bidden to sup with the Emperor in a sumptuous illuminated bower at the garden's end. The ground here had been paved in wood, and this again was spread with eastern carpets. The bower projected over the water, and under overarching boughs that were entwined with flowers and bore a constellation of delicately coloured lamps was spread a long table capable of seating fifty guests.

On whitest napery and Venetian lacework choice crystal from Murano sparkled alongside the gleaming gold plate, massively carved candle-branches in gold and silver, from the workshops of Florence, and massively carved gold dishes laden with sweetmeats from Spain and fruits brought from afar.

From under the feet of the seated company, miraculously, as it seemed, from the very bowels of the earth, came strains of music, of viol, rebec and flute. A regiment of silken-clad, turbaned, Moorish slaves hovered to serve the most delicate of meats, to pour the choicest Rhenish wines procured out of compliment to the Emperor.

And then, suddenly, the bower began to move. It detached itself from the remainder of the garden, and travelled slowly out over the darkly gleaming water, where gentle breezes tempered the heat of the summer night.

The surprised and delighted guests realized that they were on the deck of a galley so artfully dissembled by ramage that its real nature had not been suspected until then. It set them in high spirits; the wine flowed freely; the laughter increased. The Emperor, enchanted, unbent. He ate voraciously and drank copiously, as was his habit, for which soon he was to begin to pay with the torment of the gout.

Queer tales were to be told thereafter of that water banquet. It was to be related, by some so as to magnify the Duke of Melfi's splendour, and by others so as to deride his ostentation, that the gold plates in a measure as they did service were flung by the slaves into the sea. To this the mockers added that a net surrounded the vessel, so that before morning all that treasure was surreptitiously recovered. You will find an allusion to this in that part of *The Liguriad* in which Prospero relates the splendours of the Imperial visit and entertainment in Genoa. It is not on that account to be accepted as historical. But that the banquet was on a scale of luxury seldom rivalled stands on sure testimony and that the gaiety presiding over it was full-hearted.

Even Prospero was haled out of his gloom by the environment. It came by way of a regretful comment from Gianna of the continued absence of Prospero's mother and of the fact that she had yet to meet her as her future daughter-in-law.

"Her delicate health may explain the one," said Gianna. "But hardly the other. It cannot be so delicate that she should not permit me to visit her as my duty demands. Had you not better tell me the truth of it, Prospero?"

He took up his cup and frowned into the wine it held. "You guess it, of course," he said.

"Of course," she agreed. "Madonna Aurelia does not approve of the alliance. Her hostility to the House of Doria remains unquenched."

"She has suffered deeply," he excused her.

"So had you."

"My fortitude is greater."

"Ah! And you have really forgiven all? There is no rancour left in you?"

For the last time he employed the old evasion. "Should I be here if there were?"

"But are you here?"

He laughed. "Visibly and palpably. Set your hand upon me."

"But there are invisible and impalpable parts that go to make a man. It is of those I ask. Your body sits here beside me. Yes. But your spirit has too often been absent in these days. You move in a cloud, elusive and vague. It makes me unhappy in the very happiness I have laboured so to procure for both of us."

The complaint went through him like a sword. It brought him sharply, suddenly, to a parting of the ways. He must choose his road, and choose it frankly and openly. Either he must accept the arguments for rendering real this sham reconciliation, or else, abandoning loathly, treacherous ways, openly declare himself the remorseless foe of the Dorias.

He set down his cup, and swung round squarely to face her, unheeded by a company engrossed in its own gaiety, his words lost in the general laughter-laden din.

"What would make you happy, my Gianna?"

Her eyes, grave to wistfulness in that pallid oval face, were steadily considering him. "Perhaps the answer to my question. I cannot say until I have it." And she repeated it. "Is there no rancour left in you? Is the past really buried?"

His glance was steady under her searching eyes. His mobile lips smiled a little. "The past is really buried," he assured her truthfully, his choice having just made the assurance true.

He had his reward in an immediate recovery of serenity. It was as if he had sloughed some dreadful chrysalis that had hitherto imprisoned him. He became the unfettered lover once again, devout and ardent, and in his recovery of happiness Gianna recovered her own, which lately had been overcast. He spoke for the first time of the nuptials that would await them when he returned from this expedition against the Moslem. On this subject which hitherto he had seemed fearfully to avoid he dilated now, mingling awe and reverence with his joyous terms in such measure as to move her to an ecstasy.

Seeing them so gay together, the Lord Andrea sent them from the distance a grave smile that was like a benediction, and raising his glass of Rhenish he drank to them.

Later, much later, when the feast was done, the lights were extinguished and the guests had all departed, and Gianna was bidding the Admiral good night, he leaned over her from his great height.

"Your eyes have a happy sparkle, Gianna. You are pleased with me, I hope."

Her voice trembled as she protested it.

He nodded his great head. "I am happy in your happiness. For your Prospero is worthy of you. And that's high praise. I'll bring him safely home to you, and with added laurels if I know him."

Chapter 17

Cherchell

On the morrow the Emperor departed for Bologna, where he was to receive at the Pope's hands the crown of Charlemagne, to which – and not without some bribery – he had won election. Thereafter the affairs of Germany would demand his presence.

On the next day the fleet sailed away for the coast of Barbary, in a splendour of banners and a valedictory roar of guns, composing a pomp better becoming a triumphant homing than a setting forth.

Leaving out of account the ancillary transport vessels, three brigantines and a half-dozen feluccas, the fleet consisted of thirty galleys, all powerful and well-found. Fifteen of these were Doria's contingent, twelve were of the Neapolitan squadron, including the seven of Prospero's own property commanded by him from his capitana, *La Prospera*, and the remaining three were Spaniards under Don Alvaro de Carbajal, a seaman held in high esteem by the Emperor.

Prospero was a man uplifted and transfigured. His change of heart had permitted him to make his peace with his own conscience as well as with Gianna. From Cardinal Adorno he had received absolution, blessing and congratulation, and for one unforgettable moment, with a lover's ecstasy, delivered of all doubts and misgivings, he had held Gianna in his arms and spoken of the marriage to be celebrated immediately on his return.

Because he did not wish in the moment of departure to incur his mother's curse, he had left her with no more suspicion that the sham reconciliation had become sincere than that Madonna Giovanna Maria Monaldi Doria was his Lady of the Garden.

We know that the poet's mind, delivered at last from its shackles, turned freely to song, and that during that crossing to Barbary he resumed work upon *The Liguriad*. He wrote in those days that score of cantos dealing with the Imperial visit to Genoa and reflecting the pomp and majesty of the fleet's departure upon its punitive expedition against the infidel Corsairs so strongly established along the North African littoral, from Tripolitania to the borders of Morocco. If in those verses there was, as we suspect, an anticipatory reflection of victory, this must afterwards have been edited down to a less exultant key.

With that well-found fleet, it was Doria's intention to descend upon Algiers. By striking a blow that should place him in possession of Kheyr-ed-Din Barbarossa's capital, he hoped to paralyse the Corsair's kingdom. He was fortunate in being warned by a French vessel met on the way that he had no hope of surprising Kheyr-ed-Din. The Corsair, it seemed, possessed a wakeful intelligence service. The expedition, making no secret of its purpose, had been too long in setting out. Informed of it, Barbarossa had assembled at Algiers a fleet more than equal in strength to the Emperor's, wherewith to give it a suitable reception.

The news, reaching Doria when he was some two hundred and fifty miles south-west of Sardinia and less than a hundred miles from his destination, gave him pause. He summoned a council of war, and assembled in the tabernacle of his galleasse, the *Grifone*, his six chief captains. The foremost place amongst these belonged to Prospero as Captain-General of Naples. The others were Gianettino and Filippino Doria, a Grimaldi, cousin of the Lord of Monaco, Prospero's old friend Lomellino, and Don Alvaro de Carbajal.

Doria expounded to them that, robbed of the advantage of surprise, his duty to the Emperor scarcely permitted him now to hazard the fleet in the proposed descent upon Algiers.

His nephews would not have thought of taking any view contrary to his own, nor would Lomellino. Grimaldi, even if he had arguments in opposition to put forward, would have put them forward tentatively and submissively, and without a lead Don Alvaro might have been in the same case. But a lead was at once supplied by Prospero.

"If," he said quietly, "the Emperor had not desired his fleet to be hazarded, he would not have commanded the expedition."

And Don Alvaro was quick to support him with a "Por Dios, so it is." He was a portly gentleman of perhaps forty, prematurely bald, swarthy as a Moor, with dark lively eyes to which high-arching brows lent an expression of humorous surprise, and a heavy dewlap behind the black pointed beard that sprouted from his chin. Whilst the two nephews and Lomellino looked reproval upon Prospero's boldness, and Grimaldi non-committally stroked his beard, Don Alvaro frankly smiled.

The Admiral showed no impatience. "There are differences between hazards. Some it would be cowardly to avoid; others rash to accept. In a soldier, I need not tell you, between rashness and cowardice there is little to choose."

"Here I do not perceive rashness in going forward," Prospero insisted.

Instantly Gianettino was bristling. "Does that mean that you perceive cowardice? If so, be plain."

Prospero sighed. It was really a labour to keep the peace with these aggressive Doria cubs. "I should be plain if I did," he answered quietly.

The Lord Andrea explained. His information was that Barbarossa had sent out messages recalling his Corsair captains: to Cherchell for their old friend Dragut-Reis; to Zerbi for that other scourge of Christendom, Sinan-Reis, the Jew of Smyrna, who was suspected of magic because he could take a declination with a crossbow; and to Aydin, who was called Cachadiablo by the Spaniards.

"These," said Prospero, "are so many reasons for pressing on before such reinforcements reach him."

But Doria shook his head. "My information is that he is too strong already."

Don Alvaro entered the argument. "I had not gathered that his fleet is in greater strength than ours."

"But behind his fleet there are the guns of his fortresses."

"In weight of metal," answered Prospero, "the preponderance of our artillery is beyond dispute." Changing his tone, he set himself to plead. "The credit of Christian valour is here at stake. To avoid the encounter is to impair it. So far unchecked, these Corsairs are masters of our sea."

"Masters!" sneered Filippino.

"Masters," Prospero insisted. "The Moors of Andalusia appeal for succour to this Barbarossa, and no Castilian ship has yet ventured to check the responses that he makes. He has carried off already some seventy thousand Spanish subjects. In the bagnio at Algiers we know that more than seven thousand Christian slaves lie at the mercy of the Infidel. To desist now from our enterprise is to earn Barbarossa's scorn and increase his audacity."

"That is well said," Don Alvaro supported him. "Por Dios! That is well said. My Lord Admiral, there can be no retreat."

"Retreat is not in my mind," was the gruff reply. "But Algiers can wait until we have dealt with the reinforcements upon which Barbarossa counts. Expected at Algiers, we descend instead upon Cherchell and destroy Dragut. What do you say to that, sirs?"

He asked the question of them all, but his eyes looked only at Prospero, and Prospero answered him.

"As a preliminary I'll not oppose it."

"Lord God! You're gracious," sneered Filippino.

"Then I am gracious, too," said Don Alvaro with his disarming smile. "For I am of Don Prospero's mind in this. We need to strike boldly, so as to show these Infidel dogs for once who is the master."

"That is just why I will take no risk of failure," the Admiral answered. "The issue is too grave to admit of risks being lightly accepted." He was quietly impressive. "It is agreed, then, that we strike at Cherchell."

And so, leaving Algiers to the south of them, it was for Cherchell that they now steered a course.

To find Dragut there, however, they came too late. That ruthless and most formidable of the fighting seamen in the following of Kheyr-ed-Din had already sailed for Algiers. Hugging the coast as he did, he had been missed by the Imperialists, whose course had lain farther out to sea.

Don Alvaro lost his good humour in rage, and Prospero was disposed to be bitter.

"Over-prudence has defeated us," he boldly told the Admiral. "What might well have been done had we kept to our intentions can certainly be done no longer now that Dragut has joined forces with Barbarossa."

"It is possible to be too prudent," complained Don Alvaro, who, like Prospero, had gone aboard the *Grifone* to hold council with the Admiral. "See the result. We turn tail and go home at the mere barking of these Moslem dogs. I like to laugh. But – vive Dios! – I don't like to be laughed at. The Emperor will not thank you, my Lord Duke."

Andrea Doria stroked his great beard, ponderously imperturbable under this outspoken reproach. With his nephews and the other two captains he stood on the poop of the galleasse, considering the rugged coast a mile away, and in the harbour all the evidences of panic which had been spreading there since the summer dawn had revealed the presence of the Frankish fleet. Silently he surveyed the sprawling town of square white buildings set amidst dark green groves of date-palms and oranges and the grey green of olive trees, the grey mass of the citadel, the mueddin's lance-like tower above the white dome of the mosque, the ruins of the Roman amphitheatre to the east, and the hazy mountainous background of the chains of Djebel Souma and Boni Manasser.

At long last he spoke. "It will not be quite so, Don Alvaro. Yonder is Cherchell, a rich place, the very storehouse and victualling port of these Corsairs. It will be no idle thing to destroy this nest of piracy, nor will it go to swell the Moslem insolence."

Gianettino's beady eyes, wandering from Don Alvaro to Prospero, surprised the smile on the latter's countenance. "You laugh!" he cried. "Why do you laugh?"

Prospero's smile broadened. "We go out to slay a lion, and we return to boast that we have killed a mouse."

That was enough in itself. But Don Alvaro, between whom and Prospero a bond of sympathy and alliance was tightening, made it worse by smacking his sturdy thigh in approval.

Gianettino frankly damned them for a couple of hot-headed fools, who like all fools were quick to condemn what was beyond their understanding.

Prospero stiffened. In his heart, even in the worst hours of his rancour, there had been a lingering regard for the Lord Andrea. He had admired his obvious courage and imperturbable force and had recognized his exceptional gifts. Towards his nephews, however, he had stood in a natural antagonism which their upstart arrogance had ever nourished.

"That is not civil," he said, in cold reproof.

"It is not intended to be civil. You give yourself too much importance, Messer Prospero. You presume upon my uncle's favour."

Prospero turned to the Admiral. "Since we came out to fight the Infidel, and not one another, I'll return to my flagship, and there await your lordship's orders."

But the Admiral had not remained indifferent to the taunt of the lion and the mouse, and perhaps because of that had not restrained Gianettino's truculence. The fundamental truth of it had stung him as only truth can sting. There was a rasp in his deep voice.

"You will await them here, sir. I will ask you to remember, and you, Don Alvaro, that the responsibility for this expedition, like the command of it, is mine."

"Time for plain speaking, indeed," Filippino approved him.

Don Alvaro bowed. His humorous eyes twinkled. "Your pardon, Admiral. I had thought that you invited opinions."

"Opinions certainly. But not on what is to do. On the manner of doing it. If you have anything to urge on that, I'll be glad to hear you."

Sternly interrogative, he looked from one to the other of them.

Don Alvaro shook his head. "I must leave it to your lordship to determine tactics."

"The responsibility, as you've reminded us, is yours," said Prospero.

Doria smiled in his beard. "Judgment is always easier than performance. Let us get to work."

Rapidly now, with a mastery of detail that was admirable, he sketched his plan of attack, and having sketched it, curtly dismissed Don Alvaro and Prospero to their vessels, each to bear his part in it, without paying either of them the compliment of seeking his opinion.

The same sloop conveyed the two captains aboard their respective galleys. If the Lord Andrea had dismissed them in resentment, their departure had not been without resentment too. Don Alvaro de Carbajal made bold to express it. To Prospero he condemned Andrea Doria's excessive care of his reputation and foretold the ruin of it in the eyes of an Emperor who would not thank him for avoiding the business on which he had been sent.

"That may follow when we have dealt with Cherchell," was Prospero's opinion.

"If it does, disaster will be certain."

"It will be very probable at least," was the extent of Prospero's gloomy agreement. He found an irony in considering that the conduct of Doria which now aggrieved him was the very conduct which would have rejoiced him and in which he would have encouraged him had he still been vindictively set upon his ruin. If success should attend this profitless attack upon Cherchell, there would be no honour in it. If it should miscarry, the disgrace would be utter and irreparable, and the high repute of Andrea Doria would be destroyed as no defeat by Kheyr-ed-Din before Algiers could have destroyed it.

Under the ardent African sun, in the growing heat of that late August day, the Imperial fleet stood in towards the bay. The open, rambling town was protected by no ramparts, and the abruptness of the shore permitted the shallow draught galleys to come right in. No Moslem fleet disputed their entrance. What ships were in the bay when the Imperial fleet was first sighted had been scuttled, either so as to save them from capture or in the hope of hindering the Frankish vessels. Aboard the galleys they could hear on the still air the rolling of rallying drums and the call of trumpets ashore, and they could see the evidence of panic in the stream of humanity flowing in haste along the road to the citadel, some driving goats, some leading donkeys, mules, or even camels. For lack of city walls behind which they might have hoped for shelter, most of the population of Cherchell was seeking refuge in the fortress.

Coming within range, Doria gave the order to open fire, and the rolling salvoes of his artillery re-echoed in thunder from the hills. Then, when the citadel replied, he abandoned the bombardment and directed the fleet eastwards to a point where they were sheltered from the Turkish guns. At this point he landed twelve hundred men, of whom five hundred were Genoese, four hundred Spaniards and three hundred Neapolitans of Prospero's contingent. He sent them ashore in two divisions, one of which included Genoese and Spaniards under Gianettino, and the other consisting of the Neapolitans and commanded by Prospero.

This landing took Alicot Caramanli, the Turkish officer in command of Cherchell, by surprise. He had expected nothing of the kind until and unless the Frankish guns could reduce the citadel, where he had shut himself up with the main body of his troops and such of the inhabitants who, temporarily abandoning their homes and possessions, had sought shelter with him. Consequently there had been no proper preparation to receive an attack ashore. Nevertheless, one of his officers, who with a force of some four hundred janissaries was in charge of the lesser fort attached to the bagnio, conceiving that if he were pinned in his stronghold the city would lie at the mercy of the enemy, intrepidly made a sally, hoping to throw the Franks into confusion before they could form their ranks to receive the charge. In this, however, he was frustrated. Gianettino with his Genoese, who had been the first ashore, received the impact, and held the janissaries until the remainder of the Christian host could order itself to share the battle. Prospero, acting independently with his Neapolitans, fell on the Turkish flank, and shattered it by arquebusades. The janissaries, reduced to half their original number and their leader slain, broke before these overwhelming odds and retreated in disorder to the fort whence they had emerged.

Gianettino, raging to avenge the loss under the Turkish scimitar and by Turkish arrows of a hundred of his Genoese, launched the Spanish contingent in pursuit under an officer named Sarmiento. Himself he stayed to provide for the removal of the wounded aboard such of the galleys as still remained at the long mole.

The main body of the fleet was moving out with flashing oars across the bay, to resume in earnest the bombardment of the citadel.

Thus by combined action of land and sea forces Doria counted upon bringing the place to a speedy capitulation, and soon a duel was engaged whose continuous rolling thunders seemed to shake the very air. But because Turkish guns and gunners, on the one hand, were inadequate, and because, on the other, the citadel was stoutly built, little damage was suffered by either side, and but for the action of the landing-party a condition of stalemate might well have followed.

Whilst Sarmiento's Spaniards hunted the surviving janissaries through the streets, Gianettino and Prospero brought their columns to the edge of the ditch that defended the lesser fort. From beyond its high wall rose a steadily repeated, wailing cry.

"In Christ's name deliver us!"

Gianettino listened. "What litany is that?" he asked.

One of his officers answered him. "It will be the Christian slaves, the captives of their cursed raids."

But Gianettino was by nature mistrustful. "And if it were an Infidel trap? They have the cunning of Satan, himself."

The wailing went on. It cut to the heart of the young Genoese officer. "The place is easily carried. The ditch is dry."

"Let it wait." Gianettino was peremptory. "Is it likely that slaves would be left unguarded? And if guards were present should we have this clamour? I'll walk into no Turkish gin."

But now Prospero, whose column had followed, was at Gianettino's elbow. "What is this?" He, too, stood listening to that reiterated wailing.

Gianettino told him what it purported to be and what in his opinion it might prove.

Prospero was contemptuous. "Their guards abandoned them so as to attack us. That was the force we routed. I am going in."

"And the citadel, then?"

"Will wait until these Christian brothers are delivered. They'll serve to swell our forces for the assault."

"The Admiral's orders were plain," Gianettino harshly reminded him.

"He would modify them if he were here."

In this Gianettino scented a reflection upon himself. "One day," he prophesied, "your self-sufficiency will lead you to an evil end. And this may be that day."

"Or it may not. But what is written is written, as the enemy would say."

"You have my good wishes," said Gianettino with a bow that was a valediction. Then ordering his trumpets to sound the advance, he departed with his force.

Prospero marched his men through the ditch at the foot of the rampart and round to the locked gates. A dozen powder-flasks were emptied under it, fused and fired. What remained of the timbers were shattered by a ram improvised from a bundle of pikes and propelled by a half-dozen of his strongest men.

There was no trap. It was exactly as Prospero expected. They came into a courtyard empty of troops. From behind a bolted and padlocked door, the chorus crying for deliverance continued to summon them. To break down that door was an easy matter, and out into the blazing sunlight of the courtyard, in the wake of an intolerable stench, poured a human torrent whose almost naked members laughed and wept as they flung their arms about the necks of their deliverers. All were men, unkempt of hair and beard, verminous and unutterably filthy. Many of them were fettered, some were hideously mutilated, and there was scarcely a back that did not show the marks of the rods that had lacerated the tanned flesh.

Prospero watched their piteous antics for a while in compassion mingled with anger against those who had reduced these Christian men, many of them gently bred, to a degradation such as no dumb beasts could ever know. In all nearly nine hundred of them, of all ages, classes and nationalities, had been herded into that bagnio and locked in on the first approach of the Imperial fleet, in darkness and in a closeness that was in itself a torment.

For some time he left the ragged wretches to dance and scream and rattle their chains in a glee that was animal and horrible. They pranced and leapt about their deliverers, rejoicing as dogs rejoice in being loosed from confinement. Presently, however, he set about bringing some order into that crazy multitude. With implements brought from sheds and workshops into which his men had broken, manacles and leg-irons were knocked off the more heavily fettered. Then he formed them into ranks, and with half his troop for vanguard and the other half to cover his rear, he marched them out of that place of horror and down to the mole and the moorings where a half-dozen galleys waited.

By far the greater number was glad enough to go. But with others there was trouble. Many among the more lusty and vigorous clamoured to make vengeance upon their captors and tormentors the first object of their newly acquired liberty. At the outset Prospero sought to contain them by force. But relaxing this after a while and yielding to a furious, ungrateful insistence that to thwart them was to replace one form of slavery by another, he suffered perhaps a hundred of them to break away with intent to join the troops that had marched to the assault upon the citadel. They would provide themselves, they said, with weapons from the houses that lay in their way. Some who had retained the shackles of which their limbs had been eased wielded these in a manner which showed how terribly they might be used as flails.

So Prospero let them go, pitying the Turks upon whom they might happen and reflecting that the fierce spirit governing them should render them valuable auxiliaries to Gianettino.

The mischief that followed resulted from the fact that Gianettino's troops, finding themselves like conquerors in possession of a city abandoned to them by the enemy, bethought them of the conqueror's right of pillage, and so as to fall upon the unguarded wealth at their mercy were deflected from their real purpose. Gianettino saw no reason to restrain them. He argued that the longer the Admiral's guns were left to batter the citadel, the more demoralized would be the defenders and the readier to capitulate to a land force at their gates. A captain of keener vision or greater experience would have foreseen the consequences of that premature gathering of fruits of victory even without the contribution to it supplied by the delivered slaves in the course of their search for arms. For they changed the character of the search when they came upon the plundering soldiery, and were at once infected by the same predatoriness. From the more romantic thoughts of righteous justice, their minds were turned to the practical consideration that it was better compensation for their sufferings to rob the Infidel dogs of their wealth rather than of their lives. Their knowledge of the city gained in years of suffering told them exactly where the greatest riches were to be found. They became the guides of the soldiery in this looting, and soon Gianettino's regiment had melted into marauding groups that were ranging the city and even straying beyond it into the outskirts, where some of the more opulent had their dwellings. If there was no wine in these Moslem households, there was gold and jewels, silks and women to intoxicate a brutal soldiery to whom the yashmak was but a provocation.

Gianettino, in the market-place, where the pillage had started among the deserted booths, waited with some fifty or sixty followers who were content to remain with him because already laden with all the booty they could carry and glad to pause and glut themselves on the fruits and sickly Turkish sweetmeats of which the souk yielded abundance.

Whilst this was happening Prospero had embarked some eight hundred of his rescued Christians, distributing them among the six galleys at the mole. Then, in a longboat from one of these vessels, he had gone off to the *Grifone*, to report to the Admiral

Don Alvaro de Carbajal was on board the Lord Andrea's flagship, and it was plain to Prospero when he emerged upon the poop that he came to interrupt an altercation.

With a shattered mizzen, which in its fall had slain or disabled a score of men, the *Grifone* had moved into the rear, out of range of the citadel's guns, and when Prospero reached her the slaves from the oars were hacking away the tangled cordage, so as to cast off a mast which had become a crippling encumbrance.

The Admiral, bareheaded, but in a polished cuirass from which the puffed sleeves of a scarlet doublet protruded stood at the rail with Don Alvaro beside him. He frowned at the sight of Prospero.

"What brings you here, sir? You were ordered ashore." With an unusual testiness he added: "Does every one of you question my authority? Before all's done I'll have each of you know clearly who is in command of this expedition."

Displays of temper were so rare with him that Prospero at once assumed that Don Alvaro had been employing arts of exasperation, and this perhaps at a time when the Admiral's temper had been soured by a wrecked mizzen. He smiled upon that burst of wrath.

"I am here to report, my lord. I have had the good fortune to deliver close upon a thousand Christian slaves whom I found imprisoned in the fort." He added how he had disposed of them until the Admiral should make known his wishes.

It was enough to make the Admiral ashamed of the ill-humoured assumptions upon which he had greeted a bearer of such excellent tidings. He handsomely commended the achievement and turned in triumph upon Carbajal.

"You've heard, Don Alvaro. A thousand of our Christian brethren redeemed from the heathen thrall. Will you still say that I waste my powder here?"

The roar of a cannonade smothered Don Alvaro's answer. Billows of white smoke screened all view of the galleys ahead, the shore and the citadel beyond. Again the cannons volleyed from the galleys. But from the citadel now there was no response. Noting it, the Admiral wondered was the Turkish ammunition exhausted, or was this a ruse to make them suppose it, and so lure them to closer quarters?

He ordered Prospero to remain a while, until he should perceive how to proceed. His trumpets blared an order to cease fire. Slowly, rolling languidly on the air of that stifling day, the smoke dispersed until the galleys ahead, seen at first like an array of ghost ships, came clearly into view again. One of them, in a sinking condition, had pulled alongside of a sister vessel and was trans-shipping the survivors of her crew. A sudden breeze from the east carried away the lingering wisps of the enshrouding smoke, and the air became as pellucid as it had been before the bombardment troubled it. The citadel, massive, grim and silent, scarcely showed a scar. From the eastern side of the bay, where the mole was situated, a sloop came through the water at frantic speed. As she came close to the *Grifone* a man leapt from her to the poised horizontal oars, and across these came clambering to the deck. A Spanish sergeant, wild of manner, he clamoured for the Lord Admiral, and being brought before him, panted a dreadful tale.

Alicot Caramanli was neither fool nor coward. Calmly vigilant from the citadel he had observed what was happening in the city, and in the disbanded state of the pillaging soldiery he had seen his opportunity. Between janissaries and citizens whom he had armed he commanded a force of some five hundred men. With this he had marched out to round up the pillagers, and the sergeant told a tale of slaughter that turned the Admiral pale. It was not yet all told when from the western end of the bay, below the citadel and from the huddle of small houses about its base, came a battling, yelling swarm of men. Those on the poop of the *Grifone* could discern the peaked morions of the Imperialists, and the gleaming spiked headpieces issuing from the turbans of the Moslems. The Imperialists, in compact order, were retreating before the fury of their assailants, and were already in danger of being driven into the sea.

Then, whilst they looked with wits half-numbed upon what seemed a prelude to complete disaster, a galley, quitting the line, sped forward at the utmost of her oars. It was Lomellino's *Liguria* gallantly heedless of a possible fire from the citadel, hastening to offer the retreating Genoese a plank of salvation. There was deep water right up to the rocks that fringed the sea, and thither Lomellino brought his galley, her ratlines and cross-trees aswarm with crossbowmen.

As Gianettino's Genoese, in good formation, reached that fringe of rocks, Lomellino's arbalests poured a hail of bolts into the pursuing turbaned horde and momentarily threw it into confusion, checking its advance. In that respite the Genoese and Spaniards crowded aboard, using the massed oars as their gangway. They amounted to between three and four hundred men whom Gianettino had succeeded in rallying to the nucleus that had remained with him in the souk.

The galley stood off again under a shower of Turkish arrows from the yelling, baffled enemy, and when Lomellino would have manoeuvred to empty his guns into that howling Moslem mass at the water's edge, Gianettino, panting and sweating in his armour, bleeding from several cuts, and in a livid fury, ordered him with imprecations to lose no time in getting alongside the flagship.

He came in a shuddering blend of rage and panic to the presence of his uncle, in the impassivity of whose aspect he was met by something forbidding.

With Prospero and Don Alvaro for witnesses, Gianettino wasted few words on the disaster that had overtaken him. But the Admiral had something to say on that score.

"Prospero, who took the risk of storming the bagnio and delivering a thousand Christian prisoners, brings off his troops without the loss of a man. You undertake nothing, and come back with half your force. That will make a nice tale. Where are these missing men of yours? Have they been massacred?"

"How should I know?" Gianettino's normally deep voice was almost shrill with fury. "The mutinous, thieving dogs went raiding."

"Had you no power to prevent them?"

"Can I restrain a torrent with my two hands?"

"With your two hands, no," Don Alvaro joined in. "But with your authority. Had you none?"

Here Prospero intervened. "Whilst we stand talking their slaughter may be accomplished. By your leave, my lord, I'll make an attempt to bring off the survivors. My Neapolitans are ashore by the galleys at the mole. They are fresh, and they…"

"There is no time," Gianettino interrupted him, raging. "We are all but in a trap. If we linger we shall jeopardize the fleet. A prisoner whom I took mocked us insolently with the threat of approaching doom for all of us. Barbarossa with Dragut, Sinan-Reis and Cachadiablo are on our heels. They had news of our passing westward, and the whole Corsair fleet is moving down the coast from Algiers. Word came at dawn to Caramanli to hold the citadel as relief would shortly reach him."

"The whole Corsair fleet?" Andrea Doria questioned. There was no expression on the boldly carved face.

"Anything from fifty to a hundred galleys," said Gianettino.

Don Alvaro looked at them, and his smile was sour. "Now you see the fruit of your policy. The bold, swift descent upon Algiers might have smashed Kheyr-ed-Din before this concentration could take place."

"Or it might not," the Admiral coldly answered him. "And in that case, we should ourselves have been smashed." He turned his shoulder upon the Spaniard, and so faced the east. Prospero, who now confronted him, saw his eyes suddenly quicken and dilate, whilst his big bony hand went to his brows to shade them.

"Lord God!" he cried. "They come."

The others wheeled, to see what had startled him into that exclamation.

To eastward at about the level of the brown jutting promontory that shelters Tipasa, a long thin line as of foam showed against the blue of sea and sky. Even as they stood at gaze the line took definition. It broke into white points, suggestive of a flock of low-flying birds, that stretched at right angles to the coast across the turquoise waters. Perhaps a half-dozen miles away, but still hull down upon the horizon, the Corsair sails, well served by the freshening breeze, increased perceptibly in size even in the few moments of stupefaction in which the four men watched them.

Prospero was the first to stir. "The more reason to make haste in what's to do. Give me leave, my lord." He was turning away, without waiting for an answer.

"It is too late already," said Doria deliberately. "Return to your capitana, and get your galleys under way."

Prospero stiffened. "And make no attempt to bring off the men ashore?"

"Leave them to perish?" cried Don Alvaro, aghast.

Stern and cold, Doria looked from one to the other of them. "I have to think of the fleet. They must take the consequence of their own rashness. I will give the signal of departure. They will hear it, and they must make their way to the sea as best they can."

From the poop-rail he called an order to the master-gunner on the gang-deck.

"But if they cannot come?" Prospero demanded. "If they are hemmed in?" Under the shadow of his black, crested morion his face was stern.

"They must take their chance."

"That is inhuman, my lord."

"Vive Dios!" Don Alvaro supported him. "No less."

"Inhuman?" Doria's big voice swelled. He threw up his great head so that the long beard jutted forward from his armoured breast. "What have I to do with humaneness? My business is generalship." He was increasingly peremptory. "To your ship, sir!"

As he spoke, the departure signal, three shots in regular, rapid succession thundered forth. Across the water came faintly in answer the jeering of the Moslem mob of soldiers and citizens, drawn up on the rising ground above the beach, where the guns of the galleys could not reach them.

The Admiral bent his frowning gaze compellingly upon Prospero. "To your ship, sir!" he repeated.

But Prospero stood resolute. "You will suffer me, my lord, to beat up the city for these men."

"You do not even know that they are alive," bawled Gianettino.

"I do not know that they are dead. That knowledge alone would prevent my going." He stepped to the gunwale.

"You have your orders," the Admiral sharply reminded him. "You will return to your capitana and get your galleys under way."

"I should be for ever shamed if I obeyed them, as are you, my lord, for uttering them."

"As I am for uttering them? Ha! The insults of ignorance do not touch me." He mastered his indignation still to reason. "Reflect, sir. I have ten thousand lives aboard these vessels. Shall I jeopardize them to save four hundred? Shall I imperil the Emperor's fleet by staying for men who may be dead already? Is that your notion of captainship? Shall we be caught between the Corsair fleet and the enemy ashore? God send me patience! You have earned some repute as a fighting seaman, Messer Prospero. Almost you make me wonder how you came by it."

Stung now to anger, Prospero answered taunt with taunt. "By not running away from danger, as you beheld at Goialatta."

On that, he turned and sprang down into the waiting sloop.

"Stop him!" roared Doria.

Don Alvaro ran to the side as the boat pulled rapidly away. "No, no, Don Prospero," he called after him. "You are mistaken in what you do." Even the Spaniard, disposed as he was to blame the lack of foresight which had brought them to their present pass, had come to perceive that, being in it, a prudent generalship left the Admiral no choice.

Gianettino stamped and raged. "Insolent, insubordinate dog! I hope this is the end of him. We should have known that the peace could never be kept with that arrogant fool. Let him go to the devil."

The Admiral, with the rattle of windlasses about him, as the anchors were being taken up, lost his resentment in a recollection of his promise to Gianna: "I will bring him safely home to you." He turned in troubled anger to quell the continuing vituperations of his nephew.

"You'd do well to remember that it is your blundering has made this trouble. Had you done your work ashore with the wit of a starfish this could never have happened. Go after him, and bring him off; by main force if need be."

Gianettino's thin lip curled. "Look!" was his answer, and he pointed eastward.

In the little time since first they had been sighted, the Corsair galleys had reduced the distance by a quarter. The big triangular sails were now plain, even to their bellying before the wind, and it needed no counting to compute their number at upwards of three score.

"Dare we delay?" asked Gianettino.

The Admiral combed his beard in furious dismay.

Chapter 18

Dragut's Prisoner

Historians differ oddly in their relations of that expedition to Cherchell. That, however, is the way of historians. Lorenzo Capello's sycophantic "Life of the Prince Andrea Doria" presents the delusive account which was rendered by the Admiral, himself, for his credit's sake. Others, more concerned with truth than with Andrea Doria's reputation, have preferred the bare facts to the interpretation which the Admiral gave them. And the facts are that in his flight from Cherchell – for as a flight it must be regarded – he headed across the seas for the Balearics as fast as sails and oars could bear him, with Barbarossa's fleet on his heels.

But not the whole of Barbarossa's fleet engaged in that pursuit, which, after all, at nightfall, was abandoned. Dragut-Reis, with ten of his galleys, detached himself from the Barbary host and entered the Bay of Cherchell to ascertain what might have happened there.

He found the place in uproar and the harbour empty of shipping save for a single Imperial galley, manned by Turkish slaves, but with none to defend her. She was the only remaining one of the three that had been moored to the mole when Prospero, chivalrously insubordinate, had gone ashore. She was one of his own vessels, and he kept her to await the two hundred followers he took ashore with him and the men he hoped to rescue. The other two, bearing aboard them the eight hundred rescued Christian slaves, he had allowed to go with the departing Imperial fleet.

Of this unguarded vessel Dragut took possession. Then he landed, and with an army of Corsairs at his heels he swept up into the city. The uproar of combat guided him eastwards, towards the old Roman amphitheatre. In this he found a Frankish force entrenched and beset by Alicot's mixed horde of Turks and Arabs. It was Prospero's band, increased by about a hundred of the missing Spaniards whom they had rescued piecemeal.

Dragut's fame, which had earned him the proud title of The Drawn Sword of Islam, made it easy for him to overbear the older and ruder Alicot. He stayed the service of the guns which had been dragged by oxen from the citadel so as to pound this little remnant of Cherchell's invaders, and instead sent into the amphitheatre a trumpeter with a flag of truce and an invitation to the Roumi to surrender.

Prospero left decision to his followers. They had seen the guns brought, and many of them were already making as best they could their peace with God, conceiving the moment arrived in which they would have to appear before Him. Eagerly they snatched at this offer of life; for although the sufferings of slavery would darken it, yet the hope of ultimate deliverance would ever be fortifyingly present.

So they cast away their weapons and in stern, silent resignation, came forth as they were bidden. The Moslems noisily surrounded them to herd them away to the pens they would tenant until the destination of each came to be determined in the souk-el-abeed.

Last of all came Prospero, in a bitterness of heart compounded of distress for the followers whom his action had doomed to this hideous fate and of anger with Doria for having abandoned him and them. He had acted upon the persuasion that once he were engaged ashore, the Lord Andrea, as a Christian knight, would account himself committed to postpone departure and compelled to remain at hand so as to bring him off again. In this he chose, unreasonably it must be admitted, to perceive only the ruthless egotism which was responsible for the old feud between his house and the House of

Doria. He had lately dwelt, he thought, in a fool's paradise, believing that so far as he was concerned the feud was dead. It had never, he found, been more alive than at this moment.

His brow dark with these thoughts, which weighed upon him even more heavily than those of the captivity into which he was going, he emerged alone from the ruins of the amphitheatre, and stood confronting the mob that yelled insults and brandished weapons in his face. Then he became aware of a princely figure in a caftan of green sarcenet clasped about his loins by a long tongued belt from which hung a scimitar hilted in ivory and gold. A turban of green silk was wreathed about a spiked helmet that shone like polished silver. Dragut-Reis, tall, vigorous and sardonic with his black forked beard, aquiline nose and piercing eyes was steadily regarding him. The vivid red lips parted, and strong white teeth flashed in a sudden smile. The princely figure advanced, cuffing aside those who stood in his way, with a sharply barked "Balak!" He came before Prospero with a deep salaam, his palm to his brow. Then he laughed.

"The fortune of war once again, Ser Prospero." He used the Lingua Franca, that queer compound of tongues more or less comprehensible to all dwellers on the Mediterranean littoral.

"And yet another change of that same fortune, Messer Dragut. Since I must be a prisoner I give thanks that I am yours."

He was unbuckling his sword-belt to make surrender of his weapons. But Dragut checked him. From his intercourse with the Franks the Corsair was acquainted with their chivalrous gestures. He loved upon occasion to adopt and display them. It flattered his vanity thus to demonstrate himself superior to the uncouth pirates in whose ranks he stood.

"Nay, nay," he cried, with a hand outflung to wave denial. "Retain your sword, Don Prospero. Between gentlemen a word is enough."

Prospero bowed. "You are gracious, Señor Dragut."

"I give as I am given. Always. From you I had courteous treatment when I was your prisoner, and, by the One, you shall have the same from me now that you fall so unexpectedly into my hands. For

I had never thought to find you in the following of that old pirate scoundrel Andrea."

"Again, the fortune of war. All things are in the chances of a soldier's life."

"All things are in the will of Allah," Dragut corrected him. "It is written that the three thousand ducats of my ransom are now to be restored. Until then count yourself my guest, Don Prospero."

Prospero had no cause to complain that the hospitality he enjoyed at Dragut's hands, first in Cherchell and later in Algiers, was stinted. But not on that account did he desire it to be protracted beyond the time necessary for a messenger to reach Genoa and return.

It was to Andrea Doria that the messenger was dispatched, for upon calm reflection, the way actually pointed by Dragut, Prospero came to take the view that once again his judgment had done the Admiral injustice.

It was days later, when, aboard Dragut's galley, he was being taken to Algiers, that the Anatolian gave him the news that Doria had succeeded in eluding Barbarossa and getting safely away with his fleet.

"I should esteem him better if he had not," said Prospero.

"So? But would the Emperor, his master? And would those who sailed with him? The praise to Allah, I am, myself, no coward. But I do not engage where I am likely to be destroyed. That is not valour. It is bad generalship. Messer Andrea goes home without credit. But the alternative, as he well knew, was not to go home at all."

Andrea Doria, meanwhile, reaching Majorca the poorer by two richly laden transports, which had lagged behind and had been caught by Barbarossa, besides the loss of some seven hundred men to set against the eight hundred delivered slaves he brought back, took the resolve that it was impossible for him to return home with such diminished credit. Something he must first do to enable him to tell a better tale than that. So on the morrow of reaching Majorca he went about again, and sailing at a venture steered a course for the Gulf of Algiers, which he supposed would at present be indifferently defended. There he fell in with four Algerian galleys on their way to

Egypt. One he immediately captured. The other three were run ashore by their commanders, in such haste as left no time to unchain the Christian rowers. They were unchained by Doria and went to swell the number of Christians delivered by Prospero from captivity.

This the Admiral accounted was enough. The captured cornship and twelve hundred rescued slaves were evidence enough of his might upon the seas. Holding his head high, he allowed his homecoming to assume the character of a triumph, and made a report in terms which led the Emperor to give little thought to the loss of a few soldiers in the course of an expedition which had yielded at least some fruit.

Prospero Adorno was assumed to have lost his life in the affair. Don Alvaro de Carbajal wrote of his end as nobly heroic, whilst Andrea Doria reported him to have lost his life in an action of great but futile and foredoomed gallantry. The Emperor, remembering him, and reminded by del Vasto, who mourned a friend, that Prospero's death represented a real loss for His Majesty, paid him the tribute of a sigh.

As for the other matter of Don Alvaro's letters: the insistence that the affair of Cherchell would merely increase the insolence of Corsairs who might account their naval supremacy established by it, was assigned by His Majesty to the jealousy of one who aspired, himself, to command the Imperial fleet.

But if the Admiral contrived to come back to Genoa with a high head, he brought at the same time a heavy heart. On the score of his withdrawal of the fleet from Cherchell, he had rightly no misgivings. There was nothing with which he could reproach himself in a prudence which had saved it from certain doom. But if as a naval commander his conscience was at peace, as a man it was deeply troubled. All things considered, and in particular his promise to Gianna, he should at need have employed all his force to restrain Prospero from an undertaking in which, no doubt, he had lost his life.

As a result, this man of granite, who lowered his glance to none, almost dreaded to come face to face with his adopted niece.

With Monna Peretta she was, as he might have expected, foremost in the great crowd of noble and simple that came with banners, flowers and trumpets to hail the victor returning from his evaded defeat.

His first glance discovered an astounding change in her. She was pale and pinched of face. The gentleness of her brown eyes was become a lack-lustre dullness. The calm deportment that argued strength of soul had been subtly changed into a listlessness. Where hitherto her placid air had suggested a perfect control of the emotions, now it seemed to announce an utter lack of them.

She submitted herself indifferently to his paternal kiss. Most oddly, she asked no questions, and thus made his task the harder. He discharged it so soon as delivered from the acclaiming crowds he was alone with her and his lady in Monna Peretta's bower in the Fassuolo Palace.

"I have grave news for you, my dear," he said, so lugubriously that it should have told her all.

Yet there was no response; no such quickening alarm as he had dreaded. She sat strangely, unnaturally impassive, her dark eyes raised as if in mere courtesy to meet his heavy glance. Monna Peretta, sitting beside her on the Persian divan, her bird-like countenance overcast, was holding one of Gianna's hands as if in sympathetic support.

Mystified, the Admiral asked for no explanation. Instead, he told his story; told it in terms which stressed only the heroism of the action in which, as he feared, Prospero must have met his end.

He was prepared for an explosion of grief. He was prepared even for recriminations, for having set the necessity of extricating his fleet above the duty of rescuing Prospero. He was not, however, prepared for what came.

There was no perceptible change in the eyes that continued dully to regard him, no awakening from listlessness in her tone.

"I give thanks to God for him that his end should have been so worthy."

Chapter 19

Monna Aurelia's Indiscretion

The explanation of the mystery, when eventually the Admiral received it from his lady, left him aghast and appalled.

Scarcely had the expedition sailed than there had been an explosion of the irritation created by the alliance into which Prospero's projected marriage seemed to be thrusting the Adorni with the Dorias and their supporters. With those Genoese nobles who were hostile to Doria preponderance in the State and who had been ready to support the Adorni in combating it, the house of Adorno was brought into contempt by the defection of its present head. Of this contempt there was such free and general expression that it began to lead to open quarrels. These culminated when Taddeo Adorno, publicly insulted by Fabio Spinoli, killed him in a duel, and was, himself, set upon and left for dead by Spinoli agents on the following night.

That took his father in a fine rage to Madonna Aurelia.

"The treachery, madam, of your worthless son begins to bear its evil fruits, and others are called upon to eat them. My boy is like to die of wounds taken in this ignoble cause. But I vow to St Lawrence that Messer Prospero shall pay for it. We'll drain the dirty blood from his veins so soon as we can reach him."

That blenched her cheek. "Do you threaten his life?"

"What else? Shall I leave the butchery of my son unpaid?"

"Take payment for it on those that shed his blood. Vent your rage on the Spinoli."

"We'll look to that, too. Be sure. But at the same time we'll stem this evil at its source. We'll cleanse us of the shame Ser Prospero has brought on us, so that we'll not again be mocked with it." And in his fury he added the announcement: "Annibale is to go after Prospero at once."

"Oh, you are mad! You and your son."

He derided her agitation. "That same madness you shall taste presently. You'll understand it once we've slit the gullet of this whelp of yours."

They faced each other in hatred; he inflamed with rage and grief at the peril of his child; she livid with panic at the threat to hers.

"My God!" she panted. "You don't know what you do, you bloodthirsty fool."

"You shall have word when it is done," he fiercely promised for only answer, and on that made shift to go.

But in terror she clutched his arm and hung her weight upon it.

"You move in blindness," she protested wildly. "It is not as you suppose, Rainaldo. Persist in this, and you'll rue it to the day of your own death. Don't you see, you purblind madman, that Prospero could do no other?"

He glowered upon her. "You're a worthy mother to him, by the living God! He could do no other, you say. Ha!" He sought to shake her off. "Let me go, woman."

But she clung, shuddering. In the extremity of her panic, she flung caution to the winds. All that mattered was to save her son from death at the hands of these vindictive murderers. Since it was beyond her power to warn Prospero, so that he might guard himself, it remained only, as she perceived it, to turn Rainaldo from his bloody purpose by a disclosure of the dangerous truth.

"Blind, undiscerning fool!" she stormed. "What could the Adorni do in exile? Before we could settle our score with these Dorias it was necessary to be back here in Genoa. And how was that to be accomplished unless we made them believe themselves secure?"

"What are you telling me? If you mean anything, put it plainly."

"It's plain enough for any but a numskull. Prospero's peacemaking is a sham. He accepted their offers of reconciliation only so that he might the more surely work their ruin."

With feet planted widely and arms akimbo he stared at her round-eyed. "And went the lengths of a betrothal with Giovanna Maria Doria? You forget that, I think. Bah! I'm not to be hoodwinked by that crazy tale."

"It's true, man, I swear it. On the Gospels."

"True! God's Passion! But this lady, then?"

Madonna Aurelia smiled cruelly. "What of her? A figure for laughter that will recoil upon the Dorias whose name she has taken."

Rainaldo was shocked. "If that be true, Messer Prospero comes out of it with no more credit than if it were false."

"You'd like it both ways, I suppose."

"Madam, I like it neither way."

"By my faith, then, you're hard to please."

"I have some decency, Aurelia."

"You give me news," said she.

"I do not tread on women when I adjust my quarrels. I go straight to the man who is my enemy."

She laughed at him. "Again you give me news. It has rather seemed to me that you set others on. If you are so bold and brave and straightforward why didn't you pull Andrea Doria's beard, yourself, whilst he was here? Or why don't you do it now on some of the Dorias in Genoa? There are plenty of them on whom you may slake your fury instead of roaring here at me like a windy bully."

"By God, Aurelia, if you were a man..."

"You'd be more civil. Prospero shall hear your opinion of him when he returns. We shall see then if you'll be so bold as to maintain it."

Only after he had gone off in dudgeon did she come to reflect that her disclosure had produced in him an effect entirely contrary to her expectations and intentions. She had thought to soothe him by it. She had supposed that he would share her own admiration for the steadfastness of Prospero's purpose in revenge, which was not to be deflected by any mawkish scruples. Instead he had gone off in a frame of mind in which he could not be trusted even to keep faith with her. She grew afraid. If he should talk, and the thing should spread and reach the ears of the Dorias, then all would be wrecked.

Talk Rainaldo did whilst his wrath was upon him, and only when he had cooled did he come to consider the mischief that might follow. It moved at the gallop, as is the way of mischief, and some three or four days later Madonna Aurelia's chamberlain came to announce the visit of the Duchess of Melfi and her niece.

Her first impulse, born of a panic, was to deny herself to these unwelcome visitors. Then her bold Strozzi spirit reasserted itself. Empanoplied in a sense of righteousness, she descended the great marble staircase to the noble pillared chamber of mosaic floor and richly frescoed ceiling. There Prospero's mother and Prospero's betrothed looked upon each other for the first time.

The older woman bore herself with stiff, disdainful dignity; the younger with a self-possessed, rather wistful inscrutability which Madonna Aurelia found at once admirable and detestable.

That calm was today a mask upon a lacerated soul; and a mask, too, was Madonna Peretta's normal, smiling vivacity.

From the threshold Madonna Aurelia greeted them, coolly formal. "My house is honoured." Then she moved forward with that miraculous grace of carriage that defied the years, whilst her visitors curtsied low with a soft rustle of brocades, Madonna Gianna's of the colour of wine, Madonna Peretta's of rose and silver with a sparkle of jewels in her stiff head-dress and at her girdle. It was the Duchess, her dark eyes lively under their arching brows, her red lips smiling, who announced their purpose.

"Because your health, madam, has, much to our distress, prevented you from honouring our house, I have thought that it would be the duty of my niece to visit you."

"The duty has been delayed a little," said Madonna Aurelia, fencing.

She offered seats, placing her guests so that they faced the windows, and herself so that her back was to the light.

"But it could be delayed no longer," said Gianna smoothly. "An urgency always present has now become acute." The music of her level voice was perceptible even to the hostile ears of Prospero's mother.

"I ask myself what can so have rendered it."

"Do you?" said the Duchess pleasantly. Gently she used the fan of peacock feathers that was attached to her girdle. "Do you really ask yourself that? Or do you ask us to tell you what you already guess?"

"I do not usually permit myself to guess. Never when I may learn by inquiring."

Madonna Peretta maintained her bright, friendly air even though a certain asperity crept into her tone. "I will confess, madam, that I have long doubted whether your health were the sole reason why you have held yourself aloof from us. The doubt is increased when I perceive the lack of warmth with which you receive a prospective daughter-in-law."

Madonna Aurelia's smile was not pleasant. "Warmth could be expected only if I approved of my son's choice of a wife. And I have never pretended to do that. It is as well, perhaps, to be frank."

"Are you being frank, madam?" came Gianna's disconcertingly steady voice.

"In what do you think I fail?"

"That," said the Duchess, "is just what we seek to learn."

Then Gianna, grown impatient of this fencing, brought the matter to close quarters by plain terms. "There is a story current, madam, and report says that it comes from you. It is an ugly story. A shameful story. So ugly and shameful that my aunt hesitates to ask you bluntly if it is true, since even to have a doubt upon it must be to offend you. You will forgive me, madam, if I lack Madonna Peretta's delicacy. You will understand perhaps my need to know the truth without equivocation. This story then…"

But there she was interrupted. Under all the implications of Gianna's words, an anger steadily swelling and blinding Madonna Aurelia to reason, exploded violently.

"I know the story. No need to rehearse it. No need to wrap the pill in honey. You speak glibly of shame and of insults. What of the insult of supposing an Adorno so base that he could enter into alliance with the murderers of his father?"

The Duchess caught her breath in pain. "Oh, my God!" But Gianna's white face was lighted by a compassionate smile.

"That insult would be less than the insult of imagining that Prospero Adorno could lend himself to the deception you suggest."

"Our points of view are naturally different," was the answer. "That insult we can bear."

"You mean that this monstrous thing is really true!" cried the Duchess. The brightness of her face was overcast by horror. It was a moment before she could speak again, and then it was as if the words were choking her. "You said that our points of view are naturally different. Naturally. I thank you for saying that." She rose abruptly. "Come, child. We have our answer."

But on Gianna's face that oddly compassionate smile still lingered. "We have a lie," she said, with quiet confidence. "A shameful, shameless lie. It springs from a malice that seeks to wound and humiliate us. That is all." She rose slowly. "Have you forgotten, madam, that your son is at the wars? Have you thought that if he should never return to denounce that falsehood, his memory will for ever lie smirched in the minds of those who are so foolish as to believe you? You cannot have thought of that. Think of it now, and in God's name, madam, unsay that vile calumny. If it springs from hatred of me and a desire to wound me in the soul, dismiss it; for you fail utterly, since I will not dishonour Prospero by believing you."

Monna Aurelia, who often in her domineering egotism had spoken so to others, but had never yet so been spoken to, stood white to the lips, her eyes blazing, her bosom in tumult. "You prefer your fool's paradise, do you?" She laughed harshly. "A calumny, is it?

A lie? Ha! How long was Prospero in Genoa that he could not find time to marry? What hindered? You'll know how he explained himself to be so cool. Weigh now the explanations of that singularly laggard lover."

In Madonna Gianna's countenance, grown deathly, her eyes were as two black pools. She trembled visibly.

Observing the sudden change, Madonna Aurelia uttered again her hateful laugh. "Not so sure now that I am lying. Are you?"

Gianna took a step towards her aunt and put forth a hand as if to steady herself upon the arm of the Duchess. "Yes," she said in a voice that had lost its steadiness. "We have our answer. Let us go."

Madonna Peretta's arm went round her and drew her away to the door. From the threshold, over her shoulder, the Admiral's lady spoke her farewell.

"Your son, madam, is worthy of his Florentine mother. God help him for being as he is, and God help you for taking pride in it."

Madonna Aurelia disdained an answer and her two visitors departed, the Duchess as volubly angry as Gianna was preternaturally calm. But hers was not now that lovely serenity of self-control. It was the listlessness of a broken spirit. If she listened at all to her aunt's scorching comments, she offered no comments of her own either then or thereafter until that day when the Duke of Melfi broke to her the news of Prospero's end.

The Admiral's enlightenment came from his lady. At first he was utterly incredulous. Madonna Peretta had listened to the ravings of a spiteful woman. His opinion was shaken when in her turn she reminded him of how the nuptials had been eluded. But he was not convinced until his nephews came to work upon him with reminders of the abusive terms in which Prospero had refused him obedience at Cherchell, urging them as evidences of the vindictive hatred by which he could never have ceased to be governed. Then, at last, that imperturbable man was moved to an anger such as his near kin could not remember ever to have seen in him.

His nephews seemed to derive from it a malicious satisfaction.

"I knew what I was doing when I set the dog to the oar," Filippino approved himself.

"You were impatient with me, sir, when I gave you reasons against the alliance with this false betrayer."

The Duke was impatient with them now. "Oh yes. You tell me that I am an old fool, do you not? And that you are both very wide-awake and discerning. But you have not the wit to see that it may well have been your own conduct – especially yours, Filippino – that kept alive his rancour."

"Even now," minced Filippino, "you can find excuses for him."

"Excuses!" roared his uncle, striding to and fro. "I find no excuses. I thank God that he disobeyed me at Cherchell, and so came by his deserts."

Gianna shivered where she sat, whilst Madonna Peretta's lips tightened in agreement with her lord.

"Not so do I," grumbled Gianettino, with a pout of his petulant mouth. "I like to settle accounts with my own hands."

And Filippino agreed with him. "Why, yes. It's a poor satisfaction to think that the Infidels have done our work for us. He should have ended with my sword in his lying throat."

But some weeks later, when winter was upon them, and the occasion was supplied him, Filippino betrayed little anxiety to make good his boast.

From a Sicilian vessel which still dared to keep the seas despite the foul weather, a young Moor named Yakoub-ben-Isar landed in Genoa, bearing as his safe-conduct letters for the Duke of Melfi.

It happened that at the time the Duke was absent from Genoa, and that in the Fassuolo Palace, Gianettino Doria, his nephew predilect, officiated as the Admiral's deputy. To him the Moor was conducted by an officer of the port. Questioned on the source of his letters, Yakoub startled Gianettino by frankly declaring them to be from Dragut-Reis and concerned with the ransom of Messer Prospero Adorno, then a prisoner in his master's hands.

It was enough. Gianettino broke the seal.

"My Lord Duke (wrote Dragut, through an amanuensis, in tolerable Italian), *I give you the glad tidings that it has pleased Allah the Compassionate to spare the life of the great Frankish Captain Prospero Adorno, who is now my prisoner. Generously I set his ransom at no more than the three thousand ducats which you had from my Lord Kheyr-ed-Din for mine. Upon payment of it I shall instantly restore Messer Prospero to liberty and send him safely back to you in Genoa. Meanwhile he remains also a hostage for the safety of my messenger, Yakoub-ben-Isar. May Allah increase your lordship's days."*

Gianettino sent for his cousin, and the pair shut themselves up with the letter to consider what should be done. Gianettino's view was that it should be worth three thousand ducats to bring the caitiff home and give him a public hanging for his insubordination. But the subtler Filippino sneered at his cousin's heavy wits.

"So that his meddlesome friend, del Vasto, shall lay an accusation against us, and that other infernal meddler, Don Alvaro de Carbajal, shall say yet again that Don Prospero's insubordination was a gallantry."

Gianettino was annoyed by the sneer. "You professed regret once that he perished at Cherchell. You talked of a sword in his throat, I think."

"If he is brought back you shall see the threat fulfilled."

"Then I shall also see that an assassination will smell no sweeter in the Imperial nostrils than a hanging."

"Assassination?" Filippino looked his contempt. "A personal encounter is not assassination. If I kill him honourably, who shall blame me?"

"Perhaps. But if he kills you?"

"He will still have to meet you, Gianettino, and after you there will be a dozen others to send him their cartels until one prevails."

Gianettino shrugged his massive shoulders. "Heroics!" he growled.

"But there's no need for them, anyway," said Filippino. "Since we can't hang him, thanks to the way his credit with the Emperor has been built up, there's only one thing to do. Let him rot in his chains."

"But for how long? Eventually deliverance may come to him."

"You're overlooking something. He remains as a hostage for this Yakoub-ben-Isar's return. What if Yakoub should not return? It is very simple." He grinned. "I'll send Messer Yakoub to the galleys and leave Messer Prospero to bear the consequences of that. I do not think that we shall hear of him again."

Gianettino pulled at his lip. "We shall have to reckon with the Lord Andrea," he said. "He'll never agree to that."

"The Lord Andrea is not in the reckoning," said Filippino. "We'll serve him best by silence. So forget this letter, as I shall."

Chapter 20

The Homecoming

Throughout the months of that winter Andrea Doria laboured unremittingly on the equipment of a fleet that should take the seas against the insolent Moslem rovers as soon as the buds were breaking in the Fassuolo gardens. The first stirrings of Spring-time when at last they came made him impatient to depart. A further spur was supplied by the Emperor, who wrote in almost irascible terms demanding swiftest and sternest measures against the Corsairs, from which Andrea Doria may well have feared that Charles V was beginning to appraise last year's expedition at its true value. That the audacity of the Corsairs had nowise been diminished was seen in Dragut's fierce raids along the southern seaboard, from Reggio to Naples, and particularly in Kheyr-ed-Din's descent upon Fondi and his notorious attempt to carry off the lovely Giulia Gorizaga so that she might become an ornament to the hareem of Suleyman.

You know the story of that noble lady's near escape, her headlong flight by night on horseback, clad only in her nightrail, with a single attendant whom she afterwards put to death, supposedly because he had been made overbold by the sight of so much beauty scarcely veiled.

Other Calabrian women, however, were not so fortunate, and as a result of these raids Andrea Doria was deprived of the Neapolitan squadron, summoned back to Naples by the Viceroy as a necessary guard against Moslem depredations.

That squadron still included six galleys that were Prospero's personal property. The seventh had passed at Cherchell into Dragut's possession. To these galleys Rainaldo Adorno was laying claim, as Prospero's heir-at-law in such matters. The Imperial courts, however, were in no haste to pronounce, since at such a time it was of the first importance that the galleys should continue under Imperial control. So to Naples they went, under the command of Don Alvaro de Carbajal, who had now succeeded Prospero as Captain-General of Naples.

Andrea Doria's preparations were still incomplete when news came that Dragut, transcending in audacity anything hitherto performed, had seized the Spanish outposts in Africa of Susa, Sfax and Monastir, putting the garrisons partly to the sword, and carrying off the survivors into slavery. Swift on the heels of this exasperating news came a summons to Andrea Doria to render himself at once to Barcelona, there to confer with the Emperor whose cup of endurance was full to overflowing.

He obeyed in an uneasiness that was not entirely dispelled by the Emperor's manner. If it was still such as to persuade him that he had not yet lost the confidence of Charles V it yet allowed him to perceive that His Majesty's infatuation which regarded him as a worker of miracles had been diluted by the events. The name of Dragut-Reis had become even more detestable than that of Kheyr-ed-Din in His Majesty's ears, and he gave Andrea Doria to understand that the continuance of the Imperial favour would depend upon the swift and complete breaking of this so-called Sword of Islam.

Doria departed from the Imperial Court with the feeling that he was now upon his trial, yet with a full confidence that he would know how to acquit himself. The means under his hand were certainly formidable. He had assembled fifteen galleys of his own, five that had been equipped by his kinsman Antonio Doria, twelve belonging to Genoa, three supplied by the Pope and a great galleasse by the Knights of Malta, making a total of thirty-six war galleys. To these were added four transport galleons and close upon a score of ancillary vessels: sloops, feluccas and light, swift triremes to act as scouts.

Spain, which had supplied the transport galleons, refused to add a single galley to a force which she accounted adequate for any enterprise. She had no galleys to spare from the protection of her own coast, which at any moment now might lie under the Corsair menace. For the same reason Doria was not allowed further to recruit himself at the expense of either Naples or Genoa. He would not have dared to insist even had he felt the need to do so, lest by appearing timid he should supply a further weapon to those who discerned their own interest in diminishing him in the Emperor's eyes.

So with that very considerable fleet, brought together in the harbour of Barcelona, he set forth with great pomp in the early summer, and steered boldly south to put Mehedia to fire and sword. This being accomplished, but Dragut having unfortunately been missed, Doria continued to sweep along the African coast in quest of him, his galleys flung out like a net, some five miles wide, with his triremes ahead and on his northern flank, to act as the eyes of the host.

At about the time that Doria was thus engaged off the coast of Africa, a stout felucca was sailing into the harbour of Genoa, bringing home Prospero Adorno with four of his Neapolitans whom Dragut had permitted him to ransom so as to form his crew, with a Genoese seaman named Ferruccio to act as navigator.

Prospero was reaping the reward of the consideration he had shown Dragut when the Anatolian had been his prisoner. Possibly he profited, too, from a fellow-feeling engendered in the days when he and Dragut had toiled at the same oar. Thus did Filippino's past spite now recoil upon him. For even when the messenger sent to collect the ransom failed to return, Dragut did not, as even a Christian might have done, visit the consequences upon a prisoner who at the time had become a hostage. Instead, when winter was at an end and the time had come to take the seas again, the Corsair had offered

Prospero his liberty against a promise to send the ransom to Algiers by the first means available, and if possible by the hand of Yakoub-ben-Isar. It was a proposal that honoured both him who made it and him to whom it was made, and so the Corsair and the Christian gentleman parted with an increase of mutual esteem.

Prospero came home to find himself mourned for dead.

Under the shock of his sudden appearance before her, his mother swooned. Later, when she had recovered, it was he who almost swooned at the news she gave him. His hurt upbraidings at her breach of faith were met by fiercer upbraidings of the faithlessness he now disclosed. So a meeting begun in swoons and tears of gladness ended in scorn and wrath; and Prospero, reckless of all else, went off to the Fassuolo Palace in quest of Madonna Gianna.

But on his way a sudden ugly doubt, begotten of what he had just learnt, turned him aside to visit the bagnio on the Ripa. The chief warden, to whom he was well known, hailed him joyously as one risen from the dead, and at his request placed the roster of the slaves at his disposal. When Prospero found there the name of Yakoub-ben-Isar, that ugly doubt of his became almost a certainty.

Yakoub was on one of the hulks in the harbour, and the warden never hesitated to obey Prospero's command that he be brought ashore at once.

To the young Moor the sight of Prospero was as a promise of deliverance. He grinned broadly and readily answered every question. It was into the hands of Messer Gianettino Doria that he had delivered Dragut's letter. His captivity had followed. That was all that he knew. But it was enough. The rest Prospero could supply, and it was with a heavy heart and in a fear greater than he had ever known that he resumed his way to the Fassuolo.

Chapter 21

Explanation

It was the duchess who received him.

From the magnificent pillared vestibule where he had waited whilst a chamberlain announced him, he was conducted by the great gallery of heroes, where first he had discovered the identity of his betrothed, to the apartments of the Admiral's lady, equipped for her with that barbaric splendour for which heavy contributions had been levied on the East.

She did not rise when he entered, and her dark eyes were sadly stern as they considered him.

He bowed low. "I suppose," said he, "that few resurrections can be convenient. The living so often take advantage of the dead."

"Death makes forgiveness easier," she answered him.

"I have not come to seek forgiveness, madam."

"What?" She frowned upon him. "So arrogant?"

"Nay. So humble. I know myself beyond forgiveness."

"Then I wonder that you should come at all."

"To tell my own story in my own way. So that my offence may not seem, as it must seem, blacker than it really is."

The Duchess gravely shook her head. "I do not think that my niece will consent to see you. If she would I do not think you should desire to see her, unless you wish to add to the pain she has already suffered through your conduct."

"You mean that she would rather know me dead than living?"

"Need that surprise you? Dead it may be possible to think of you with some kindness. The nobility of your supposed death made amends for much that was ignoble in your life."

"If my action is accounted noble, that nobility cannot be diminished by my survival."

"Where your life offended, your survival will continue to offend."

"But perhaps less when all the truth is known. Of your charity, Madonna Peretta, suffer me to see your niece."

"Can you insist when I have said that it will merely increase her torment, reopen wounds?"

"If I believed that, I should not ask it." Quickly he added: "I love Gianna better than life or honour or anything that the world holds."

"You have proved it. Have you not?"

"You may come to think so when all is told."

Her dark eyes searched his countenance, and the expression of her little face grew kindlier. She was, after all, a very gentle-hearted lady, ever reluctant to credit evil; and there was not only the prayer he made; there was himself. He stood so straight and virile, so elegant in the simplicity of his dark raiment, his head held proudly high, his glance so direct and frank, that it seemed impossible to believe him utterly a felon.

"Would you be content," she asked, "to see Gianna in my presence?"

He inclined his head. "It is all that I ask."

She yielded, and soon Gianna was confronting him, with the Duchess at her side to lend her strength.

From her diamond-shaped head-dress, to the velvet hem of her satin gown, Gianna was all in black. By contrast the whiteness of her neck and face was dazzling. There was a wan, pinched look in that sweetly grave countenance that smote and startled Prospero. Instinctively at the first sight of him, her slender arms were raised and thrust forward from her ponderous half-sleeves. Then they fell heavily to her sides, and her face lost all expression.

"Why are you here?" was her first question, to which in a glow of vehemence she added a second: "Why are you alive?"

"Because a Barbary Corsair showed more chivalry than the Christian gentlemen who twice left me to perish: once when they abandoned me in the dangerous enterprise which honour imposed upon me; and again when they suppressed the messenger sent to Genoa to procure my ransom."

"Of whom do you speak?" the Duchess sharply challenged him.

"Of some gentlemen of the House of Doria."

The colour deepened in her face.

"You have deceived me, I think. I believed you came as a suppliant, not as an accuser."

"Have patience, Monna Peretta. I do not accuse. I do not reproach. I merely state, whilst deploring these acts of rancour which revive a feud that I was prepared to bury."

"Let me understand you. Do you dare to say that my lord or any of his house knew of your survival? That they had any part in this suppression of a messenger?"

"I can produce the messenger. A Moor named Yakoub-ben-Isar, whom I found in the bagnio here this morning."

"I would not take the word of twenty Moors for what you say."

"Then there is little hope for me. If I cannot be believed where I bring a witness, how shall I hope for belief where my word is all I have to offer?"

"Your word on what?" Madonna Gianna asked him suddenly. "Can any word explain the... Oh, I will not qualify it. Hard words are as unprofitable as false ones. Why do you stay, Ser Prospero? You lose your time."

"My time is no matter. Not all the time I may yet have to live. Of yours, madonna, I beg but some few moments. I have that to say which may help at least to heal your pride."

"My pride?" Her voice was hard. "Do you think it was my pride that you offended?"

"I desire you to know the exact sum of my offence, against whatever it may have been."

"You think it is not known already? You think there is anything you can still bring to light?"

"I know it. Things are not always what they seem. It was the Cardinal, my uncle, who reminded me of that in allusion to the Adorno grievance against the Lord Andrea when in my despair at the trick fate had played me I sought his help."

"We are to hear, then, that it was you who were tricked," said the Duchess, with asperity.

"If you will listen to me," he begged.

And now, at last, whilst the Duchess drew Gianna to a couch that glowed with Persian tapestry, he told his tale: confessed to the duplicity with which he had accepted the Doria offer of alliance, so that he might be the better able to avenge upon them the murder – as he deemed it – of his father; painted his despair upon discovering that the Giovanna Maria Doria to whom he had spuriously betrothed himself was his Gianna Monaldi. Then he spoke of his interview with the Cardinal on the eve of sailing for Algiers, and how the Cardinal had helped him to the ardently desired resolve to bury all thought of the feud, whatever the consequences in Adorno scorn and wrath. What had followed – the wretched affair of Cherchell and the rest – was of little consequence now. All his hope was that Gianna should understand in what a tangle of ugly circumstances he had been trammelled, and to believe that he would have had himself torn in pieces before he would consciously have subjected her to the indignity of that spurious betrothal.

He paused a moment at the end of his tale, as if hesitating.

That he had deeply moved the warm-hearted Duchess was plain from the tearful distress in which she looked at him. Of his impression upon Gianna he received no hint. She sat with folded hands and bowed head, immovable.

Silence endured. It was as if they waited for him to resume, whilst he waited for some word from them.

At last, "That is all I came here to say," he told them, softly. "I thank you for having heard me out in patience. I take my leave."

He bowed with solemnity, and he was already turning to depart, when Gianna quietly spoke. "You have confessed. You do not ask for absolution."

"I do not. I told Monna Peretta that I know that what I have done is beyond forgiveness. The circumstances have made it so. It is too late for the penitent's disclosure of hidden things. Mine is the admission of a discovered crime."

"The explanation," Gianna amended, still in that oddly quiet voice. "I have memories to inform me." She was thinking of the oddness discovered in him when first he came from Naples, when, as she had told him, he was hardly the Prospero she knew. She was remembering how, at the last, he had changed and quickened into himself again, free and unconstrained. That, she now understood, would be after he had taken counsel with Cardinal Adorno. "I have memories that bear witness to your truth." She rose suddenly, a sweet wistfulness in the eyes that steadily regarded him. "My poor Prospero, you do not need to ask for forgiveness. It is yours." Her eyes filled with tears. "Could I deny you, now that you have made all clear? You have restored to me something that I had lost and for lack of which I thought I must have died."

"Gianna!" was all that he said; but with such a wonder in his voice and eyes that not all the sonnets he ever wrote could have said more.

She was smiling at the bewildered Duchess through her tears. "Would you give us leave for a little while, madam?" she begged.

Madonna Peretta was scared by this transfiguration into a sense of duty. "To what purpose, child? Will you deceive yourself by false hopes?" She turned almost sternly upon Prospero. "This tale of a message? This Moor whom you say you have discovered in the bagnio?"

"Not only shall he come, himself, to testify, but the warden with him, to tell you how he was sent there six months ago."

"Six months ago?" she questioned. "Precisely when?"

"Early in November last."

She seemed relieved. "Then, Prospero, my lord can have had no hand in it." She was definite. "From October until after Christmas he was away with me at Acqui."

He remembered then that Yusuf had said that it was Gianettino Doria to whom he had delivered the letter. He confessed it, adding, however, that in such a matter the nephews must be their uncle's deputies.

She shook her head. "You have no cause to say so, or to think it."

"There is the harmony that I have always found between them."

She curbed impatience with him. "I'll not dispute the point with you. It is not worth while, for... Don't you see?" She looked from Prospero to Gianna, and distress softened the sternness of her glance. She slipped an arm about Gianna's waist, and held her close. "Whoever it was – whether my lord or Gianettino – he acted so for Gianna's best, as he supposed, knowing only the falsehood of your reconciliation. I do not justify him. Neither do I blame him. I ask you only to consider what is, and not to delude yourselves with the hope that there can ever again be a question of your marriage. The Dorias would never trust you again. Nor dare you blame them."

"I don't," he said. "The feud I would have bridged stands overwide. But if Gianna wills it, the betrothal may be renewed in spite of that."

"A betrothal which is an offence now to both sides – the Adorni and the Dorias?"

"They are not the world," said Prospero, and he repeated: "It must be as Gianna wills."

Her eyes were piteous. "My dear, I am frightened. What Aunt Peretta says is true. You would provoke the resentment of both my people and your own. Between them you would be crushed."

"My bones are hard," he said.

"But Gianna's are not," the Duchess answered him. "And she would share your danger."

"That is not what frightens me," Gianna protested.

"But it frightens me and should frighten Prospero."

And here they were interrupted by a more immediate scare.

Madonna Peretta's chamberlain came to announce that her lord's cousin, Lamba Doria, asked to see her. She commanded her alarm, and calmly ordered the servant to conduct Messer Lamba to the long gallery, where she would presently join him.

Then she came breathlessly to Prospero. "He must not find you here, or suspect your presence."

He would have argued, but she cut him short with reminders of Lamba's violent nature, and prayers that for her sake and Gianna's he depart at once. Because it was impossible not to yield to her frightened intercessions, he took his leave. And thus an interview begun in blackest cloud, ended, although abruptly, in pale, timid sunshine.

Chapter 22

The Way Out

The violent nature of Lamba Doria was advertised by his exterior. Red as a fox of hair and beard, and of a fiery, freckled complexion, with eyebrows so light as to be scarcely perceptible above eyes as pale and glittering as agates, he looked the hot, aggressive man he was. His age was not above forty, his stocky, muscular figure not above middle height. He dressed like a soldier, with a deal of steel and leather about him. Few men were more readily moved to anger, and in the display of it few put on a more terrific aspect.

It was in anger, seething and bubbling like a human cauldron, that he was ushered into the gallery of heroes after Prospero had gone.

From the warden of the bagnio word had gone forth that Prospero Adorno, risen from the dead, was in Genoa; and in bearing news of it to the Duchess, Lamba bore also an injunction to her forcibly to detain the rogue should he have the temerity to present himself at her palace.

The Duchess was now as cool as Gianna was agitated.

"To what end should I detain him?"

"To what end? Lord God! Do you ask me that, Peretta?" There was a deepening glow in the furnace of his face. "So that we may supply him with a winding sheet. The hunt is up. There is not a kinsman or friend of ours who is not on the watch for him. We've sought him in his own house. He is not there. But wherever he skulks we'll find him. And this time there'll be an end to his foul buffoonery at our expense. We'll settle your score with him, Gianna. Trust us."

Gianna controlled herself to speak. "You mean to do murder?"

"No," he bellowed. "Execution. And he shall have an imposing funeral."

Madonna Peretta's generous bosom was in tumult. "I cannot think that my lord will approve of such a deed."

Lamba showed his teeth in a grin. "His disapproval will not raise the dead."

"But it will fall heavily upon the living who've had part in this. And I'll not be of those. So expect no help from me."

He stormed in vain against her, and finally, still storming, that messenger of wrath departed in quest of the object of this wrath.

Because, whilst fierce, Lamba was also prudent, he enlisted the assistance of another kinsman, Flavio Doria, and four of his own followers, and thus reinforced set out to hunt his prey. It was in the nature of things that they should prefer the darkness for the work they had to do, and it was not until they had lain in wait for two nights outside the Adorno Palace that their victim walked into their midst, as he was homing. He was not quite alone, which is how they would have preferred him. He was accompanied by Ferruccio, the Genoese navigator who had been the master of his felucca, and was his devoted servant. But as there were six of them in the Doria party, Lamba did not hesitate to give the word, and in a moment the street was noisy with the clash of steel.

Be it from confidence in their numbers, be it from sheer stupidity, the Dorias had neglected caution in their approach. Their sudden rush had made Prospero halt, and the livid gleam of their naked weapons in such light as lingered had advertised their purpose.

Both Prospero and Ferruccio were armed, and they were prompt to draw their weapons and to square their back to a wall, so as to thwart any attempt to envelop them. Ferruccio was not only a navigator of skill. He had practised piracy in his time, and had kept a whole skin by the briskness of his swordplay and the toughness of his sinews. Also he was of that peculiar kind of courage which discovers exhilaration in a rough and tumble.

He displayed his quality at the very outset, and even as he backed to the wall, to stand shoulder to shoulder with his master on the defensive, he whirled his blade at the foremost assailant and all but clove one of the fellow's arms from its shoulder.

"By the Mother of Heaven, there are still too many of you," he complained derisorily.

The effect of his prompt action was that whilst the wounded man fell back with a scream, the other five, as if obeying some herd impulse, directed their attack upon the seaman.

Prospero heard and recognized the voice of Lamba, blasphemously urging on the others, and he advanced a pace, so as to deflect some of that wholesale charge from Ferruccio. Crouching, he drove his unopposed blade through the flank of the man nearest, and thereby brought the assailants to a division of their force.

Thereafter the six of them fought bitterly across the body of the fallen man, Prospero and Ferruccio strictly on the defensive, but alert and watchful in the uncertain light for any opening that might present itself. Sword and dagger met sword and dagger at lightning speed; steel ground on steel, clashed, parted and clashed again in a fury that could not long endure. But though they fought in silence now, grimly intent, there had been clamours at the outset and the ring of metal vibrated on the silent eventide. The delay in making an end was enraging Lamba. This went not at all as he conceived it. His intention had been a swift surprise attack that would have stretched Prospero lifeless before he realized that he was beset. That he and the three who remained him must presently make an end of the two as soon as their defensive energy began to weaken he could not doubt. But already the engagement had lasted too long. Doors were opening, voices were calling, lights were stirring in the street, and these four who were too obviously the assailants must presently find themselves overwhelmed by those who would account it their duty to interfere.

Lamba fell back to take stock of the situation, and perceived at once that it had become dangerous to linger. With an oath that he would not blunder next time, he gave the word to retreat, and before the advancing rescuers, the Doria party, including the man Ferruccio had wounded, backed away into the darkness, plunged down a narrow alley-way and was lost to sight. The man brought down by Prospero was left to lie where he had fallen, and the lights of those who came up revealed him to be Flavio Doria. He lay in a pool of blood, unconscious and seemingly in desperate case. But he evoked no sympathy from any in the crowd that was very soon assembled.

"He is well-served for an assassin," was an old man's angry comment, which, from what else was said, seemed to express the mind of all.

Prospero and Ferruccio, putting up their weapons, stayed for no more than to recover breath and mop the perspiration from their brows. Then, with a word of thanks to these timely saviours, they disengaged themselves from that friendly press, and made off in their turn.

Yielding to Ferruccio's urgent persuasions, Prospero descended with him to the port, and went aboard the *Gatta*, his felucca, at her moorings beyond the Cow Gate.

"I've been as near my end tonight as I find it comfortable," Ferruccio protested. "And so have you, my lord. Luck may not stand our friend again if we give Ser Lamba another opportunity. You heard his parting threat. A man of blood, and the death of Ser Flavio will not soften him. Take warning, my lord, and do not wantonly expose yourself."

Prospero took heed for that night, and slept aboard the felucca. In the morning, when he would have departed, he learnt from one of his men who had been ashore that all the talk on the quayside was of certain doings in Genoa that obviously concerned him. In the night his house had been invaded by an armed party under Lamba; failing to find him there, the fiery Doria had forced an entrance to the Cardinal's palace in quest of him. Frustrated there again, and threatened by His Eminence with grave consequences of this violence, he had withdrawn, swearing for all to hear that wherever Prospero hid himself, he would know how to find him.

Prospero sat down to consider, and came presently to the same conclusion that since there was nothing now to keep him in Genoa, there was no purpose in risking his life by lingering a moment longer than it need take him to order matters for departure. He realized the futility of sending a cartel to such a man as Lamba Doria. Lamba would never consent to meet him in single combat, and Prospero was not disposed to another encounter with a band of assassins.

Yet when he had taken his resolve, the necessity to go ashore was increased in urgency. He must provide for the voyage ahead, and whilst he could leave the victualling to Ferruccio, only he, himself, could deal with the matter of gold supplies. So ashore he went, soon after the hot noontide, at the hour at which men are taking their siestas, when the quays are empty of all but those who sleep upon them. He went muffled in a cloak, with a wide-brimmed hat to overshadow his face, and he was attended by two of his knaves, who presently returned with him, staggering under the burden of a chest fetched from the Bank of St George. Yet for all his precautions he was seen and watched aboard. Lamba had stirred the vigilance of needy idlers by a widely-proclaimed promise of twenty ducats to the man who brought him word of where Prospero Adorno lurked.

The rogue who had spied upon him made haste away with news of his discovery. Lamba, however, was from home when the informer got there. He was away on his relentless hunt, and was thought by his people to have gone towards Carignano. Fretted by this, the spy had betrayed more of his purpose than was prudent, thinking thus to spur Lamba's people to tell him where their master could be found. These had talked in their turn, and before sunset it was known in more than one quarter of the city that Messer Prospero Adorno, so fiercely sought by Messer Lamba Doria, was in hiding aboard his felucca. What they did not know was that the felucca, hurriedly made ready for the voyage, was on the point of setting sail.

News of it at least reached Lamba, when he came home belatedly to dine, wearied by a fruitless search. At about the same hour it reached the Fassuolo Palace, and so troubled the Duchess that she was for dispatching at once a messenger to the felucca. Her niece, however, in a trouble deeper far than Madonna Peretta's, yet preserving an outward semblance of self-mastery, insisted upon going, herself, upon that errand.

"I could trust no other," was her answer to her aunt's protests. "And there is more to do than merely warn him of this fire-eater's threats. He must be persuaded to leave Genoa. He is not safe here."

Monna Peretta looked at her wistfully.

"I understand, my dear. God send a speedy end to this wretched tangle. Go, then, Gianna, and prevail upon him to be gone, at least until my lord returns. Then, at last, I hope, peace will be made."

And so, at about the hour of sunset, a closed mule-litter emerged from the Cow Gate and clattered over the kidney-stones of the pier below it, past an untenanted trireme that was moored alongside, and past a fishing-boat aboard which men were singing as they stowed their nets. It came to halt beside a broad felucca that announced its identity by the gilded cat's head on the prow, and Madonna Gianna was handed from it by one of the two grooms who escorted her.

A premature dusk overhung the city as she stepped forth. Overhead the sky was black, and out of the west came a mutter of distant thunder, whilst the first raindrops fell scattered upon the stones in splashes broad as ducats. This made her hurry across the gangplank, at the end of which a man rose to challenge her. Scarcely had she begun an impatient answer than the sound of her voice fetched Prospero himself to the entrance of the tabernacle. In a bound he was below her, helping her aboard, then swept her from the increasing rain into the shelter of the cabin in the stern.

He was as breathless as was she. "What miracle accounts for this, my Gianna?"

Her terrors for him drove her as if by instinct to his arms. There was no further word between them of his offence or her forgiveness. It was as if no cloud had ever stood between them. Held thus, she delivered her message. He must set sail at once. He must go from

Genoa. He smiled upon her pallid fears. "This anguish is so flattering that I could almost thank Messer Lamba for inspiring it."

He led her to the divan. He stood observing her, a glow in his dark eyes to make it plain that danger was far from being the subject of his thoughts. He was contrasting this agitation on his behalf with the tranquillity he had always known in her.

"Let me behold you calm again," he exhorted. "Calm as my placid Lady of the Garden."

"Can I be calm, Prospero, when death hangs over you? Think of me if you will not think of yourself."

This brought him down at her side. "Dear love," he murmured.

"Will you go?" she asked. And added: "If you love me, you will not let me be tormented further by my fear for you."

He paused, as if a hesitancy beset him, before replying. His eyes, looking deeply into hers, were very tender, yet as if haunted by a wistful hunger. "I have thought of it," he confessed, and heard her gasp of relief. "Indeed, I have prepared for it, and it is in my mind to sail for Spain, where I shall not want for friends." He pointed to an iron-bound coffer that was ranged beside the divan. "I have shipped gold enough for my needs already…"

"Why, then," she broke in, "what can detain you?"

"I might have sailed some hours ago. But at the last moment I was seized by a reluctance to depart. Can't you understand it? Am I to go from you again after all that has happened?"

"Will you stay to be murdered? Will that help or comfort me? Go now, and leave me to make your peace with the Lord Andrea when he comes home. Then all will be well."

But to this he shook his head. He knew the Lord Andrea and these Dorias too well, he said, to suppose that they would ever consent to their union.

"Their consent is not necessary. I am no Doria, save by adoption. I took the name at the instances of Aunt Peretta. I would now that I had never done so. It has been the source of all the trouble. But I remain, nevertheless, Giovanna Maria Monaldi, mistress of myself and of the little that my father left me. I may bestow one and the other as I please. If you cannot come back to Genoa to claim me, none can prevent me from going to you wherever you may be."

That was to provoke the answer that he made her.

"Then none could prevent you from sailing with me now."

It robbed her of breath. Round-eyed, in a sort of apprehension, she stared at him. He answered the question of that glance. "It is a dream I have been dreaming, Gianna. Your coming now is like the miracle of its fulfilment. Why should we suffer the torment of yet another separation? I vow to Heaven," he added in a sudden passion, "that I will not. Whether I go or stay is now in your hands. For I will not go without you."

"Will you be mad, Prospero? What are you asking?" It was a demand, and the hushed voice was stern.

"That you marry me at once, and sail with me. The Cardinal will tie the knot. He loves me well enough to set the Dorias at defiance, and he understands. Afterwards you can make our peace with the Lord Andrea. Or not. It shall be as you please."

The rain thrashed down upon the cabin roof. Overhead the thunder rolled and crackled. It had become so dark within the tabernacle that they could see each other only dimly. Yet as he waited he felt the trembling of the hands he held.

And then their ears were assailed by a brazen voice outside.

"Bestir, there, you lubbers! Get forward, and clear the sail."

Made suddenly aware that the vessel was moving under their feet, Prospero sprang to the entrance. He saw that the felucca had been unmoored at the prow, and was swinging at the end of the rope that held her stern.

Ferruccio, labouring at a sweep, did not wait to be questioned by his master. Unbidden, the hairy giant gave him the reason for this sudden, frenzied urgency. By the grace of God he had sought shelter in a wine-shop of the Ripa, when Messer Lamba Doria, marshalling a band of cut-throats, had come there to inquire where a felucca named the *Gatta* might be moored. Ferruccio had not stayed to hear him answered. He had slipped out of the tavern and had run his hardest, and, by all the devils, he was no more than in time; for yonder came that murderous crew.

Prospero followed the fellow's indication, and through the streaming rain beheld a band of a dozen men or more, approaching swiftly down the quay.

"Hold there!" was Prospero's sharp, instinctive command. "Are we to run from those dogs?"

"Are we to stay to be savaged by them? Faith, I already know something of their mettle, and there are too many of them. There always are when Messer Lamba leads." He dropped the sweep, caught up an axe, and went climbing round the tabernacle to the stern to hack at the mooring rope. "There's a time to fight, and a time to run," he growled. "And if I'm not the man to run at fighting-time, neither am I the man to fight at running-time."

The felucca swung free, just as Lamba and his band came abreast of her. For an instant it looked as if Lamba would risk a leap; but the widening gap deterred him. Instead, brandishing a naked sword, he hurled threats and insults across the water.

"Don't think to escape me, you Adorno dog. I'll find you if I have to follow you to Hell." Then he and his knaves went swarming aboard the fishing-boat, slashing at her mooring-ropes with the clear intent of compelling her to give chase.

"Wait! Wait! A plague on your panic, Ferruccio! To what will you commit me?" Prospero shouted. "Avast there! Devil take you! We have a lady aboard, who must be put ashore."

"A lady? Ohe! The devil!" But the seaman was nonplussed only for a moment. "First to shake these bloodhounds off our heels. Then we'll go ashore at San Pier d'Arena, at Portofino, or where you will. Give way there!" he roared.

Prospero was angry. "Hold, I say!" He was moving from the cabin entrance when Gianna's hand fell upon his arm.

"Let be, Prospero. Let be. Your seaman is in the right. See!" She made him turn and look back. "Lamba's boat is moving out to follow. Even now we may not be in time to escape."

"Escape was not in my mind," was Prospero's hot rejoinder.

"Then I thank God for the better wisdom of your seaman."

Sail was hoisted now and made fast, and the freshening breeze from the land sent them rippling forward towards the harbour's entrance, between the moles. Behind them aboard the fishing-boat they were still busy at the tackles. But it was certain that in sailing power she would prove no match for the felucca.

Prospero shed his indignation, and resigned himself with a half-laugh as he drew Gianna once more within the shelter of the tabernacle from the steadily increasing rain. "I do not care to have any cut-throat boast that I ran away from him. But there! It's done, thanks to Ferruccio and you. It only remains now to land you at San Pier d'Arena, and find means there to convey you back to the Fassuolo."

Thus he proposed. But Fate was disposing otherwise. Just as they drew level with the Old Mole, the storm that had been gathering broke upon them with a sudden and devastating fury. Under the first fierce blow of the mistral that smote them almost without warning, the felucca heeled over until her gunwale was awash. Only Ferruccio's promptness in slashing through the halyard saved them from foundering there and then. The sail came down in a heap, to balloon forward, thudding and drumming and shaking the craft from stem to stern until they had it close-reefed to the yard again. After this there was nothing to be done but suffer themselves to be driven bare-masted before the hurricane out into the open sea where none would now dare to follow.

The felucca was broad-beamed and sturdy, and so long as their sweeps kept her headed into the wind, she should be able to ride out the tempest. But no conjectures as to where the end of it might find them could now temper Prospero's regrets that he had not preferred to stay and meet Lamba's onslaught, whatever the odds.

Chapter 23

Capture

To Dragut-Reis in the stronghold of Mehedia, which he had made his own, had come the news of the formidable expedition sailing from Barcelona for the proclaimed purpose of exterminating "the pirate Dragut, a Corsair hateful to God and man".

Dragut laughed in his forked beard. He bethought him of the loud Frankish boasts that had heralded the adventure of Cherchell, and the sorry Frankish end of that adventure. That the Emperor's famous Admiral should come now in greater force must merely render more disastrous the defeat which by the mercy of Allah the All-Knowing would await him.

There was a heavy score to settle. Dragut's back was still, and would ever be, a lattice-work of scars from the wardens' whips in the days when he had heaved at the oar of a Doria galley. It might be mere murder to chain an old man of between sixty and seventy to the rowers' bench; but Messer Andrea would have some of his pestilent nephews with him, and they should be his deputies at the oar, whatever the ransom they offered. So Dragut laughed, and planned the strategy by which the will of Allah should be wrought upon the unbeliever. For its swift execution he sailed away to Algiers, so as to enlist old Kheyr-ed-Din. But there a check awaited him. Kheyr-ed-Din, himself, was on the point of putting to sea on a command from Suleyman the Great to render himself at once to Istanbul.

As impressed by the prowess of the old Corsair as he was contemptuous of the incompetence of his own admirals, Suleyman, projecting maritime action on a large scale, was bestowing the supreme command of his fleet upon the Basha of Algiers. It was in the orders of the Exalted of Allah that Kheyr-ed-Din should take his fleet with him to the Golden Horn. Therefore, Kheyr-ed-Din could spare Dragut none of the reinforcements so urgently required. The Anatolian must shift for himself. That he would do so successfully Barbarossa could not doubt. His address would supplement his valour. Let him but temper both with prudence, and it was certain that Andrea Doria would again be cheated of his hopes.

Against commands from the Sublime Portal it would have been idle to argue. Therefore, as submissive to the will of Allah as his sick heart permitted him to be, Dragut saw the imposing fleet of Kheyr-ed-Din Barbarossa sail away from an Algiers so fortified that rash, indeed, would be the enemy who would attempt to cast anchor in its harbour. Because of this, Dragut was tempted to lie snug there for the present, and from that inexpugnable stronghold defy and deride the Imperial might. And of this mind he might have continued but for the news that presently reached him from Mehedia. For it was now that seeking him there, and failing to find him, Doria had put the place to fire and sword.

This was a blow at Dragut's heart. Like Barbarossa he had sovereign ambitions. It was his dream, too, to build himself an independent kingdom, and at Mehedia he counted upon its realization. Now, for the present at least, his hopes of a bashalik had gone up in the smoke of that conflagration.

In his anger he disregarded Kheyr-ed-Din's parting injunction of prudence. He put to sea in the scorching heat of mid-July, with all his force, which amounted to three galeasses, twelve galleys and five brigantines. He was not so rash as to conceive himself in strength to meet the mighty host with which Doria was seeking him. But at least he could give himself the satisfaction of reprisals, and take elsewhere such payment for the ravages suffered by Mehedia that the plunder of that city should by comparison look like the robbing of a hen-roost.

So whilst Andrea Doria nosed along the African coast in quest of him, Dragut made a sudden swoop upon the south-west coast of Sicily. Beginning at Girgenti, he carried his raid as far north as Marsala, leaving ruin and desolation behind him. At the end of a week he stood off again with the spoils of six townships, and some three thousand picked captives of both sexes, destined, the men to slavery and toil, the women to the seragli of the Faithful. He would teach the Genoese dog to allude to him as "the pirate Dragut, a Corsair hateful to God and man". He would so, by the Beard of the Prophet!

He packed his captives aboard two of his brigantines, and sent them in charge of one of his captains, Yarin Sabah, straight to Algiers, there to be sold in the Souk-el-Abeed. With the proceeds new galleys were to be acquired; at need, new keels were to be laid down; and these vessels were to join him at Djerba, where he would await them. Until his little fleet should be thus reinforced, he judged it well to practise caution. And having gathered from a Greek ship he met that Doria was belatedly hunting him along the Sicilian shores, he headed his galleys north-west for the Straits of Boniface, beyond which it was his intent to turn south again, giving his pursuers a wide berth.

Let his Sicilian activities be reported to the Emperor whilst the Infidel bells were pealing for the victory of Mehedia, so that His Majesty might ask himself what his great Admiral was about.

Towards sunset of the sultry July day on which he had sent off the brigantines to Algiers, sky and sea assumed the hue of copper. A dull ominous glow suffused them, which gradually deepened to a pall-like blackness overhead. From the north-west, to punctuate the almost breathless calm, scurries of wind, as brief as they were abrupt, whipped up the now oily bosom of the sea and angrily rattled the sails.

Dragut, whose sea-craft was no whit inferior to his generalship, stood on the poop lifting his nose to these whiffs of mistral as a dog lifts its nose to a scent. He ordered the sails of his capitana to be furled, and saw that the example thus set, which was in the nature of an order given, was immediately followed by the other vessels of his fleet. Then he waited, studying the sky which grew ever blacker, and observed the sooty clouds edged with that hint of copper, moving ever faster against the fitful wind. Suddenly the heavens were rent by streams of fire, and the deafening artillery of the storm was loosed. The rain descended in steady, glassy sheets, and the mistral came no longer in cat's-paws, but shrieking through the shrouds with all its terrifying might. On one of the galleys the mainmast cracked with a report like that of a gun, and went down in a tangle of rigging to crush a dozen slaves by its fall. The wardens were hard put to keep their feet upon the gang-decks whilst the oars were plied so as to supply the steering-way that should hold each vessel straight downwind. The sea rose. It broke over their decks and poured from the scuppers as from fountains, and the tormented, frightened rowers were pounded, drenched and blinded by it.

Night fell, a night of howling wind, of roaring thunder and heaving seas. The darkness encompassed them like black velvet, intermittently illuminated by livid lightnings which revealed one to another the labouring galleys.

The three lanterns on the poop of the capitana, tossed against the blackness by the roll and pitch of the vessel, served as a rallying point to the fleet, and ever and anon Dragut would order a gun to be fired as a further precaution against scattering. Nevertheless some scattering there was in that wild sea, and one galley, acting upon the independent judgment of her commander, deliberately disregarded poop-lights and cannon alike.

This was the galley whose mainmast had come down at the first impact of the storm. She was commanded by the eunuch Sinan-el-Sanim, esteemed by Dragut above any other of his captains, for Sinan's was an unbroken record of successes won by an uncanny ability in estimating chances and a shrewd aversion to unnecessary risks. This was not pusillanimity, for when a risk was unavoidable none could be bolder in accepting it.

It may be that as a result of the loss of his mainmast, in the confusion ensuing whilst it was being cut adrift, and in the deepening darkness, Sinan had been blown out of touch with the remainder of the fleet. Be that as it may, two astute considerations governed him which appear to have been overlooked by Dragut. By riding before the gale they must come ever under the increasing force of it and they would be driven towards the Calabrian coast and so quite possibly right into the arms of their pursuers. The way to avoid both dangers was to hold to the course that had been theirs before they were struck by the storm. At whatever cost to the rowers the galleys must be kept headed into the wind. If they made headway against it, they would find the going easier in a measure as they came under the lee of the Sardinian coast. If they did not, at least they would avoid the risk of being blown within the reach of Andrea Doria.

Such a course seemed to Sinan to justify the risk of going about in that heavy sea, a risk he took despite the protests of all aboard. There was a dreadful moment when the galley slid sideways down a black wall of water into a trough where she was pounded and smothered by another similar black wall that fell upon her. A man was smashed to death against the foremast, two others were swept overboard, a warden was lifted from the gang-deck and hurled among the slaves, and of these more than one sagged forward unconscious upon the oar against which his ribs had been crushed. But the binding-strakes were tight upon the scuttles, and no water reached the hold. The galley rose like a cork through the engulfing waters, and like a cork was tossed to the crest of the next billow, even whilst under the pull of the starboard oars her head was pivoted into the wind, taking yet another heavy sea before the manoeuvre was complete.

By then the main of the fleet was a mile to the south-east, and Sinan could account himself alone. Gradually he recovered breath, and gradually the quaking of his enormous body settled down; for if all aboard had known terror in those moments, none had known a terror as great as he by whose orders the thing had been done.

Before the end of that dreadful night, in the course of which Sinan died a thousand deaths, he came to regret the course which wisdom had led him to adopt. For all his years aboard, his too sensitive stomach had never become reconciled to the ruder vagaries of the sea; and as the galley heaved under him to each succeeding crest, and fell shuddering away with crashing impacts into the succeeding trough, he lay prone on the divan in his tabernacle, a quivering, quaking mass of flesh that groaned and sweated in anguished nausea. And all about him, to clutter what little sense his sickness left him, the din was infernal: the shrieking of the wind they breasted, the groan of straining timbers, the rattle and clatter of blocks, the thud and crash of the seas that swept over them, the grinding creak of the oars on their tholes, and through all, the groans, the invocations and imprecations of the labouring slaves.

Nor did these labours result in much more than holding the position. Of progress there was little. In all that night of toil the galley advanced but a few miles, and when the dawn broke clear after the storm, all that they could see of Sardinia was the hazy peak of Monte Severo to the north of Spartivento. Something else they saw as the sun broke forth from the ragged clouds that scudded eastwards. Not a mile distant a green and white felucca with a bare mast was drifting helplessly, tossed on the ground-swell that was the legacy of the now abated storm.

The trivial craft was not trivially regarded by Sinan, who neglected no chance of picking up information.

Although the waves were still long and heavy, the wind had fallen to a mere breeze, and against this the galley was making as much headway as could be expected from the lassitude of her rowers. The helmsman veered a point, heading the vessel straight for the felucca.

There was some stir aboard the little craft. Men rose to view from the shallow depth of her and one was seen to emerge from the gabled structure, like a hen-coop, that made a cabin in the stern. Sweeps were thrust out, but remained idle. It was as if an impulse to flight had, on the score of its futility, been abandoned even as it took shape.

When not more than a dozen yards of heaving water separated them Sinan's kayia, the burly Hisar, made a trumpet of his hands, and in the Lingua Franca bawled an order to the crew of the felucca to bring her alongside. She came, of course, being without alternative. The idle sweeps were plied at last, and in a moment she was at the short entrance ladder from the vestibule of the poop. As she rose and fell there beside the greater vessel, Hisar leapt down into her, followed by a couple of his Moors.

He was confronted by five men, wearily pallid and blear-eyed, whom only panic now seemed to keep awake. His dark eyes went contemptuously over them and came to rest upon the man and the woman standing in the gabled entrance of the cabin. Gazing his fill upon the pallid beauty of the lady, Hisar gave thanks to Allah for the Christian indecency which permitted its women to go bare of face.

"Who are you?" he asked.

The man, proclaimed by dress and accoutrements a person of consequence, and of a countenance that bore the same signs of exhaustion discernible in his sailors, answered composedly: "I am Prospero Adorno, of Genoa."

There was not an officer in the following of Dragut to whom that name was not known. Hisar raised his brows. "And whither bound, Messer Adorno?"

"To be truthful, I no longer know."

Hisar grinned. "In that case, you had better come aboard. We may put you on your way."

"You are kind," said Prospero. "But we will not abuse your kindness. We can shift for ourselves now that the wind is easing."

"You'll be safer with us, nevertheless."

Prospero's weary face turned a deeper grey. He had been under no illusion as to the end of all this. For himself, he could face Moslem captivity, as he had faced it before, with comparative equanimity. But the thought of it for Gianna stirred him to frenzy. Less than ever could he now thank Ferruccio's furious zeal to save him from the murderous Lamba. Better a thousand times to have faced his onslaught than that Gianna's merciful errand to him should end in this. In momentary madness he carried his hand to his sword.

The gesture was enough for Hisar. Before Prospero could draw an inch of blade, there was a blast from the silver whistle that dangled on the Moslem's breast, and such a swarm of bare-legged, brown-faced children of Mahomet fell aboard the felucca that they almost swamped her. There was no fight or room in which to wage it. Overwhelmed by numbers, Prospero and his men were made fast and heaved aboard the galley.

With Madonna Gianna the Corsairs dealt more gently. The intrepid calm in which she cloaked whatever emotions may have been astir in her produced an effect of awe upon Hisar. He handed her to the deck, and conducted her to the tabernacle.

There, on a divan, she beheld a mountain of a man. Seated cross-legged, he seemed to lose all human shape. He was an almost globular mass of apparently boneless flesh packed into a scarlet gold-embroidered caftan, surmounted by a smaller globe under a white but unclean turban. His swollen, puffy face with its sagging chins was this morning of a sickly yellow, and his little eyes, sunk deep into their fleshy settings, had the shape and glittering malevolence of a hog's.

Intently and at length those eyes considered her fair, clean-limbed height and the noble countenance that endured with such contemptuous tranquillity his evil gaze. Then, without having addressed her, he shifted his eyes to a chest that had been hoisted from the felucca and under the load of which two of his men had staggered into the cabin. Hisar had raised the lid, to display the gleam of the newly minted ducats with which it was filled. Sinan thrust into the mass a hand each finger of which was like a monstrous yellow slug. Through these he let a handful of the gold trickle back into the chest. His voice, absurdly reed-like issuing from that great mass, was twittering orders in Arabic, pointing to a corner of the cabin. Thither, in obedience, Prospero's treasure-chest was conveyed, the lid snapped down.

Next Hisar drew Sinan's attention to a long stole of pearls with tasselled ends visible about the lady's neck now that her cloak hung open. The pearls, of great size and brilliant lustre, represented a prince's ransom.

Sinan grunted an order, and, with a grin of mock apology, Hisar removed the necklace from Gianna's neck. She suffered it in apparent insensibility. But when she beheld Sinan's horrible fingers caressing that shimmering rope, her calm was in danger of breaking down. There was a pain in her throat, from the sobs that she repressed. For these pearls stirred memories, ordinarily lovely, but now poignant. She had worn them that evening in the Carreto garden when Prospero had sought sanctuary of her, and because of that she had worn them again on the day when first he came as her betrothed to the Fassuolo.

She was recalled by Sinan's absurd voice addressing her in Italian. A lady who hung such a fortune about her neck must be, he chirped, of high degree. He desired to know to whom he had the honour to offer the hospitality of his galley.

She did not hesitate to answer him. She thought, indeed, by her answer to empanoply herself.

"I am the niece of the Lord Andrea Doria." Her voice was steady. "You were wise to remember it in your treatment of us."

He caught his breath, and for a moment his face was blank. Then he smiled evilly, so that his little eyes vanished. "Verily the ways of Allah are unfathomable." He swung to Hisar, and was chattering to him again in Arabic, his glance ranging the while over Madonna Gianna, from the hem of her rich gown to the crown of her dark head, and an odious leer creased his yellow, oily face.

As he ceased, the kayia opened a scuttle in the deck, and with his exaggerated mock-courtesy, invited the lady to descend to the little cabin that was disclosed below. She drew back, stiffening. Then, commanding herself, she did as was required, in a serenity that was wholly histrionic; and in that serenity she remained until the scuttle closed again over her head. Then, at last, she raised the stern barriers she had imposed upon nature, and allowed despair to have its way.

Chapter 24

A Prize for Suleyman

Prospero Adorno lay where they had flung him, amidships by the stump of the lost mainmast, half-stunned, partly from the rough usage he had received and more from the horror of having brought Gianna into the hands of these Moslem dogs.

He lay on his side, his wrists pinioned behind him by a thong of bullock hide. His five knaves lay about him similarly bound. Ferruccio, only half-conscious, moaned softly ever and anon from the pain of a broken head. He had been so foolish as to offer resistance, and a Moslem cudgel had felled him. Of the other four, three were actually asleep, so utter was their exhaustion. Swarthy, turbaned Corsairs came to make a ring about them, chattering and laughing.

Slow, ponderous, slip-slopping steps approached along the gang-deck. The human ring opened to admit a newcomer, and the curved toe of a Turkish slipper prodded Prospero urgently in the flank. He beheld the loathly obesity of Sinan.

"Well-returned, Messer Prospero," the eunuch mockingly greeted him. "We did not look to see you again so soon. Dragut-Reis will be rejoiced. He'll require news of Yakoub-ben-Isar, and of a ransom he was sent to fetch. Meanwhile I, too, require some news. News of Andrea Doria. Tell me what you know of him."

"That I can answer in a word. Nothing."

"Therein, of course, you lie; which is what you have taught us to expect from you. For one thing, you know his niece."

Prospero blinked, and recovered. "True. And several others of his family. But I supposed your question to concern his movements. Of those, all that I know is that he is upon the seas hunting your kind, which is no more than you know yourself."

Sinan smiled, and became thereby more repulsive. His flute-like voice was gentle. "Do you think that with a match between your fingers you might remember more?"

"You would waste your time. I can tell you nothing. But I might advise you, if you would listen."

"Advise me?"

"How to make yourself safe from the wrath of Doria when he catches you, as catch you he will."

"Let me hear you."

"You have a priceless hostage for yourself in the Admiral's niece. Upon your treatment of her your fate will hang. If you are content to be her rescuer, you will find Doria generous. But if any harm should come to her it will go very ill with you. Doria is not above adopting your own barbarian methods. You'll have heard how the Venetian Bragadin was flayed alive by your Turkish brethren. That is what you may expect. And I ask myself, how should you look, Sinan, if you were flayed."

There was a glitter of rage in the little eyes. "Do you think I tremble at the name of Doria?" He was contemptuous. "He'll first have to take me; and that's a miracle he's not been able to perform in years."

"Opportunity has never favoured him as now. You are alone upon the seas. Doria's sails may come up over the horizon at any moment."

The eunuch set a slippered foot on Prospero's flank and cruelly leaned the whole of his vast weight upon it. "Wait till they appear."

"So I do. But if you wait until then to show his niece the respect due to her rank, you'll have waited too long."

Sinan leered. "How should he know that she has been my prisoner? And if he does not know that, what shall he have to avenge, even should that happen which Allah knows I do not fear?"

But from the very question Prospero inferred a certain anxiety in this man who never took an unnecessary risk of any kind. He laughed, and sat up, bringing his shoulders against what remained of the mainmast. "Is there in all that mass of you but wind and tallow? Is there no brain to that elephant body? Haven't I said that in the hour of your need Madonna Giovanna Maria Doria could be a hostage in your hands, provided that meanwhile you give her no cause to complain of you?"

Sinan kicked him viciously in the ribs. "May Allah wither thy malapert tongue. That hour is not yet."

"But you know not when it may strike."

Sinan kicked him yet again, muttered an imprecation in Arabic, and waddled away, leaving him, however, easier in mind, persuaded that for the present at least Gianna would be safe, if only out of consideration for the use to which he had shown their captor that she might be put if Sinan should encounter, as well he might, the Genoese Admiral's fleet. That this might come to pass was Prospero's present fervent prayer, despite the dread consequences it must have for him.

When presently the course of the galley was changed, Prospero conceived that this reflected Sinan's apprehension of his peril in those waters. Hisar had announced that they were making for the Straits of Boniface. But now the vessel was headed south, with the shadowy Sardinian coast that had loomed ahead fading again on their starboard quarter. The north-westerly wind had veered a point or two northwards, and the heave of the sea was rapidly diminishing. The great brown triangular foresail was hoisted, and the galley ploughed ahead, whilst, the oars being lashed down, the weary slaves slept like the dead on their benches.

The morning advanced, the sun rose higher in a sky now cloudless and the heat increased. The jovial Hisar paid a visit to the prisoners. He was accompanied by three of his men and a negro from the Sus, all but naked, who carried a bucket of water and a wooden platter on which there were some dates and biscuits. The prisoners' wrists were unbound, and this lean fare was placed before them. Pleasantly Hisar informed them that for the present they might consider themselves free of the forward half of the deck, and as pleasantly added that the least abuse of that freedom would result in their being pitched into the sea.

To rejoin the fleet from which the storm had separated him, Sinan proceeded by that shrewd reasoning which never failed him in emergency. Doria, from what they knew, should be somewhere off the northern coast of Sicily. That was the direction in which the storm must have swept Dragut. But it could hardly have swept him four hundred miles, which was the distance to Sicily; and the storm itself, from which Doria must have run for shelter, would preclude a meeting far out at sea with the Imperial fleet. The altered circumstances in which this morning he must find himself should lead Dragut to abandon the notion of the sweep through the Straits of Boniface. Instead it was almost certain that he would head directly south for Tripoli, which was their destination.

It but remained for Sinan to lay his own course thither. The wind veering farther north served him so well that soon his galley was moving at a rate of some three leagues an hour and could hardly have carried more canvas than was spread on his foremast.

Late in the afternoon of the morrow the man in the look-out cage on the foretop sighted land ahead, and a little while later reported ships, hull down on the southern horizon. When he had counted the sails with the aid of a telescope, Sinan's assurance was confirmed that this must be Dragut's fleet, and so they held confidently to their course.

They anchored that night in a cove under Cape Bona, and were off again at sunrise, as soon as the Mueddin's call from the poop and the prayer that followed it had been uttered. The tramontana which so far had driven them had now died down. But the slaves were well rested and in renewed vigour, and the oars creaked on the tholes at the rate of twenty-four strokes to the minute. Sinan was in haste.

It still wanted some two hours to noon when, as they were passing between Pantellaria and the Tunisian coast, a red galeasse emerged from the south of the green island to intercept them. From her masthead floated a banner of red and white bearing a blue crescent, to proclaim her Dragut's own flagship.

At a distance of perhaps a half-mile the Corsair captain had recognized one of his missing galleys – for he had lost two others in the storm – and a clarion summons rang across the water, to cause Sinan's helm to be swung more definitely to larboard.

Prospero, looking out from the steps of the rambade to which he had ventured to climb, remembered those neglected matters of which Sinan had reminded him, yet hoped against hope for some advantage from this meeting. He was doomed, however, to disappointment.

No sooner had Sinan cast anchor with the fleet sheltered in that little natural harbour on the southern side of Pantellaria than Dragut stepped aboard his galley, and climbed to the poop, where the eunuch awaited him.

The Anatolian was imposing in a caftan of green satin that descended to his knees and was richly wrought in golden arabesques; his red knee-boots were of finest Cordovan, each decorated by a golden tassel; a cluster of rubies glowed in the snowy turban that seemed to deepen the swarthiness of his bearded hawk face.

He came in anger to reproach his captain for having strayed, but checked when he heard what Sinan had to report. The eunuch displayed the treasure chest and the rope of pearls. "These and the men we captured," he said, "you may take as prizes of the fleet. For my own share I claim only the woman that was with them."

Dragut opened wide his dark eyes. There was amusement in the fierce depths of them.

"The woman! Bismillah! What wouldst thou with a woman, Sinan? Is she of a beauty to have wrought the miracle of making thee a man?"

The eunuch curled a malevolent lip. He did not relish jests of this nature, and Dragut was much too free with them. In Sinan's opinion they were the offspring of a paltry wit. But he answered with composure.

"She is of a beauty fit to grace the hareem of the Commander of the Faithful. She should find favour in his eyes. It is my hope to offer her as a gift to the sublime Suleyman."

Dragut grinned. "Art deep as the sea in craft, Sinan."

The eunuch raised his tallowy palms. "I would not go empty-handed into the sublime presence. It is my fortune to have found this lovely gift. So take the men and the rest, Dragut; but leave me this peri-faced houri for my share."

"Nay now. Nay. If this be such a key to the Sultan's favour, why shouldst thou have the advantage of it rather than I?"

Sinan curled his thick lip again. "Would the gift be as acceptable from thy hands?" His leer was eloquent.

Dragut understood. He laughed. "Maybe not. The thanks to Allah! So, be it as thou wilt. But let me at least behold this pearl that's fit for a Sultan's wear."

Sinan protested in horror that male eyes must not defile a face destined to gladden Suleyman's hareem. Dragut, however, was peremptory, and so, reluctantly, Madonna Gianna was bidden to ascend from her cabin in the hold.

Dragut seemed to hold his breath whilst he considered her, and his smouldering eyes aroused the uneasiness of Sinan, who knew the Anatolian's lustful ways.

When, with her head high and her expression so self-contained as to seem scornful, she stood before them, Dragut spoke.

"My captain tells me of his good fortune in serving you in your need."

"The need was none so urgent, nor the service required. But it shall be paid for. You have my word for it. The word of the Lord Admiral Doria's niece."

By this she thought to give him pause, and seemed to have succeeded. For a moment he continued to regard her with those fierce eyes. Then he uttered a soft laugh. "By the splendour of Allah!" He swung to Sinan. "That should add savour to her for Suleyman. Thou fat slyness! To have said naught of this! And the men taken with her? Who are they?"

The mention of Prospero's name moved him to such fresh and gay astonishment that, to Sinan's immense relief, it dimmed his interest in the lady. In the next moment Dragut was gone, leaping down the companion and striding along the gang-deck in quest of the prisoners.

For Prospero's seamen, huddled together near the kitchen, he had not so much as a glance. His eyes went beyond them, to rest on Prospero, himself, and there was laughter in them, of a kind that was not reassuring. It held something fierce and malicious.

"The praise to Allah, Who delivers you into my hands again, Messer Prospero. There was – was there not? – a matter of a ransom we agreed, of a hostage to be returned to me."

"You'll not suppose that I would willingly break faith." Prospero spoke with quiet dignity. "Circumstances have conspired against me. But you may now have the gold, Ser Dragut. It is in my chest that was taken by Sinan."

"Allah preserve your wit, Ser Prospero." Dragut laughed aloud. "You'll pay your ransom out of a prize of war. No doubt you'll require me to return what's over."

"Not even that. So that you'll let me have my felucca again, and those my knaves, you may keep my treasure chest."

Dragut still laughed. He brushed a hand over his forked beard. "There is a woman, too. I wonder that you do not also ask for her."

"But I do. That is understood."

"Ah! Understood? Then understand this: Sinan is fortunate. More fortunate than Kheyr-ed-Din at Fundi, when he thought to take the Lady Giulia for the Sultan's hareem. That was a piece of flesh to have gladdened the eyes and heart of Suleyman; but not so fine, I dare swear, as this one. Sinan shall have great honour when he lays this gift at the feet of the Commander of the Faithful."

Prospero was white to the lips. "But, Dragut, she is…" He checked on a sudden thought. It was scarcely a lie to anticipate intention, and it might be of effect. "She is my wife, Dragut. My wedded wife!"

"And is it so? Ah! A pity, of course. A pity! A maid would find more favour in the Grand Signor's eyes. Still, she's of a loveliness to make amends."

Horror brought Prospero's pride to the dust. He humbled himself to plead with the Corsair. "Dragut, when you were my prisoner you had generous treatment from me."

"As you had from me when you were mine. There we are quits."

"We have toiled at the oar together. Does that common suffering make no bond between us? Once you accounted that it did."

"You ended that when you broke faith with me."

"I did not break faith. It is the one thing I may boast that I have never done. Payment you would certainly have had from me, as you still shall have. Listen, Dragut. Name the ransom you'll require for both of us. Whatever it may be, at all costs it shall be procured."

"You think that I would trust you again?"

"I do not ask it. We remain your captives until the ransom comes. But as captives to be ransomed."

Dragut grinned. "If I were to say ten thousand ducats?"

"Agreed!" Prospero was eager. In his relief he felt the blood returning to his cheeks. "The money shall be fetched from Genoa. The means shall be found. These knaves of mine shall carry letters to the Bank of St George."

Broader grew Dragut's grin. "But I have not said ten thousand ducats. Nor twenty. Do you think a hundred thousand would tempt me to part with Andrea Doria's niece? Do you forget all that lies between that old sea-wolf and me? By Allah's Splendour! Perhaps he'll remember it – the infidel dog – when he hears of his niece, a daughter of his house, in the seraglio of Suleyman. Perhaps at last he'll know regret for having chained me to an oar and made me know the lash of the wardens' whips when I whip his wicked old soul with the thought of that."

"And I, then?" cried Prospero. "Do I count for nothing? I have told you that Doria's niece is my wedded wife."

Dragut raised his shoulders. "Shall I forgo so rich a vengeance because of what you may suffer? I owe you nothing. And if I did, is it not in the will of Allah, the All-knowing, the All-pitiful, that the punishment of the guilty be often shared by the guiltless? I commiserate you, Ser Prospero. But not so far as to deny myself so sweet a cup, or the Sultan so sweet a gift. It was well thought of by Sinan."

Then Prospero's self-possession left him. He cursed Dragut for a misbegotten scoundrel in the most virulent terms supplied by East and West. And all the while Dragut stood before him like a laughing devil, refusing to be moved to anger by this invective even when it reached its envenomed worst. When at last the storm was spent, and Prospero stood shamed by his own fury which had but made him an object of mockery, Dragut spoke.

"So, so. Words draw no blood. But having uttered them, be content. For less another would send you to the oar. And so may I if you begin again. You and your fellows will come aboard my galeasse, and you'll suffer no harm so long as you are circumspect. But circumspect, by Allah, you shall be."

Chapter 25

The Trap

One glimmer of light there was for Prospero in all this darkness. Since Gianna was to be reserved as an offering for the Grand Signor, it followed that meanwhile she would be jealously guarded and considerately used by her captors. Intolerable to contemplate as were their intentions, at least fulfilment was not imminent. There was time, and in time there is always hope because of the incalculable element in the flow of the events.

When Dragut had come to consider the great strength of those who hunted him and to realize how hot was the chase upon his heels, he resolved at last to seek the assured safety that lay in following Kheyr-ed-Din to Istanbul. There, merging his navy with the Sultan's, he would place himself once more under the orders of his old commander. First, however, he must await at Djerba, to which he had bidden him follow, the arrival of the reinforcements Yarin Sabah had been sent to raise in Algiers; this because those additional galleys, unless incorporated with his fleet, might be imperilled, and further because, swollen in strength by them, he would be more assured of a welcome from the Sublime Portal.

So they weighed anchor at Pantellaria, and steered a leisurely southern course that took them past Dragut's ravaged seat of Mehedia. Whilst accounting it imprudent to enter the port, yet Dragut committed an imprudence almost equal by going within less than a half-mile of it, from a natural anxiety to behold the place at close quarters and estimate the ravages. Thence he launched a bitter curse upon the unbelieving pigs who had despoiled his stronghold, and slowly coasted on.

He was in no haste. There was small likelihood of pursuit in these waters, and he must linger in them until the reinforcements came. This, he knew, could not be yet for some weeks.

In a broiling heat from which no breeze brought relief, over a sea of glass that mirrored every shroud, the galleys crawled south with the brigantines in tow. Past Sfax and the Karkennah Islands they crossed the vast Gulf of Gabes, and came at last to the shallow waters about Djerba, Homer's Island of the Lotophagi. With all the precautions which the place demands, and not until the tide was flowing, did the galleys thread the channel through the shoals of the bottle-neck into the bight beyond. Twenty miles in length by fifteen miles across, this great and almost circular lagoon lies between the rugged mainland of Syrtis Minor and the green, flat Djerba which is called an island. Strictly, at the highest tides, it does just answer the description; for then, on the south-east, a thin skin of water is spread over a couple of miles of the marshy lands where flamingoes feed and nest. Even then, however, a causeway known as Tarik-el-Djemil supplies a safe road across this marshland; so that Djerba properly is not an island at all, but a peninsula.

Coming within the great lagoon Dragut's fleet followed the shore of Djerba, as far as the village of Houmt Ajim, a huddle of houses about a white domed mosque, some of stone, some of clay tiles mortared with dung and roofed with the reeds of which the marshes yielded abundance. Here in a pellucid bight that was fringed with feathery tamarisks above the line of silvery beach the Corsair fleet cast anchor. Its coming was hailed as an opportunity for trade by the dwellers of that land, flat and fertile as a garden, in which the shining green summits of the date palms towered everywhere above the grey green of olives and the lustrous green of fig and loquat. Berber women, light complexioned and unveiled, came down to the water-side with osier baskets on their heads, laden with great golden plums, syrupy locust beans, dates and water-melons which ripen early in that favoured clime, cereals, eggs, chickens, and the like. They put off with their men in high-prowed boats and came to offer their wares with importunate cries that did not go unheeded. If the fruit of the lotus was to be sought in vain in this lotus-eaters' island of the ancients, the fruits that did grow there were luscious and welcome to the Corsairs. In the days that followed even the wretched slaves knew something better than the hard biscuit and the handful of beans of their daily fare.

Dragut, being assured that hidden away in this bight he might wait undisturbed for the coming of his reinforcements, took the opportunity to careen his galleys, five at a time, so as to tallow their keels. Amongst the first to be dismantled and hauled up the gently shelving beach were those which had suffered in the storm and were in need of some repair. A forge was set up ashore, and the slaves were put to work. For five days their labours proceeded serenely and unhurried. Then a messenger, dispatched on a swift camel from the village of Houmt-es-Soum on the northern coast, rode across to the anchorage with news of a great fleet approaching from the north across the Gulf of Gabes.

Startled and uneasy, Dragut called for horses, and with a few of his officers went off, himself to survey the reported vessels.

They were within a mile of the straits when he beheld them, and in the shallow water which they had reached they were casting anchor: thirty-six galleys and galeasses with ancillary and transport vessels, numbering nearly as many. Some flew the red and gold of Spain, others the red and white of Genoa; but it needed no banners to tell Dragut with whom he had to deal. Already at his anchorage, when word had been brought of this fleet's coming, he had known that it could not yet be the supplement he expected from Algiers, and that be it by some compact with Shaitan, be it by some other form of evil Nasrani magic, Andrea Doria had tracked him across the trackless ways of ocean.

Later, in a calmer moment, he was to remember how near the coast he had sailed in passing Mehedia and what traces he had, therefore, left. On his first sight of the enemy, however, he was filled with a superstitious dread, that turned him pale under his deep tan. The infernal Genoese held him at his mercy. The accursed lagoon in which he accounted himself so safely and unsuspectedly hidden was now become a trap from which there was no issue. And those unbelieving children of the Pit were aware of it, or they would not be content to anchor there, guarding the only gateway by which the Corsairs must come forth. He raged like a madman before his officers, gesticulating wildly, calling down curses on Andrea Doria, on the Lagoon of Djerba, and on his own folly in having placed himself in a position to be thus trapped. Then, having exhausted himself in imprecation, he wheeled the mettlesome Arab barb that carried him, and with his officers, rode back at a wild gallop to his anchorage, ten miles away.

His return made some stir in the fleet. Word of Doria's coming ran through the ranks of the fighting men to strike them into consternation. From these it spread to the slaves, and awakened hope in the bosoms of some two thousand Christians of all nations who were at Dragut's oars.

To none, however, was the news so welcome as to Prospero. He had lived through days that were to form the ugliest memories of all his life, days of listless, stunned despair, most of which had been spent in the utter idleness to which his numbed condition doomed him. His few men had been incorporated in the slave gang of Dragut's galeasse. He, himself, however, had been left at liberty within the confines of that prison. Dragut had assigned to him a cabin in the hold, and had given him, moreover, the freedom of the tabernacle and of his own table, treating him in spite of the past with the consideration due to a prisoner of his rank until he should finally take orders about him. Prospero had remained not merely insensible to this consideration but resentful of it. He shunned the tabernacle, so as to avoid the Corsair's company and courtesies, which in all the circumstances seemed no better than a studied mockery. Yet since he was served at the Corsair's table, he could not entirely avoid him save at the cost of going without food, and of that table Dragut did the honours with a joviality which took no account of his prisoner's torment, his grim silence and increasingly haggard air.

If he had been concerned to consider himself, Prospero would have had little cause to give thanks that Doria was at hand and Dragut trapped. But since he could now dismiss the unspeakable horror hitherto constantly before him of the fate Sinan had intended for Gianna, his spirit soared in thankfulness, and it was an almost airy Prospero who confronted Dragut on his return from Houmt-es-Soum.

Preoccupied by his own peril, Dragut did not at first remark this change. He brooded measures to be taken, even whilst he believed them futile, so as to parry the blow that threatened him. He ordered and supervised the landing of a dozen of his most powerful cannon. He sent for the old Khadab, the Sheik of Djerba, and induced him to impress into Corsair service a couple of thousand Berbers to aid Dragut's own slaves in the swift construction of a fort on the promontory at the entrance of the straits, where the landed ordnance was to be mounted. Then, without staying to dine, he was away again to supervise in person the erection of that stronghold. Under the hard-driven labours of Berbers and slaves swarming there like a colony of ants, the earthworks seemed to rise out of the ground before the eyes of the beholder. Date palms were felled, and the tough brown boles, over sixty feet in length, went with even tougher, age-old tamarisks, to make a parapet behind a breastwork of osier gabions which Berber men and women were feverishly weaving and filling with earth as soon as they were in position.

In a matter of hours, almost by the time that panting, sweating, naked slaves had dragged the ordnance to the site, the work was miraculously accomplished, and it remained only to emplace the ponderous guns. To this task the slaves were set before they could rest their aching limbs and breathe at ease again.

Dragut's officers moved in brisk relentless supervision, bawling orders, plying whips, driving gangs to work at this point or at that, whilst Dragut himself was everywhere, his dark fierce eyes missing no detail, his voice harsh with impatience, correcting errors, commanding improvements.

It was finished at last, and Dragut came down from the broad parapet whence he had made a last survey of the whole. The satisfaction that he took in it was no sooner born than it was dimmed by reflection of how utterly inadequate it was to his real need. A crisp voice at his elbow was almost an echo of his thought.

"So much toil to so little purpose, Messer Dragut."

He swung round to find Prospero at his side. He scowled in fierce surprise.

"You here? By whose leave? What brings you?"

"Curiosity. None hindered my coming." He was at ease, whilst Dragut breathed fury through distended nostrils. "I was deploring such vain effort and wasted ingenuity." He smiled. "You but fortify the door of your own prison, Messer Dragut."

It needed no more than this to make Dragut aware of it; therefore was his rage the hotter at conceiving himself mocked. "May Allah cast thy soul into the Pit!"

He would have gone on but for the prayer with which the curse was met. "May Allah send thee sight to see where safety lies."

Dragut's anger was checked by sheer astonishment. A moment he stared, round-eyed.

"Do you see that?" he asked at last.

"I might if I were concerned to save you from this doom."

"Doom? Where is the doom?" Dragut was breathing fire again. "Let that misbegotten Genoese attempt to enter the lagoon, and you shall see whose is the doom."

"Oh yes. If that were all, you have provided well. But why shall Andrea Doria trouble to come in, when all his need will be served by waiting until you go out? And he'll wait patiently. Patiently. As a vulture."

To Dragut the image was infelicitous. He answered it with a foul imprecation, and followed that by a question: "Under what need am I to go forth?"

"To be sure, you could settle down to agriculture in Djerba."

Dragut clenched his hands. Yet the very doubts that troubled him made him curb his rage and argue with this mocker. "If I cannot stay here forever, neither can Doria; and I have the advantage of being in shelter. At need I can wait until the winter storms come to drive him away."

Prospero laughed, reckless of the anger he provoked not only in Dragut, but in the growling, scowling Corsair captains who stood about them. "And of course Doria is a fool. He will not think of that."

"Thinking of it will not help him."

"Will it not? I know what I should do were I in Doria's place. When weary of waiting for you, I should land a force over there on the east of Djerba, in sufficient strength to seize this fort of yours, and after that sail in to make an end of you. Do you suppose that Doria will not think of it?"

It was the Corsair's turn to laugh. "May Allah so inspire him to his ruin. He will need half the strength of his fleet for that. The moment he puts it ashore I'll go out to smash the other half long before he can be master of the gateway. That's why I build this fort. Now perhaps you'll account it less idle."

On that, conceiving it the last word, he would have turned away. But Prospero's rejoinder stayed him. "Why must you still suppose that Doria is blind to what you perceive so clearly? He will be content to hold you trapped here until he is reinforced by the troops he'll require for a landing. He need send no farther than Naples for them, and I'll wager that he has sent already. It's a long while yet to winter, Dragut, and Doria, as I've said, knows how to be patient." And to gall the Corsair, he repeated the ominous phrase: "As a vulture."

Momentarily there was dismay on Dragut's hawk face. That presently he should grin was merest bluster. "Build your hopes of deliverance on that," he mocked, "and you'll have a fool's wages." Then, weary of this colloquy which stirred the wondering anger of his captains, he grew stern. "Get you back to my galley, and see that you stay aboard. Let me find you ashore again without leave, and I'll have you in irons. Irja! Away!"

He waved an angry hand, and turned on his heel abruptly. Prospero went back to the flagship under the escort of a couple of Corsair officers. But for the moment he was content. That they would return to the subject he was persuaded, and also that when they did he could ensure Gianna's safety, if not indeed her immediate deliverance.

In the three days that followed he scarcely had a glimpse of Dragut. The Anatolian came aboard his galeasse only to sleep. His waking hours were spent at his fort, watching with eyes that grew daily more blood-injected the Imperial fleet at anchor a full mile away, just out of range, in a great arc that stretched from the mainland to a point in line with the easternmost spur of the island. Under the steely azure of the sky, immovable upon the glassy sea of those breathless July days, the Genoese galleys were content to drowse, waiting until the trapped foe should be driven by despair to make the first move.

And the trapped foe, observing their cursed immobility, found himself regarding them in the evil image Prospero had invoked, as a flock of waiting vultures. Daily his face grew more drawn, his eyes more haggard, his temper more fretful and his invective more virulent. Never since the affair in the road of Goialatta, when he had fallen a prisoner to the Genoese, had Dragut-Reis found himself in so desperate a situation. And at Goialatta there had been the chances of battle, whilst here, such were the odds that there was no chance at all.

In the lagoon, meanwhile, the careening and the greasing of keels had been abandoned, since at any moment Dragut might need his every ship. The crews idled without occupation, putting their trust none too hopefully in Dragut and Allah to extricate them from a situation whose desperate nature was perceived by all.

On the evening of the third day, the pride which had kept Dragut from asking a question prompted by Prospero's own words at the fort broke down under the strain. Coming aboard his galeasse, he sent for the Genoese.

Prospero was conducted to the tabernacle, where Dragut sat cross-legged on his gaudy divan awaiting him. He had flung off his caftan, and save for his dusky bearded face, he was all white from head to foot.

"The other day you hinted... At what did you hint, when you prayed that Allah might send me sight to see where safety lies?"

"At my friendly desire to see you delivered from the net that Doria has spread for you," was the soft answer.

"To be sure. To be sure," snarled Dragut. "So Allah prosper you! The friendly desire should beget in you the will to assist. You might find it worth your while."

"I hoped that you would realize it." Prospero found himself a low Turkish table inlaid with ivory and mother-of-pearl, and using it as a stool, sat down upon it. "You are fortunate beyond your deserts, Dragut, that in this extremity, probably the most desperate you will ever know, you actually hold the price of deliverance. I wonder you had not thought of it for yourself. Send word to Andrea Doria that you hold his niece, and propose to him that he ransom her by according you a free passage out to sea."

Prospero spoke easily, dissembling his anxiety. In the breathlessness of the gambler who has staked his all, he awaited the result of the throw. Dragut's eyes had opened a little wider, and for a long moment he was content to stare at the Genoese. Slowly, at last, he spoke, and there was a sneer in his tone.

"You unbelievers set a high value on your women, I know. But that one woman should suffice to ransom Dragut-Reis and all his fleet is too much to believe."

"I do not ask you to believe it. But to test it."

"Jahil! A waste of time."

"What other use have you for time just now? Test it, Dragut. If no good comes of it, at least your case will be no worse."

"Save that this Genoese dog will have the laugh of me."

"What is the risk of that against the risk of the greater laugh that will be his if you do nothing?"

"May Allah rot thy tongue!" growled Dragut. But he added: "I'll think of it."

Though the thought he gave to it brought him no conviction, yet it sent him betimes on the morrow aboard Sinan's galley. He was in no case to neglect any chance, however desperate. He met Sinan's greeting with a demand that the woman be brought to him.

The eunuch roused himself from the listlessness in which he had sat during most of these days like a gross incarnation of fatalism itself, and his little eyes glittered suspiciously as they scanned his captain's face.

"What dost thou want with her, Dragut?" He curled his lip, and slowly shook his head. "This woman is not for thee. You know the destiny I give her."

"I may have another for her," was the dry answer.

It was enough to stir the anger of Sinan. It set the loose mass of him trembling. "She is mine," he screeched. "My prize. My share of what was taken. That was agreed, and we will keep to it."

"May Allah send thee wit. Before you can offer this pearl to Suleyman we must get away from Djerba." Shortly he announced the purpose Madonna Gianna was to serve in this; and so, partly by argument, partly by despotic insistence, constrained a reluctant Sinan to bring her forth.

She came, bearing herself with that placidity which was beyond the understanding of these men. She was mantled, as when taken, in grey samite with a hood to cover the under-cap of grey velvet with a jewelled edge that confined her dark hair. Her countenance was of a pallor deeper than normal, there were shadows under her eyes and lines of suffering drawn by her confinement and anxiety. But she stood before them without plaint or prayer, with something of scorn in the almost unnatural aloofness that acted as a challenge upon Dragut.

He had seated himself upon the divan, at some distance from Sinan, and from a goose-quill demanded of the eunuch, he was cutting a pen. He suspended the task, so as to regard her, and thus continued for some instants with such a kindling in his dark eyes that Sinan, grown uneasy, leaned over to pluck at the sleeve of his caftan, squealing an admonition in Arabic.

The Anatolian roused himself, and in quiet, even tones informed the lady of the purpose for which he sought her. She was required to write a letter to her uncle, the Admiral Andrea Doria, the terms of which he announced to her. It was necessary that she, herself, should write this letter so that it should supply the evidence of her presence on the Moslem galley.

It was her first intimation that Andrea Doria was at hand and in such strength that he held her captors in a check that drove them to this expedient. The news robbed her of her statuesque calm. Under its gold-laced corsage her bosom heaved in an excitement she could not repress, her eyes widened and quickened with a sudden eagerness, some colour crept into her pallid face. But very soon, upon reflection, these signs of hope were put aside again. Her consent to write the letter was given impassively. She was, she said, too well acquainted with the Admiral's high sense of duty to suppose that he would permit her to become the object of such a barter.

"So I, too, supposed," said Dragut, glooming now. "But the notion is Messer Prospero's."

Gathering from this that at least all was as well with Prospero as in the circumstances could be expected, she took heart. Of Sinan's intentions concerning her she had mercifully been spared all suspicion, so that even failing succour from Andrea Doria, she could not regard as hopeless their situation.

But that she had well-judged the Admiral's mind was seen when Doria's answer came that evening. It was couched in such insulting terms that Dragut went near to venting upon him who had inspired the proposal the rage aroused in him by its rejection.

However taken aback to discover that his niece was in Dragut's power, Doria mocked the Corsair by the assertion that he was under no necessity to bargain with him for something that he would presently take for himself. He contented himself with a warning that if in the meantime any harm should befall Madonna Gianna, Dragut would not receive at his hands even such quarter as a Corsair might expect, but would be dealt with like the scoundrelly thieving pirate that he was. He should know what it was to be flung on the hooks and left to perish gradually through days of torment. He ended by giving Dragut the choice between coming forth to surrender without further waste of time and waiting until the Imperial Admiral should have completed his preparations to come in and take him.

Dragut ground his strong teeth as the letter was read to him by one of his Christian slaves. At the end he tore it from the cowering reader's hand, and crumpled it as he would have crumpled the writer had he held him at that moment. Next he bade one of the wardens fetch Prospero to the tabernacle, and when Prospero came he regaled his ears with the astoundingly passionate fluency with which he cursed the Imperial Admiral. He pronounced authoritatively upon the evil reputation of Doria's mother and the inevitably shameful destiny of his daughters and their female offspring. He foretold how dogs would certainly defile the Admiral's grave, and he called perfervidly upon Allah to rot the bones and destroy the house of that unbelieving pig.

Having thus spewed up some of the gall that bubbled in him as he paced the narrow limits of the cabin, he smoothed again the crumpled sheet. "Behold the answer of that misbegotten bastard of Shaitan. Read the foul insolence your advice has earned me. Ay, and worse than insolence. It has disclosed too much to Doria. The situation is worse than it was, thanks to your cursed counsel."

Prospero took the letter, and stood to read it in an affected calm, whilst the tall figure of Dragut, all in white, moved about the cabin with the lithe fury of a panther.

"At least," said Prospero coolly, when he had read, "you know what to expect if any injury should be done to her."

The Corsair checked in his pacing, swung about and faced Prospero in a half-crouching attitude, as if about to spring upon him. His teeth were bared and his eyes baleful.

"And that is what you played for, when you persuaded me with your smooth lies to disclose her presence to Doria. That was all your crafty aim."

"Not all of it. No," was the quiet answer. "I was not without hope that Doria might be led to treat with you. But I'll confess that I perceived how Doria, once he knew that his niece is in your power, might put a bridle on your intentions for her." And he proffered the letter again.

Dragut snatched it from him, crumpled it as before, and tossed it aside. There was a foam on his lips and flecks of it on his black beard.

"You think to have succeeded, do you? You think to have fooled me finely with your infernal Italian subtlety. But, by the Beard of Mahomet, it shall not profit you. If I thought it would, I'd hang you out of hand for this." He flung about the cabin again, his voice pitched high by his consuming rage. "You smugly think with Doria that I have to choose between going out to be destroyed and waiting here to be destroyed. You think there is no issue for me. But, the praise to Allah, I, too, have my subtleties." He laughed savagely. "There's a way out that has occurred to neither of you, and tomorrow I take it.

"I pay a bitter price; but at least there shall be no gain either for Doria or for you. Not a ship of mine, not a man of mine, shall fall into his swinish hands. Least of all shall he ever again see this niece whom he so insolently boasts that he can come and take when he pleases."

It was a vindictive fury that made him disclose all, so as to smother in despair the hope that Prospero had betrayed. "Tomorrow we cross the lagoon and land at Bou Ghara. There I'll scuttle my fleet before setting out on an overland march of three hundred dreary leagues to Algiers. When Doria, weary of guarding an empty trap, at last discovers what has happened, do you think he will regret his insolent refusal to make terms? And when he hears that his niece, who might have graced the Sultan's hareem, is gladdening mine, will he regret it then?"

For a moment Prospero was as stunned as if he had been bludgeoned. Then he braced himself to answer almost mechanically: "Not half so much as you will regret your scuttled fleet."

It was a shaft in the very vitals of the Corsair. His face was distorted. Almost he seemed to Prospero on the point of tears. "Haven't I confessed the bitterness of it?" he cried out. Then commanding himself, he added more quietly: "But since it is the will of Allah, I must console myself as I can."

Greatly daring in the face of the Corsair's dangerous mood, Prospero displayed scorn. "To speak of this as a way out! What more could victory give Doria? Your fleet sunk, yourself and your followers a fugitive errant band in the desert, driven from the seas for many a long day! In your place, Dragut, I would go out and set all upon the hazard of a battle. Your defeat would be no more costly to you."

"Do you advise, or do you merely mock? Of your advice I have had a surfeit. Your mockery will make an end of the little patience I can still use with you. Be warned."

On that, he strode past Prospero, flung down the short companion, and bawling for his sloop, departed the galley and went ashore.

He rode away at once to his fort at Houmt Soum, and seeing some of the Imperial galleys moving, as if on a reconnaissance, at a distance of rather more than a mile, he childishly vented his spite by emptying all his cannon at them, knowing well that there was no hope of reaching them at that range.

That cannonade, which seemed to shake the very island, filled the hot sky with screaming sea-birds, and brought the Berber inhabitants in flocks to discover what might be happening. But it also served to warn Doria of the extent of Dragut's fortifications and of the might and number of the guns of which he would have to run the gauntlet if he should attempt to force the passage of the straits.

The Imperial Admiral, however, had no thought of that. He was proceeding exactly as Prospero had assumed. Already one of his fastest triremes was speeding north to Naples for troops with which to force the issue by a landing on Djerba should Dragut not come forth meanwhile. And at the same time, in his impatience to repair any damage his credit might have sustained in Imperial eyes, the Admiral ventured to anticipate events in the report he sent the

Emperor, by announcing that Dragut-Reis was held fast and could already be accounted taken and destroyed with all his fleet. To this splendid piece of news he added a relation of the raid upon Mehedia in terms which, making an epic of it, were calculated to gild the fame of Andrea Doria.

He could laugh at the roar of Dragut's guns as he might have laughed at the puerile grimace of an ill-mannered urchin; but he ordered his galleys to see to it that they kept themselves at a safe distance from the shore.

Chapter 1

The Plan

"La Illaha Illa Allah!"

So sang the mueddin at sunrise reciting the Shehad from the poop of Dragut's galeasse, and on the morning stillness the cry rang plaintively across the water. It awoke the line of anchored galleys to life, and brought the Faithful to prostrate themselves, their faces turned towards Mecca. It disturbed a flock of sea-birds, and set them circling and mewing in the flushed sky overhead. It awoke Prospero where he lay in chains on the platform amidships.

From the paralysis of horror in which yesterday Dragut had left him, he had roused himself to the frenzy of a man battling for his life. Even the factor of time upon which he had been resting his faint hopes was now denied him, since Gianna, no longer guarded for ultimate consignment to the Sultan's hareem, was to pass at once into the power of a Dragut whom lust and vindictiveness would strip of that thin veneer of chivalry with which it was his vanity to adorn himself in Frankish eyes.

For a full hour and more after Dragut's departure Prospero had desperately plied his wits to discover an issue from this horror that produced in him a sense of physical nausea. Now huddled upon the divan, with his elbows on his knees and his chin on his fists, now pacing as restlessly as Dragut had erstwhile paced, he brooded, whipping the poet's inventiveness in vain and with ever-mounting despair. Then, suddenly a glimmer of light had come to him, in an idea so wild that he must have put it from him if his case had not been such that he could discard no hope however extravagant.

Scarcely daring to reflect upon it lest its futility should become too apparent, he quitted the tabernacle in a fever of sudden haste, and defying the ban which forbade him to quit the galley, he had himself pulled ashore in the long-boat which waited alongside. There, at the encampment on the beach, on a pretence that he required it in the service of Dragut, he obtained after some argument a horse. He was without hat or doublet, in trunks and hose of a deep wine colour, with grey boots of soft leather, laced at the side and turned over at the knee. To protect his head against the ardour of the sun, he tied a white kerchief about his long chestnut locks, and thus accoutred rode away south along the shore.

He came back after some hours, to be met by a raging Dragut, who, refusing to listen to anything that he might say, ordered him incontinently to be put into irons for his disregard of the condition on which he enjoyed the freedom of the galley.

Prospero had resigned himself. He was the better able to do so because his quest had been far from fruitless, and in the hours of darkness, as he lay there on deck in his chains, he gave his mind to a perfection of the notion with which he had been inspired. Overnight he thought Dragut would have cooled from his anger, and he was confident that a word that he would send him must compel the Corsair's attention. To this thought he awoke at the mueddin's call, and lay listening to the murmur of the breeze in the tamarisks and the silken rustle of the tide on the silver strand.

Soon followed other and more violent sounds. After the pious opening of the new day came a bustle through all the fleet in preparation for departure from this station.

An air of sullenness reigned aboard Dragut's galleasse, and would be reigning similarly, no doubt, aboard the others. The Moslem crews could not look complacently upon an escape that was indistinguishable from defeat, or upon a three-hundred-league journey overland, which most of them would have to perform on foot, since such camels and horses as they might procure at Bou Ghara and elsewhere would be used by the officers and the baggage they might save.

Dragut, fierce of aspect, made intermittent appearances on the poop to issue his ill-humoured orders, and it was as a result of one of these that presently a sloop came alongside, out of which Prospero beheld the vast bulk of Sinan-el-Sanim heaving itself aboard. Wheezing and squealing, the eunuch rolled across the vestibule towards the companion, and there checked as Dragut appeared at the head of it to apostrophize him savagely.

"What make you here, Sinan? I did not send for you. Back to your galley, to make ready to take up anchor, and send the woman to me here at once, as you were ordered. At once. Do you hear me?"

"I hear you, Dragut," the eunuch raged back at him, squealing. "I hear you. But I am not to be abused. She is all that I claimed as my share of the booty, and, by the Beard of the Prophet, I'll not be robbed."

Thus began an altercation between the Corsair leader and his subordinate conducted in a jargon that mingled Arabic with the Lingua Franca, and was as intelligible as it was audible to Prospero where he lay. For he was not the only soul aboard who was attentive, and a silence had fallen on the vessel.

Dragut was contending that since Sinan's purpose with the woman was now frustrated by the events, she was no longer of any consequence to him. For himself Sinan could not want her; and as an offering to Suleyman, Allah alone knew now when they would come to Istanbul. To this in reason there was no answer. But Sinan in his spluttering wrath cared nothing for reason. He continued to clamour until Dragut, completely losing patience, threatened to have him thrown into the sea if he continued to pester him, and dispatched his kayia to Sinan's galley, to fetch the woman.

"But I'll not cheat you, Sinan," he protested. "Set a fair price on her, such as she would fetch in the souk at Algiers, and I will pay it. Now begone with my kayia, and trouble me no more. Away!"

Dragut's intentions left no room in Prospero for any doubt. The quick hot lust of the man aroused by Gianna's beauty, stimulated by her very aloofness, was reinforced by the vindictive satisfaction he perceived in the possession of Doria's niece. The very kinship that should have been her protection was become a provocation.

Raging, Prospero rose in his irons, and raging yelled: "Dragut!"

In the act of re-entering the tabernacle, Dragut turned at the call. He looked down the vessel at his prisoner, a smile of ineffable malice parting the red lips within his black beard. "Is it you, Messer Prospero?"

Prospero mastered himself. "I have something to say to you." He began to move forward, slowly and painfully, hobbled as he was, his chains clanking and thudding on the deck. With a shrug Dragut was turning away again, when again Prospero checked him. "If you do not listen and at once, you will regret it all your life, Dragut. I bring you your salvation."

He had reached the foot of the companion. From the head of it Dragut sneered down upon him: "I've had enough salvation of the kind you offer, my friend. I'll find my own, in my own way."

"The way of ruin and defeat. The way of shame. What I offer you is the next thing to victory: the way to save your fleet."

For a long moment Dragut continued to sneer at the incredible boast. And yet, his desperate case being such that he must snatch at any hope, even as he sneered he was telling himself that he would be a fool if he did not at least hear this man.

"To save my fleet, do you say? Bismillah! If you trifle with me, I will so deal with you, as Allah hears me, that you will never trifle in this world again."

"I am no trifler, as you should know." Laboriously Prospero dragged himself step by step to the poop under the stare of the turbaned mob that stood about. He clanked into the shadow of the tabernacle, signing to Dragut to follow him. As he went the Corsair could only renew his warning.

"Be warned, Messer Prospero," he said, and the intensity of his tone showed how little strain his patience was capable of bearing.

Nevertheless, Prospero, with all that he valued in life at stake, played his game in his own way without regard for the Corsair's fierce impatience.

"There is a possibility that I was studying yesterday, when I disregarded the ban under which you placed me." He indicated his fetters. "This is a poor return for the service I was seeking to do you. But last night you would not listen. You are so hot and rash, Dragut. One of these days it will be the end of you."

"I am listening now," Dragut reminded him savagely. "Speak out. If you are not at your tricks, if by Allah's light you have seen a way to save this fleet, let me hear it."

"You shall hear it when you agree my terms."

"Terms? Y'Allah! Do you bargain with me?"

"Would you not bargain for so great a service? What would you not offer to the man who can show you how to win out of this trap in all the pride of your strength, instead of slinking back to Algiers, a stripped and discredited fugitive? What would you give for that, Dragut?"

Dragut showed his teeth. He gripped Prospero by the shoulders in his steely fingers. "What's in your mind, man? Let me have it."

"You have not answered my question."

"Mash'Allah!" Dragut shook him. "How can I answer it until I know your thought?"

"How can I disclose it until you pledge yourself?"

"May the Pit receive thee! Shall I pledge myself before I know that you can make good this boast?"

"A conditional pledge, Dragut. No more. You do not pay until the thing is done, until you have regained the open sea with your fleet, and cheated Doria by eluding him."

Dragut glared at him. He was breathing in gasps and his complexion had assumed a greenish tinge from the excitement such a prospect stirred in him.

"I am in your hands," Prospero reminded him. "You shall do with me as you please if I fail."

"Aye, aye!" This was an argument that persuaded Dragut. "Your terms, then? What do you ask?"

"I'll be easy with you. I might ask the half of your possessions, and you'd not dare refuse me. But I am modest. First, there is the ransom that I owe you from Cherchell. You'll acquit me of that."

"Yes, yes. And then?"

"The ransom that you would now exact for me and my wife."

Dragut glared more fiercely still. "The woman is not for ransom."

Prospero curbed with iron will the impulse to take Dragut by the throat. He smiled. "In that case I have no more to say."

Again Dragut took him by the shoulder, and thrust a livid, furious face within a hand's breadth of Prospero's. "We have ways to make men talk."

Now Prospero laughed. "They are the surest ways to make me dumb. Bah, Dragut! I have accounted you both wise and generous; and you are neither. You disappoint me. You covet my woman," he continued. "Has the Prophet no law against it? And even if he had not, is she worth more than all your fleet to you?"

Dragut loosed his grip of Prospero's shoulder and turned away. With clenched hands he strode the length of the cabin and back. "What else do you ask for this service you pretend that you can render?"

"The life and liberty of the poor knaves that were with me when Sinan captured us."

"That is naught. You may have them. Now! Your plan?"

"Wait. Wait. I am not yet at the end of my requirements. You'll restore my ducats. So far I have but asked for what is rightly mine. You will add a vessel in which we may resume the voyage you interrupted. I will accept a galley of six-and-twenty oars, suitably armed and equipped, and furnished with a proper complement of slaves."

"May Allah blot thee out! And is that all?"

"This galley you shall place at my disposal as soon as you are satisfied that I can do as I promise. And that will be today. I shall take up my quarters aboard her together with my wife, my treasure and my knaves." To meet the suspicion darkening Dragut's countenance, he added: "You may leave aboard what troops you please, to guard against any treachery you may fear. That is all, Dragut, for a greater service than any man has done you since you took to following the sea."

"Your plan?" barked Dragut.

"To open a way out of this trap for you."

"Yes, yes. Y'Allah! Will you drive me mad? But how? How?"

"You have not said that you agree my terms."

"I agree them. Yes. May Allah strike thee dead! Do you need an oath? Show me the way hence, so that I may be spared to wield the scimitar against the foes of Islam and increase the glory of the Prophet's holy law, and I swear to you upon Alcoran and by the Beard of Mahomet that I will faithfully keep those terms. Is that enough?"

"It is enough," said Prospero. For Dragut was known to be as faithful to his word as any Christian knight.

"The praise to Him! Now let me hear what you would do."

"Ride with me to the strip of land that joins Djerba to Syrtis, and I will show you."

The hope faded from Dragut's expectant glance. "If you think there is an issue that way, you are in a fool's dream."

"I am in no fool's dream. I have surveyed the place and I have well considered. Come with me, and I will show you where the issue lies."

Chapfallen, Dragut continued to stare at him, as if again suspicious that he jested. At last he hunched his shoulders, spread his hands. "To be sure all things are possible to Allah," he said, as if to remind himself of that article of faith. But his tone was gloomy. "Let us go, then."

Relieved of his fetters, and still dressed as yesterday, booted, but without doublet or hat, Prospero again rode south, with Dragut beside him, and a half-dozen mounted followers behind.

They went by groves of olive trees, which the Romans had first planted in Djerba, through Berber villages where naked children scuttled into hiding at their approach, whilst shawled women stood to see them pass. By more than one pile of sculptured stones and broken pillars to remind men still that here had been once an outpost of mighty Rome, they came in the burning heat of approaching noon to the edge of the marshlands, where an imperfect isthmus, two miles in width, raised a yellowish green bar between blue sea and blue lagoon. The tide was making, and the rising waters were creeping about the tussocks of the boggy ground and lapping against the edges of the causeway. On this a troop of Bedouins, with a dozen camels and as many horses, made noisy haste to cross before the waters overtopped the solid way.

From among the tall reeds at the edge of the marshes, where Dragut's party drew rein, a flock of flamingoes arose with vibrant beat of their great wings, circled, and sped westward, a rosy cloud against the steely blue dome of heaven.

Prospero, upright in his stirrups, shaded his eyes with his hand and surveyed the isthmus. Then he waved that same hand. "There lies your way, Dragut," he said.

This was to exasperate the Corsair. "There is no way. May Allah blacken thee! Should I be in a trap if there were an outlet on this side? Don't you see the camel-road, unbroken from end to end."

"Unbroken, yes. But not unbreakable. And we might break it."

"Insh' Allah! But even then? Can I float my galleys through those puddles in the marshes?"

"We will go on," said Prospero, and led the way farther towards the ruins of El Kantara that may well once have been the Roman capital of Djerba.

Disgruntled, with hopes now dead, Dragut, nevertheless, still followed.

They reached the outer end of the isthmus, and drew rein again by the open sea, on the golden sands where the wavelets curled and broke in froth. On their left was a great bay, and beyond it a coastline running north-east, the only high ground of Djerba.

"This is your way out," said Prospero again, his eyes as bright as the Corsair's were gloomy.

"Do you repeat that parrot-cry? Is it a jest? If so it may be your last. Are we flamingoes?"

"Almost as poor-witted."

"So, so! Ha! Find me a way through that for my fleet, and as Allah hears me I'll be as the dust beneath thy feet. Fail to find it me, and…"

But Prospero cut the menace short. "Give me a free hand, and in six days, if not in less, I'll have your fleet here in this bay, whence on the first dark night you may weigh anchor, and with the open seas before you slip quietly away. You'll be hull down on the horizon before the following dawn, whilst Doria continues to guard the mouth of an empty trap."

It was a boast that made every man of the company catch his breath. Dragut, however, needed more. "A dream," he condemned it. "A Nasrani's drunken dream."

"A dream, to be sure. That is the beginning of all things. The world was a dream before Allah made it a fact, as I will make this dream of mine. We'll need for that, in addition to your slave-gangs and all the hands aboard your galleys, seamen and soldiers, every able-bodied man that Djerba can supply. I estimate that there should be five thousand of these Berbers. Win the assistance of their Sheik, and let your soldiers round them up, at the point of the sword if need be, and let them bring every spade and pick and mattock on the land. You shall see what can be done."

A glimmer of the project broke on Dragut's mind at last, and almost scared him by its vastness. He took a deep breath, and his voice was muted. "You'll set them to dig a way? A canal nearly a league in length?"

"No miracle with some seven thousand hands to do the work. The canal need not be deep. We lighten the galleys of all gear until only the shells remain, and we refurnish them again here in deep water."

He enlarged upon it, and in a measure as he did so the practical nature of that colossal enterprise became more and more apparent, until at last Dragut, himself, exclaimed his belief that Allah, the All-wise, the All-knowing, had sent Prospero to him so that the Sword of Islam should be set free to continue to uphold the glory of the Prophet's law.

Chapter 27

The Reunion

In the cool of that evening Prospero and Gianna, reunited, sat on the poop of the *Aswad*, the twenty-six-oared black galley which Dragut, faithful to his word, had assigned to Prospero at the end of that day of incredibly active preparatory toil. For from the moment of taking the decision to act upon Prospero's plan, not an instant had been lost.

They had begun by a visit to the leathern-cheeked, grey-bearded old Sheik at Roumt-es-Soum and expounded their need of all available hands for certain labours, the purpose of which they did not disclose. The crafty old Khadab made difficulties at first. These Dragut conquered partly by bribery and partly by appeal to racial feelings, with the hint of a threat in the background. When at last the Sheik yielded, which was when he conceived that he had wrung the last ducat from the Corsair, he did so with such enthusiasm as to make Dragut free not only of all the able-bodied men on the island, but of all the women and all the children of an age to bear a share in the labour that was planned. His messengers went forth, carrying in his name the summons from village to village, and with the messengers went Dragut's Saracen soldiery, so that the natives should have a glimpse of what might happen to those who were reluctant to obey.

A couple of thousand of these impressed Berbers were conducted that same afternoon to the spot where the operations were to begin, and thither the slave-gangs, another couple of thousand, were ordered; all were to encamp there in the open, so as to be ready to start work at peep of day upon the morrow.

Next a score of wardens, being appointed overseers, were taken to the marshes, and received from Prospero very precise instructions as to where and how to set about the cutting of the channel. Already before this, Prospero, with Dragut and some of his officers, all of them now in an enthusiastic fever that made them fawn upon the inventive Genoese, had carefully surveyed the camel-road and determined the point at which it should be cut.

Lastly there had been a hurried visit to the fort near Houmt-es-Soum, and a shot fired at one of the galleys that was a little in advance of the wide crescent which the Imperial fleet preserved. It did no damage, but would serve to show the Lord Andrea that the keepers of the fort were alert and vigilant.

By the time they came back to Houmt Ajim and the Corsair fleet, whose earlier orders to cross the lagoon had been suspended, the afternoon was well advanced. Among the troops remaining there the excitement had been running high ever since the slave-gangs had been landed and marched away south; for the rumour had spread that they were being taken away to be employed upon works that would deliver the fleet. Whilst it was an impenetrable mystery to the Corsairs, yet they gave it faith and were lifted out of their gloom. Those ashore surged about Dragut and his companions clamouring for confirmation of the report.

"The praise to the One," Dragut had answered them, "it is even as you have heard. The Nasrani dog shall be cheated of his prey."

He laughed as he made the announcement, for his mood was exultant now. It was, Prospero judged, the moment in which to claim fulfilment of Dragut's promise, and Dragut in his jubilation had acquiesced without any manifest reluctance. It may have been not only that he desired to practise that loyalty to his word that was his pride, but also that he realized that whilst Prospero had now parted with his secret, yet in the execution difficulties might arise, to resolve which it would need the shrewd wit of the man who had invented that colossal project. Like Henry IV of France, consoling himself by the reflection that Paris was well worth a Mass, so now Dragut must have comforted his thwarted lust by the reflection that his fleet was well worth a woman.

He ordered the *Aswad* to be made ready for Prospero, leaving aboard her for the present only her Turkish commander, Usuf-ben-Hamet, and a score of his men as a precaution. Whilst she was preparing, he took Prospero with him aboard his own galeasse, where Gianna, brought thither earlier in the day waited without knowing for what she waited, and little dreaming that it was for reunion with her lover. Sinan was there, too, for the purpose of renewing his disgruntled arguments. But Dragut was short with him. In twenty words he told the eunuch how all was changed, and by the prospect made an end of Sinan's discontent. He squealed loud praises of Allah for this sign of favour to the True-Believers, and on that departed to his galley, understanding now why the slaves had earlier been withdrawn from her.

And whilst Dragut had been offering that explanation to Sinan, Prospero had as briefly conveyed to Gianna the sudden alteration in their circumstances, and Gianna in her unutterable relief at news so incredible and uplifting had not then stayed to ask him how this miracle had been brought about.

Dragut had kept them to sup with him, and it was in the course of this that she obtained her first glimpse of the price that Prospero was paying for their sudden emancipation. They sat in his tabernacle, waited upon by a couple of his Nubian slaves, whose ebony bodies were clothed for the purpose in blue-girdled white caftans, each woolly head covered by a blue and white kerchief held in place by a twisted cord of camel-hair. Dragut, his mind bubbling with satisfaction at the trick that was about to be played on Doria and admiration of him who had invented it, was moved to speak of the glories of Islam and of the honour that would await a man of Prospero's endowments in the armies of the Faithful, in the service of the Sublime Portal. He spoke of Ochiali Pasha and other renegades who had risen high in the service of the Sultan, and ventured the opinion that it must be impossible for Prospero to return to the ranks of the Unbelievers, who trod the path to the Pit, after having laboured for their defeat as he was now doing.

To Prospero this came as a daunting revelation of the real nature of what he did. It was something that had gone unconsidered in the singleness of his purpose. But even now he put consideration of it aside.

"Not for their defeat, Dragut; nor even for your deliverance."

"But for what, then?"

"For what you pay me. For the price of my hire as your condottiero in this service."

Dragut's fine eyes were momentarily saddened, then scornful. "The fruits are the same. But there! What is written is written."

On that he dismissed the subject, and gave his attention to the stew of chicken dressed with eggs and olives in the silver dish which was their common platter.

Later, after the Nubians had poured rose-water into silver bowls, so that each of them might wash his fingers, Dragut escorted them to the sloop that was to convey them aboard the *Aswad*. And here now, alone with Prospero, in the descending dusk, Gianna sought and obtained a fuller explanation of the words Dragut had used and of the activities by which Prospero had won them this emancipation and reunion.

Dismay grew in her gentle eyes as he made clear the thing which she had only half-suspected. When he had done, she sat rigid, her hands locked in her lap, her face set, staring straight before her into the deepening shadows. Her attitude and her silence filled him with a very definite uneasiness. He could not avoid the sense of her unvoiced reproof. He leaned over, and placed his hand on hers.

"You say nothing, Gianna."

"Sweet Mother in Heaven! What can I say? What can I say?" Affliction, almost despair, vibrated in her deep voice. "You do not need me to tell you what you are doing, Prospero. You are ruining yourself for ever, my dear, by this betrayal. For it is that, Prospero."

"Betrayal?" he echoed. He shook his head, stifling a growing uneasiness. "Where no loyalty is due, there can be no question of betrayal. And God knows I owe no loyalty to the Doria. Not after Cherchell."

"I am not thinking of the Doria, but of the Imperial cause, of which you are a servant, and of Christendom, against which you act when you contrive that Dragut, now caught in this trap, shall be let loose again to ravage Christian lands. That is your betrayal, Prospero. That is something for which you can hope for no forgiveness. Well might Dragut propose to you that you become such another renegade as Ochiali. What else remains for you?" And then, clutching between her own the hand that he had placed on hers, she swung to face him, and her voice was broken. "Prospero! Prospero! What have you done?"

In his distress he still could do no more than seek arguments to palliate his action. "Dragut would have escaped without me. He had planned to land at Bou Ghara, over there, scuttle his galleys, and march to Algiers. All that I have done is to save his fleet."

"But it is his fleet that matters. His power is in his fleet, as you well know. You are not being frank."

"We were in danger," he answered. "And I saw no other way to extricate us. I acted quickly, desperately, and I did not give thought to all that was involved. I think I am only beginning to realize it. But even had I realized it sooner, I must still have done as I have done."

"Is life so very precious that we should buy it at the price of being a dishonoured outcast? Will life be tolerable so?"

"Life!" he echoed, and now his voice rang fierce. "Life! If life had been all! When have I feared to risk mine? Did I set a high value on my life at Goialatta, at Amalfi, at Procida, at Cherchell?"

"I know... I know." She spoke more gently. "I was not thinking of your life, Prospero, but of my own. I did you the justice to suppose that this is what had weighed with you."

"If it had been only your life..." he was saying wistfully, and there broke off. "Dear love, you do not yet know for what I am paying by my service; you do not know what I have bought with it." And now he conveyed to her the knowledge that hitherto, so as to save her from madness, she had been spared by a merciful Heaven: how Sinan had first intended her for an offering to Suleyman; how, later, Dragut had destined her for himself, partly because he had cast eyes of lust upon her, partly because in the possession of her he perceived a voluptuous vengeance upon Andrea Doria.

She uttered a little moan of shame as he spoke, and bowed her head until her chin was resting on her breast.

"Could I stay then," he cried, "confronted with that abomination, to weigh my duty to the Emperor or to Christendom? My heart and brain were all but broken at the contemplation of it. I was on the rack to find a price at which I could ransom you. And let follow what may, in despite of Emperor and of Christendom, to the hour of my death I shall thank God for the inspiration which supplied the means."

She had covered her face with her hands. He knelt beside her, and his voice was lowered again to a pleading tone. "Tell me, Gianna, tell me of what else at such a time would Heaven or honour have me think but of your salvation?"

She uncovered her face. It shone palely in the deepening dusk. She bent over him, and took his head between her hands. She was weeping.

"Forgive what I said, my dear. I did you such wrong as to think that your feud with the House of Doria might have had some part in this. I did not suspect..." She broke off, and then with pain quivering in her voice, she added: "But afterwards, my Prospero? Afterwards? When this is done, and Dragut has escaped from the trap, will you not be called to account for your part in it?"

"Let that wait. One thing at a time. If I am to consider future difficulties, I shall be overwhelmed by present ones. My first concern is to fulfil the task to which I've set my hand. If thereby I cheat the Lord Andrea Doria of his prey, why so much the worse for the Lord Andrea Doria. Neither that, nor any other consequence shall stay or trouble me. Do not let it trouble you, my Gianna. Rest content for the moment in what is done, and in thankfulness that you go neither to Algiers nor to Istanbul. As these Moslems have it, what is written is written. We but follow our destiny." His arms enfolded her, his cheek was against her cheek that was wet with tears. "We are together, dear love. Miraculously together. And, God helping us, together we'll remain whatever the sequel to this queer adventure."

Chapter 28

At a Venture

Unrepentant in the matter of all that was involved, and unconcerned in the matter of ulterior consequences, Prospero guided the labours by which at the price of betrayal of his cause, Gianna and he were to win deliverance.

"Never," he told her, "was life so dear as now that it is shared with you. It has grown too precious to be yielded to Doria vindictiveness, which is what would happen if we fell now into his hands. For you perhaps a convent; for me a yard-arm, or an even less exalted exit. It is not my notion that our story should end thus."

Only the deep devotion he expressed sustained her in those days, when from dawn to sunset she sat alone aboard the *Aswad* with Prospero's five knaves for bodyguard, whilst he was away directing the vast operations he had planned.

He apportioned the labour amongst the slaves and the army of Berbers which had been forcibly enlisted, a third of which was made up of women, so that the total number exceeded even his original computation. They began the cutting at the causeway, working backwards towards the lagoon, so that not until the last wall of earth was broken down would the water flow into the canal. So that no time be lost, it was not a yard wider or a foot deeper than necessity decreed for galleys which being lightened of all gear would not draw more than five feet of water. Along that length of marshy ground the army of toilers hacked and dug and heaved in the blazing sunshine, relentlessly driven by the wardens and the soldiery, whilst Prospero, himself, constantly moving hither and thither, overlooked nothing, anticipated and provided for every difficulty the ground presented. Progress was so rapid that by the evening of the second day the canal from the lagoon to the causeway was complete and the water flowing in it. The causeway, itself, in which there was a deal of rock, must have proved an infinitely more difficult and laborious matter; and had Prospero kept to his original plan the work could never have been accomplished in the time he had prescribed. But he had improved upon it. It would no longer be necessary to cut the causeway. By means of rollers, for which trees were even then being felled and planed, and by harnessing a whole slave-gang to each galley, he would drag the vessels across those fifty yards of solid land.

This determined, he let it wait until the outer canal, from the causeway to the bay near El Kantara, should be dug. Not only because the distance was shorter, but also because he had profited by the experience gained in cutting the inner channel, this labour was completed quite early on the third day from the commencement of operations, and at once a start was made to bring the vessels through and haul them over the causeway.

Already whilst the cutting was in progress, Prospero had set other gangs to the work of lightening the galleys by removing not only their guns, their ballast, their stores, but every object that was movable or could be easily detached. Dragut, himself, had supervised and directed this part of the operations once the need had been indicated by Prospero; and now the galleys, riding high in the water, stripped even of their oars, were ready to be hauled. The slave-gangs, squelching their way on both sides of the canal through ground rendered tolerably firm by the excavated earth piled into banks which the sun had partly baked, drew on the ropes, and the lightened hulls moved forward. By nightfall, all of them were in the canal, the foremost already at the causeway. Dragut's own galeasse came last, immediately behind the *Aswad*. And these were the only two that were still tenanted.

On the morrow came the difficult and most toilsome of all their labours, that of hauling the galleys to the causeway and across it on the rollers, and of launching them again in the cut beyond. The whole of the day was consumed in this, and it wanted less than half an hour to sunset when the last of the thirteen galleys, Dragut's own flagship, was relaunched in the outer canal.

The two brigantines had to be abandoned. But not on that account did Prospero suffer them to be entirely wasted. He had them warped to the mouth of the lagoon, and anchored at a little distance from each other opposite Dragut's fort, where they would be just within sight of Doria's vessels. Thus, whilst offering Doria delusive evidence of the continued presence of the Corsair fleet, they would suggest to him a further fortification of the entrance to the bight, and a precaution against surprise. Whilst this might move Andrea Doria's scorn by its ultimate futility, yet it should meanwhile supply additional reason why he should continue to keep his distance. The vessels had been stripped of everything of value before being anchored in that station, and the sparse crews that had remained to handle them were brought off under cover of night.

On the morrow Prospero had yet another demonstration for the Imperialists. Before the heavy basiliscoes were removed from the fort, so as to be restored to the fleet, he fired six shots at different points of Doria's line as if some hope were entertained of reaching them. He intended it merely as a last sign of activity and vigilance. Lest the silence of that fort which must afterwards ensue should be rendered suspect, no shot had been fired, on Prospero's instructions, since Dragut's idle display of rage. Also the futility of this last cannonade would supply a reason why the guns should be idle in the days that followed.

After that the guns were hauled away from the fort by teams of oxen, and conveyed across the island to be re-embarked on the galleys when they reached the bay below El Kantara. Here, too, was re-embarked all the other gear of which the vessels had been eased for their voyage through the cuttings.

Prospero's miracle was accomplished, and in one day less than he demanded. The Corsair fleet, re-equipped, freshly victualled and re-manned, was assembled in the bay with the open sea before it, awaiting only the coming of night so as to go forth.

Dragut in high glee, making a jest of the pertinacity of Andrea Doria which, no doubt, would keep him for weeks in his present station guarding an empty trap, stood with Prospero on the poop of his flagship in the gathering dusk. At the entrance ladder the sloop from the *Aswad* waited until Prospero should have taken his leave of the Corsair.

Dragut's gratitude moved him almost to affection.

"I part with you in regret," he confessed. "But a bargain is a bargain, and you have kept your part. May Allah shield you if ever the Admiral of Genoa should come to learn of it."

Prospero proffered his hand. "Once you were my prisoner. Twice now I have been yours. It is enough. I pray we never meet again as foes."

"Ameen," said Dragut. He salaamed, touching brow and lip. "May Allah send you a safe voyage."

The sloop bore Prospero away to the *Aswad*, a shadow among shadows, for not a light showed that night on any of those galleys. A half-hour later she was stealing out of the bay with the fleet and heading eastward. She carried a full complement of Christian slaves, who, slaves no longer, and unfettered, would henceforth serve as buonevoglie, volunteers ready to exchange the oar for the sword, the crossbow or the arquebuse if needed in their ship's defence.

The *Aswad* held to that eastward course with the rest of the fleet until some time after midnight, when being fully twenty miles from Djerba, she was headed north.

On the following morning, when Prospero emerged by a scuttle in the vestibule from the cabin in the hold which he had made his own, his galley, moving gently now under sail before a breeze from the south, was alone upon the sparkling sea. Not another vessel was in sight.

In addition to his rowers, who still slumbered on their benches, the *Aswad* carried only a dozen hands as sailors including the knaves, who had left Genoa with him in the felucca, whilst to Ferruccio had been entrusted the mastership of the galley.

As Prospero appeared now below the poop and the tabernacle in which Gianna had her quarters, Ferruccio detached himself from the little group amidships, about the kitchen, and came aft. His only garments were a pair of loose linen drawers and a belted cotton tunic striped red and white. His head was covered by the red woollen cap, shaped like a bag, that was common to galley-slaves, and his legs and feet were bare. Nevertheless he carried himself with the conscious dignity of the office bestowed upon him.

"If this wind holds," he said, "we should make a landfall at Malta by tomorrow morning. If not, we should still reach it before tomorrow night."

Prospero inquired what had become of Dragut.

"The fleet veered west again two hours before sunrise."

The information was surprising, for Dragut's last avowed intention had been to steer at once for the Golden Horn, so that he might rejoin Barbarossa without delay. Clearly he had changed his mind, and Prospero's assumption was that he would now be making for Algiers, there to incorporate into his fleet the new vessels that his kayia had been sent to assemble.

It was an assumption only partially correct. Actually, Dragut had been on the point of detaching a galley and dispatching it to Algiers with orders for the reinforcements to follow him to Istanbul, when Sinan had brought him an alternative suggestion.

"Would you quit these seas at the very moment when their shores lie unguarded at our mercy?" Sinan had asked, and because Dragut had not readily understood him, the crafty eunuch had gone on to make his meaning plain.

"Whilst by the mercy of Allah that misbegotten son of a dog is held by his fool's dream before Djerba with all his might, what hinders us from falling upon the Unbelievers? Will you go empty-handed before the Sublime Portal when rich spoils are so easily to be gathered? Do you not perceive the rare chance that Allah sends us?"

Dragut perceived it, and took shame that Sinan, who was less than a man, should show him a man's part in their present situation. So he veered west, that he might carry the glory of the Prophet's law to Frankish shores, putting in at Algiers in passing, so as to pick up the reinforcements that should increase his strength.

This, however, was more than Prospero could guess. It could not enter his speculations that a Dragut who had so lately and so narrowly escaped annihilation should be other than in haste to make the most of his deliverance by placing himself as speedily as possible in the safety offered him by a junction with Barbarossa. He was expressing his wonder that Dragut should even delay to seek, as he supposed, his reinforcements in Algiers, when Madonna Gianna emerged from the tabernacle.

Cool and placid in the dove-grey gown that remained miraculously unimpaired by its owner's tribulations, she came to lean upon the poop-rail, giving them good morning.

Ferruccio withdrew at once, to provide for breakfast, whilst Prospero went up to join her on the poop, and give her an account of their position and the hope of being at Malta on the morrow. There was more than ordinary gravity in the eyes she turned on him. This mention of a destination reawakened all her slumbering fears.

"And then, Prospero? After that, whither?"

He knew the unspoken thought. It brought a hesitancy into his reply. "Why, to Spain as we planned. To Barcelona."

It was a plan suggested by his faith in del Vasto's friendship to find him employment there in the Imperial service. And it was within the plan that they should seek a priest to marry them at the first port of call.

But Gianna, sad-eyed, answered him now as he feared she would.

"Is that still possible? How will they receive you in Spain when they learn what you have done?"

"Will they learn only that, and no more?"

"What more is there to learn?"

"The motives from which I acted. When all is known…"

"It will be known," she interrupted him, "that you have saved two lives: yours and mine, at the cost of what? The Lord Andrea's victory would have delivered some two thousand Christians from Moslem slavery at the oars. Dragut's escape may yet bring all the horror and bloodshed of Moslem raids on many a Christian shore. Who can yet say how many lives may have to pay for our deliverance?"

Prospero sighed. "A hero, I suppose, would have reckoned this. But, you see, I am not heroic." He was faintly ironical. "I fear I disappoint you, Gianna."

Her hand closed firmly on his arm. "I was not passing judgment, Prospero. I was reminding you of how others will judge, especially in Spain. You know the Emperor's anger at the ravages of Dragut, his impatience to see that evil Corsair destroyed. What favour will be shown you when it is known that you have frustrated that destruction?"

"What need that it ever should be known?" was Prospero's desperate question.

"Would you conceal it?"

"Honour places me under no obligation to accuse myself."

"Can it be hidden? Are there no others to accuse you?"

"Be sure that when Dragut comes to boast of what happened at Djerba, he will not diminish himself by saying that he was helped by a pig of an Unbeliever."

"There are these slaves here, whom you have freed. There are some two thousand more, mostly Spaniards, who toiled on those canals under your direction. At any time some of these may win to freedom. Will they be silent?"

"They will if they have any gratitude. How many of them would have survived the onset of Doria's fleet? You had not thought of that when you accused me of sacrificing two thousand Christian lives to our own deliverance."

"Do not say that I accuse you, Prospero. God knows, my dear, how far I am from that."

He set an arm about her, and drew her close. "Meanwhile, dear heart, in thankfulness for what we have, let us trust to fate for what's to come."

Her eyes were tender. "I will try. Fate cannot have thrust us so irrevocably together merely to destroy us. But we must help Fate. That is why I warn you again of the dangers ahead, so that you may provide."

"Yet Fate must point the way. Meanwhile, we sail at a venture."

At a venture, then, they sailed, and very gently and unhurried before the soft August breezes that slowly wafted them north. They were two days in reaching Malta, at which they did not touch, for Prospero was in no mind to meet questions from the Knights of St John. So they left the fortress island a couple of miles to westward, and after that for two days they had the coast of Sicily on their starboard beam. It was on the sixth day after leaving Djerba that they entered the Straits of Messina, and ran without warning into a fleet of galleys proceeding south. Coming suddenly upon this force as the *Aswad* was rounding a headland, and with not more than a half-mile between them, Prospero caught his breath to recognize in the stately three-masted galleasse that led the line, with the Imperial standard at her maintruck and the cornucopia carved and gilded on the prow, his own flagship the *Prospera*. Nine more he counted, all of them powerful galleys of twenty-eight banks, and in their wake followed four galliots and three round ships that would be in use as transports.

He perceived that he was confronted with the Neapolitan squadron, and it was not difficult to guess its destination. These were the reinforcements summoned by Doria to enable him to force the trap in which he held Dragut. The round ships would be conveying the land forces he had requested for the purpose.

He did not know whether to laugh or groan as he thus explained to Gianna the long line of vessels approaching, to the rhythmic flash and sweep of the long oars.

"Our sailing at a venture has brought me home to my own fleet. For I am still the Captain of Naples, and the half of those vessels are my own property."

Ferruccio came bounding to the vestibule deck for orders.

"Take in sail, and stand hove to, the oars at the ready."

Ferruccio's whistle summoned the hands, sails were furled and oars unlashed.

The capitana of Naples came steadily on, converging towards them. At close quarters they saw a line of arquebusiers at her larboard pavisade, and so understood the mistrust in which they were being approached, as was natural, since they displayed no flag. At a distance of a half-cable's length a hail came across the water. On the poop of the *Prospera*, a portly gentleman in yellow, in whom Prospero recognized Carbajal, made a trumpet of his hands.

"Ho there! Who are you?"

The answer which the Spaniard received was the last he could have expected.

"God save you, Don Alvaro! This is the Captain of Naples, Prospero Adorno."

Chapter 29

The Return

From the long-boat that brought him alongside, Don Alvaro de Carbajal climbed, puffing and sweating in his clumsy haste, aboard the Turkish galley. Surprise it was, as much as the exertion, that robbed the portly Spaniard of his breath.

On the vestibule, where Prospero stood to meet him, Don Alvaro struck an attitude.

"The Virgin and all the Saints sustain me! Is it, indeed, you, Don Prospero, flesh, blood and bones?" He opened wide his arms, to swoop forward and engulf in them the Genoese. "Here to my heart, my friend. This is a resurrection that will bring joy to many a mourning heart."

In the smother of that embrace, Prospero laughed, warmed by the Spaniard's warmth.

"You reassure me," he said, as they fell apart again. "A return from the dead is not always welcome."

"Always for one who survives the noble death we were told that you had died. You come back, my friend, to reap the honour earned. The Emperor has mourned you. I have it from del Vasto, who wrote to me, himself inconsolable."

"And the Imperial Admiral, too, should rejoice," said Prospero dryly. "For not a doubt but he will have shared that grief."

Don Alvaro looked at him for confirmation of the irony he suspected.

"That man," he said, with a grimace of anger, "should have wept tears of blood for his part in the loss of you. Perhaps he may yet, when all the tale is told. I burn to hear it, Don Prospero."

Prospero took him by the arm, and drew him up the steps of the companion to the poop. As they were entering the tabernacle, the Spaniard drew back and hung heavy on his companion's arm, taken with fresh astonishment at the sight of Madonna Gianna.

The slim grey figure stood straight and tall before them, gravely smiling, whilst Prospero presented their visitor and by the terms of the presentation completed Don Alvaro's surprise. He dissembled it only for so long as it took him to bend over the slim fair hand, whilst a cool, pleasant voice gave him welcome.

He straightened himself and looked from the lady to her lord with bewildered inquiry in his full dark eyes. "I go from amazement to amazement," he complained.

"Yet all is simple when explained." Prospero waved him to a seat on the stern-locker, and took his stand beside the chair in which Monna Gianna was now seated. "At Cherchell I fell a prisoner to Dragut-Reis, an old acquaintance, who once had been my prisoner and received courteous treatment at my hands. He repaid the debt. He agreed my ransom, and permitted me to go home to Genoa in quest of it. When I reached home the expedition had already sailed, and my own galleys had gone back to Naples. Events for which I will not pretend to be entirely without blame had aggravated an old feud between Doria and me. Nor was I well viewed by my own people because of my betrothal to Madonna Maria Giovanna Doria. So I had virtually decided to go to Spain, and meanwhile I kept my quarters aboard the felucca that had borne me to Genoa." He added the tale of Gianna's warning visit to him there, of Lamba Doria's sudden attack, of Ferruccio's high-handed action to elude it, and the rest. "The storm that began by saving us and then almost destroyed us, ended by blowing us into the very arms of Dragut. Again I made terms with him, and... And that is all. At least, all that matters."

In anxiety Gianna watched Don Alvaro's countenance for indications of the impression made upon him by Prospero's account with its rather lame conclusion.

The Spaniard stared round-eyed from one to the other of them. "By my faith, it's plain that Destiny meant to join you in spite of all the Dorias. The Admiral will be the first to wish to see you married. So give you joy of each other, children. As for Dragut-Reis, that Moslem rogue is not likely ever to trouble us again."

"Not likely to trouble us again, you say?"

Don Alvaro savoured the pleasure of communicating great tidings; and they were tidings which by now were spreading along the Christian shores of the Mediterranean. Unctuously he told of Dragut bottled up in the Bight of Djerba by Andrea Doria, to whom the Neapolitan fleet was now convoying the transports bearing the land forces and the artillery that were to make short work of the trapped Corsair.

Instead of surprising by his news, it was he, himself, who was surprised by the answer to it.

"Don Alvaro, if that be your mission, you may go about and return to Naples. Positively Dragut's fleet is not in the Bight of Djerba. I left it nearly a week ago, somewhere off the Tunisian coast and steering westward."

For a moment Don Alvaro was dumb. Then his comment came explosively.

"By the eyes of God, you must be at fault, Don Prospero."

"That is impossible. I was in the Bight of Djerba with Dragut. And I left it with him, by the way out that was found at its southern end."

"What are you telling me?" Don Alvaro was almost impatient. "I know the place. There is no such way out."

"One was made. I speak of what I saw. A channel was cut through the isthmus. Doria has been fooled. He was left sitting at the door of an empty trap."

"Por Dios y la Virgen!" swore Don Alvaro under the shock of the news. Then suddenly the bulk of him shook with laughter. But this only for a moment. Soon, as he digested the matter, he became grave.

"If that be true, he has been more than fooled. He is ruined. Nothing less. The Emperor's patience has been growing short. This will completely end it. And Dragut cut a channel through the isthmus to the south, you say? Vive el cielo! Of course Doria would not think of that. Who, indeed, would have thought of it?"

"I would," said Prospero, and earned a glance almost of terror from his lady.

The Spaniard made a dubious lip.

"Maybe you would," he agreed, without conviction. "But what's to do now? My orders from the Viceroy are to join Doria before Djerba. That becomes useless."

"It is worse. I have told you that Dragut has gone westward, naturally to seek reinforcements at Algiers. You've to consider that he is loose upon the seas, and that with Doria out of the way, our coasts are defenceless. It follows that your place is back in Naples."

"Whilst Doria sits at Djerba guarding nothing and writing smug, self-laudatory letters to his Imperial master." Despite the gravity of the situation, Don Alvaro's bulk was again shaken by a half-repressed convulsion of mirth. "Faith, it's a well-deserved lesson for that self-sufficient Genoese, and, as you say, it is not for me to leave the Italian littoral unguarded."

In that clear perception of duty, Don Alvaro presently took himself back to the *Prospera* to order the fleet to go about. Setting their lateen sails to the following breeze the galleys headed north, and the slave-gangs rested. But later in the day the wind veered round and freshened, and in the teeth of a tramontana they took to the oars again, and progress became slow. The wind continuing from that quarter, the fleet, creeping along the coast by day and anchoring in shelter at night, consumed the greater part of a week in coming again within sight of Mount Vesuvius. But it was a week of pleasant voyaging under bright skies and in weather agreeably cooled by the steady breeze.

Gianna's anxieties had been diminished by Don Alvaro's unquestioning acceptance of the account that Prospero had rendered. Prospero, himself, with faith in his fortunes, and enheartened to find himself once more with his own fleet, refused to entertain misgivings. He paid a visit of inspection to each of his own six galleys, and received upon each of them a welcome almost affectionate from the captains of his own appointing and their crews. He learnt of the claim which on the presumption of his death had been laid to these vessels by his uncle Rainaldo, laughed at Rainaldo's coming disappointment and approved the delay of the Imperial Courts in satisfying the claim.

So carefree, indeed, did his mind become in those days when they hugged the green coast of the Terra di Lavoro, that he composed some fifty stanzas of his lately neglected *Liguriad*. They are those which deal with Doria's exploits at Mehedia, the ironical undertone of which, from the first line,

"*Tuonò con prepotenza l'ammiraglio*",

was long a mystery to his commentators.

Once Gianna questioned him on his present intentions, supposing that this meeting with the Neapolitan fleet should have given them shape. He answered with a laugh that he had taken "Sequere Deum", for his motto.

"Dragut was wont to say that Allah has bound the fate of every man about his neck. Why labour then to ponder it? I follow my destiny, and I know that it is kindly, for it has united us and it has delivered us already from one great peril. So have faith in it as I have, my Gianna."

On a sigh she answered him: "My faith is in you, Prospero."

And so, she trusting to him, and he trusting to fortune, they came at eventide on a Sunday of August into the spacious Bay of Naples, dominated by Vesuvius, whose crown of lambent flames set a fierce, orange glow against a sky that was like polished steel.

They were soon to realize that it was not only the volcano that was here unquiet. As they crept forward in the dusk, the silence of eventide was shattered. Across the water came to them an uproar of rolling drums and braying trumpets, to which presently was added the distant clang of alarm bells. Last of all from the vast dark square mass of the Castel Nuovo the deepening gloom was split by a shaft of flame. The roar of a gun shook the air, and from the plunging shot a shower of spray was flung up ahead of the leading galley.

Trumpets called now from the capitana, and "Sia scorre!" was the command running from vessel to vessel, to bring the slaves to their feet, their faces turned to the prow, straining to back the galleys.

It happened that Prospero and Gianna were aboard the capitana with Don Alvaro. They had been his guests at dinner that day, and with their destination in view they had lingered on through the afternoon. Don Alvaro's table had been sumptuously spread for them. There had been a choice Falernian to accompany the meats, and a dark syrupy Malaga for dessert, with strange sweetmeats confectioned out of fruits from the New World. Don Alvaro, who denied himself no luxuries, carried a troupe of musicians aboard, and these had made music for them whilst they ate and afterwards. Thus his guests had been in no haste to leave him.

He turned to them now, simmering with indignant excitement, shoulders hunched and arms outflung. "Will someone tell me what is happening in Naples? Have they gone mad at the Castel Nuovo? A hundred yards nearer and I should have had a galley sunk."

"Yours, Don Alvaro, is the last fleet Naples will be expecting to see. You are imagined to be at Djerba by now."

"But to fire on us!"

"It argues a state of panic."

"The devil take their panics. What should cause it?"

A sloop was dispatched to the Castel Nuovo, and at the end of something over an hour, a twelve-oared barge, with a lantern glowing above the little cabin in the sternsheets, came swiftly through the water to the *Prospera*'s side.

A tall man in a dark cloak came up the entrance ladder; the cloak fell open and the poop-lanterns glowed on a rich dress and the fair golden-bearded countenance of the Prince of Orange, himself.

"How come you here, Don Alvaro?" His greeting was sharp.

"I learnt, Highness, that we are no longer required at Djerba; that Dragut has eluded Doria's trap."

He thought to create surprise. Instead: "I felicitate you upon having so soon discovered it," said the Viceroy. "Your return is most timely. God be thanked! Dragut has already made us aware that he is at large. Three days ago he raided Corsica. Between Tarignano and San Nicolao he has laid waste a half-dozen townships, stripped the churches, sacked the houses, and carried off over a thousand souls into captivity."

"God save us!" ejaculated Don Alvaro.

The Prince's tone grew bitter. "And this at a time when 'Te Deum' is being sung for his reported capture. For we have believed the fatuous boasts of Doria that he holds the robber trapped." The indignation deepened in his voice. "Not for a kingdom would I stand under Doria's hat when the Emperor hears of this. But there! When first we sighted your fleet in the dusk, we concluded that the damned Infidel was upon us. We could not believe in the good fortune of your return. I have been assembling such vessels as I could, for our defence in case of need; and the Holy Father has sent me three galleys from Ostia. But I have been in no case to oppose Dragut if he should take it into his evil head to descend upon Naples."

"He would never push audacity so far."

"Are there limits, then, to his audacity? If so, I have yet to learn them. But whilst I talk, I keep you waiting. Give the order to go forward to the harbour."

Don Alvaro's trumpeters wound a flourish, and with thud and creak of the great oars and the rustle of water to their blades, the galleys began to move again.

The Viceroy turned to mount the poop, and became for the first time aware of the two figures standing at the rail. The light from the lantern on the mainmast was beating full upon Prospero's face. The Viceroy recoiled.

"God's mercy! Do you carry ghosts aboard, Don Alvaro?"

Don Alvaro's laugh began an answer for which his Highness did not wait. He sprang up the remaining steps to the poop.

"Prospero Adorno!" It was an exclamation of glad amazement. He was laughing as he held out both hands. "Alive! But by what miracle?"

Chapter 30

Reparation

In the chamber of the angels, in the Beverello Tower of the Castel Nuovo, where a year ago Moncada had presided over the council which determined the ill-starred action of Amalfi, sat the slim, fair young Viceroy and the portly, swarthy Don Alvaro de Carbajal, whilst Prospero, sitting with them, rendered a full and exact account of the events at Djerba.

It was the morning after his arrival. A night's reflection had brought him to the view that whatever the consequences, no other course was possible. In this, Gianna had stoutly if fearfully supported him, perceiving that if the truth transpired in any other way Prospero would be for ever disgraced.

The tale produced widely different effects upon the two members of his audience. Carbajal, naturally prone to a humorous outlook, and holding Doria in no affection, was disposed to be merry over this fooling of the Admiral. The Prince, however, was appalled.

"But that you tell me this, yourself," he said, "I could not believe it." His tone was magisterial. "To lend assistance to that scourge of Christendom, to show this pirate scoundrel the way of escape, so that he may continue to devastate our shores! Frankly, sir, even from your own lips the tale's incredible."

"Until you reflect upon my peril," said Prospero.

"The peril would make your story credible in the case of a coward."

With a muttered, "Ah! Por Dios!" Don Alvaro made a gesture of dismay.

Prospero inclined his head. "Let that explain it to Your Highness."

"But it does not explain it," cried Orange. "For you are not a coward."

"All the world knows that," said Don Alvaro, and what he added was not without point. "If there were not Goialatta, where you saved Doria, and if there were not Procida, there would still be Cherchell, where I saw you left by Doria to pay with your life for your heroism. Come, Don Prospero. Be frank with His Highness. In what you did at Djerba you had some thought of squaring the account. Is it not so?"

But the Prince did not wait for the admission.

"Ah! Now I begin to see," he exclaimed. "It's this old feud between your houses, lurking ever behind your associations, and making of your reconciliations a pretence. In paying off the score you took no account of what or whom you might be sacrificing to your rancour. It did not weigh with you that you betrayed the Christian cause and thwarted the Emperor's dearest hopes. That is the truth, Messer Prospero, is it not?"

Prospero shook his head. "It is not. I will confess that I am chained to this feud like Ixion to his wheel. Had I taken this chance to settle the account, who that knows all could blame me? There was Cherchell, of which Don Alvaro has spoken. But afterwards there was more. The news of my survival was suppressed together with the messenger who sought the ransom that would have set me free. It was intended that I should rot in Moslem chains. Not to have frustrated the victory of those who had done this, and a victory that would have placed me in their power, would have been to bare my throat to my enemy's knife. And that is not all. There was Monna Gianna to be saved from Dragut. He, too, has a score to settle with Doria, and my affianced wife's kinship with that house rendered her doubly and evilly desirable in his eyes. She was destined for his seraglio. Her ransom was the price I exacted from Dragut for his deliverance." Almost scornfully he summed up: "I had not heroism enough to leave her in his power. To expect it of me is to expect me to be more than human."

Don Alvaro, deeply moved, exploded. "By all the devils, it was enough to justify you."

But the fair face of Orange remained overcast. He stirred and sighed. "You have certainly brought your feud to the issue you desired. For you have certainly ruined Doria. Discredited, brought down to the very dust of contempt, he can never rise from this again. Together with the Admiral's premature announcement of his triumph the Emperor will be receiving my reports of Dragut's ravages in Corsica. Thus the Admiral will appear a vain, presumptuous boaster, and that the Emperor will break him is certain." Sourly he added: "And so the victory is yours, Ser Prospero. You have certainly conquered in this long, bitter duel."

"So I perceive. But what Your Highness still does not perceive is that this is the result of chance, not of design. The ruin of Andrea Doria had not entered into my calculations."

"But you'll not pretend that you deplore it?"

Prospero raised his shoulders in deprecation. "In my place it would need a saint to do so much. And I am not that. The very chance of which I spoke is but the recoil of the murderous aims of the Dorias against me. Poetic justice has overtaken them."

The Prince struck the table with his clenched hand. "The devil take your factions and your feuds! See where your quarrelling brings us. A hundred ravaged Corsican homes; murder, rape and slavery for their unhappy tenants; the Emperor's hopes deluded; Christ's Cross trampled under the heel of Mahomet's followers. Poetic justice, you say! These are the fruits of your feud. Fruits to be smugly contemplated, are they not?"

"I do not contemplate them smugly. But that is no matter. What I did you know, and why I did it. The feud was not concerned. In my own view I was justified, although I may not hope to be justified in that of Your Highness." And he ended: "I am in your hands."

The Prince gloomed at him. "It will need grave thought," he said, and on that dismissed him.

But less than an hour later he was summoned again to the Viceroy's presence in that same chamber, and found with him not only Don Alvaro but also a stranger, squat and rough of shape, who proved to be a French shipmaster, just landed in Naples. He came with a report that two days ago he had sighted, a hundred miles or so off the western coast of Sardinia, a strong fleet of galleys, which he believed to be Corsair, steering westwards.

The report had left the Viceroy aghast; for the instant thought suggested was that this would be Dragut, and that he would be making for the coast of Spain.

Don Alvaro was as profusely blasphemous as he was inconclusive. The Prince lost himself in despondent surmises of what must be the Emperor's feelings if in this moment in which he was accounting Dragut destroyed, the Corsair should appear on his very threshold.

When at last they had exhausted their vehemence, Prospero quietly offered a practical opinion. "Whatever may be Dragut's destination, he must be engaged before he can regain the African coast."

The Viceroy, who, in a white heat of passion was pacing to and fro, turned upon him irritably. "What means have we, with Doria at Djerba or thereabouts? A week to reach him. A week or more to fetch him thence. Dragut is reckoning upon that. He would never otherwise dare so much." With flaming eyes he glared at Prospero. "You begin to see what you have done."

"Rather," said Prospero, "was I concerned to consider what I might do."

"What you might do?"

"I, or another if I am no longer trusted."

"But what is it possible to do with the force at our disposal?" The Prince turned in exasperation to the shipmaster. "Of what strength do you say was this Corsair fleet?"

"Between galleys and galliots we counted twenty-seven keels, noble lord. And of these, twenty-two were royal galleys."

His Highness swung again to Prospero. "God's light! You hear? And what do we command? Thirteen galleys, including the three we have from the Holy Father. What can we hope to do with such a force? What could we look for but defeat?"

"Even so," said Prospero, coolly, "whilst suffering it, we could at least so maul Dragut as to leave him in no case to continue his depredations. Would not that be something?"

Don Alvaro breathed noisily. The Prince, taken aback, looked at him in a sort of awe. "You would deliberately sacrifice the Neapolitan squadron?"

"At need why not? We immolate a part to the profit of the whole. In a desperate pass, that seems to me commendable strategy."

"Yes," said His Highness slowly, as he absorbed the notion. "That I can perceive. But…" He paused at fault, and resumed his uneasy pacings. Then he dismissed the shipmaster, and continued only after he had departed. "Even if I should consent to so desperate an employment of this squadron, who is there to command it? Whom could I send to certain death?"

"Death is by no means so inevitable," Prospero objected. And Don Alvaro agreed with him. "No, vive el Cielo! There is always the fortune of war. Queer things can happen in an engagement."

Prospero stood up. "If, now, I were to beseech you to give me this command, would that resolve some of your misgivings?"

The Prince's sharp, clear glance found him calm and resolute. "You have a high confidence in yourself, Ser Prospero."

"Shall we say, a sense of what is due from me? Your Highness has said that this situation results from what I did at Djerba. It remains, then, for me to repair it as best I can."

Orange bowed his head, gloom on his fair countenance. He flung himself down again in his armchair at the table, and chin in hand sat thoughtful, whilst the others waited. He turned at last to Carbajal.

"What do you say, Don Alvaro? After all, you are now the Captain of Naples, and the squadron is under your orders."

But Don Alvaro took a more generous view. "Hardly, since Don Prospero has returned. Half the galleys are his own personal property. Those also he risks in this affair. But I'll answer you this way: I'll be glad to share the venture with Don Prospero if your Highness decides in favour of it."

"You, too?" said Orange.

Don Alvaro smiled, and spread his hands. "There is much honour to be won. Vive Dios! I shall be proud to serve with Don Prospero."

"Less proud," said Prospero, "than I to have your company and counsel."

Orange, looking from one to the other, turned peevish. "Very fine and gallant, to be sure." His own indecision marred his temper. "But you take too much for granted. I must have time to consider."

"With submission, Highness," Don Alvaro reminded him, "there is no time to spare. Never was haste more necessary. While we think, Dragut strikes. We should sail today."

This was so stoutly supported by Prospero that between them Don Alvaro and he swept the Viceroy into a reluctant consent. Having won it, they went to work at once to make ready for departure.

All through that day the quays of Naples vibrated with the activity of swift preparation and equipment, and in the dead calm of that summer evening the fleet set out, and laid a north-westerly course for the Straits of Boniface.

Madonna Gianna was left behind, in the care of the Prince of Orange and his sister, the Countess of Nassau-Chalons. Because of the difficult situation in which she found herself, the chivalrous prince and his warm-hearted sister were at more than ordinary pains to treat her as an honoured guest. In that sombre Angevin fortress she was lodged with the Countess in the noble apartments that once had been del Vasto's, and all the Vice-Regal resources were at her command, to supply her every need.

To those apartments Prospero had gone in quest of her with news of the desperate enterprise upon which he was to set forth.

If it relieved the fears in which she had encouraged him to render an exact account of the events at Djerba, it replaced them by others even more appalling. Yet whilst alluding to them she gallantly preserved her calm.

"You go to face great dangers, Prospero," she said.

"It is no new territory for me. I know my way in it."

She shook her head. "It was never like this. They have told me of the strength of Dragut's fleet. The odds are such that I must stay you if I dared. Yet I dare not. Standing where you do we must accept it." And then, shedding some of her calm, and allowing passion to appear, she added: "See whither this ill-starred pursuit of vengeance has brought you. You have encompassed the Lord Andrea's ruin, as you vowed; but how terribly it recoils upon you."

He answered her as he had answered Orange. "The Admiral's ruin has resulted from the circumstances. It was no part of my design."

"But you! Would you undo it, Prospero? Would you, if it were not for the harm resulting to you?"

He was wistful. "It is easy to affirm it. Yet it is true. For your dear sake and for my own, I would make peace with Doria if it lay within my power."

"Too late, dear love," she lamented. "All that you can now do is what you are doing. Though I should lose you, I cannot repine the step you take. For it offers you the only chance of redemption from the ruin to which that accursed feud has brought you."

He sighed. "Redemption will depend upon the measure of the amend that fortune will enable me to make. It will need to be enough to restore my honour, or else more than honour will be lost to me."

"What more?"

"You, my Gianna."

She smiled with a touch of scorn. "Do you think I am concerned for the world's opinion of you, Prospero? There can never be dishonour for you in my eyes. Come what may, I am yours whenever it be your will to claim me."

He held her close. "Brave heart, I shall claim you as soon as I can offer you a name that I have placed beyond the reach of all reproach. I stake all I have and am upon the board to win it, and so win you."

"Yet if you should not…"

He interrupted her. "If I should not…" And there he checked. He smiled very tenderly into her widening eyes. "We'll not consider it. If I should fail where so much waits to reward success, I shall have proved that I do not deserve you."

But she was not deceived. She knew that what he meant when he spoke of staking all was that he would not survive failure; and considering what she knew there would be for him if he failed, her distress could scarcely bring her to any other wish for him.

Her eyes were dimmed by unshed tears, for it was in her mind that she might be looking her last upon him. "I shall never be more proud of you than I am now, my Prospero. I shall be on my knees in prayer for you until you come back to me."

"What mightier buckler could I have, dear love? Trust you to my fortune as I trust to your prayers."

On that he had her close in a farewell embrace, and there was almost a gay note in his parting assurance that he would not be long away.

But now, seated alone in the luxurious tabernacle of the *Prospera*, as in the fading daylight the little fleet crept with creak and splash of oars past the headland of Posilipo, his confidence was lost in the pain of the reflection that only by a miracle would he ever see her again.

There was a heavy step on the poop, and the portly figure of Don Alvaro filled the arched entrance of the cabin. Prospero sighed, and spoke his thought aloud.

"Love should have no place in a soldier's life. For love renders life too desirable and makes a man fear to lose it."

"But also," said the light-hearted Castilian gentleman, "it lends the soldier a fury to preserve it that makes him victorious against every odd. That, at least, is the lesson life has taught me, and I think it is the lesson you are now to teach Messer Dragut. His Highness of Orange may regard us as sacrificial offerings." He chuckled. "Not so do I. We go to reap laurels, Don Prospero."

Chapter 31

Mars Ultor

The oars were plied all through that Monday night without surcease, and the Neapolitan squadron ploughed a course in line, the capitana in the rear. Immediately ahead of her, in tow of four of the galleys, went a heavily armed Andalusian galleon, which Prospero had been inspired to include in his fleet. The Prince of Orange had at first opposed it, on the ground that if there should be a continued absence of wind this galleon would delay them at a time when speed was the paramount consideration.

Prospero, however, with intent to reduce the heavy odds against him, and possessing in Don Alvaro a captain experienced in the handling of round ships, had insisted. And Don Alvaro had supported him, claiming that in command of her in action he could render her worth any three galleys. So the Viceroy had yielded, and this galleon, the *Imaculada* from Malaga, a floating fortress, suitably manned, went to reinforce the little fleet. Prospero added also to his strength the Turkish galley he had received from Dragut. Her banks were manned by buonevoglie. Nor was this the only vessel on which, in action, the gangs would exchange the oars for lethal weapons. Prospero had conceived the notion of separating Moslem from Christian slaves. As a result five of his galleys, in addition to the *Aswad*, were rowed entirely by Christians of different nations. Some of these were prisoners of war, some were heretics, judaizers and the like, sent to the galleys by the Spanish Holy Office, and some were common malefactors from Spain or Italy, expiating their crimes by servitude at the oars. All of them were informed that they would be unchained before going into action and supplied with weapons, and that every Christian survivor of this expedition should at the end of it be given his freedom. Thus to compensate for the heavy risks of this forlorn hope, they were afforded the chance to fight for their own liberty. Also the measure, by almost doubling the number of fighting men, made the hope far less forlorn.

The dawn of Tuesday broke rosy and dismayingly calm. With gloomy impatience Prospero considered a sea of glass through which his prows were cutting their sluggish way under the propulsion of arms grown weary from the unceasing labours of the night. In an hour or so half the toiling gang would be relieved by fresh slaves; but even then there was little increase of speed to be expected, for the wardens, aware of the urgency, were keeping the pace to twenty-four strokes a minute, which meant the maximum maintainable rate of a league an hour. As from the poop-rail Prospero looked along the benches, a warden, moved perhaps to display zeal because the Captain's eye was upon him, swung his whip aloft. Prospero's voice arrested the lash.

"Hold there! That will not serve. The men are but men, and weary. Serve wine, instead."

And whilst the slaves were gratefully drinking from the cans that were passed along the benches, the gods, as if to reward Prospero's humaneness, sent a puff of air from the east to ruffle the glassy surface of the sea.

It proved the harbinger of a steady breeze that soon was blowing from the Levant, and with creak of blocks and rattle of shrouds, the triangular sails were hoisted. The oars lashed down, the weary gangs could now sleep and renew their strength against the later need of it.

The wind increased as the morning wore on, and only the haste that spurred him made Prospero refuse to allow sail to be shortened even when the long spur at the prow was submerged at every forward heave and the scuppers ran like fountains. Perforce the other galleys must follow the example of their capitana. The formation had changed with the recourse to sail, and the fleet was advancing now in an irregular line abreast, the *Prospera* in an almost middle position, and the galleon, now under her own canvas but with topsails furled lest she should outstrip the remainder of the fleet, on the right flank.

By noon land loomed ahead, and Prospero, with his second-in-command, a lean, middle-aged Genoese named Adriano Allori, and Don Alvaro, was dining in the tabernacle when the squadron entered the Straits of Boniface. They surged through at a speed of between three and four leagues an hour. Emerging off Cape Ferro, they spoke a French brigantine, whose captain gave them news of having two days ago sighted in the distance the Corsair fleet some fifty miles east of Minorca, still going west.

Neither Prospero nor Don Alvaro hesitated to conclude that Dragut would be making the Balearic Islands his destination.

"A raid on the very doorstep of Spain!" was the Spaniard's description of it, and he swore with choleric variety. "And we, too late to prevent it. God help the High and Mighty Duke of Melfi when the news reaches the Emperor."

Prospero prayed that the wind might hold for another twenty-four hours, so that they might at least be in time to avenge what they could not hope to be in time to prevent. For all that day at least it not only held, but increased to such a blast that only Prospero's furious impatience made him still take the risk of carrying full sail. When, however, it eased towards nightfall the fleet had taken no harm beyond the continuous drenchings endured by the gangs. The oars were unlashed, so that manpower might supplement the light airs that came to blow soon after sunset, and all through the night they thrust westward, pitching on the heavy groundswell left by the day's Levante. With the coming of Wednesday's dawn the wind rose again, and Prospero's fretted spirit revived with it. Their speed was much as yesterday's and fully as perilous, but the friendly gods who sent it to blow so opportunely were watching over their safety.

An hour before dusk a cloudy mass on the western horizon proclaimed the good landfall they were making, whilst away to the north, a speck upon the heaving ocean being identified as a boat, the *Imaculada* veered away from her place on the extreme right of the line, and, crowding sail, went in pursuit. She came back to the fleet in the dusk, with the boat in tow. It proved a fishing-craft of the felucca type, with a crew of five, which had been attempting to cross from Minorca to Spain. Her master was brought aboard the *Prospera*, a sturdy, hairy little ruffian, whose natural fierceness was now intensified by the tale he had to tell.

In a Catalan dialect incomprehensible to Prospero but fortunately understood by Don Alvaro, he violently related how two days ago a fleet of Saracen swine had descended upon Palma de Mallorca, and for six-and-thirty hours had ravaged the place until they had converted it into a likeness of Hell. They had sunk or burnt all the shipping in the harbour, including two fine galleons from Barcelona, and then landing they had first seized the fort and butchered its garrison, and after that, at their leisure, they had proceeded to sack the city. They had despoiled the Cathedral of every piece of gold and silver plate. They had murdered the Bishop and left the Episcopal Palace in ruins. For a day and a night they had been pillaging the town, killing ruthlessly wherever opposed. As a climax to that tale of robbery, slaughter and rape, they had that morning shipped close upon a thousand captive youths and maidens aboard their accursed galleys, and not content with all this plunder, they had headed for Minorca, and were even then in Port Mahon, which no doubt would suffer at their foul hands the same fate as Palma.

News of this had come to Minorca ahead of them, brought by fugitives who had crossed from the farther island in open boats, and the narrator, himself, had set out from the Gulf of Anfos as the Corsairs were approaching Port Mahon. It had been his desperate hope to reach Barcelona, so as to bring thence, if not help for the unfortunate islanders, at least vengeance upon their heathen ravishers. He thanked God and the Saints for the unexpected arrival of this Christian fleet, and he prayed that it might prove strong enough to dispatch those sons of pigs to the fires of eternal Hell. He warned them that the Corsairs were in great strength, outnumbering them by almost two to one. But he would blaspheme if he did not believe that the Lord God must be on their side to give them victory in despite of numbers.

"And so pray we," said Prospero, who in a measure as Don Alvaro had translated that tale of horror, had quivered with an anger sharpened by a dread sense of his responsibility.

He ordered at once the furling of all sails, content for the present to let the galleys drift before the wind, which, again as yesterday, was sinking at sunset to a gentle breeze. Then with Don Alvaro he held a conference, to which Allori was bidden, so that he might help their council out of his knowledge and experience as a navigator. Whilst they pored over a chart, Allori described in detail the south-east coast of Minorca which they were approaching. Prospero was measuring with a pair of calipers on the chart the length and width of the creek within which Mahon is situated. In length he ascertained it to be some three and a half miles, and in width a mile at its widest, whilst at the entrance it was not more than three hundred yards across. The land enclosing it on the north-east was a narrow precipitous peninsula, Allori told them, some two hundred feet in height. He also knew that the city of Mahon standing on high ground above the creek was well fortified, and unless Dragut had taken it by surprise, which was hardly to be feared, considering the timely warning received, its capture was likely to delay him.

It was Don Alvaro's proposal, in view of this, that they approach the island on the north and make their landing in the Gulf of Anfos, unperceived by the Corsairs. Thence they could carefully reconnoitre, and postpone attack until the enemy should have landed. That would be the moment to surprise a virtually undefended fleet and destroy it. The plan was further recommended by the fact that by the time Dragut had effected his landing, his galleys must perforce be low in ammunition. But whilst commending its strategic excellence, Prospero incontinently rejected it on the ground that if they waited for the moment urged by Don Alvaro they would have waited until Dragut's devils had repeated at Mahon what already they had done at Palma. "Our task is to prevent any more of that."

"If we can," Don Alvaro agreed. "But can we?"

"We have advantages. We are unsuspected, and now the night will cover our approach."

"You do not hope to enter the inlet unperceived. Dragut will have his sentries at the entrance."

"Even so, if we are not perceived until we are entering, we may be perceived too late. As you have wisely said, Dragut's powder will be running low. This gives us an advantage in ordnance, and this advantage we must preserve by avoiding action at close quarters."

"For such tactics," Allori wisely objected, "an engagement in the open sea would be better. In narrow waters it will easily miscarry."

"Agreed. But for an engagement in the open we should have to sacrifice the advantage of surprise." Prospero paced the length of the cabin in his agitation. Don Alvaro on the divan, his hands folded across his paunch, watched him with pretended imperturbability. "My friends, ours is a choice of evils. We have to determine which is the lesser."

He came back to the table, flung himself into his chair and renewed his brooding over the chart. At last he decided that they must hold a fuller council. He would divide his force into three squadrons, appointing a commander to each, whilst Don Alvaro must transfer himself to the *Imaculada*. He named his three best captains: Allori; another Genoese, named Capranica; and the Neapolitan Sardi, who had been in charge of one of the galleys at Procida. He sent out a sloop to summon them aboard the *Prospera*, and to convey at the same time his orders that all lights be extinguished and the galleys keep as close together as possible.

Night had by now closed down, dark and moonless, and they put their distance from land at about five miles. At the rate of their drift they should be under the bluff of Minorca and at the entrance of the creek in five or six hours.

One of these hours was spent by the five men in discussions that proved inconclusive. Each plan put forward was ultimately rejected. Don Alvaro's remained the only one upon which it seemed desirable to act, and almost Prospero was persuaded to alter their course and head for the Gulf of Anfos to the north. Only the loss of time that would now be involved made him reluctant. So he postponed decision until the last moment, meanwhile ordering Sardi and Capranica to take command each of a division of five galleys, whilst retaining under his own immediate direction the remaining four which included his capitana. Upon that he dismissed them with a promise of definite orders to follow, and applied himself again, alone, to the consideration of what those orders should be.

For another hour he paced the length of the gang-deck, to and fro, from the poop to the bastion of the prow. Amidships, where the kitchen occupied the larboard, and the two heaviest guns the starboard quarter, the cook and his assistants mingled in hushed somnolent chatter with the gun crew. Below the gang-deck, on either side, came the heavy breathing of the slumbering gangs, whilst in the deadworks beyond, where the wooden pavisades had already been erected preparatory to action, the arquebusiers could be heard in talk and movement. Dimly in the clear, starry night were to be discerned on either beam the shadow of the nearest galley, a score of yards away.

These things went all unnoticed by the absorbed captain as he paced there with his problem. He saw nothing but the mental picture he had made of Port Mahon: the long, narrow inlet between high cliffs, with its exiguous entrance and expanding middle, and the close press of Corsair galleys at anchor a mile or so within it. In fancy he took his fleet a dozen times to the attack and each time he pursued a different method, only to follow an initial success by a bitter engagement that ended in his final defeat and extinction, yet left Dragut so crippled that he must run for home so as to save the little that was left him. This was the best that came of all his musings, and it was the least that he had promised to perform. To this least, it seemed, he must resign himself: content to go down in a blaze of glorious defeat that should make some amends for Djerba.

He was at this conclusion – putting from him all thought of Gianna that might yet weaken him into playing the coward – when in his pacings he came to a sudden check. He was standing by the kitchen. The fire was out, and the cauldrons stood cold upon the bed of fire-clay, ringed with iron so as to protect the deck. He had been brought to a halt by the figure, dimly seen, of the master-gunner, who squatted there between a powder-keg on one side and a bucket and a bale of tow on the other. Aloof from the others he was at work, dipping a hand ever and anon into keg or bucket.

"What are you at?" Prospero inquired.

The man came to his feet. He was a Greek named Diomedes, an elderly little fellow, wiry and almost ape-like, but of great skill both in pyrotechnics and ballistics. "I am making matches, my lord."

"Matches?" The word was to prove, itself a match, to fire a startling train of thought. At the end of a long moment Prospero spoke again. "Come with me," he said, and led the way to the poop.

As he raised the heavy leather curtain that masked the entrance to the tabernacle, and came into the light of the slush-lamp suspended from its ceiling, Don Alvaro, who had been dozing on the divan, awoke and gathered himself up.

"Time I should be going aboard the *Imaculada*," he said, "whatever the decision you may have reached."

"A moment." Peremptorily Prospero waved him back to the divan, and turned to the Greek who had pattered barefooted after him. "What is the slowest match that you can make?"

"The slowest match?" Diomedes scratched his grizzled head. Calculation deepened the network of wrinkles in his brown face. "I could make a match of five yards that would take a minute to burn."

"Or one of ten that would last two minutes?"

"Oh yes. Or longer still, my lord, to burn at the same rate."

"I could depend upon that? You'd answered for it with your head that the match would burn no faster?"

Diomedes took an instant to consider. "I would, my lord."

"How long would you need to make me a hundred yards of such a match?"

Again the Greek took time for calculation. "Three hours," he said, "with a man to help me. Three hours at most."

"Take as many men as you need, and see that you keep your word. It is close on midnight. In less than five hours it will be daylight. I can give you four hours for the work; but not an instant longer."

Diomedes swore fulfilment, and pattered out to set about the task, whilst the mystified Spaniard asked a question.

"It means," said Prospero, "that I shall command a round ship for once." He was smiling, and his lean face was alight with excitement. "It is I who will go into action aboard the *Imaculada*. You, Don Alvaro, will remain with Allori to command the capitana in my absence."

Chapter 32

The Battle of Cape Mola

The first pallors of the dawn revealed the Neapolitan squadron to the Moslem sentinel on the rocky headland of La Mola, like a line of ghost ships in that pearly light.

He heaved himself from the scrub on which he had lain comfortably asprawl, rubbed his eyes, and asked himself whence, in the name of Allah, such a fleet could have sprung.

Leading the line by a couple of cables' length, and riding high in the water, came a great galleon of unmistakable Spanish build.

The light grew even as in his moment of amazement the watcher continued petrified at gaze. Before he had kindled a match, to fire the alarm signal, the pearly grey of the sea was already shot by the first rays of the sun into a fiery opalescence. Sounds came to confirm the watcher's vision. With thud and splash of oars the galleys quickened suddenly into life, whilst from the galleon came the creak of blocks as she increased by topsails her spread of canvas to the freshening morning breeze. Then, close-hauled, she veered for the entrance of the creek.

Blowing frenziedly upon his match, the sentinel snatched up his arquebuse and its crutch, and at that very moment the stillness of the morning was shattered by the roar of a cannonade.

A mile and a half away, opposite Mahon, Dragut, who in the dark had crept within range of the fort, loosed upon it that terrific volley from a score of guns. With the cloud of dust that rose from sandstone walls reduced to rubble mingled the smoke of a reply so faint that it revealed how sadly reduced already were the defenders. Dragut's galleys, having discharged their heavy pieces, had gone about, and were pulling out of range again as the few hasty shots from the fort splashed harmlessly about them. Even at that distance could be heard the rousing cheer with which the Corsairs greeted the result of their bombardment. As it died down, the sentinel on La Mola discharged at last his piece, to give the alarm, and then, flinging down his arquebuse and crutch, so that he might run the faster, sped yelling, "Y'Allah! Y'Allah!" to carry the warning to the next outpost.

But it was no longer necessary, for from his station Dragut had already sighted the galleon at the mouth of the creek, and after a moment's incredulous gaping pause had roared his jubilation at this vision. His trumpets sounded, and in a moment a dozen of his galleys had quitted the main body of the fleet and were advancing at the utmost speed of the gangs.

Sinan-el-Sanim was in command of this detachment, with orders to board and seize a vessel supposed – as Prospero reckoned that it would be – a richly laden prize, perhaps from the New World.

Dragut, himself, with the remainder of his fleet, keeping under the peninsula of La Mola, where no shot from Mahon could reach him, followed leisurely at a distance.

The galleon, notwithstanding this rush to meet her, with an overweening confidence, as it seemed, that provoked the mockery of the Corsairs, held steadily on close-hauled, with a gentle list to larboard. The main body of her crew, having made all secure, had dropped over the side into the attendant longboat just as she was heading into the creek, an operation this which had gone unperceived by the Moslems. Aboard her now there were none but her master, who remained at the helm, dressed only in shirt and drawers, Diomedes, who was busy on the main deck below, and Prospero, who armed with a linstock had stationed himself at the forechasers in the prow.

The galleys came on in line abreast, the platforms behind the rostra thronged with yelling turbaned devils who counted the galleon as good as taken already since she was too far committed in that narrow place to attempt to go about. Indeed, to leave the western shore to which she clung would be to lose the little breeze that reached her over the heights of La Mola.

When not more than three-quarters of a mile lay between the Corsairs and the *Imaculada*, Diomedes suddenly surged at Prospero's side, with the announcement that all was ready.

Prospero nodded in silence, his face set, and handed the linstock to the Greek. A moment only the master-gunner spent in laying the chasers, then touched them off, more or less at a venture, in quick succession. The first shot flung up a harmless shower of spray in the space between two of the galleys; but the second, by great good fortune, ricocheting from the water, broached the flank of one of the Corsairs between wind and water, compelling her to fall behind and, in a leaking condition, seek safety ashore. With redoubled yells of fury the remainder continued an undeterred advance.

"Away with you, Diomedes. Bid Gastone lash down the helm, then take him with you. Away!" Diomedes looked at him, hesitating. "Away!" Prospero repeated, more peremptory. "You know what is to do."

Still Diomedes lingered to utter a warning, grave with fear. "You'll not delay overlong?"

"Be sure I'll not. Away!"

Diomedes departed. On his way aft he was joined by the master, who had lashed down the helm. The two passed into the coach, and from the stern window climbed down into a sloop that the galleon was towing. They cut her adrift and got out the oars; but they did not pull away; they sat idle on the thwarts, watching the stern of the great ship as it drew steadily away from them to meet the advancing galleys.

Prospero remained at his post for only a moment after Diomedes' departure from the forecastle. He estimated at eight miles an hour the rate at which the distance between galleys and galleon was diminishing, and so judged that in five or six minutes now the Corsairs would be alongside. It was time to set about what yet remained to do.

The *Imaculada* carried twenty guns on two decks. Eight of these were in the waist, four on each quarter, whilst twelve were on the main deck below. To the four starboard guns in the waist time-fuses of varying lengths had been attached by Diomedes. Since the galleon was sailing with her other quarter close to the land, those were the only guns worth firing for purposes of demonstration. It could hardly be hoped that they would serve any greater purpose, for their fire would prove harmless to the enemy, and would probably be derided as a sign of panic aboard; but it would supply apparent evidence that the ship was manned, and disposed to fight.

So, as he sped aft, Prospero ignited each match in turn, and as he was dropping through a scuttle to the main deck, the galleon shook with the discharge of the first of them. Two more went off at intervals of a minute whilst he was busy below. The gun-ports of the main deck were all closed, and he was compelled to work in the dim twilight from the open scuttle overhead.

Every powder-keg the magazine had contained was stacked here in a great pyramid from deck to deck, and close about the base of this pyramid the black contents of a couple of kegs had been heaped. In this loose powder were buried the ends of the fuses upon which Diomedes had laboured through the last hours of that night. Each fuse was twenty yards in length and there were three of them, so even if two should chance to fail, there would still be a third to do the work.

Quickly Prospero lighted them, stayed a second to watch their spluttering start, then leapt for the scuttle-butt, and hoisted himself swiftly to the upper deck, rammed down the scuttle, and made fast the binding-strake.

One glance ahead showed him that, quick though he had been, the distance separating him from the Corsairs had been halved since he had left the forecastle. He raced down the gangway astern, reached the coach, and lifted himself to the sill of the open window.

In the moment that he balanced there, the fourth of his guns went off, and drew a derisive cheer from the approaching Moslem galleys. Then, naked save for a pair of drawers, he dived into the eddying wake.

When he rose to the surface, the galleon was already fifty yards away from him, but was still interposed as a screen between himself and the Corsairs. He set out to swim towards the sloop, which remained more or less at the spot where she had been cut adrift.

A moment or two later the galleys closed about the *Imaculada*, and hurled their grapnels, so as to clutch her bulwarks, her bowsprit, and her fore and after chains, just as Prospero had reckoned that they would. With oars lashed astern like folded wings, they hauled themselves close, knowing that once alongside, the galleon's guns could not be depressed to a level at which they could be brought to bear upon them. Hanging on to the flanks of the great ship, they retarded, but did not arrest, her stately progress. Grappling her, they were towed slowly along. Three of the Corsairs had tackled her to starboard and three to larboard, whilst a seventh galley passed under her counter, and attached itself by a grapnel to the coach. The remaining four had slackened speed, and hung a little in the rear, forming a reserve, to close in when the crews of the leaders should have boarded.

If the majority of the Corsairs crouched behind their pavisades waiting for the first arquebusades from the galleon to be spent, others had swarmed the ratlines to the cross-trees, whence they could command the *Imaculada*'s decks, and sweep them with the bolts of their arbalests or the shafts of their steel Turkish bows. It was these who, perceiving in amazement the emptiness of those decks, were first aroused to a vague sense of peril. Scarcely, however, had they begun excitedly to clamour the news to those below, when all sound was lost in a roar that was like the volley of a hundred guns. The sides of the great galleon were thrust out and her decks rose up, borne, as it seemed, on walls of fire; and in a devastating explosion the *Imaculada* disintegrated into far-scorching flame.

The sea in convulsion as of an earthquake in its depths, heaved itself up in curling walls of water that ran like tidal waves in that narrow place, and battered one against the other the galleys of the main body of the fleet, off Mahon.

Prospero, at a distance of some two hundred yards from the explosion, was lifted high on a mountain of water, and then sucked under by the swirl of it, whilst a hundred yards farther out the sloop that waited for him, within an ace of being capsized, was left half-swamped in the trough of that terrific wave.

When Prospero re-emerged it was into a shower of fiery wreckage that fell hissing about him.

Where the galleon had been there was now a fiercely eddying, smoking whirlpool in which timbers, masts, oars and spars were wildly tossed. The galleon, herself, had gone, and with her had gone the seven galleys that had grappled her, whelmed in flame, and crushed by the toppling ruin of her. Of the four that near at hand had formed the reserve, two had been flung so violently against each other, that with splintered oars and smashed bulwarks, both were sinking, whilst a third was on fire and the fourth engaged in rescue work that was already overcrowding her.

Nor was this the whole of the disaster that had so suddenly and swiftly overtaken a third of the Corsair fleet. Yet another of their vessels, a big galeasse, which had been creeping along the shore of La Mola, as if to observe the action, was lifted by the great wave, borne helplessly landwards, and smashed down inextricably upon the jagged rocks. The fact that she flew the blue crescent on a white and red standard proclaimed her Dragut's own flagship.

Whilst in the main body of the fleet they were recovering from the dismaying astonishment of that inexplicable catastrophe, the water-logged sloop was crawling to meet Prospero, who rode astride of a baulk of wreckage. The shipmaster pulled, whilst Diomedes frantically baled. Coming up with him at last, they helped him over the side into the ankle-deep water within. He slid down, a little exhausted, into the sternsheets. Then he sat up with a laugh that was all grimness.

"That has levelled up the odds a little. We may improve them further if we don't hurry."

It was in his calculations that the Corsairs must see the sloop and, attributing to it the cataclysm in which eleven galleys had been lost, must presently be in pursuit of them. If he miscalculated at all, it was to underestimate their vindictive rage, for soon no fewer than six galleys were racing after that one small boat. Two of these paused by the one survivor of Sinan's squadron to lend a hand in the work of rescue; but the other four came on at speed, lessening the distance at every stroke of the oars.

In the sloop Diomedes and Gastone were now both rowing, and rowing frantically.

"Easily!" Prospero admonished them.

"By all the demons!" swore the shipmaster, panting. "We shall be flayed alive if they catch us. I saw a man flayed once in Aleppo by these Saracen dogs, and I've no mind to look as he did."

Prospero glanced over his shoulder. "You're in no danger of it yet."

The galleys were four hundred yards behind them and the mouth of the creek two hundred yards ahead. Along the heights of the peninsula, and level with the pursuers, two sentries ran screaming and gesticulating furiously, in an attempt to convey a warning of the Christian fleet that lurked waiting in the open. But their frantic outcries were misunderstood and went unheeded.

The main body of the Corsair fleet was now moving towards the spot where the disaster had overtaken Sinan's squadron. One galley, ahead of the others, made for Dragut's galeasse, piled up on La Mola. And as she reached her, one of the yelling sentries slithered down the declivity to the same spot. The sloop was almost at the mouth of the creek, when from the disabled galeasse came the boom of a gun, and from her cross-trees a frantic waving of flags.

These were intended as warnings to the pursuing galleys. But they were interpreted as demands for help, and were left unheeded by the four pursuers, now racing one another for the satisfaction of making the capture.

The sloop cleared the entrance, swung round the headland to the north and found itself among the vessels composing Sardi's and Prospero's own divisions. The five galleys under Capranica hugged the shore on the opposite side of the inlet.

Prospero had barely climbed aboard his capitana, and received, wet and naked as he was, the bear-hug of an embrace with which Don Alvaro expressed relief at his safe return, when the four Corsairs came racing out of the creek into the open sea.

Their only chance, once they perceived into what an ambush they had blundered, lay in keeping to their course with all the speed of which their oars were capable. Thus they would have avoided, at least, being surrounded, and might have created the occasion for their rescue by the main body of their fleet. But in that moment of consternation, their instinctive thought was to retreat, and by yielding to it they completed their instant undoing.

Even as the scourged slaves rose in their places and turned, to face the prow, Sardi's five galleys slid in behind them, to cut off their retreat, and the gunners ready at their stations, with matches smouldering, touched off the heavy pieces amidships. Ten guns pounded those galleys at point-blank range, and three of the Corsairs received amongst them the stone projectiles of those ten guns. One of them broached in two places between wind and water, listed, filled and began to sink. Two other reeled, crippled, with shattered pavisades and broken oars, their decks cumbered by dead and dying. The fourth, which had gone unscathed, and had contrived to turn about, was headed in fury at her assailants, and with rending crash of oars drove her rostrum on to Sardi's own galley abaft of the middle platform. But taken unawares as they had been, and all unprepared for action, the Corsairs could not bring their guns to bear in time. In a frenzy of despairing rage, scimitar in hand, they flung themselves aboard Sardi's vessel. The foremost of these invaders were mown down by a file of arquebusiers, and then, as hand-to-hand fighting began, the Corsair was herself entered by another of Sardi's galleys, and swept by arquebusades from the rear. Caught thus, between two fires, the fight went out of those wild children of Islam. Within five minutes of boarding Sardi, they clamoured for quarter, and threw down their arms.

Capranica, meanwhile, was ensuring the surrender of the other two, and packing aboard the survivors of the vessel that had been sunk. Swiftly they went about the work of disentangling the galleys that had been interlocked, of disarming the crews of the three captured vessels, and of putting aboard each a sufficiency of arquebusiers to ensure submissiveness and order. Gladly did their slave-gangs, with the scent of freedom in their nostrils, bend to the oars, to convey those galleys to the Christian rear, which was established to the east of Cape La Mola. Already these gangs, armed with the weapons of which the Corsairs had been deprived, were ordering the captives to the benches which they had themselves vacated. The prisoners remaining over were set to clear the decks of the ugly vestiges of battle, and temporarily to repair as far as possible by the means available the damaged deadworks.

Whilst this was doing, Dragut, who had transferred himself from his grounded galeasse to one of his galleys, was leading forth what remained of his fleet to the task of vengeance that Allah imposed upon him. It was in this light that the Anatolian, with hell raging in his soul and infecting his following, viewed the situation.

From the distance he had seen the discomfiture of the four galleys that had pursued the sloop. Into his field of vision seven stranger galleys had moved during that engagement, and he had supposed that this was the entire force with which he had to deal. Deal with it he would, by the Beard of the Prophet, in a way that should make his name remembered. Hereafter the terror of it should exceed any yet inspired among these Nasrani swine. They should pay dearly, these presumptuous, unbelieving pigs, for thus ruining his fine enterprise and reducing to naught the profit of his raid. He would roast alive every man of them that survived the fray to which he moved with the thirteen galleys that remained him of the proud fleet which Nasrani treachery had cut in half by now. But whilst fury turned to fire the blood in his veins, it did not blind him to essentials, or dull the keenness of his mind. Some of the loss in men, in galleys and in slaves might yet be made good by the capture of these his rash assailants. Reckoning himself as of still twice their number and of a vastly superior address in an ordinary encounter, it should not tax either his strength or his skill to reduce these Frankish vessels into possession, and so partially make good his loss. Therefore, as they raced to battle, the word went forth from him, that, so as not to damage this prospective property, the Corsairs were to refrain from using guns, confining themselves to laying the Frankish vessels board-and-board.

But when in the leading galley, the *Rakham*, he raced out of the creek, and beheld the enemy's full array, he saw that he was not merely outnumbered in vessels but outmatched in weight by ships that in the main were superior to those of his that remained afloat. When from the maintruck of the *Prospera* he beheld the standard of the double-headed swan, and knew that Prospero Adorno was his adversary, fresh anger and amazement clouded his wits. They cleared again when a thirty-six-pound shot swept the deck of the *Rakham*, smashed the rambade into fragments and laid low a score or more of his crossbow-men assembled upon it.

Dragut stood at the poop-rail, a glittering figure in chain mail, scimitar in hand, his black-bearded hawk face swart and fierce under the white turban that swathed his steel cap, and in a hoarse voice croaked the order that sent his galley in a charge, blind as that of a wounded bull, at the nearest enemy. Driven home, the charge entered Capranica's galley towards the prow, and a wave of Corsairs swept over her with a fury which beat down all resistance until they were amidships. Here they found a barrier stretched, and beyond this a steady line of arquebusiers, whose fire cut a bloody swathe in their serried ranks. But Dragut himself was at hand to steady the staggering of his men. Under his fierce urge the barrier was overcome, and in hand-to-hand fighting with cold steel, the poop itself was reached, its defenders cut to pieces and Capranica himself laid low.

Whilst guns roared about him, smoke billowed over the galleys, and the acrid stench of powder caught him in the throat, Dragut swung round before the tabernacle of the vessel of which in that fierce charge he had made himself master. Momentarily intoxicated by blood-lust and the success gained into a delusion of victory, he uttered a fierce yell of triumph, waving aloft his bloody scimitar. But even as he so turned, and his glance pierced the eddying cloud of smoke, he had a glimpse that sobered him. Ten yards away one of Dragut's stoutest galleys was sinking by the head, whilst close at hand the *Rakham*, on which only a few fighting men had been left, had been boarded in her turn, occupied, and was now a bridge across which Volpi, one of the captains of Capranica's division, was bringing a strong force of arquebusiers to rake the invaders of Capranica's galley. Taking cover along the larboard pavisades and behind the wreckage of the rambade, Volpi's men poured volley after volley into the dense ranks of those who had followed Dragut. Torn and stung by this pitiless fire, the Moslems sought shelter in the deadworks whilst preparing to use their crossbows.

Dominating the hellish din of vocal fury, the rattle of small arms, the hum of bowstrings, the clash of metal and the crash of rending timbers, came the steady thunder of artillery both Moslem and Christian. For in the pass in which the Corsairs found themselves, the original notion of reducing the Frankish galleys into possession had perforce been abandoned. They fought desperately, instead, to destroy so that they might, themselves, avoid being destroyed, and the more desperately because the measure of surprise at the outset had given the Christians an advantage which further weighted the odds against the Moslems.

Capranica's galley, which Dragut had so rashly accounted won, was not only in danger of being recaptured by those who made a bridge of the *Rakham*, but if recaptured now would leave the *Rakham* also in Frankish hands. And half recaptured Dragut already beheld her, for his diminished followers were unable to stem the rush of Volpi's boarders, who stabbed and hacked their way forward with pike and sword.

Dragut upon the poop, shouting orders that none heeded between calls upon Allah the Omnipotent for assistance, watched the battle sweeping towards him as his men gave way or went down on a deck slippery with blood and cumbered by the bodies of the fallen. He was accounting all lost and about to spring forward into that mêlée, to die as he had lived, when the *Jamil* came board-and-board on his larboard side, and from her decks to the platform below the poop surged a horde of Sinan-el-Sanim's men to reinforce his own faltering followers.

Above the uproar Dragut could hear the piercing falsetto of the colossal eunuch, urging his men on. But they came too late. Dragut's forces were beyond salvation. What remained of them in their retreat of exhaustion and panic of perceived defeat hindered the advance of those who would have come to their assistance. Vainly did Dragut curse them for dogs and cowards to yield before the unbelieving offspring of Shaitan. Panting, sweating, bleeding, they gave way until they blocked the entrance platform. As vainly did Sinan's men, at his shrill bidding, leap down upon the oars which the Turkish slaves of Capranica's galley held firm for them, so as to supply a gangway by which they might reach her decks. Some were shot from the oars by Volpi's arquebusiers, who had now established themselves in the deadworks, some were plunged into the sea by a sudden releasing of the oars that followed upon the merciless slashing of the slaves who had sought thus to help their Moslem brethren.

When from his poop, the shrill voice of Sinan summoned Dragut to save himself by retreating aboard the eunuch's galley, the raging, despairing Anatolian perceived no alternative to compliance. It was his only chance to extricate himself, and so, by resuming command of the entire action, repair the fatal error of having yielded to the lust of a personal engagement which he had imagined would have been triumphantly brief. He thrust his way to the galley's edge, and whilst the last line of his men held the unbelievers in momentary check, he leapt aboard Sinan's vessel. In the need to think of his fleet as a whole, rather than of what might survive of his immediate following, he gave the order to pull away for the open, whence he might survey the action and determine the direction of it.

At a distance of a hundred yards from the spot where eventually he halted the *Jamil*, he beheld the battle now concentrated into two struggling interlocked masses, with a clear space of perhaps fifty yards of sea between them. At such close quarters the heavy guns had ceased to function, but the rattle of firelocks was continuous through the clash and roar of combat, and about the antagonists hung a thin mist of smoke which the freshening Levante was dispelling as fast as it arose. Thus Dragut was enabled to cast up the account.

In the westward battle four of his galleys were besetting three of the enemy's, and one of the latter, overrun by his turbaned fighters, seemed already as good as captured. In the other battle, however, five Corsairs were interlocked with six Imperial galleys, and at the stage at which Dragut surveyed it, the encounter there showed little advantage to either side.

In sickness of soul Dragut realized that during the hour which the engagement had now lasted, since his issue from the creek, three of his vessels had vanished, sunk by gunfire, whilst on the side of the Imperials only one was missing. The water, churned by the strife, was littered with their wreckage.

Some eighty yards beyond the two battling groups, and at an equal distance from either, the *Prospera* stood aloof, watching, directing where possible, and poised to swoop to the assistance of either battle as its development might demand.

In the westward group one of the Imperial galleys ran up at that moment the red oriflamme, which was the call for succour. With blare of trumpets to answer and encourage her, the *Prospera*'s oars flashed in the sunlight, and she began to move. But she checked again almost at once. For Volpi, having now disengaged his own and Capranica's galleys, thrust them into the mêlée, leaving the captured *Rakham*, now manned by Frankish slaves, to follow. Thus the odds were changed from four to three to four to six, and the Moslem onslaught instantly turned into defence.

Dragut was giving the word to go in and save the day there, when Sinan clutched his arm, talking rapidly and pointing to the eastern struggle. He urged that it would be easier to turn the fortunes of battle there, and after that, with a greater striking force, retrieve what might meanwhile be lost in the other group, where their weight at present would have less effect. Dragut recognized the shrewdness of the advice, and was deciding to act upon it when suddenly, to his joyous surprise, he beheld three of the Turkish galleys which he had accounted lost swing out from under Cape Mola, racing to join the battle in that same group.

"The praise to Allah, the Mighty, the Strong, Who sends succour to the Faithful!" he chanted. "All is far from lost, Sinan. We outnumber the unbelieving dogs. Allah sends victory to His children."

Sinan enlightened him, his shrill voice hoarse as a jay's. These were vessels that the unbelievers had captured, rowed now by their own Moslem brethren and manned by their erstwhile slave-gangs. In answer the eunuch received the full blast of Dragut's wrath and bitterness.

"May Allah strike thee dead, thou bladder of unclean lard! What were you doing to let them fall into Frankish hands?"

"I was not there when it befell," protested the indignant eunuch.

"To be sure you were not. You were preserving your worthless greasy carcase. You are never to be found where you are needed."

"Bismillah! Had I lately not been where I was needed, and desperately, by you, I should not now be offended by unjust reproaches."

Dragut, however, remained untouched by this lament. "As Allah hears me, you shall be found for once where swords are clashing." He pointed with his scimitar to the eastward battle. "There lies our work."

Sinan's soft, large hand fell on the extended arm. "There lies our death," he amended.

"What is written is written. When all else is lost shall life still matter to this handful of vile dust? Are you afraid to die, Sinan?"

"I am if I must die in the displeasure of Allah; and that is how they die who waste His gift of life to no good purpose."

Dragut's smouldering eyes scorched him with their scorn. "A coward will never want for reasons to cling to his worthless life."

The fat mass of Sinan was agitated by anger. "Have your petulant way, then. Let the Sword of Islam be flung away in childish rage rather than preserved to avenge the disaster of this day of woe."

Here was an argument to touch Dragut. That the day was lost beyond hope of redemption there could no longer be any doubt. In one of the still battling groups four Corsair vessels were hemmed about by six of the Imperials; in the other eight Frankish galleys were opposed to six of the Moslems, and to render the odds there still more overwhelming, Prospero's great galeasse, which beyond the execution done at the outset by her guns had not yet been in action, was moving into the encounter with her fresh fighting men.

With a groan Dragut covered his face, and vanished into the tabernacle. Dropping his sword, he flung himself prone upon the divan to curse and weep in one at the ruin that confronted him. Two hours ago he had been master of a mighty fleet, laden with the plunder and slaves that Palma had yielded to him and with the clear prospect of adding to these at Port Mahon. And now that fleet was being destroyed and his prizes were being lost to him. His own great galeasse was fast on the rocks of Mola, her hold stuffed with treasure and some three hundred captives, among whom were a hundred Balearic maidens he had destined to grace the hareems of the Faithful after enriching him by the fat prices they would have fetched in the souk-el-abeed of Algiers or Tunis. Of all this in two brief hours had he been cheated by a misbegotten Genoese dog whom Shaitan protected and endowed with his own Satanic craft. But by Allah the All-Knowing, the All-Wise, Who had created man of clots of blood, there must be a day of reckoning, and for that day Dragut must consent to live.

Sinan, at the entrance of the tabernacle, despite his own quaking, could yet observe with eyes of scorn this breakdown of the pride and strength of the great Corsair regarded by Islam as of tempered steel.

"Is it your will, then, that we go whilst yet we may?" he softly asked.

Dragut ceased his lament. He heaved himself up. "Impatient for the order, art thou not?" he snarled. "Give it then, and may blackness cover thee!"

In silence the eunuch vanished.

Without any blast of trumpet or display of flags, the oars were dipped, and the *Jamil* headed south, and slunk away at the best of her speed from that lost fight. Unpursued by the Imperialists who were still heavily engaged in garnering the fruits of an action now determined, she was of all Dragut's great fleet the only Corsair galley that escaped from the Battle of Cape Mola.

Although it would not be known that Dragut himself was on board the *Jamil*, yet her flight was a signal to the surviving Moslems to save their lives by flinging down their arms.

Chapter 33

The Rehabilitation of an Emperor

Before noon of that memorable Thursday, Prospero was able to cast up his accounts of the battle that had begun at dawn. He had come into it with fourteen galleys. He went out of it with twenty-six. He had lost only one vessel of his own, whilst he had captured thirteen of Dragut's. And this excluded the crippled Corsair galley that had never issued from the creek and Dragut's flagship, which had gone aground. The first was too seriously damaged to be worth appropriating. But her crew was made captive and sent to the rowers' benches, and her Christian gangs were set free. The second was left impaled upon the rocks of the Mola; but from her, too, the gangs were removed and delivered of their chains, whilst from her hold was recovered the great treasures of gold and gems of which Dragut had plundered Palma and the three hundred captives – the youths and maidens of Majorca – destined to the slave-markets of Barbary. In addition to these, and including in the count the slaves released from the oars, it was computed that Prospero had that day delivered from captivity upwards of three thousand Christian slaves, whilst taking prisoner some two thousand Moslems to man the Imperial galleys.

With the captured vessels now rowed by their erstwhile masters, under the whip of those who yesterday had been their slaves, Prospero's augmented and now imposing if battered fleet entered the

Port of Mahon with banners flying, drums beating and trumpets flourishing.

The Minorcans, who from the headlands on either side of the inlet had watched the battle, crowded to the quays of Mahon to receive, embrace and caress these gallant warriors to whom they owed their own preservation and the deliverance from captivity of their Balearic brethren.

Whilst the captains were banqueted by the Spanish Governor, the troops were feasted by the townsfolk, filled with wine and laden with gifts. On Friday a Te Deum was sung in the Cathedral, to return thanks for the preservation of Mahon, and the Archbishop came over from Majorca, to preach a sermon in which he superlatively lauded the valour of the little squadron that – in his own happy phrase – had dealt with the Barbary ravishers as David had dealt with Goliath. On Saturday a Requiem Mass was sung for some four hundred Christians who had fallen in the fight, and again the Archbishop preached, on a text this time of "Dulce et decorum est pro Patria mori".

Three days the Neapolitan squadron remained in Mahon, overwhelmed by Minorcan hospitality, whilst the galleys, many of which had suffered damage more or less severe, were being restored to a seaworthy condition, re-equipped, victualled and reordered in the matter of their crews.

On the following Monday, at last, just one week after leaving Naples, on a hope regarded as forlorn, they weighed anchor, leaving behind them in the care of the Minorcans some three hundred wounded who were unfit to travel. On the same day a Minorcan frigate set out from Mahon for Barcelona, with letters for the Emperor from Governor and Archbishop. In these they sent His Majesty an account of the glorious victory of Cape La Mola and the annihilation of Dragut-Reis and his formidable fleet, in terms which painted the achievement as even more fantastically splendid than it actually was.

Don Alvaro de Carbajal, who swore himself from that day in all but blood Prospero's own brother, would have had him sail for

Barcelona, too, so that he might receive from His Majesty the Imperial thanks that were his due. But Prospero would not be persuaded.

"There is a lady who waits in Naples in more fear than hope. To ease her gentle spirit is more to me than the thanks of all the emperors of the earth. But if I do not go to render my accounts in person, I can render them by letter."

And so he went to write. But it was not, as he had said, to render his accounts. Abundantly Governor and Archbishop would be rendering those for him. His purpose was quite other. It was to prove to Gianna the sincerity of his parting assurance that if the chance were his he would reject the fruits of vengeance that in the end had been thrust by chance upon him. His mission, the forlorn hope upon which he had come, facing self-immolation, was to undo as far as might yet lie in his power the wrong that at Djerba he had done to Christendom. Now that success far beyond all reasonable hope had crowned his endeavours, he would do more. The amend to Christendom was made. It remained to make amends to Andrea Doria, by an effort to avert the ruin that all of those few who knew the facts foresaw for him.

In that spirit he sat down to pen his letter to the Emperor. In the course of it he wrote:

Whilst as Your Majesty will have learnt, the Corsair Dragut-Reis succeeded in eluding the trap in which a month ago my Lord Admiral, the Duke of Melfi, had counted upon seizing him, yet by Heaven's grace he has not succeeded in avoiding the far-flung net that was cast to take him before my Lord Admiral could account fulfilled the enterprise upon which last he sailed from Genoa. Whilst the Duke of Melfi kept the seas to the east, it fell to me, with the Neapolitan squadron, to the command of which I was lately restored, to be in charge of the western end of that wide net, and it was my good fortune here at Port Mahon to fall in with the Corsair fleet and completely to destroy it, in fulfilment of my Lord Admiral's design.

Lest Don Alvaro should be tempted to write anything that should contradict it, Prospero showed him the letter. It left him gaping.

"But this...this is not true!" the Spaniard protested.

"Come, come, my friend. Should I write falsehoods to the Emperor? What word of untruth do you discover?"

Don Alvaro studied the letter again.

"I can put my finger on no untrue word. But the implications are all false. What has Doria to do with this?"

"Was it not Doria's design, when he sailed, to make an end of Dragut? And is not that the design that is accomplished? And is it not true that he keeps the eastern end of the Mediterranean, and that the Neapolitan squadron is a part of his fleet?"

"But for what will you deny yourself the glory of an achievement that is entirely your own, that deserves the Golden Fleece?"

"To pay a debt; a debt of honour."

"From what I have seen, the debt between you and Doria is of a different order."

"You have not seen all. Humour me in this, Don Alvaro. Say nothing that will detract from the credit that I gladly give to Doria."

"Since you ask it, my friend. But neither will I say anything ever to detract from the credit that is yours."

"It is possible to compromise, which is all that my letter does."

To please him Don Alvaro agreed. But to none but Prospero would he ever give the credit for the masterly tactics which had won the amazing battle of La Mola, beginning with the invention which had converted the *Imaculada* into a Titanic bombshell and had blown a third of the enemy's fleet out of the water before battle was joined.

"When a condottiero trained to the sea happens also to be a poet with a poet's vision, it follows," Don Alvaro would conclude, "that he must be invincible."

If that view was exaggerated, yet it was not Don Alvaro's only. An age which set craft far above mere valour was ravished by the details of the sea-fight of La Mola as earlier it had delighted in the guileful strategy that had earned the victory of Procida.

From such evidence as we possess it is to be doubted if the Balearic achievement produced in any man an admiration greater than that which the Emperor was to express. And this because a feat which at any time must have earned the rich approval of the warlike Charles V was peculiarly welcome to him happening when it did.

A fortnight earlier His Majesty had come to Barcelona with the intention of taking ship for Italy, jubilant over Andrea Doria's rashly anticipatory report of the capture of Dragut and his fleet at Djerba. There was reason why this should be a source of personal pride to him. He was well aware that his acumen in appointing the Duke of Melfi his Mediterranean Admiral in preference to any of the Spanish seamen among his nobles had been secretly impugned. Its vindication by this glorious achievement was a personal triumph for His Majesty. But at Barcelona, on the very eve of embarcation, the dreadful news that this Dragut whom Doria boasted that he held captive was at sea in force and ravishing as ruthlessly as ever the Christian coasts came to prick that bubble of Imperial pride. The Emperor was not only dismayed, he was filled now with angry doubts of that very acumen of which he had been boasting so as to avenge himself upon those who had presumed to question it.

To feed his misgivings there were about him not only those who at the time of Andrea Doria's appointment had advised His Majesty against it, but there were also those who could not forgive him for not having found his admiral among themselves. He was rightly persuaded of their covert, wicked satisfaction in this conspicuous failure of the Genoese braggart. Upon their countenances they might set masks of grave concern, and they might utter sighs of "Que lastima! Que desventura!" But His Majesty was not deceived. He felt himself mocked and diminished, and inwardly he raged the more bitterly because pride forbade him to display resentment. Soon it was worse. There were innuendoes subtly assailing the Genoese Admiral's worth. To be sure he had been successful in the past. But how much of this success might not be due to the sheer fortune of war? How much of it might not have resulted from the incompetence of those who opposed him? How much of it was not the work of the captains who served under him?

Even the Marquis del Vasto, in the Emperor's following, because mourning a friend he accounted lost, as he believed, by Doria treachery, spoke openly of Goialatta and the glory with which Andrea Doria had emerged from it. But analysing this glory, he reminded men that actually the Admiral had been all but lost by rashness on that occasion, and that he had been victoriously extricated by the heroism of one of his subordinates, a Genoese named Prospero Adorno, who had afterwards ended his career in a heroic deed at Cherchell, in which Doria had failed to support him. These grandees shook their noble heads, and concluded with sighs that the world had been sadly deceived in the merits of a seaman whose true worth was now revealed.

That was as near as they dared go to an indictment of the Imperial judgment; but it sufficed to fill the Emperor with secret shame, discovering himself belittled by this failure of a foreign Admiral, appointed in the teeth of the opposition of elderly experienced counsellors.

To drive the iron deeper into his proud soul came then the appalling news of the horrors wrought by Dragut in His Majesty's own dominions, here at Majorca, on the very threshold of his Spanish kingdom. Such was his anger that when he attempted to speak of these things his stammering became too acute to leave his words intelligible. Others about him, however, whose speech suffered no physical impediment, overcame any spiritual impediments that might hitherto have restrained it. They now spoke openly of Andrea Doria as an impudent charlatan, a man who covered paltry deeds with big words and a thrasonical swagger, a bald man who accounted himself hairy because the Emperor had given him a wig, and they laid at the door of his imposture the murdered men, the ravished women, the slave-raiding, the sacrilege, the pillaging and the incendiarism that had tormented the Emperor's Balearic subjects.

To the Emperor it was as if they laid the blame upon himself. He admitted it to his confessor, the Cardinal Loyasa. "Qui fecit per alium, fecit per se. I appointed this man to his command. His failure is my failure. In their hearts men hold me answerable for these dreadful sufferings of my subjects. And I cannot contradict them."

In deep dejection, the projected voyage abandoned, he quitted Barcelona, and set out lugubriously to return to Madrid; and his every breath became a despondently sighed "Mea culpa!"

And then, like a glorious sunburst upon the black gloom of his despair, had come the startling news of La Mola, the utter annihilation of Dragut's fleet, the recovery of the plunder of Majorca, the deliverance of the Balearic captives and of countless Christian men besides from the slavery of the Barbary rowing benches.

It was that sentence in Prospero's letter, curiously confirmed by a phrase in the Governor's report, which you may suspect Prospero to have inspired, which completely restored the Emperor's fading self-respect.

This glorious feat of arms [the Governor had written] *is the work of the Neapolitan squadron, led by Messer Prospero Adorno, the ablest of the lieutenants of Your Majesty's Captain-General. We, Your Majesty's faithful subjects in these islands, commend to Your Majesty both the Duke of Melfi and his gallant subordinate for the timely dispositions which resulted in the salvation of Minorca and the reparation of much of the harm lately suffered by Majorca.*

In these blessed words His Majesty discovered not only the rehabilitation of the Duke of Melfi, but, what was much more important, his own rehabilitation also. In the uplifting reaction His Majesty turned upon those who had increased his load of shame by their unsparing denunciations of Andrea Doria, and he rent them, condemning them for spiteful calumniators. To silence criticisms of Doria, which had seemed unanswerable criticisms of his own Imperial self, he gave the letters the widest publication. The critics, he declared, had been foolishly rash and presumptuous in their recent censures. Upon whatever grounds the Duke had supposed at Djerba that Dragut's destruction was accomplished, yet that destruction had followed so promptly and so completely that he must be accounted justified.

One audacious gentleman about the Emperor's person still caustically ventured the opinion that, in the matter of the dispositions resulting in La Mola, it was an assumption that the Duke of Melfi was responsible for them.

The Emperor gloomed upon him out of his long, pallid face.

"The only assumption I perceive, sir," he stammered, "is your assumption that Captain Adorno should seek to crown another with the laurels he has won. That, sir, is something better than human nature at its best, and therefore, as Euclid would say, absurd. Besides," he ended scornfully, "have you never heard that 'qui fecit per alium, fecit per se'? La Mola is Doria's triumph since it was achieved by an officer of his appointing to it, just as in a sense it is my triumph, being an Admiral's of my appointing."

After that clear expression of the Imperial view not even del Vasto would take the risk of incurring displeasure by voicing his conviction that the victory of Mahon might have been achieved not in collaboration with, but in despite of Andrea Doria. He knew his world and something of the hearts of princes, and he perceived that to insist here would be to produce in the Emperor an irritation which might actually find its ultimate expression in hostility to Prospero. So for his friend's own sake he left uncontested for the present the great share in that victory which His Majesty assigned to Andrea Doria.

Chapter 34

The Discovery

Had Andrea Doria at this time known of the view that Charles V was taking of his activities, it might conceivably – though not certainly – have supplied a salve for the laceration which his pride had suffered, a laceration so deep that it did not seem to him that he could ever recover from it.

On the very day that Prospero delivered battle to Dragut at Mahon, a swift galliot from Naples reached the Imperial fleet before Djerba, bearing Messer Paolo Caracciolo, with messages from the Imperial Viceroy.

Messer Caracciolo, a spoilt darling of fortune, was young, audacious and of a humour that in its indulgence rarely spared the feelings of others. The manner he adopted for the purpose of conveying the Prince of Orange's message was one that provided him with some malicious amusement. A tall, handsome fellow, florid of complexion and red-gold of hair, carrying himself with a swagger in brilliant garments, suggestive, in the shortness of his vermilion doublet, of the flamboyant Venetian mode, he stepped airily aboard the Admiral's galley at a moment when the Admiral was sitting down to dinner with his nephews.

"His Highness the Prince of Orange," announced this envoy, "sends your lordship his deferential greetings, and desires to know what keeps you in the Gulf of Syrtis at this present time."

The three had risen, and their three pairs of eyes in staring at him seemed to ask was he a lunatic. From the Lord Andrea came a rumbling echo of Messer Caracciolo's question.

"What keeps me?"

"By God!" said Gianettino in his throat.

"What keeps me?" the Lord Andrea repeated.

"That is the Prince's question," minced the envoy.

"But, sir...sir..." The Admiral's voice quivered between astonishment and indignation. "Has, then, no message of mine reached Naples demanding troops? Troops to be set ashore on Djerba yonder?"

"Oh, that! But that, my lord, was nigh on three weeks since, when Dragut-Reis was in the Bight of Djerba."

"When he *was* in the Bight?"

"Perhaps," suggested Filippino, with a withering sarcasm, "you'll inform us where he is at present."

"Precisely, sir, I cannot say. But I can tell you where he is not. And that is in the Bight of Djerba."

"Not at Djerba?" said the Admiral. He scowled on the exquisite from under his craggy brows, and shrugged his massive shoulders. "It must be that you are mad," he concluded. "Just mad."

Gianettino's behaviour was odd. He laughed. He flung his arms upwards as in a gesture of invocation, and let them fall again resoundingly to his sides. "There!" he ejaculated.

But from Filippino came the harsh demand: "Are you from the Viceroy at all, sir? Or are you some buffoon impostor?"

Being annoyed by this, Messer Caracciolo became the more merciless in the indulgence of his humour. "That is not civil," he said. "I have letters here to vouch for me. You will apologize when you have read them. They will inform you that ten days ago Dragut-Reis was pillaging the coast of Corsica."

"That is impossible. A lie," bellowed the Admiral.

"Oh no. A fact."

"Some other rover impersonating him," said Filippino.

But Caracciolo insisted that the identity of the raider was beyond doubt.

"It follows, therefore," he ended, "that ten days ago Dragut was no longer at Djerba. That is, if he was ever here at all."

"If he was ever here?" This brought the blood to the Admiral's face. "Did I not chase him and all his fleet into that lagoon? Have I not sat here since on the watch by day and by night? Could he have flown out?"

"It is a Moslem saying," murmured Messer Caracciolo, "that all things are possible to Allah. If you are sure that he was here, I am no less sure that he is here no longer. Explanations will be for you, my lord; and I've no doubt," he added, with smiling affability, "that they will be such as to allay the wrath that you'll conceive in His Imperial Majesty."

"Give me your letters," cried the goaded Admiral, and snatched them rudely when they were proffered.

Messer Caracciolo found himself a seat. He fanned himself with his cap. "I have never believed until today that the Genoese are as mannerless as they're reputed."

But none of the three heeded his pertness. He had given them something else to think about.

The Admiral had spread the sheet, and with a nephew at either elbow to share the reading, his glance raced over the written words. Filippino stood like a man whose pulses are suspended. Gianettino's jowl was thrust forward, and his small, woman's mouth was curled in a bitter smile. For it happened that for a week now Gianettino had daily been protesting that there was something suspicious in the stillness of Djerba and the utter lack of movement about the earthworks Dragut had thrown up. But that his uncle sternly forbade it, he would have moved in to test the matter by offering himself as a target for the Corsair's fire.

"And thus fulfil that pirate's very hopes," the Admiral had told him. "He plays the fox, and looks to us to act like geese. We'll wait until the land forces arrive. Meanwhile let him pretend to slumber. It shall not deceive us."

"Unless we're deceived in supposing just that," had been Gianettino's retort.

"What else can he be doing?"

"I would I knew the answer. I feel it in my bones that all is not well."

"In your bones, maybe," he was mocked. "But I'd sooner trust my brains than your bones, Gianettino."

Now, however, with the letter before them, it seemed as if those despised bones had displaced the greater intelligence.

"There!" cried Gianettino, when they had read. "What have I been saying these days?"

It was the only thing wanting to complete the infuriation of the old Admiral, who so seldom could be moved to anger. In the look he bent upon his nephew there was a dangerous wildness such as Gianettino had never yet encountered in it.

"The guesses of a fool may sometimes hit a truth that's hidden from the wise. But who would heed the guesses of a fool?" Then, with a change of manner, and a wild stare at the suave and composed envoy, "This, sir," he faltered, "passes all understanding." His legs began to shake, and he sank, limp and spent, to a stool beside the table. For the first time in his tough, virile life, that sexagenarian was conscious of his age. He set his elbow on the board, and took his head in his hands, shading his eyes. Something like a groan escaped him. "It can't be true. It can't. How, in the name of God, can it be?"

Gianettino stood forward. "Look, my lord. I'll do now what you would not let me do before. I'll land on Djerba, and set a term to doubt."

He did not even wait for consent, but stamped out, and was gone.

It was dusk when he returned. In the tabernacle of the Admiral's galley he found his uncle and Filippino alone with their dejection. The tale he brought did nothing to dissipate it. He had discovered on Djerba that whilst the Imperial fleet had watched the front entrance, Dragut had slipped out by an unsuspected back door. The Sheik of Djerba had shown Gianettino the canals that were cut.

"They were cut, he tells me, under the direction of a Frank who was with Dragut. A Frank named Prospero Adorno." He laughed bitterly at the sudden amazed stare of his audience. "We should be proud of the ingenuity of our compatriot. Properly applied it might have enhanced the fortunes of our house. Applied as it has been, it has no doubt accomplished our ruin. And so that treacherous dog has fulfilled his infamous purpose."

He cleared up obscurities out of what else he had learned from the Sheik, and when to his tale Messer Caracciolo had presently added something more, they came to understand in precisely what circumstances Prospero had been with Dragut at Djerba, and how Gianna had come to be there with him. The fate of Gianna, which at another time must have weighed heavily with the Lord Andrea, was an almost negligible consideration to a mind under the shock of this revelation.

Whilst the Admiral sat like a man stunned, Filippino widened his thin-lipped mouth. "Faith, we deserve no less. Had I had my way with that treacherous villain this could never have happened." He turned to his uncle. "Mortuis non mordent. As I warned you."

"Yes, yes," the Admiral growled. "You all warned me, and I did not heed you. I should be in leading-strings, I think. And now all that I have ever done may go for nothing. The meanest hind shall henceforth have the right to laugh at me."

Filippino asked a question of his cousin. "How comes it that in all this time no word was brought to us from Djerba? Did you ask the Sheik?"

"Of course I did. His answer was that Dragut, on the advice no doubt of his Frankish mentor, burnt or sank every boat on Djerba before he left. It may be true, or it may not. What does it matter now?"

"What, indeed?" said Messer Caracciolo. "What matters is the fact you have verified." And he added: "You'll be weighing anchor at once, no doubt."

Andrea Doria reared his massive, leonine head. "To go whither?"

"Why, sir, to Naples."

"To be laughed at?"

"Oh, sir! To take order with His Highness the Viceroy for the pursuit of Dragut-Reis."

With angry, blood-injected eyes the Admiral looked keenly at the airy envoy to see whether he dared to mock. For a bitter mockery it seemed to Doria that anyone should urge him to take instructions for the pursuit of a pirate whom his letters to the Emperor had announced as already captive.

Chapter 35

The Last Hope

The easterly winds which had served Prospero so excellently in the pursuit of Dragut persisted to fret him now that his prows were turned eastward, and impatience consumed him to reach Gianna and by his return bring peace to her anxious soul. In the teeth of this Levante the galleys could make no better progress than some three miles an hour for sixteen hours of the twenty-four. For the remaining eight they must lie at anchor, so that the gangs could rest. At this tortoise-pace if the Levante should continue to blow, or any other than a westerly wind, two weeks and more would be necessary to row a distance that had been sailed in little more than three days. Therefore, in his natural impatience, Prospero turned north for the Gulf of Lyons, and from Marseilles, by swift overland couriers, sent his news to Naples, with a request to Gianna to come to him at Genoa, where he would land.

> *Since, my beloved Gianna* [he wrote], *it is not my intention that we should remain exiles from our country, I judge that for our return no moment could be more propitious than the present. I recall the affection with which my fellow-countrymen received me after Procida, and how that reception tamed my enemies, silenced calumny and left in their sheaths the daggers that had been sharpened for me. Remembering it, I can have no doubt of the*

welcome that will await me when I sail into the harbour with fourteen captured Moslem galleys, three thousand Moslem prisoners and as many Christians delivered from captivity, among whom I count at least a thousand Genoese, and the glory of having annihilated Dragut-Reis and his fleet and weakened by so much the Moslem menace to our shores. I do not think that the boldest of my enemies will venture to test the panoply of public esteem that should be mine. Hasten to me there, then, my Gianna, so that we may be joined at last and I may lay this triumph at your feet. His Highness of Orange will provide you with an escort and all else that you may need.

What else he wrote, in a more fervid strain, need not concern us. To the Viceroy he sent at the same time an account of the events at Port Mahon. It was a succinct and baldly modest statement of the facts. But if it did them less than justice, more than justice was done to them by Don Alvaro de Carbajal's lyrical version of the matter, which was dispatched at the same time.

If Prospero's letter bore relief and thankfulness to Gianna yet she sighed a little over the complacent confidence in which he wrote of his return to Genoa. It was true that having made so full an amend for the part he had played at Djerba, it must seem inconceivable that on that score more could be exacted from him. But that his bitter enemies at home would be palsied by his triumph was in her view a dangerously rash assumption. It spurred her to set out at once, so as to be at his side in whatever trouble he might have to face.

The events proved that he had chosen his moment with that clear-sighted opportunism which was his strength in strategy, and which, had he not also been a poet, must eventually have established him as the foremost sea-condottiero of his day. So free was his estimate from the faults of optimism that it fell far short of the actuality. The news of the battle of La Mola and the destruction of Dragut-Reis with all his fleet – for at the time it was believed even by Prospero that Dragut had perished – was already in Genoa when the victor landed there. There was no port of the Christian Mediterranean littoral to which the news when it came did not bring relief, rejoicing and honour to the name of the Genoese captain to whom the extinction of that Moslem scourge was due. In his native State, national pride magnified him in that hour into the greatest hero of all time, and the appearance of his fleet in the Gulf let loose a very frenzy of enthusiasm.

There had been little leisure in which to prepare a reception commensurate with the public view of his achievement; yet enthusiasm, working at fever pitch, had accomplished miracles.

A triumphal arch, of ramage and bunting, was raised outside the Cow Gate through which he must pass. A flourish of silver trumpets saluted him as he stepped from his galley on to the quay which had been strewn with flowers and green boughs to make a carpet for him. Here to receive him stood the Doge with the scarlet-mantled senators and a flock of patricians representing every noble house in the Republic. For their mouthpiece they employed a little maid of the house of Grimani, who read a sonnet of welcome. If it bore signs of a hasty composition that made the author of *The Liguriad* wince, yet, as he afterwards told Gianna, since it hailed him as the greatest of Liguria's sons, only a churl would have permitted a critical faculty to cavil at the scansion.

As he listened, and marked those who came to honour him with these superlatives, he was moved to inward laughter at the contrast between this return to Genoa and his departure thence less than two short months ago. Then every man's hand had been against him, those of the Doria faction accounting him as much a traitor as those of his own. Now every man's hand was extended in loving welcome. And beyond the patricians was the deliriously clamant multitude, confined by the files of archers of the Ducal guard. He would be bold, indeed, thought Prospero, who in such an hour would proclaim himself his enemy.

Very different was the landing in Naples at about the same time, almost to the very hour, of the Lord Andrea Doria, Duke of Melfi and Knight of the Golden Fleece. For that great Admiral there were no silver trumpets, no flowers, no sonnet, no fawning patricians and no acclaiming populace. There was a frigid Viceroy who did not even descend to the mole of the Castel Nuovo to receive him, but awaited the Admiral in the audience chamber of the fortress.

Thither the Lord Andrea and his nephews repaired in no good humour. They went in resentment of the lack of courtesies which they accounted the Admiral's due. They had by now recovered, it will be seen, from the shock of the news received at Djerba and the humility it had induced in them. Reflection had shown them that things were far from being as desperate as they had at first supposed. Certainly the harm was not beyond repair. Since Dragut was so rash as to remain at sea, the Lord Andrea was supplied with the opportunity to hunt him down and destroy him. Once this were accomplished, the relief and thankfulness of Italy would be more than enough to obscure the mischance at Djerba. And even should it be remembered, it could be turned to account by a disclosure of the author of it. At least, that was Filippino's subtle notion.

"When we make known the treachery that saved Dragut, we shall be plagued no more by the Adorni. Messer Prospero will be held answerable for the desolation of Corsica that followed upon the Infidel's escape, and he will certainly answer for it on the gallows."

The Lord Andrea displayed no enthusiasm. "I have observed," he said gloomily, "that every action taken against that rascal recoils by an odd fatality upon ourselves."

"This will not be our action, but the Emperor's," Gianettino reminded him. "Justice will at last overtake the dog."

"I suppose so." The Duke passed a hand wearily across his brow. "It will hurt poor Gianna," he deplored.

"She earns the wages of her disloyalty," was Filippino's sour comment.

"Your mind runs ever on paying rancour's wages. We have had little good of it so far."

"Are we to give quittances for affronts?" Filippino was hot with indignation. "Perhaps you would spare Messer Prospero by taking on yourself the blame for Djerba and becoming a laughing-stock to the world."

The Duke winced. "No, no."

Cruelly, so as to spur him in vindictiveness, Gianettino turned the knife in the wound in his uncle's pride. "Even when all the truth is known, how shall it make us less ridiculous?"

The Admiral reared his great head, to roar like a maddened lion: "When I've sunk Dragut and all his galleys there will be little fear of ridicule."

In that confidence he came now to Naples, seeking there the latest news of the Corsair's whereabouts. Stung by the absence of any sort of reception to a person of his consequence, he fumed into the Viceroy's presence at the heels of the officer who conducted him, his nephews following indignant in his wake.

The Prince of Orange was seated at his table, writing, when the three were introduced. He laid down his pen and rose. But he did not quit his place. He extended no welcoming hand, and his blue eyes were ice-cold, his countenance as bleak as his words.

"You arrive at last. You have been a long time on the way."

The Duke's resentment swelled under this cold reception. Once again this sorely tried man discarded his habit of imperturbability. His voice was loud and harsh. His words uncivil.

"Criticism of a seaman comes easily to landsmen who know nothing of the sea and its hazards. We had the wind abeam, and we were forced to depend upon our oars. Yet we made all speed."

"You made all speed. I see." His Highness was dry. Offended by that lack of deference for the viceregal office, he sat down again, but forgot to invite his visitors to sit. "And how," he asked, "do you explain the events at Djerba?"

"By treachery. We were deceived by the tricks of a traitor so shameless that he did not scruple to show Dragut the way out of the trap in which I held him fast. Prospero Adorno used his craft in the service of the Infidel, and he shall answer to Imperial justice for the ravages since committed by that accursed Corsair."

Whether because of his dislike of the Duke's manner, or because of his friendship for Prospero and his full knowledge of all that had befallen at Djerba and since, the Prince's frigidity increased.

"And the proof of this?"

"Proof?" Doria stared, a black frown darkening his glance. The colour deepened in his face. "There is my word."

Orange shook his head. "Your word? An opinion, no more. Were you on Djerba, so that of your knowledge you could swear that Prospero Adorno was a party to the tactics that defeated you? He was with Dragut. Yes. As a prisoner. That is all that you dare swear, I think."

"But I have been on Djerba, Highness," Gianettino exploded. "I have the word of the Sheik for what we assert."

"The Sheik of Djerba!" Orange smiled. "Is that Infidel a witness for a Christian court against a valued officer?"

"Against a proven traitor," Filippino stormed in, unable longer to contain himself. "If Christian witness were needed, there are enough of them. The slaves who were set to do the work under that rogue's directions."

"Where shall you find them?" wondered the Viceroy.

"But does Your Highness doubt our word?" demanded Gianettino. "Do you defend this man?"

"I?" The Viceroy raised his brows. "I merely caution you to tread warily. You may not improve matters for yourselves by sheltering your blunder behind such an accusation. Nor does it make your blunder less. Whether you were fooled by Dragut himself or by Prospero Adorno, fooled you were; and that is all that matters."

This was to drive the iron deep into the Admiral's soul. He drew himself up to the full of his towering height and threw back his lion head so that the great beard jutted forward. "I will render my accounts to my master, His Imperial Majesty."

"Of course you will. You will be asked for them. But let me warn you again to beware what accounts you render."

"I am grateful to Your Highness for this solicitude," was the answer, tart with irony.

The Prince inclined his head. "That, then, is all, I think. I know of no reason why you should remain in Naples, unless, of course, it is your wish to do so."

"My wish, sir? I have no time to waste here. All I seek is the latest news of Dragut."

And from Filippino came now a raging detailed menace of what must befall Dragut at their hands with assurances of how little anyone would dare to mention Djerba when that was done.

The ever frigid Viceroy listened, and may have been moved to malice by this arrogant ranting. "You ask me for the latest news of Dragut. You shall have it. From Corsica he steered a westward course, and went to ravage the Balearics on the Emperor's very doorstep." Briefly, to the mounting horror of his audience, he gave details of those ravages. "News of that dreadful raid reached His Majesty at about the same time as your report that you held the Corsair fast and that his destruction was assured. You conceive, my Lord Duke, His Majesty's emotions."

The Admiral stood with clenched hands, his breathing quickened and behind his nephews stared in goggle-eyed panic at the Prince of Orange. Then the Lord Andrea loosed a dreadful imprecation.

"All the more to avenge," he exclaimed. "And avenged it shall be if I leave my life in the business."

He realized that unless he could now find and destroy Dragut, his own reputation was for ever blasted and his life henceforth useless. In the utter defeat of Dragut was his only chance to rehabilitate himself. "What are this Infidel dog's present whereabouts?" he demanded. "Do you know?"

"Not positively." There was a bleak smile from the Viceroy. "But I trust that he's in Hell."

Conceiving this a flippancy, the Admiral was angry in his reproof of it. "Highness, I am serious."

"Faith, so am I," said the Prince. "Messer Dragut and all his fleet – some six-and-twenty galleys – were destroyed off Port Mahon three weeks ago by Prospero Adorno with the Neapolitan squadron amounting to half the Moslem strength. A feat of arms that has made some stir along the seaboard from here to Cadiz."

There was utter silence. Palsied, the three Genoese seemed to have ceased to breathe. Slowly the blood drained from the Admiral's weathered countenance until it looked like a face of wax. It was some moments before he found his voice, and then it came hoarse and unsteady.

"If that is true..." he began, but got no further.

"It is true. Be sure of that," the Viceroy answered him, and he added details: the recovery of the plunder of Palma, the deliverance of the Majorcan captives and of some thousands of Christians from the Moslem oars, besides the capture of galleys to swell the strength of the Imperial fleets.

But the Admiral scarcely listened. With wits benumbed he waited until the Viceroy's tale was done, then, mastering himself, he bowed and spread his hands. "In that case there remains no reason why we should linger in Naples or further waste the time of Your Highness. I take my leave, Lord Prince."

Doria's dignity in a calamity that crushed his last hope moved the Viceroy's compassion. He rose, but he could find no words that might serve to comfort.

"I'll wish you a safe voyage, my lord, and you, sirs," was all that he actually found to say, but the gentleness of his voice conveyed something more.

Doria stumbled out, his nephews following.

On the staircase Filippino muttered fiercely in his ear: "As I reminded you long ago, my lord, mortui non mordent. Now that this snake has bitten you to death, perhaps you'll give me reason."

Chapter 36

The Investiture

Aboard his flagship again, Andrea Doria asked himself in bitterness whither he should now steer a course. Then he put that question to his nephews who sat with him in the tabernacle, sharing his dejection.

Both were disposed to be sardonic at their uncle's expense, and to blame for their present misfortune his past weakness and credulity where the crafty, treacherous Prospero Adorno was concerned.

"The riddle, sir," said Gianettino, "is what remains for us to do. When you've resolved that, the question of our destination will resolve itself."

"Riddle?" said the Duke. "There is no riddle. All is clear." Dejected he might be; but at least he had resumed his mantle of calm dignity. His words were as dispassionate as if they concerned another. "In this long duel with Prospero Adorno the victory is at last with him."

"Treacherously fought and treacherously won," said Gianettino.

The Admiral shook his head. "You may say that if it comforts you. But in war all is fair. When our own guile succeeds, we call it strategic talent. When the enemy's succeeds we call it treachery."

"As God's my life," swore Filippino, "I do not yet admit defeat."

"Why! What remains?"

"Justice upon this miscreant. When the Emperor knows of his work at Djerba, his triumph is likely to be converted into something else."

"Are we not ridiculous enough already? Shall we set the world rocking with laughter by denouncing Prospero Adorno for having outwitted us? Will that diminish my shame or repair the ruin under which I am crushed, a ruin that effaces now in my old age all that in my lifetime I have achieved? Besides, don't you yet see that by forestalling me and destroying Dragut, Prospero has not only robbed me of my only chance to redeem myself, but by that great feat of arms he has purged the offence that might have been held against him?"

"It shall be tested, nevertheless," said Filippino through his teeth.

"We may test it. Yes. Having nothing left to lose."

"And if we fail in that, there is still this." Filippino struck his hilt viciously. "I do not bow in defeat before this Adorno swagger."

"Nor I, by God!" swore Gianettino. "In one way or another Messer Prospero shall pay for the havoc he has wrought."

In that resolve they came home to Genoa; but for once without any ostentation. Such was their dread of a derisory if not actually hostile greeting that they landed at Lerici, and from there took horse. They timed their arrival in Genoa so as to ride into the city under the friendly mantle of an August evening.

His approach unheralded, the Admiral's abrupt advent startled not only his servants at the Fassuolo Palace, but his Duchess, herself. She had been on the point of retiring for the night when her lord strode booted and dusty into her bower, whose sumptuous eastern furnishings were so many trophies of his past triumphs, evidences of a great career that was now miserably closed.

She sprang up breathless in surprise. "My dear lord! Andrea!" With that glad cry she ran to him, and cast herself into his sturdy arms.

He bowed from his towering height over that lively, sweetly fragrant lady, and in the contact she sensed an unusual weakness and lassitude, almost a frailty, in this man of granite.

"You are travel-weary, Andrea." All tenderness, she drew him to a chair.

The Sword of Islam

"Aye, weary," he agreed, and in the candlelight she saw how grey and drawn was his face, how lack-lustre his deep-set eyes. In appearance it was as if he had abruptly reached the years he counted.

She knelt beside him, taking his rugged hands in hers. "Whence are you, Andrea?"

"From Lerici. I left my galleys there."

"In your haste to come to me?"

He smiled wistfully. "I would, by the grace of God, that I could say so." He shook his head. "In my shame. So that I might creep unnoticed into Genoa. So that I might escape the derision that will be waiting to greet me. I have accounted myself brave, my dear. But I am not brave enough for that."

She set her soft hands on his shoulders and pulled him round so that she might regard him squarely. "Derision?" she said.

"Aye. Have you not yet heard?"

"Heard what? All I know is that the Marquis del Vasto is here in Genoa, awaiting you, with letters from the Emperor."

"Ah!" It was an indrawn breath as of apprehension. "Already, eh?"

"The Emperor, they say, is always prompt to give honour where it is due."

"Where it is due. They say well. And as prompt to give whatever else may be due in the Imperial judgment. Where is Messer del Vasto?"

"At the Adorno Palace. Lodged with his friend Ser Prospero."

The Admiral's was a crooked smile. "Of course it would be so. And Gianna?" he asked.

"She is here with me. You'll have heard of the queer trick of Fate's by which she and Prospero sailed away together, and what came of it. There was, of course, much idle talk and horrid calumnies. But that is now happily overpast. Their marriage awaits only your return."

"It becomes something necessary," was his sour comment. "Her honour will stand in need of patching." He uttered a short grim laugh that set his Duchess staring.

"That is not kind, Andrea. You cannot know the facts, or how Lamba's murderous fury…"

"Aye, aye! I've heard the tale. It is no matter now."

"Why no," she agreed. "And I give thanks for her, dear child, that all is now so happily concluded and that Prospero is safe in the public esteem from the enemies he had made. I would she had arrived in time to witness the triumph of his return."

"So all is happily concluded." The Admiral's grimness deepened. "Happily! And this Prospero is in great esteem. His return was a triumph. Well, well!"

She told him of the delirious reception given by Genoa to the conqueror of Dragut. He sat with elbows on his knees, his big head in his hands, his face invisible.

Then she went to summon servants, and soon, by her orders, supper was spread for the Lord Andrea there in her bower. Herself she waited upon him.

He ate little, and that little mechanically. But he drank thirstily and copiously of the rich Greek wine she poured for him, and whilst she ministered to his needs she begged of him an account of himself.

"We heard of your great victory at Mehedia and that you were on the heels of that vile Corsair Dragut. But nothing since."

He was silent awhile, considering the terms in which he should convey his evil tidings. But reluctance and lassitude defeated the weak intention. "Let the rest keep until tomorrow," he said. "You shall hear it then. You shall hear it from Alfonso of Avalos, the messenger of Majesty. Let word go to him betimes that I am here and shall be honoured to receive him."

That word reached del Vasto next morning as he sat at breakfast in the colonnade above Prospero's garden. With him were his host and that other guest, Don Alvaro de Carbajal. Madonna Aurelia was fortunately absent, at Prospero's country house of Verdeprati, whither she had gone to escape the August heat of the great city.

Del Vasto had reached Genoa with the Imperial letters within a day or two of Prospero's arrival there. Informed as he was of the terms in which the Emperor wrote, he had communicated them to

Prospero. Don Alvaro, who was with them at the time, was moved to uproarious laughter.

"I guess what is amusing you," the Marquis told him.

"Not the half of it." Don Alvaro choked. Tears stood in his eyes. "If you did you must share my laughter."

"I think I do. Keep faith with me if I talk treason. The clay under the Imperial purple is just as common as yours or mine. The same weaknesses torment it. In the blundering failure of his Admiral, His Majesty perceived the failure of his own judgment in appointing him. He saw that the contempt and derision into which Doria was falling recoiled upon himself. Therefore he was eager enough when we had news of the victory of La Mola to give the credit for it to Doria. For in rehabilitating his Admiral, he rehabilitated himself. He accounts the victory of La Mola his own. In his own words: Qui fecit per alium, fecit per se."

Don Alvaro was indignant. "And is Prospero thus to be eclipsed?"

"It is Prospero who has eclipsed himself by his too generous report. Who shall contradict it?"

Don Alvaro stormed. "Was I not at Mahon? Do I not know what happened? And are there no others? All the captains serving with us in the Neapolitan squadron. We can all testify. And, as God lives, we will." Don Alvaro raged on. "It is time that His Majesty's eyes be opened as to the true worth of this Genoese whom he has preferred to so many able gentlemen of Spain; time that His Majesty be cured of his infatuation."

Here Prospero intervened. "To see in Andrea Doria the first sea-condottiero of the age is not infatuation."

Don Alvaro blew out his cheeks. "But even if he were that, is it a reason why he should take the credit that belongs to you for the greatest action fought in our time at sea?"

"That has nothing to do with his ability."

"Need we dispute on it?" asked del Vasto. "I have to discharge by Andrea Doria the embassy on which I am sent. It includes for you, Prospero, the cross of St James of Compostella, which the Duke of Melfi, very properly as your Admiral, is commanded to hang about your neck in his Imperial master's name. Considering the error under which he is charged with that investiture, you may, if you so choose, as properly refuse to receive it at his hands."

"Aye," Don Alvaro approved. "That would be the way to open up the truth."

"If that were my aim should I have written as I did?" Prospero had asked them. "And am I now to go about diminishing and humiliating the Emperor by robbing him of his personal pride in Doria's victory, as he accounts it? How shall that serve me? And you may be rash to suppose that Doria will accept commendation for deeds in which he had no part. It may be necessary to persuade him."

Don Alvaro had laughed this to scorn, and they had left the matter to be decided by test when Doria should return.

Now the testing hour was come. Del Vasto sent word by Doria's messenger that he would follow him within the hour to the Fassuolo Palace.

Thoughtfully Prospero fingered his chin. "By your leave, Alfonso, I will go with you."

"You do not need my leave for that."

"I would give a deal to be of the party," chuckled Don Alvaro with malice.

"There is no reason why you should not be," Prospero assured him.

The Duke of Melfi received them in the great gallery of five arcades that gave access to the terraces, a gallery made dazzling by the recently completed frescoes of Pierino della Vega. Here under an azure ceiling glowed in rich colour such scenes of Roman history as Brennus dictating the laws, Mutius Scaevola before Porsenna and the like. There were tapestries of Ispahan and Teheran; carpets from the looms of Smyrna softened the tread on the floor of wood mosaics; Moorish vases, damascened in gold and silver, and richly sombre Spanish furniture from the workshops of Seville and Cordova.

The Duke was leaning by the great cowled fireplace in Carrara marble into which Guglielmo della Porta's chisel had brought the life and movement of Promethean scenes. Filippino and Gianettino were with their uncle, and whilst the Admiral carried himself proudly erect, his countenance as calm and cold as if it, too, were a product of della Porta's chisel, the hangdog looks of his nephews betrayed their conviction that they stood there to receive sentence.

The Marquis del Vasto, very elegant, as became the arbiter elegantiarum of the Imperial Court, in an azure mantle lightly worn over a suit of lighter blue that was slashed with white, followed the ushering chamberlain, and was followed in his turn by Prospero and Carbajal.

At the unexpected sight of Prospero, the Admiral shifted his position and perceptibly stiffened. Gianettino's head was craned forward, his eyes bulging. From Filippino came a sound inarticulate as the growl of an animal, and his hand dropped eloquently to the knuckle-bow of his sword. The three conceived, of course, that Prospero was come to feast his vindictiveness on the spectacle of their humiliation.

The Marquis bowed low. "Greetings, Lord Duke, in my Imperial master's name. I bring you these."

He proffered a package of some bulk, whose silken fastenings bore the Emperor's seal.

Mechanically Andrea Doria took it. But he did not look at it, or even at the Marquis. His deep-set eyes continued from under their craggy brows to stare at Prospero, who, self-contained, stood in slimly athletic contrast to the bulky and gaudy Don Alvaro. He cleared his throat.

"I had not expected that Your Excellency would be accompanied. Least of all by Messer Prospero Adorno."

Del Vasto was suavity incarnate. "When you have read my master's letter, your lordship will understand the occasion of Messer Prospero's presence."

"Ah!" said the Duke, and by a gesture repressed Filippino, who would have spoken.

He broke the seals of the package. Out of it fell a little lily-hilted sword all wrought in rubies and attached to a ribbon of red silk.

Gianettino stooped to recover and restore it. But he was left to hold it whilst his uncle conned the letter from which it had dropped.

As he read, the Admiral's breathing became faintly audible; some of the colour faded from his rugged countenance. He frowned at the end, and paused to read it a second time, pulling at his beard the while.

At last he raised his eyes and looked squarely at Del Vasto. "Your lordship knows what is written here?"

"His Majesty honoured me with his confidence."

"And… And…" The Admiral hesitated before plunging on. "And you believe what is written?"

"Should I disbelieve what His Majesty asserts?"

"But His Majesty? His Majesty believes this?"

"Would he write it else?"

"By your leave." Andrea Doria passed the letter to Gianettino, and the two nephews fell to reading it, their heads together. The Admiral advanced a pace or two, carrying himself very erect, his face set in sternness. "There is in all this so gross a misapprehension that almost I ask myself am I being mocked."

This was no more than the exordium. But here Prospero intervened, to check whatever might be about to follow. "Give me leave a moment with my Lord Andrea," he begged the Marquis.

"With me, sir?" cried the Admiral. "What can you have to say to me?"

"There is an investiture with which you are charged, my lord. I can understand that you may be unwilling to perform it."

"More than unwilling, sir. Much more than that."

"Yet I do not despair of persuading you. If," he turned again to del Vasto, "you'll give me leave, Alfonso."

"Why…since it is your wish," agreed the understanding Marquis, and he led out the reluctant Don Alvaro.

"I vow to God, Don Alfonso," he complained, "I am cheated of the richest entertainment I could ever hope to witness."

Within the gallery Doria was challenging Prospero's intentions. "Well, sir? What can you have to say to me? Do you perhaps venture to make this opportunity to mock me with the havoc you have caused, with the shame and humiliation in which you have brought me down? Is that your purpose?"

"You speak of shame and humiliation, my lord. Nothing of that is to be discovered in the letter which you hold."

The Duke's answer was fiercely impatient. "I have said that this letter is the fruit of a misapprehension."

"So much of life is the fruit of that. So much of what has passed between us has been misapprehension growing from misapprehension."

To this Filippino yet more fiercely supplied the answer. "On the score of your persistent treachery, at least, there has been none."

"Nor on the score of your persistent rancour, Filippino. But it is to my lord your uncle that I address myself. This duel has endured long enough."

"Now that you conceive the victory to lie with you," sneered the old Admiral,

"Have it so, if you will. I have been under a vow made when my father died in exile, renewed when Filippino set me to the oar. But that is now behind me."

"Now that you have fulfilled the vow to your satisfaction. I am to end my days as a laughing-stock to the world. The glory so hard-earned in sixty years of honourable life is quenched in derision by your contriving. Oh, you have paid yourself, Messer Adorno. Take joy in it whilst you may. But get you gone. This mockery has endured enough."

"Too long, by God!" snarled Filippino.

"And so say I," agreed Gianettino. He stepped forward, peeling off his slashed glove as he came.

Prospero raised a warning hand. That and his stern gravity checked the menacing advance. "A word, before you cast that glove. Consider that as yet all the hurt you have suffered lies between you and me. The world knows nothing of it. That letter from His Majesty is the proof. Your native Genoa waits at this moment feverishly to welcome the great Admiral whom the Emperor honours. Who is there to tell the world that I was not under your lordship's orders, as the Emperor supposes, when I broke the Sword of Islam at Port Mahon? The Prince of Orange, perhaps, and Don Alvaro de Carbajal are the only ones who can speak positively, out of their own knowledge. But will they dare to tell the Emperor that he is wrong if I do not?"

"If you do not?" the Admiral echoed, and the three Dorias looked at one another, passing from amazement to amazement.

Gianettino was the first to reach a conclusion. "You hint at a bargain."

"Aye," agreed his cousin. "You have something to sell."

"Something to give. Something that I have, indeed, given already. Sirs, you cannot carefully have read the Emperor's letter. It runs, I believe, that His Majesty learns by reports from your lordship's captain Messer Prospero Adorno that as a result of the measures taken by your lordship the Corsair Dragut-Reis has been destroyed and his fleet annihilated. Is it not thus that His Majesty writes?" He paused to add solemnly: "If he writes so, it is because I so reported. That is the gift I offer, my lord. A peace-offering."

The three had listened in a growing wonder that was by no means free from anger. As Prospero paused the Admiral turned again to the letter. Cursorily read, it had not conveyed the full significance of the phrase that Prospero quoted.

He recited aloud the material passage:

"I learn by dispatches from my Governor of Minorca and more particularly by reports from Messer Prospero Adorno, commanding the Neapolitan squadron of your lordship's fleet, that as a result of your lordship's glorious design in which Messer Adorno so valorously performed his part..."

He read no farther. He reared his great head, squared his mighty shoulders, and cast off his calm as if it were a garment. He stormed in wrath. "I am to take shelter behind your reports? I am to accept a cloak from you to cover my nakedness? I am to be a party to an imposture, and receive praise for deeds that are not my own? Lord God! Do you dare to stand calmly before me and offer this? Of all the affronts you have put upon me, sir, this is the least forgivable...this assumption that I am so mean and venal that such a proposal may be made to me." Then his tone changed. "All the answer needed to this letter from the Emperor is ready for dispatch. I wrote it last night. It conveys my resignation from his service and from all services. It gives him the true facts of what occurred at Djerba. It marks the inglorious end of a career that has known some glory, wrecked by a vindictive treachery so reckless that it delivered Dragut from the trap in which I had taken him, and let him loose to ravage Christendom anew."

"Is that your monstrous view of it? You believe that it was to vent my spite on you that I did what I did at Djerba?"

"Would you dare to deny it?"

"It needs small daring. There was no thought of you in what I did. Little thought even of myself. Have you forgotten that Gianna was with me in Dragut's evil power? You were given the chance to save her, and you declined it."

"Is that a reproach? You saved her, you will say. And the cost? A holocaust in Corsica. Another in Majorca. How many hundred lives went to pay for Gianna's? Was that not to be foreseen? Knowing the cost, could I dare to face it?"

"Gianna is not to you what she is to me. You'll grant so much. There are not even ties of blood between you and her. And what followed was by no means to be foreseen. Dragut's avowed intention was to set a course for the Golden Horn and join Barbarossa. Either he lied to me or he afterwards changed his mind. And in no case would you have captured him, though his fleet would have been lost." And in a dozen words he told them of Dragut's resolve to march his troops and slaves overland to Algiers.

"I should have gone with him in the chain gangs, and Gianna, my Gianna, would have gone to his hareem." His voice shook with the pain and wrath of that memory. "Gianna, my lovely, gracious Gianna, your godchild and adopted niece, in the arms of a filthy Turk! The victim of a loathly rape! Was that a thought I could endure? Was I to stay and count the cost of saving her from such a fate? And if I could save her should it matter to me that the world might crack to pay for it? Answer that honestly, my lord. Imagine yourself in my place. Imagine Madonna Peretta in Gianna's. Would your thought of duty to the Emperor or to all Christendom have held you back?"

He paused for an answer. But the Admiral had none for him, nor had his nephews. The three stood abashed, the Admiral's eyes almost scared.

Observing them subdued, Prospero's lip curled. Scorn rang in his voice when he resumed.

"And you conceived that it was merely out of spite against you, in pursuit of the vengeance sworn that I betrayed the Imperial cause by showing Dragut how he might escape! The ruin and humiliation that face you as a consequence were never in my reckoning, as you may now believe. But since they have brought you where I had vowed to bring you perhaps it will reassure you to hear me say that I count the vow fulfilled. And so, perhaps, you will account sincere the reconciliation that I offer. And the hand I hold out to you is not empty. Accept it, and you may burn the resignation you have penned, and continue to serve the Emperor and Christendom with the honour that is due to you."

There the Admiral answered him at last, and now that he had recovered, indignation was again rumbling in his voice. "Do you dream that I can profit by a misapprehension? Shelter myself behind the false assumption under which the Emperor writes? Do you venture to suggest that? Is that the sting in the tail of your fine-sounding phrases?"

"If you do not, you will humiliate the Emperor with yourself, and you will deprive him, in the hour of his need, of his most valued servant. To my knowledge Barbarossa is at Constantinople building and equipping a powerful fleet for Suleyman. You can guess the purpose of it. In all the Frankish ranks only you, my lord, are a match for Kheyr-ed-Din. Will you desert your post at such a time out of a false sense of pride?"

"Is it false pride to disavow praise that is not earned? Is it false pride to refuse to be a party to an imposture? Besides – Bah! – It would be discovered in the end, and the disgrace would be the more bitter. The truth of Port Mahon is known to too many."

"Suspected perhaps. Not known. It is known positively only to the Prince of Orange and Don Alvaro de Carbajal; but they will never dare to utter a thing so unwelcome, so offensive, to the Emperor unless I confirm them; and that I should hardly dare to do in the face of the report I sent the Emperor."

The Admiral's troubled eyes considered him more kindly. "You persuade me that you mean well. Better, perhaps, than we deserve from you. But it is impossible. At all costs the truth must be known."

"And a bitter cost it may be to Christendom. Will you think only of your pride?"

"There is my honour, too, I think."

"Then regard it this way: When at Port Mahon I shivered the Sword of Islam, I repaired not only the fault I had committed against Christendom, but also the fault committed against you at Djerba. But since I am by my commission one of the captains at your orders, and what I did was done with the Neapolitan squadron, which is one of the divisions of the Imperial fleet of which you are the Admiral, the responsibility for what was done is yours. That is the Emperor's view. Is it not plain?"

"More specious than plain."

"But – by God! – " cried Gianettino, "none will dare to say otherwise if Prospero does not."

"I am glad that you begin to perceive it," said Prospero.

The Admiral wheeled to regard his nephew. "Why here's a change! An advocate in my own house!"

"Two advocates," Filippino made bold to answer him. "For I am of Gianettino's mind. If Prospero is honest now."

"You may believe me honest. Gianna will answer for me. Since we are to be in some sort kin, my lord, should we not stand together? And, if you can bring yourself to make peace with me, does not this become a family affair?"

The Admiral paced away to the threshold of the terrace. He stood there, looking out upon the magnificent gardens that with his house made up the monument to the glory he had so laboriously earned, but which now, if he rejected the proffered hand, would be burst like a bubble by a single breath.

They watched him, waiting, until Gianettino's impatience could wait no longer. "My Lord uncle, decision should be easy."

"Easy?" growled the Admiral. "Lord God!"

"As Prospero has told you, at Constantinople Kheyr-ed-Din is forging another sword for Islam. Your sacred duty is to preserve yourself so as to meet and destroy the menace of it."

"In the alternative," Filippino hotly reminded him, "you profit no one."

"Are you so sure?" Ponderously their uncle seemed to sneer at these two, to see them so suddenly converted by interest from that malice to which the protraction and exacerbation of the feud might be accounted due. He came slowly back, heavy-footed, to the marble fireplace. "The glory of Port Mahon is all yours, Prospero."

"So is the shame of Djerba, my lord," Prospero was prompt to answer. "If I cheat you of one, I must relieve you of the other. I agree for once with Filippino. Not to continue in your office is to profit no one. And do not overlook that to publish all is to ruin not only yourself, but me as well. In this we stand or fall together. In serving the other each of us serves himself. So you see, my lord, that on every count we must accept the judgment in the Emperor's letter, remembering, too, that thus we shall best be serving him."

The Admiral stroked his long, fulvid beard. His eyes were moist. The great rugged face was overcast as he pondered that mass of argument. There was no escaping the conclusions drawn. He sighed, at last, and looked up. "Will you believe me, Prospero, that I never broke faith with you when we took Genoa in the service of France?"

"I came to believe it before we sailed together for Cherchell."

"Ah! Cherchell!" The gloom deepened in the Admiral's face. "For that, too, I think that you have blamed me. It was done with a sore heart. I had no choice. In like case I must do the same again, or be false to the duty of my office."

"That, too, I understand. It was not so much Cherchell that I resented, but something that followed after, for which I now know that the blame was not yours, my lord."

"What was that?" the Admiral demanded.

His nephews looked guiltily disquieted. But Prospero shrugged. "Does it matter? So many of the blows we have exchanged in the course of this long duel have been out of mistaken judgments."

"It matters that the sword be sheathed at last."

Prospero advanced towards him. "I have sheathed it, my lord," he said, and held out his hand.

The Admiral's powerful grip closed over and held it a moment looking into Prospero's clear eyes. Then he turned to the Moorish table and took from it the little fiery cross of rubies. "It will be my honour, then, to invest you with the order of St James of Compostella in my Imperial master's name." But there he checked, and for a moment frowned, considering. "No, no," he said at last. "This is no thing to be done in secret. The investiture must be publicly made."

"Why, yes," Prospero agreed. "And the public that we need is waiting."

"How?"

"Gianna is with your Duchess, in anxiety to know that the peace is made which she so much desires and for which she has always striven. If then you will send for the ladies and bring in my friends, del Vasto and Don Alvaro, we shall have all the public that need matter to us."

Rafael Sabatini

Captain Blood

Captain Blood is the much-loved story of a physician and gentleman turned pirate.

Peter Blood, wrongfully accused and sentenced to death, narrowly escapes his fate and finds himself in the company of buccaneers. Embarking on his new life with remarkable skill and bravery, Blood becomes the 'Robin Hood' of the Spanish seas. This is swashbuckling adventure at its best.

The Gates of Doom

'Depend above all on Pauncefort,' announced King James, 'his loyalty is dependable as steel. He is with us body and soul and to the last penny of his fortune'. So when Pauncefort does indeed face bankruptcy after the collapse of the South Sea Company, the king's supreme confidence now seems rather foolish. And as Pauncefort's thoughts turn to gambling, moneylenders and even marriage to recover his debts, will he be able to remain true to the end? And what part will his friend and confidante, Captain Gaynor, play in his destiny?

'A clever story, well and amusingly told' – *The Times*

Rafael Sabatini

The Lost King

The Lost King tells the story of Louis XVII – the French royal who officially died at the age of ten but, as legend has it, escaped to foreign lands where he lived to an old age. Sabatini breathes life into these age-old myths, creating a story of passion, revenge and betrayal. He tells of how the young child escaped to Switzerland from where he plotted his triumphant return to claim the throne of France.

'…the hypnotic spell of a novel which for sheer suspense, deserves to be ranked with Sabatini's best' – *New York Times*

Scaramouche

When a young cleric is wrongfully killed, his friend, André Louis, vows to avenge his death. Louis' mission takes him to the very heart of the French Revolution where he finds the only way to survive is to assume a new identity. And so is born Scaramouche – a brave and remarkable hero of the finest order and a classic and much-loved tale of the greatest swashbuckling tradition.

'Mr Sabatini's novel of the French Revolution has all the colour and lively incident which we expect in his work' – *Observer*

Rafael Sabatini

The Sea Hawk

Sir Oliver, a typical English gentleman, is accused of murder, kidnapped off the Cornish coast, and dragged into life as a Barbary corsair. However Sir Oliver rises to the challenge and proves a worthy hero for this much-admired novel. Religious conflict, melodrama, romance and intrigue combine to create a masterly and highly successful story, perhaps best known for its many film adaptations.

The Shame of Motley

The Court of Pesaro has a certain fool – one Lazzaro Biancomonte of Biancomonte. *The Shame of Motley* is Lazzaro's story, presented with all the vivid colour and dramatic characterisation that has become Sabatini's hallmark.

'Mr Sabatini could not be conventional or commonplace if he tried'
– *Standard*

TITLES BY RAFAEL SABATINI AVAILABLE DIRECT FROM HOUSE OF STRATUS

Quantity		£	$(US)	$(CAN)	€
FICTION					
☐	ANTHONY WILDING	6.99	12.95	19.95	13.50
☐	THE BANNER OF THE BULL	6.99	12.95	19.95	13.50
☐	BARDELYS THE MAGNIFICENT	6.99	12.95	19.95	13.50
☐	BELLARION	6.99	12.95	19.95	13.50
☐	THE BLACK SWAN	6.99	12.95	19.95	13.50
☐	CAPTAIN BLOOD	6.99	12.95	19.95	13.50
☐	THE CAROLINIAN	6.99	12.95	19.95	13.50
☐	CHIVALRY	6.99	12.95	19.95	13.50
☐	THE CHRONICLES OF CAPTAIN BLOOD	6.99	12.95	19.95	13.50
☐	COLUMBUS	6.99	12.95	19.95	13.50
☐	FORTUNE'S FOOL	6.99	12.95	19.95	13.50
☐	THE FORTUNES OF CAPTAIN BLOOD	6.99	12.95	19.95	13.50
☐	THE GAMESTER	6.99	12.95	19.95	13.50
☐	THE GATES OF DOOM	6.99	12.95	19.95	13.50
☐	THE HOUNDS OF GOD	6.99	12.95	19.95	13.50
☐	THE JUSTICE OF THE DUKE	6.99	12.95	19.95	13.50
☐	THE LION'S SKIN	6.99	12.95	19.95	13.50
☐	THE LOST KING	6.99	12.95	19.95	13.50
☐	LOVE-AT-ARMS	6.99	12.95	19.95	13.50
☐	THE MARQUIS OF CARABAS	6.99	12.95	19.95	13.50
☐	THE MINION	6.99	12.95	19.95	13.50
☐	THE NUPTIALS OF CORBAL	6.99	12.95	19.95	13.50

ALL HOUSE OF STRATUS BOOKS ARE AVAILABLE FROM GOOD BOOKSHOPS OR DIRECT FROM THE PUBLISHER:

Internet: www.houseofstratus.com including author interviews, reviews, features.

Email: sales@houseofstratus.com please quote author, title and credit card details.

TITLES BY RAFAEL SABATINI AVAILABLE DIRECT FROM HOUSE OF STRATUS

Quantity		£	$(US)	$(CAN)	€
FICTION					
☐	THE ROMANCE PRINCE	6.99	12.95	19.95	13.50
☐	SCARAMOUCHE	6.99	12.95	19.95	13.50
☐	SCARAMOUCHE THE KING-MAKER	6.99	12.95	19.95	13.50
☐	THE SEA HAWK	6.99	12.95	19.95	13.50
☐	THE SHAME OF MOTLEY	6.99	12.95	19.95	13.50
☐	THE SNARE	6.99	12.95	19.95	13.50
☐	ST MARTIN'S SUMMER	6.99	12.95	19.95	13.50
☐	THE STALKING-HORSE	6.99	12.95	19.95	13.50
☐	THE STROLLING SAINT	6.99	12.95	19.95	13.50
☐	THE TAVERN KNIGHT	6.99	12.95	19.95	13.50
☐	THE TRAMPLING OF THE LILIES	6.99	12.95	19.95	13.50
☐	TURBULENT TALES	6.99	12.95	19.95	13.50
☐	VENETIAN MASQUE	6.99	12.95	19.95	13.50
NON-FICTION					
☐	HEROIC LIVES	8.99	14.99	22.50	15.00
☐	THE HISTORICAL NIGHTS' ENTERTAINMENT	8.99	14.99	22.50	15.00
☐	KING IN PRUSSIA	8.99	14.99	22.50	15.00
☐	THE LIFE OF CESARE BORGIA	8.99	14.99	22.50	15.00
☐	TORQUEMADA AND THE SPANISH INQUISITION	8.99	14.99	22.50	15.00

ALL HOUSE OF STRATUS BOOKS ARE AVAILABLE FROM GOOD BOOKSHOPS OR DIRECT FROM THE PUBLISHER:

Order Line: UK: 0800 169 1780,
            USA: 1 800 509 9942
            INTERNATIONAL: +44 (0) 20 7494 6400 (UK)
                or +01 212 218 7649
            (please quote author, title, and credit card details.)

Send to: House of Stratus Sales Department   House of Stratus Inc.
            24c Old Burlington Street   Suite 210
            London   1270 Avenue of the Americas
            W1X 1RL   New York • NY 10020
            UK   USA

PAYMENT

Please tick currency you wish to use:

☐ £ (Sterling)   ☐ $ (US)   ☐ $ (CAN)   ☐ € (Euros)

Allow for shipping costs charged per order plus an amount per book as set out in the tables below:

CURRENCY/DESTINATION

	£(Sterling)	$(US)	$(CAN)	€(Euros)
Cost per order				
UK	1.50	2.25	3.50	2.50
Europe	3.00	4.50	6.75	5.00
North America	3.00	3.50	5.25	5.00
Rest of World	3.00	4.50	6.75	5.00
Additional cost per book				
UK	0.50	0.75	1.15	0.85
Europe	1.00	1.50	2.25	1.70
North America	1.00	1.00	1.50	1.70
Rest of World	1.50	2.25	3.50	3.00

PLEASE SEND CHEQUE OR INTERNATIONAL MONEY ORDER.
payable to: STRATUS HOLDINGS plc or HOUSE OF STRATUS INC. or card payment as indicated

STERLING EXAMPLE

Cost of book(s):..................... Example: 3 x books at £6.99 each: £20.97
Cost of order: .... Example: £1.50 (Delivery to UK address)
Additional cost per book:............... Example: 3 x £0.50: £1.50
Order total including shipping:.......... Example: £23.97

VISA, MASTERCARD, SWITCH, AMEX:
☐☐☐☐☐☐☐☐☐☐☐☐☐☐☐☐☐☐☐

Issue number (Switch only):
☐☐☐

Start Date: Expiry Date:
☐☐/☐☐   ☐☐/☐☐

Signature: _____

NAME: _____

ADDRESS: _____

COUNTRY: _____

ZIP/POSTCODE: _____

Please allow 28 days for delivery. Despatch normally within 48 hours.

Prices subject to change without notice.
Please tick box if you do not wish to receive any additional information. ☐

House of Stratus publishes many other titles in this genre; please check our website (**www.houseofstratus.com**) for more details.